GOD'S
MONSTERS

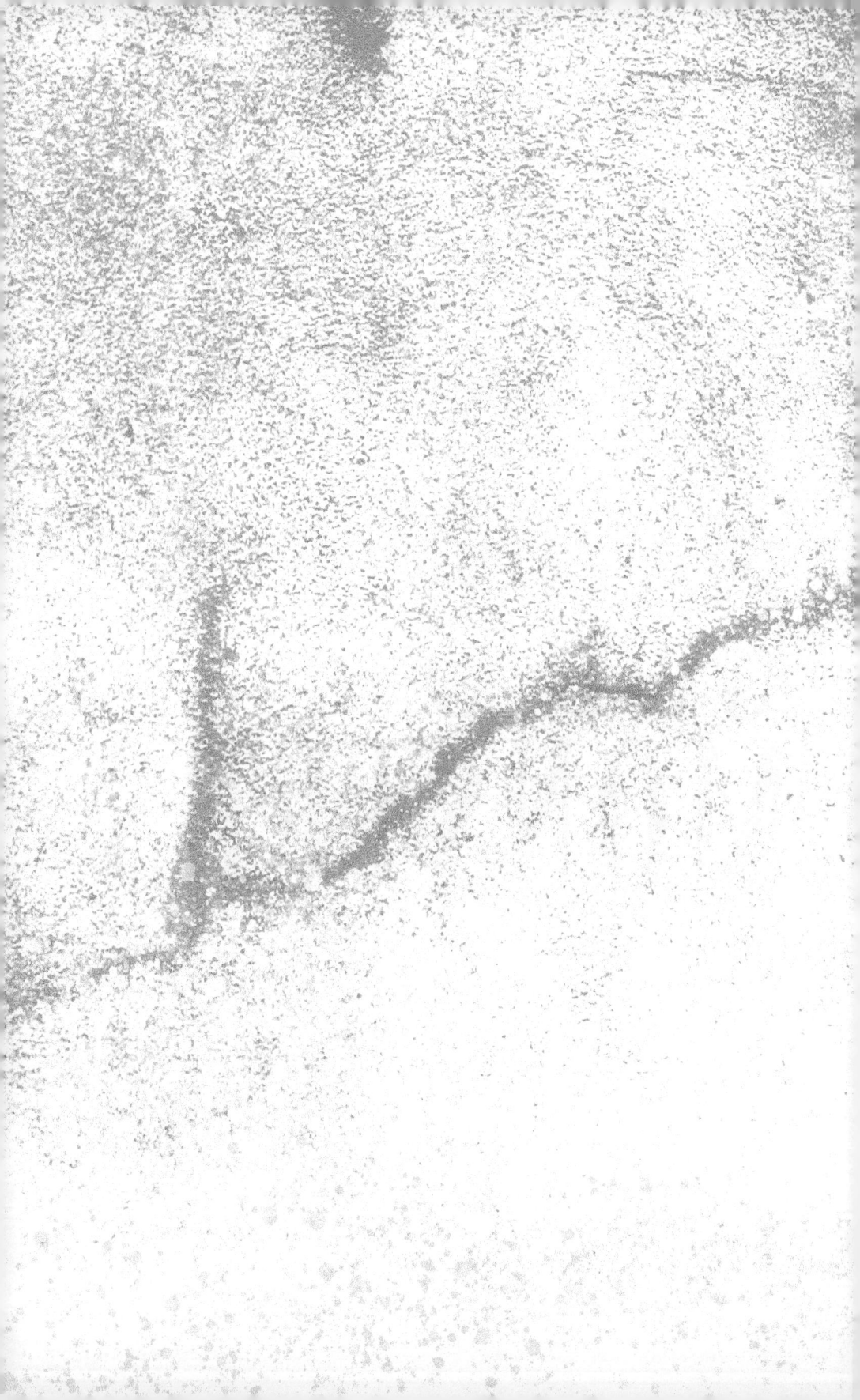

ODYSSEYS OF AN ETERNAL CREATURE

GOD'S MONSTERS

SINARA ELLIS

4 Horsemen
Publications, Inc.

4 Horsemen
Publications, Inc.

Published By: 4 Horsemen Publications, Inc.

4 Horsemen Publications, Inc.
PO Box 417
Sylva, NC 28779
4horsemenpublications.com
info@4horsemenpublications.com

Cover & Typesetting by Autumn Skye
Edited by Isabelle Reynolds

Library of Congress Control Number: 2024938006

Paperback ISBN-13: 979-8-8232-0435-4
Hardcover ISBN-13: 979-8-8232-0436-1
Audiobook ISBN-13: 979-8-8232-0521-4
Ebook ISBN-13: 979-8-8232-0434-7

I write this for my friends, Shannon J., Will, Lady Carol, Terri, Marcus, D'Ann, Geoff, and all those who seek out the monsters in the closet and embrace them without question or fear.

&

For Wayne, who has been the light in the darkness and the maker of lovely pancakes.

Do not judge the capacity of a man or beast to love or be loved without first hearing his story, for you cannot genuinely grasp everything about him until you have traveled all of his miles with him, cherishing the journey no matter its twists and turns in the darkness and the light.

Shall we walk?

~ Noble Lincoln

CONTENTS

1712

He watched as the beauty of seventeen danced barefoot across the ballroom floor, her long white dressing gown's skirt floating on the breeze her spinning created.

Lit candles gave the high arches of the ceiling a faint golden glow. Dark wood showed only where her feet disturbed the dust. Her long golden curls rose from her shoulders as she spun around. Smiling, she laughed as she became dizzy. Blue eyes sparkled, lit by candlelight, as hers met his again and again.

A sudden foreboding filled him as, unbeknownst to the girl, a large looming shadow on the wall consumed hers.

Alarmed, he quickly moved toward her as the candles flickered, threatening to go out. He reached out to her, and she stopped spinning. Her smile changed to an expression of pure fear. As he stepped closer still, her hands rose to the sides of her face, and she backed away from him, screaming.

"Elizabeth!" The name escaped Noble Lincoln's cracked lips in barely a whisper as he was startled from his dream by distant screams. Dull pain in his gut clashed with the sickening roll of the ship, mixed with the smells of rot and human waste which filled the moist air, attacking his senses. Noble rolled to his side and vomited. Groaning, he sat up, his legs splayed out before him.

Swallowing the bile in his throat, he wiped his mouth on the crusted shirt-sleeve he did not remember being dirty. Startled, he opened his eyes. He blinked slowly, trying to make out anything; instead, he found complete darkness.

Noble's hand reached out into the blackness. His fingers found the riveted bars of what he realized were the cells *below* deck—cells of the slave ship on which he had purchased passage.

Pulling himself to his feet, ignoring the pain in his gut, he stood and turned in his prison, searching for any sign of light. There was none.

What am I doing here?

"Hello," he called out, his voice weak. "Is anyone there? Why have I been confined? Is someone there?"

Rough fingers grabbed him through the bars. Noble cried out and pulled away instinctively.

Whispered "Quiet!" noises came from the dark.

"Hush! You'll call that beast back here to kill us all," whispered the familiar voice of the ship's captain, John Allsopp.

"Captain?"

A scream filled the putrid air. For a few moments, everyone seemed to hold their breath.

"What's happening?" Noble asked in a whisper.

"Be quiet. It'll hear us," the captain whispered back.

"I don't understand," Noble pressed.

The captain sighed and responded, "Something has taken over the ship. It keeps the lot of us locked up down here."

"What do you mean, 'something'?"

The ship bobbed side to side as the storm started sending flashes of light through the cracks of the doors above and somewhere else on board; something struck the ship's bones with a loud crash and the splintering of wood. For a few moments, the men sat silent.

Thunder crashed, giving the men a start.

"That thing keeps at it, we're all done for. It'll sink the boat," whispered another familiar voice to Noble.

"What is it?" demanded Noble in a whisper.

"Dunno what you'd call it. Ain't human."

Another voice shushed them again as an additional crack sounded, startling them once more into silence. The men held their collective breath, leaving only the sounds of the storm rocking the ship to and fro.

Then another man dared to speak, whose name Noble did not know. "It wanders, killing the rest of the night. It is unlike any creature I've ever seen. All black and covered in hair, wings like a bat... teeth so big, claws more like huge hooks. It smells like death."

"It's killed most of the crew, passengers, and cargo. Some of us, what was wise, just jumped overboard. I will, iffen I get the chance," whispered another frightened man.

"Tell me when you might have had one ounce of your mind when that thing speaks, James," said Captain Allsopp.

"It controls men with its eyes, it does," said another frightened man.

"I said, 'iffin I get the chance,'" James whispered.

"I cannot recall the last time I saw the sun. There's been only this darkness we wake to and the stink of your rot and waste, Barson," whispered the captain.

"I don't want to die," whispered another sailor.

"Me neither," whispered Barson.

"Quiet," commanded the captain, startled by his raucous direction.

The thrashing of metal upon wood moved closer, and the sailors fell silent once more.

The foul breath of the men breathing into his face made Noble's stomach lurch.

"I don't feel quite myself," Noble whispered, backing away from the bars. He doubled over again and fell into his mess; in too much pain to care, he blacked out.

In the dim light of a single lantern, they yelled and fought. The creature reached in with long hooked feet, wrapping around the necks and limbs of each man as it cleared the cage. Its red eyes seemed to glow, and it spoke in a tongue that had never fallen upon Noble's ears. Some of the men grabbed on to the bars, fighting whatever fate had in store for them outside of their captivity.

Noble rolled over on his back, his eyes opening and closing, hoping the nightmare would fade. He wailed as if suffering the other men's fate.

Samuel Barson, the captain's second in command, a skinny man with a sea-worn face, grabbed tight to the bars and kicked at the creature as it pulled him out by one foot. The beast screeched and pulled harder still while the man screamed, "Father, save me!" The sailor released the bars with one of his hands and struggled to reach out to Noble through the bars. Noble raised a shaking hand toward the outstretched crewman's, his eyes full of tears and his brow heavy with sweat.

Noble's arm fell back on his chest from exhaustion, and the man looked up, still holding tight to the iron bars. "God, grant me mercy so I may die quickly!" he sobbed.

Barson whimpered as the creature sank its teeth into his thigh, snapping his femur as if it were nothing more than a twig. The monster pulled harder still at the sailor, who lost his grasp. His outstretched arm hooked the bars, filling Noble's ears with the loud sound of breaking bones. A hideous death cry echoed through the hull as the monster crushed the sailor's throat with jaws that opened like nothing Noble had ever seen. Teeth gnashing through the soft tissues, striking the cervical spine with a crunching noise that made Noble wince. Red eyes looked up at him through the bars, and Noble froze, his stomach sinking. He sat staring back at what he could imagine was Death in its physical form.

The creature cocked its head to the side, studying the other man behind the bars, its nostrils quivering as it sniffed the air for a moment. It moved closer to the bars that separated the two cells before flinging the broken body in its grasp out of the cage, bored with it. Noble watched as the corpse flew through the air past the shadow of someone holding a lantern over their head. The body dropped to the deck and looked with unseeing eyes toward Noble.

Fear sent Noble into the black again, and the nightmare left.

Noble awoke and tried looking around, only to have his eyes meet the darkness again. The dank smell of his own sick and the familiar coppery scent of blood sent him to his knees. The pain returned. "Captain, how long have we been down here? I feel as though I have not eaten in a fortnight," he whispered toward the next cell.

Noble's ears met with silence.

"Captain?"

Noble's hands reached through the bars, feeling emptiness in the next cell. The eight men crammed there earlier were gone.

It was merely a dream, was it not? What I saw could never be real.

His heart started racing in his chest, and he felt dizzy.

Reaching his hand outward, he sucked in his breath as he reached out to the screaming man who had begged for his help in his memory; it had not been a dream. Noble's mind started sorting through what he had seen and what was possible. None of it was possible, but the horror of what he had seen troubled him. *Am I losing myself to madness?*

He listened, but no sound outside of the sea met his ears.

Taking a chance, he called out, "Hello... Hello? Is anyone there?"

Noble felt around in the darkness of his cell, finding nothing but an unforgiving lock, puddles of piss, and vomit. He sat in the corner, leaning on the bars. The scent, a heady mix of death, salt, and rotting vomit, hung heavy in the air. The squall pushed the ship through the never-ending Atlantic, and the waves slapped against the walls around him in a melodic song, numbing him. He rubbed his rough, chapped lips together and felt the roughness of his hands against his face. Usually close-shaven, he was confused to find a beard. The thickness of it startled him. *How long have I been down here?*

Deciding to take inventory of himself, he felt his clothes. They were familiar, but torn in places and stiff in others with what he guessed was his own stomach contents and waste.

The clink of metal striking metal and wood gave Noble a start. Shuffling feet dragged something metal and heavy behind them. He quickly scooted to the back of his prison cell.

A light suddenly appeared from behind a wall across the way, which hid the stairs that led down to the slave cargo. The lantern was shoulder-high, so Noble could not make out its carrier.

Finally able to see within his cage, he rose to his feet and moved to the bars. "Hello... Who's there?" he whispered.

The figure moved closer, dragging its chains and shuffling as though there was no hurry.

As the lantern approached, he looked down at the floor where the light fell upon two dark black feet with chains at the ankles. His eyes scanned up the dark pair of legs, to the dark patch of hair of the woman who stopped before him. Then his eyes met hers; the whites made paler by their black centers. He knew those eyes. They had looked into his when she boarded. Although no longer frightened, they seemed off. Then she spoke, and this startled him. "I am for your eat."

He looked at her. "You speak English?"

As she closed in on Noble's cell, the hand behind her back produced a brass key and placed it in the lock. Meeting his eyes, she said, "I am for your eat."

"Do you have food?"

The heavy lock fell to the floor with a metallic *thud*, and she dropped the key, and the brass bounced out of the light. She backed away from the door, still holding the lantern high.

Noble observed her. Desperate to be out of his prison, he slowly opened the door. She backed farther away until he could step out of the cage.

Setting the lantern on a water barrel outside the cell, she turned to him. Her face was without expression; her eyes stared without blinking.

"Can you tell me what is happening? Where are the captain and the crew?"

There was no response, only an empty gaze.

Noble motioned to himself. "More people... people like me, but not... the tall, cruel man, the captain," he said, holding his hand above his head, hoping she understood.

For a moment, there was nothing, and then she turned toward the steps leading to the main deck; her arm rose, pointing to the door.

Noble pointed at the lantern. "May I have your lamp? I must speak to him. I must know what is happening."

The woman picked it up and handed it to him.

Looking into her eyes, he saw nothing but blackness. "What is your name?"

"I am for your eat."

"You've said that, and I am quite afraid I don't understand what you mean. Your name. What are you called?"

She moved closer to him and held her arm up. Blood ran down her arm from an open gash on her wrist. The coppery smell wafted into his nostrils, causing a wave of nausea.

"Your wound is most terrible." Noble quickly tore off the cleaner of the two sleeves of his shirt and ripped the fabric into strips, tying it over her injury. "Are you hurt anywhere else?"

She stood silent and unmoving. Noble's eyes followed the blood that had run down her arm to her chest, where fresh blood covered her dark breasts, down her stomach, and dripped down past her waist. He noticed more blood running from a wound on her neck. Looking at the wound closely, he noted it was deep and free-flowing. The pain in his gut returned, and his heartbeat pounded in his ears. "Who did this to you?"

"I am for your eat."

"Please stop saying that. I don't understand."

Tearing another strip of fabric from his sleeve, he took her hand and placed it on the material on her gaping neck wound. "Keep your hand upon this, and be still. Do you understand?"

Her expression remained unchanged, her black eyes staring through him.

Worried about her condition, he persisted. "You need to sit; you've lost a lot of blood, and I'm without my bag of medicines."

He tried to help her sit on a barrel, but she stood rigid against him, repeating, "I am for your eat."

Shaking his head, he sighed. "I'm going to find my bag. Please, please stay here. Do you understand?"

She repeated the same words.

Noble left the girl at the bottom of the stairs with the lantern, afraid he would never find her in the darkness without the light. He ascended to the deck doors. Noble stood for a moment, closing his eyes, trying to chase away the nightmares. *None of it was real, not the monster, not the death, none of it. The woman is simply injured, and when I push open these doors, I will find only the pirates who have made me do things outside of my conscience. All will be well. I will retrieve my bag and treat her wounds just as I have been doing on this ship these three months. I do not believe in monsters who eat men.*

Opening the doors, Noble was met with an almost starless sky and a full moon hampered by heavy clouds. A light at the steering deck caught Noble's attention. Noble started toward him, glad to see the captain standing at his post.

"Captain, I am most relieved to see you here. What has happened?"

The captain's eyes did not meet his, and he made no move to acknowledge him.

"Captain?"

Confused by his silence and his face mostly hidden under long, stringy hair, Noble moved closer, picking up the lantern that lit the ship's compass and raising it in front of the *Buscador De Alma*'s captain.

The man's steely eyes looked straight ahead as if Noble was not there. His skin, once tanned and roughened by the harsh seas he had sailed upon his entire life, now looked gray and hung as though he were wearing it like a too-large costume. His ankles, wrists, and neck were bound to the wheel with shackles.

"Captain?"

Reaching out his hand, Noble started to touch the man's face when the steering wheel turned slightly in the man's hands, and the chains rattled together, startling Noble. He was alive.

"Captain Allsopp?"

The man remained silent, staring at nothing as he steered the waves in the darkened seas. Noble backed away from him.

Remembering the injured woman below, Noble started for his bunk in the ship's living quarters. He met two other men, seemingly guarding the captain's quarters' door, but neither spoke nor acknowledged him. They stood rigid as statues in the shackles that had once kept the slaves in the cargo hold below, now slaves themselves to whatever magic or malady held them.

Feeling his way in the darkness from memory, Noble grabbed a lantern hanging on a wall in his quarters. Running his hands over the small writing desk, he found matches and lit one. His trunk lay broken and rifled through; his clothes and his papers littered the floor around his feet. Catching a glimpse of a face he did not know, he almost dropped the lantern.

Looking into the mirror, he picked up from the mess on the floor, his reflection struck him. His face filled with confusion, seeing a very dirty and haggard-looking man.

Usually well-kempt, the young man of twenty-eight looked much older. Noble's dark, naturally wavy hair, usually tied back at the nape of his neck, instead hung loose and much longer than it had been. It was grimy and matted with bits of vomited food and the pungent smell of waste. His skin had layers of filth from his indiscernible time below decks. A dark and dirty beard covered his usually clean-shaven face. He ran his hand over it. Even his light-blue eyes seemed different, but he could not put his finger on what it was.

Remembering why he was here, Noble dropped the mirror and dug through his scattered belongings. His hands fell upon his journal, and without an idea of the current date, he opened the book to find his last entry.

WHAT DEMON
IS THIS?

July 24th 1712

I lack the understanding of cruelty in men, and had I known this kind of barbarianism existed amongst the crew, I would have never set foot on this ship.

We found port today at a great fortress of stone and clay. Captain Allsopp had me set out upon the shore with him to assist in selecting his cargo.

He is a slave trader who carries what sounds like one-quarter of his mass in coin about his neck. I know this from the sound it makes as he takes weighty steps. Behind us followed the loud footfalls of several sailors carrying crates of flintlocks and blunderbusses, while I carried a small barrel of gunpowder.

After I had climbed half a hundred stairs, the wall opened, and I saw a large crowd surrounding a stone block where Africans in rope and iron stood glaring down at those interested in purchasing them. Their muscles glistened in the sun from the oils slathered all over their skin. The captain showed no interest in these slaves and instead passed through the crowd, who shouted at the auctioneer bids for the "livestock" he intended to sell without conscience.

Allsopp meant to buy in large quantities and had no interest in the larger boys and men intended for house slaves and sport. Passing through to another large area of the fortress, I was startled by the sounds of women and inconsolable children, and it sickened me. Looking into their faces, all I could think about was my own Elizabeth, Yancy, Mira, and unborn child, and how I would defend them to my death if ever such a fate as this threatened them.

I reached out to aid a struggling child trapped beneath the body of a dead woman when I was suddenly struck between the shoulders and screamed at in a tongue I did not recognize. Cringing in pain, I crossed myself, praying for her soul, an old habit that has not been shaken by my leaving the cloth. The trader shouted at another man who went and unchained the dead woman and beat the child before dragging away the mother's body. The captain laughed at me and said, "Don't touch what ain't yours, Doctor."

Although angered by the inhumane tone, I nodded and followed the slavers and the ship's captain through to an area set up for showing slaves in large quantities. They stood shackled to one another in long strands of ten and twenty. Most cried at us; I can only assume they were begging for freedom while the slavers whipped them into silence. My heart ached for them, but I kept quiet, for I was among thieves and murderers.

The captain selected the Africans he believed hardy enough to make it across the sea. He then commanded me to examine each, one after another, checking their teeth, eyes and skin for injuries that mighty hinder their ability to work. I was hurried along by Allsopp, who rested his hand on a pistol in his belt. Each time my eyes met a new dark pair of eyes, I saw fear, anger, and confusion. Some whispered words I did not understand. All I could do to quell them was to whisper in return, "I am sorry."

There was one man, his eyes unlike the rest. He smiled at me, and I felt most unsettled. When I pushed my fingers into his mouth to look at his teeth, I swear I saw something odd about his eyes. They stared into mine with a darkness that rattled me. Everything fell into silence for a moment, and I could not breathe. Looking into my eyes, he uttered the words, "A lost man of God," in a very thick accent. The short hairs on my neck stood as my mouth barely managed to respond in a whisper, "How…" Suddenly, the noises of the slave trading post returned, and a sharp pain in my fingers caused me to cry out. Blood dripped from the mouth of the man with the strange eyes, my blood. I tried with all my strength to pull my hands back, but his teeth bore down harder still as he sucked the open wounds on my fingers. The trader shouted at him and then clubbed him until he released me and fell back, his eyes still staring at me while that foul smile continued to play upon his lips. I stumbled back into one of the sailors, trying to keep from falling to the ground, but he pushed me back hard, and I caught my footing.

Captain Allsopp merely laughed at me and said, "He thinks you taste good, Doctor."

The African's eyes felt as though they were trying to carve through to my very soul. Even now, I feel as though he is staring through the decks, still watching me.

What demon is this?

Noble paused to look at his hand; the wounds from the bites had healed. He dropped his journal into the mess and continued his search. Tossing aside his belongings quickly, Noble found his father's old medical bag, thrown amongst dirtied clothes and fallen open, emptying the contents. The doctor pulled clean shirts from his trunk and tore them apart to make bandages for the woman below deck. He then shoved them in with the few medicines he had brought on his trip across the Atlantic.

Finding the hidden dark-amber bottle of powder, he uncorked it and eyed an amount of opium that might settle the pain in his gut. He tipped his head back and emptied it into the back of his throat. He then removed enough for the injured African woman, who he hoped was still where he left her. He measured out a bit more into another fold of paper if saving her was not possible, for he wished no amount of suffering on her.

Please, God, forgive me. I only mean to allow her a painless passing from this tortured life if it is required, Noble prayed, looking upward and crossing himself.

Stuffing the folded squares of paper into his bag, he headed for the door to the deck.

The sky opened. The captain remained at his post, his face without expression, hands tight to the wheel of his ship as raindrops slapped his pale skin.

Rushing to the door leading below deck, Noble held tight to his bag and fought to keep his footing on the rain-slicked wood.

Pulling the door open, he looked down into the circle of light at the bottom of the stairs and saw nothing but the feet of the nude woman. Yanking the door closed behind him, he quickly moved down the stairs.

Reaching the bottom step, he picked up the lantern and held it up above his head to get a better view of his patient, but dropped his bag and fell back onto the steps. Glowing red eyes met his gaze. Noble looked into its dark face—which resembled a bat more than a man—as teeth bit into the woman as if she were a roasted pig. Claws dug into her shoulders as they ripped at her throat with a ferocity Noble had only seen in dog fights.

Having gotten its attention, he set the lantern down and pushed himself back up the stairs. The red-eyed beast screeched. Noble shuddered and continued up the stairs slowly, as if backing away from a rabid animal.

The sound of the dead woman's body falling to the floor had Noble on his feet, running for the door.

Slamming the door behind him, Noble pushed his full weight against the weathered oak, helped by the crashing waves coming over the sides of the rocking deck, splintering wood and banging coming from the other side of the door behind him.

"Captain Allsopp!" he shouted, but the slapping rain and wind drowned out his voice. Allsopp was still subdued and unmoving at the wheel.

Noble realized he was alone to face the beast tearing quickly through the door. He started praying as the wood gave way. Picking up a shattered board, he held it up above his head and backed away from the entrance to the middle of the deck.

"You will not have me, demon!"

The black beast screeched loudly and bounded toward Noble. Raising a clawed hand, it batted at him, knocking him on his back. He fought to get to his feet as it slammed him into the rail, breaking it but grabbing him before he could fall overboard. The oak board flew from Noble's hands and splashed into the rough waters of the Atlantic.

Noble groaned out in pain as the beast pushed him to the deck and sat upon his chest, its red eyes aglow. The foul breath of the creature reminded Noble of the putrid stench of the dead house he had seen his parents' bodies in over a month earlier.

He could not help but shake as the beast seemed to study him. Its long teeth were much too large to fit beneath closed lips. It sniffed, its thinned lips almost sneering as it took in his scent. A clawed hand brushed his face and ran down to his throat.

Noble's adrenaline-filled muscles twitched with the sting of the scratches left behind, immediately cooled by the falling rain.

The beast ran its claws over him as if entranced. A strange chanting sounded from under its breath.

Finished with the torment, Noble shouted at it, "Kill me already!"

The creature seemed to smile before it pulled Noble's head roughly to the side and attacked his throat. The excruciating pain, blood loss, and fear made his head feel like it was swirling into a cold, dark abyss. His eyes closed, and he felt no more.

Noble woke unable to breathe, his nostrils pinched shut by two fingers. Opening his eyes, Noble opened his mouth wide and sucked in the hot air around him, just as a newborn babe might take its first breath. Crying out, he exhaled and looked around, hoping to find the nightmare gone. An oil lamp swung back and forth as the ship rocked in the hard waves, allowing him to see a little of the cargo hold where he now lay. Noble's eyes met those of the man who still held his nose. The familiar face of the man who had bitten him in Africa looked down with a wide smile. Noble tried to slap away the hand of the slave, but found his wrists and ankles shackled. The chains clanked as he fought to free himself.

"Please help me loose these chains. There is a monster upon this ship; we must kill it or flee."

Releasing his nose, the man chanted in words unknown to Noble and picked up a knife from the chest of a dead body next to him.

Noble took a deep breath through his nose and immediately regretted it. The stench from the rotting corpses surrounding them made Noble ill again, but he found the courage to ask hoarsely, "What are you doing?"

The African raised the knife above Noble, and Noble's heart began to race. He shouted, "I mean you no harm! Release me! I am no danger to you; I swear it! Do you understand me?"

Dropping the dagger, the African leaned in close to his face, and a wicked grin opened as his teeth grew longer right in front of Noble's eyes. The doctor struggled harder against chains, but they held fast.

Black hair grew from the man's skin, and his ears extended high above his head until he no longer resembled a man. Long claws replaced fingernails and raked down Noble's cheek, leaving long, painful scratches. Its tongue lolled out of its mouth and licked his cheek, tasting the blood dripping from the wounds.

"Kill me, demon! Be done with it. Kill me!" Noble shouted, ready to be done with the taunting of the creature.

Red eyes stared at him for a moment as the beast cocked its head to the side. It seemed as if it wanted to speak but screeched instead. As it stood upright like a man, Noble saw long black hair covering most of its body. Large leathery wings loomed behind it, settling on its back, folding inward. Where there were once feet, talons jutted out from thick black hair; it was as if a large bird had lain with a demon, creating the beast standing over him.

"How did you escape hell?" asked Noble under heavy breath.

The demon leaned down suddenly into the chained man's face until Noble could feel its breath reeking of death. Gripping Noble's face with one clawed hand, it forced his mouth open. The demon ripped into its limb with its teeth and poured its blood over Noble's face and into his mouth.

Choking on blood, Noble tried to fight the creature drowning him. Between the pain and weakness from lack of food and his blood loss, he blacked out and dreamed of a life not of his own.

MAKING A MONSTER

The sun peeked over a desert horizon. An African man squatted near the fire for light and wrapped sinew around his spear while a small boy squatted next to him, watching. A woman holding a baby sat across the fire from them, her proud eyes on her older son.

"Father, I want to hunt with you," said the boy.

The father smiled. "You are very brave, my son, but you are too young to hunt."

The boy's eyes filled with disappointment.

The father patted the boy on the knee and grinned. "But you are not too young to help protect the village."

"Lions do not attack the village, Father. How will I learn to hunt the big lion?"

Laughing, the man clapped the boy on his back. "You will be big enough someday, and soon enough, you will tire of hunting."

"I will never get tired of hunting. I want to be a warrior for the people like you."

"You will be soon." He pulled open the skin lying on the ground at his feet and pulled out a small spear. The little boy's eyes grew large.

"A boy needs a weapon to protect his family while the hunters are away."

The boy nodded as his father handed him his very own spear.

"Tabansi, do you think he is old enough for such a brave weapon?" the mother teased her son.

"I will protect you, Mother, and Rasul. I am his big brother, and I will teach him to hold a spear like a warrior," the boy said, smiling, his front teeth missing.

"He is a baby still. You can teach him when he gets a bit bigger," his mother said, smiling down at her son. "You will be a great teacher, Diallo."

The boy grinned and stood up, holding his spear over his head.

Children ran behind the hunters walking out into the desert, waving and calling out their goodbyes and cheers for a successful hunt.

They hunted until the sun started to set. Then they started for home, carrying antelopes. The hunter laughed until he noticed many large birds flying over their huts. Tabansi stopped in his tracks, catching the other hunters off guard with his strange silence. Something about the village was not right. Suddenly, they all understood. The lack of firelight while large whirls of dark smoke rose from the huts caused alarm amongst the hunters.

Dropping their kills, they all ran toward their home, shouting the names of their loved ones. When there was no response or movement, they ran faster.

Dashing between the huts, Tabansi saw the embers of a dying fire and spotted the burned remains of a leg. A partially burned infant's hand lay palm up. The smell of burned flesh filled the air around him. Falling to his knees, he cried out as he picked up the head of his son's spear from the edge of the fire.

The other hunters ran from hut to hut, looking for survivors. A scream drew Tabansi from his grief. He ran to the fire on the other side of the village. An older man, dying from deep wounds and burns, forced out words between charred lips as one of the other hunters tried to give him water. "Save my son. Kill me ... and ... save my son."

"Who did this?" demanded Tabansi, kneeling next to the old man who had told him stories as a boy.

"The ones from the east. They have spears that throw fire and stone from their tips. They used them against the ones who fought. They chained those who could walk and killed the ones who could not. The men made mothers throw infants on the fires and pushed the old onto the flames. They chained the rest and made them walk to the south." The old man grabbed Tabansi's spear with his unburned hand and shook it. "Find them, Tabansi. Kill them and save our wives, sons, and daughters." He took a ragged breath, saying, "Please kill me, Tabansi, and return me to the earth."

With his eyes brimming with tears, Tabansi wiped them away and nodded at the old man. Tabansi stabbed him fast and sure through the heart.

The elder's breathing slowed and stopped, and then his eyes stared at the sky, never to look upon his family again.

With great sadness, Tabansi pulled his spear from the old man's chest. He had learned enough. Two of his brothers returned the dead man's body to the flames. They sang for their dead under the early evening stars.

Tabansi sat on his heels, his mind running between anger and grief, hitting his head with his hands. The memory of his son's face from that morning kept flashing in his mind, Diallo waving and cheering his father as the warrior waved back and the hunters left the village.

He stood up, shouting his frustration and rage at the sky. "Why!" Walking out of the village, heading south, he found himself followed by the rest of the hunters.

The battle lasted mere minutes, but felt like years as they attacked. His brothers of the hunt fell against the men with fire spears, even as they struck by surprise with their stone-tipped weapons. The men holding the chains and stones had their skulls crushed or were stabbed in the chest before they had a chance to take many shots. Women and children cried out and tried to help by beating the men with open hands and closed fists.

His son, Diallo, beat a man angrily with his tiny fists as the slaver fired a gun toward his father. The man then turned and fired at the boy. Diallo's small body fell limp, and Tabansi pounced, mortally striking the stranger's chest with his spear. He could not stop, even as other men fired their weapons around him, hitting more of his people, who were chained together by wrist and ankle. He watched them all fall, pulling down those ahead and behind them in the line.

Screaming, cries of pain, and gunfire filled the air as a man holding a rifle pulled Tabansi from his victim and shouted at him in a language he did not understand. Tabansi felt the hot end of the gun at his head, and then he yelled as he pulled the weapon from the man's hand and started to beat him with it. He heard the crunching of the man's skull as it caved in. Tabansi continued to beat him until the dying man's nose and upper teeth broke and sank into a bloody mess. Blood bubbles blew from his nostrils and throat as he struggled to breathe. His arms flailed about, finding no aid.

Men around him screamed and shot their weapons up in the sky, hoping he would flee. When he didn't, they ran up to Tabansi, pulling at him and screaming. Anger-spurred adrenaline seemed to explode within him as he turned on his heels and hit another and another, knocking them back, beating them down as they tried to stand. One of them struggled to reload his weapon as Tabansi brought the butt of the rifle down on his head. The man fell, and his body twitched as death took him.

Tabansi screamed at them, spittle flying from his lips, for killing his sons and slaughtering his people.

Running into the crowd of slavers, Tabansi swung his newly found weapon and cried out a hunter's cry of triumph. Then a familiar cry came from the chained line of his people. Looking over his shoulder, he saw her pulling against the chains, trying to get to him, but under the weight of the dead, she barely moved a step.

More gunfire erupted as the slavers ran from the front of the caravan of chained prisoners toward Tabansi, felling more of the hunters.

"Tabansi!" she cried out for him, her face wet with tears: "Tabansi, do not die for me! Run! Run! Live for me! Live for Diallo and Rasul! Run!"

Looking around, he found clarity in her words, and then ten men all ran, pointing their fire spears toward him. His fallen brothers now lay strewed across the ground, either dead or dying. He was alone in the battle.

He saw the fire coming from the ends of their weapons as they stopped midway between him and another bunch of running men.

Turning, he looked toward his wife, who screamed again, "Run, Tabansi, run!"

Unable to fight so many so far out of reach, he turned and ran.

Blood spurted from his battered and beaten body. With gunfire behind him, Tabansi ran as tears fell. He moved his feet as fast as he could in no particular direction. Tabansi ran and ran until the sun sank into the horizon and darkness fell behind him. He ran until the sounds of his people and their captors were no more and blood marked his every step. Exhaustion finally took over, and he fell forward into the dirt.

Smoke and chanting woke him; his body, no longer face down in the dirt, now sat slumped up against a boulder. The fire sparked up between him and something moving on the other side.

"Who is there?" he demanded to know, although his voice was weak.

The fire seemed to answer him as it died down a little, and he could see over it. A small man with lion's fangs pierced through his nostrils, paint on his face, and long dirty locks of hair covering his head looked through the flames, laughing.

"The dead demand knowledge so far out of his reach," the man cackled.

"Who are you?" repeated Tabansi, coughing.

"In the day, I am the man from under the sand. At night, I am the creature that hangs from the trees, snatching men bigger than you from their lives, feeding on them until the screams stop."

Tabansi coughed again; his chest heaved painfully. "What does that mean?"

The old man cackled and stood up on the other side of the fire. His eyes stared at Tabansi, but the light did not reflect upon their shiny surface as it should have. Suddenly, his teeth grew longer, and hair started to cover his body as he gained height. Jumping into the fire, it leaped out again and landed on one knee, holding up a clawed hand over Tabansi.

"Stop," Tabansi cried out, but without fear.

The glassy eyes of the creature studied his face. Then the hair vanished, and the teeth receded. He placed his raised hand upon his knees and sat back, staring at Tabansi.

Looking curiously into his eyes, the small man looked puzzled. "You do not fear death? You do not fear the beast of the trees, the Asasabonsam!"

Tabansi's breathing was becoming more labored. "I do not fear what is already coming. But I must try to live for my sons who lay slain upon the earth and the wife taken from me today. She commanded I live for them. I did as she said. But if you want to see me dead, I will join my people, the ones who have returned to the earth."

The small man took a deep breath and grabbed Tabansi by the shoulders, quickly biting into his throat. Tabansi did not scream or struggle. He only wished to die.

Tabansi woke and found himself lying on his back on the ground. The fire was high, and the small man kneeled over him, chanting. He leaned down closer to him and whispered, "I saw the death in your blood. From this night on, you will walk the earth. Men will drop at your feet as you drain them of life, but you will not meet death."

Tabansi's head felt like he was floating as the small man raised a hand of claws above his head and plunged them deep into Tabansi's chest. He screamed in pain and felt his beating heart being pierced. The man, who had again become the beast, pulled his heart out. Tabansi did not know why he still lived. Tabansi could not breathe, he could not move, he could not scream, but he watched in terror as the beast bit into his still-beating heart. The creature consumed the still-beating organ, chanting between bites, and then plunged its claws into its own chest and pulled a black, beating organ from the large, ragged opening, then shoved it into Tabansi's chest. Opening its wrist, it let its blood spill into both Tabansi's mouth and his gaping chest wound.

Tabansi lost consciousness for what seemed like only a moment.

When he came to, the small man had his hands on either side of Tabansi's face and spoke quietly. "You will not become the beast until you have tasted the blood of a living man. Until then, you will walk in the day and be like the man you came to me as. Know that you have only seven sunsets to do this, or you will be the dead thing I found in the desert. On each of those seven days, a spirit may challenge your will. The spirits of the animals, roots, earth, fire, water, sky, and finally, man, will decide the fate of your body. If, by the seventh day, you are still alive and a man offers you his blood, you will become the Asasabonsam. Drink the blood. Avenge your family."

The beast appeared again, screeching into his face before taking flight and vanishing. Tabansi blacked out again.

Noble woke and sat up, breathing heavily. He saw the man rocking on his heels next to a lit lantern as the ship swayed beneath them. "Still a lost man of God, No-bell Leencoln," he said, smiling widely, teeth red with blood.

Wide-eyed and scared, Noble looked down at his chest and, with a trembling hand, felt under the tattered material of his bloodied shirt as a gaping chest wound closed.

"What have you made me?" he asked as the African began laughing.

VIRGINIA

The shore was sighted on the evening of the third night after Noble's awakening. Captain Allsopp collapsed as the ship sailed into the bay of Virginia, starvation and dehydration having taken him from any further suffering as the zombie navigator of the sea.

The few remaining deckhands, little more than mindless slaves, set the ship's anchor as Noble sat on the rail, writing in his journal in the moonlight.

> I assume it is somewhere near the end of October 1712 since the weather has cooled, and my home lies just across the water.
>
> After awakening to the awful reality that is mine, I found the African languages spoken by Tabansi and his victims are now common tongues to my ears. I could even understand the Frenchman, who worked as the ship's navigator before Tabansi, the beast, tore out his throat.
>
> I am now resigned with the horrors of the ship. Fear has passed, leaving me numb. I am confused by what will happen to me. Will I become that thing, so black and evil, that monster that tore out my now-healed throat and killed so many others?
>
> I have no idea why I still write in the journal of a dead man. I do know I am finally home, but to what end?

I fear what I am. What I am, I know not. I hunger not for the remaining crew's food to stay alive: moldy oranges and herring. Those smells send my stomach lurching over the rail, although the only thing that comes up is blood, so much so I cannot explain why I have not died from this malady, so much like the consumption that killed my parents.

I have refused the Africans Tabansi sends to me. Looking into their eyes, he speaks to them, and they stop thinking as men do, instead following his every word as if it is of their own mind.

I have never seen such evil craftiness. Tabansi must be one of the demons the Bible warns of. Now I fear I am that demon as well. I do not feel any less love for God or his for me than I did in my days in the church. I pray, and it causes me no harm. However, looking skyward to the heavens, I find the sunlight burns my skin, and I feel as if there are flames in my skull, and I am forced below decks until it has set again.

The sky spirit denied me my end, so Tabansi has told me.

Tabansi believes this will stop when I finally take of my first kill. I cannot bring myself to do so. I look upon the Africans he sends to me not as food but as children following the cruel instruction of an evil father. I tell them to return to the hold while I wretch over the ship's side.

I asked Tabansi why he chose me to make this beast. He tells me he needs me to get him around in the New World, filled with men who would see him as nothing more than a slave. He also believes that since I made him what he is with the letting of my blood, he is only giving me the same chance at greatness in return.

He wants to find his wife, Siti. I have no idea what he thinks will come of finding her when he dines on or lays with other women from the cargo hold so freely. He is undoubtedly damned for that sin, less the sin of murder as he feeds on what remains of the Africans. Tabansi drains them almost to the point of death and then sends them to the top deck to jump overboard. Sometimes, they walk, while at other times, they crawl because they are too weak to stand.

Tabansi sees them as cattle going to slaughter rather than slaves to cruel white men.

'I asked how he would know of something he has never seen, never having left Africa.

He told me he sees the fate of them when he feeds on the ship's crew and the other white passengers. Everything that bleeds tells him a story: what kind of people they are, where they are from, whom they love, and their deepest secrets and wishes. Blood cannot lie as the lips do.

Though I saw Tabansi's life and loss flash through my mind as if they were my own memories, I cannot believe it so. I asked how it was possible. Tabansi told me it is a gift of the blood he shared with me, and he, in turn, saw mine when he drained me near death. He has seen my Elizabeth and our children. Of this, I am frightened.

Initially, I tried to stop the people from throwing themselves overboard, but his words must contain some black magic more potent than sense.

Last evening, I grabbed a woman as she climbed the rail, and I saw the look on her face as she peered down into the moonlit water. I watched a tear spill down her cheek, and then she jumped, taking us both into the sea. I slowly sank to the bottom with her, my arms around her shoulders on the gentle descent, until the moon shone no more and blackness overtook us.

I felt no pain, no urgency to fight for my life. I felt peace as I came to rest on the ocean floor. It was short-lived as the winged beast pulled me roughly by my coat up from the deep and deposited me back onto the deck. I coughed up ocean water for what seemed like hours. Tabansi said the spirit of the water denied me death as he smiled, patting my back, before returning to the women he keeps below.

I wonder how long I have left to live as a man still of my thoughts and not those whispered by whatever demon I am starving inside me. Tabansi has told me that the hunger grows fiercer in the days before the seventh sunset, which will mean my end. He swears I will feed and becomes angry when I turn away yet another would-be victim.

Tonight, we will set upon land. I watched in the early evening as the remaining crew poured barrels of gunpowder all along the *ship's bulkheads and over the bodies of those who were unable to make it to the top deck railing, strewn about the lower decks.*

Grasping what remains of my humanity in the guise of normalcy, I have packed my bags, and they sit in the boat tied up in the water below. After washing himself, Tabansi dressed in stolen clothing more suitable for a servant.

I dread what lies ahead, seeing his voracity played out upon this ship; I can only imagine what kind of extermination he plans for the colonists innocently waiting across the bay.

I desperately pray he brings no harm to my family and our home west of the village.

As a young, hollow-eyed African rowed the boat away from the *Buscador De Alma*, the first of several explosions set the ship ablaze. With tears welling in his eyes from fear and illness, Noble crossed himself. Sighing, he quietly prayed for those lost as the mast fell forward on the deck of the schooner that had been his home—and nightmare—for three months.

"Do not cry for them, No-bell Leencoln. They are free."

Noble ignored Tabansi and looked to the shore. Men on the docks sounded the alarm for the ship burning in the bay. Noble was envious of those men, for they were too far away to witness the vestiges of the horror suffered on his voyage home.

They pulled the boat ashore in a dark area of the beach. Noble picked up his bags and started for the lights of town.

Tabansi followed close behind, while the young rower walked into the ocean with a blank look. Noble envied the final peace the boy was allowed in the sea.

The inn smelled of dank sea air. Two prostitutes followed the well-dressed gentleman with a dark-skinned servant at his heels.

One was large and barely dressed, her heaving bosom all but hung out over her bodice. The other was skinny and pretty until she opened her mouth, revealing a black-toothed smile.

"Bugger off, you bloody harlots. He's not buying," said the innkeeper, shooing them away.

"I want the fat one," Tabansi said to Noble in his native tongue.

"No," responded Noble as the innkeeper walked them to the rented room.

Eyeing Tabansi, the innkeeper grunted. "The African has to stay in the horse stalls."

Noble turned on his heel. "I require my servant in my quarters for now, but I will honor your wishes and send him down when I've finished with him." He put a coin in the innkeeper's hand and unlocked the door.

The innkeeper walked away, mumbling about the growing number of Negros in town.

Tabansi set the bags down and closed the door of the room. "We shall feast on white women tonight."

Noble sat upon the bed, and fleas jumped about in the blankets. "I shall have no use of them."

Smiling, Tabansi sat on the bed beside him. "You want that woman in your head, the one with eyes like the sky and the hair gold like the desert grass."

"Yes, but not for the purpose you would have those whores serve."

"Then go and have her," he said, motioning to the door.

No longer surprised by his master's knowledge, Noble knew Elizabeth was no longer his alone to dream. "I am no longer her husband. I am a beast like you."

"You are just a man, the simple man I met in my country. You will not be the beast until you have taken blood from the living."

"I don't want her to be that source."

"Why not? She can be yours forever."

"I could not force another human being into this or the depths of hell that are sure to follow it. And I certainly would never subject my love to such a deplorable existence."

Tabansi shook his head.

Noble laid his gloves on the bedside table. "We have three days to find your wife before I can no longer help you."

"You say you will not feed," Tabansi said, kneeling before the white man and placing his black hand flat against Noble's chest, "but my heart is strong, and it will make you. Unlike you, it wants to live."

Looking into the black eyes that did not reflect candlelight, Noble pushed Tabansi's hand away. "God will not allow me to fall at the feet of a demon, for I serve him and him alone. You should not have chosen someone as faithful to God as I to become your companion-murderer."

Noble looked through the window, taking a long look at the bay. Boats rowed out, close as they dared, to the ship sinking in flames. He knew none would bring back survivors.

Scoffing, Tabansi growled, "I'm going to find food. You can stay here and pray that your God takes your life before you are caught up by the fate set upon you."

Tabansi slammed the door and was gone.

Dreams of Elizabeth and a strange pounding in his head woke him in the darkened room on the fourth day. The pounding stopped, then started again as he stood up, unsteady on his feet. His head was filled with a rhythmic pounding, which came closer and then moved away again. Footsteps outside of the inn door passed by, and so did the pounding. Noble realized the incessant pounding was nothing more than the heartbeats of the people outside of his room. He fell upon the bed and covered his head with blankets, hoping to dampen the torture drilling through his skull. His stomach begged in his gut, and the heart of the beast beat hard and fast in his chest.

Giving up, Noble pulled back the curtains and found the sun had set. Tabansi was not in the room. Noble assumed he was no doubt enjoying the cuisine Virginia had to offer.

Digging through his bags, he found a small painted picture of Elizabeth. He wished to meet her gaze and see her smile again before his death. Closing his eyes, he thought of her.

He helped her down from the carriage; her hand gently held his as she looked up at the grand house on land he had purchased with his parents' wedding gift. She pulled back the loose blonde curls blowing about her pretty face in the breeze while her bright blue eyes stared in wonder at the place that would soon be her home.

"Our home is beautiful, Noble."

"I hoped you would like it. A French architect who draws for my father drew it up for me. Father paid a king's ransom to get him to come here and see it built."

"The sun is so bright and shining. And the wildflowers are pretty. I never thought you would leave London. I'm so happy you did."

Noble looked into her eyes, taking her hands into his. "I left the church for you. It's a much smaller thing to leave one's home for someone you love."

"There is no greater want than of love and someone with which to share one's life. You have built a perfect place for us, and you have made me most happy, Noble. Your sacrifices have been great, but there are greater rewards still ahead. We will have babies, and gardens will bloom around them."

Noble looked at the sky and then at her. "There is no greater wish in my heart."

Staring out at the street lanterns, he furrowed his brow. "There is no harm in looking upon one's love before finding what is on the other side of death... even with a demon's heart pounding in your chest," he said to no one.

After sitting in the darkness of his room, trying to block out the bombardment of heart sounds around the inn and being unable to get Elizabeth off his mind, he decided to go to his homestead, even if it only meant peeking in her window.

Noble purchased a horse from the stable in town. He raced west out of the city and into the countryside. His eyes found no challenge in the darkness. For miles, he kept the horse's head low until he saw the familiar fields of his plantation home.

Noble tied the mare's lead to a tree and walked up to the edge of the woods near the house. He looked up at the French doors leading to the bedroom he had once shared with his wife. He listened to the night until he heard it over the sounds of the wind, insects, and animals in the woods behind him, the rhythmic, relaxed sound of her beating heart.

Seeing no movement, he climbed a trellis leading up to the balcony and peeked into the windows.

Elizabeth sat at her dressing table, her back to him, pulling a brush through her long blonde hair. She paused and looked up at the painting of her husband on the wall above the fireplace. "Where are you, Noble?" she asked the air.

He longed to be with her, to run his fingers through her hair, to comfort the loneliness the portrait brought her.

As she turned to the mirror, Elizabeth's eye caught the movement of something through the windows behind her, and she turned to the doors. Caught off guard, Noble stepped back from the glass out of the light.

She stood and walked quickly across the room toward him; her heartbeat quickened.

He jumped from the balcony and into the edge of the woods.

"Who is there?" she asked, opening the doors.

Noble stepped back into the trees out of her sight. He watched her lithe fingers set upon the rail as her eyes searched the grounds below. Her figure had slimmed since the last time he had seen her, and there was sadness in her eyes.

The sudden cry of an infant caused her to look back into the room. "Silas, I'm coming," she said, entering the room, careful to close the doors behind her.

He watched as she walked back to the windows, rocking the child in her arms, her eyes trained on the panes of glass. Noble smiled. Elizabeth had given him another son. *Silas.*

Leaning against the trunk of a birch tree, Noble's hand rested on his chest as his aching heart fell into rhythm with hers.

"I do so love you," he whispered, watching her walk away from the doors, hoping to be heard without being seen.

He closed his eyes and sank to his knees as he listened to her quietly whisper sweet words to the child suckling at her bosom. Tears streamed down his face as he remembered.

Laughing, she ran from him through the trees of her parents' orchard. He gave chase, finally catching up with her as she looked at him around the trunk of an apple tree. Placing his hand on hers lying on the smooth bark, he grinned. "I've caught the lady."

"But can you keep the lady, Mr. Lincoln?" She laughed and ran again with him following.

Elizabeth ducked behind another tree and stood quietly, biting her lip. Noble ran up behind her, catching her hand for a moment before she ran again, holding up her skirts a few inches to keep them out of the dirt.

"How is it the lady who was so eager to chase me now demands I chase her?" he called out behind her.

She stopped and turned to him, out of breath. "You must court me; you said you would."

He shook his head and smiled. "I said I would marry you because you made me promise. We have surely surpassed courting now, Lady Darby," he said, walking toward her.

"I should simply marry without the enjoyment of your courting me. Did you not know courting is what a woman lives for?"

"Is that so?"

"Yes. You bring me pretty flowers and trinkets of your affection to make me wonder how well you know me—if you are a true fit for my hand and family."

He put an arm around her waist and gently laid her on the grass. "I've come here, leaving my family, leaving my church, my faith, shaken by love ... for you. And still, you question my worth, Elizabeth Darby?"

She smiled up at him. "I'm only toying with you because you get that look in your eyes that I so adore."

"What look would that be?"

"The look that says you mean to kiss me."

"I've meant to kiss you for quite some time, but you always have me chase you as if you do not wish to be kissed."

Elizabeth looked up into his eyes and placed her hand on the side of his face gently. "I live for the day my lips become your only wish and your kisses never stop."

"Since I renounced my place in the church, your lips are all I have wished for. I pray the chase ends and you become mine in the eyes of God."

Smiling up at him, she replied, "My lips are yours forever, Noble. You only need to take back your name and titles from home to be found a proper suitor by my father, Lord Lincoln, my love."

Leaning down, he kissed her lips. They closed their eyes, not wanting to wake from the dream.

Noble sat beneath the tree, wishing he could feel the memory upon his lips and her hand on his face. Tears flowed from his eyes, and then the light from the balcony window was extinguished.

Walking on the grass below the windows, he prayed silently to God to return to the life he'd had before setting foot upon the *Buscador De Alma*.

As Noble walked toward the trees where he had tied his horse, he heard it whinny in alarm. He ran until the trees parted, and he saw a dark form standing near the gelding. "These things, they do not like me," he said, walking toward Noble.

"Horses sense danger, Tabansi."

"I have no taste for these beasts."

"What are you doing here?"

"I came to see the woman from your head and to find out if you still control yourself or if you were dying out here alone."

"You have nothing to worry yourself about. I am still able to travel in search of your wife. I merely looked upon my own and dreamed of my old life."

"I am scared for your future. You must be hearing the people's heartbeats so loudly in your ears."

Noble took hold of the reins of his horse and climbed into the saddle. "I do, but I will not give in to it."

"Then you will die, lost man of God."

"If it means one less demon on this earth, I will. Though lost I may be, I will not be forced into corruption. No matter how terribly this heart of yours begs for me to kill. The mind can overcome the heart, no matter the evil buried within it."

Tabansi laughed. "If the heart were weaker than the mind, you would still be a holy man in your church."

Taking a deep breath to keep from lashing out at the monster, Noble gently kicked the horse and rode off into the night.

SEARCHING
FOR A GOD

Though ill, Noble woke at first light and set out to the slave markets, seeking Tabansi's wife, Siti. No one questioned a well-dressed gentleman about his queries of an African woman. He looked like a man willing to pay well for what he sought.

Cages kept the newly arrived segregated. Chains kept them controlled. At first sight, most would believe they were under arrest for some unknown crime. They dressed as though they had always lived in the colonies. Looking into their eyes, however, told another story.

These Africans' eyes differed little from those he saw in Africa. Once on the ship, the men would try to stand taller than their captors and intimidate the sailors. Though they were chained, they were angry and shouted in foreign tongues, demands that would never be met. Now in the new colonies, their once booming voices had been silenced into mere whispers. The Africans' faces, once filled with anger and fear, had turned into expressions of defeat and sadness brought on by the loss of family and familiarity, now separated by an ocean. Strange men—pale-skinned men—spoke to them in tongues they did not know, followed by the stinging of leather lashes they did not understand.

Given only a blanket, clothes, and shoes—strange upon feet having never had something between them and the earth—they awaited buyers or shipment down the winding rivers.

Stepping into a cage of a dozen or so women, Noble freely walked as they moved out of his way, fearing more lashes from this new stranger.

"Looking for a housemaid... or maybe something else?" asked the slaver, licking his chapped lips and stepping behind him. Two more waited at the door, ready to strike if the slaves decided to do anything threatening.

Turning to him, Noble grimaced. "You are a foul man. Leave me."

"These are my Africans, and you won't be touching my property, 'less you mean to pay."

"Leave me, trader. I mean no harm or foul upon your property," he said, holding up a large gold coin in front of the rotten-toothed slave trader, whose eyes sparkled with greed.

Noble held fast to the gold as the trader grabbed the coin. "Leave me; I will not be long."

"Whatever you say, mister."

The man then took the coin and bit into it while he slowly backed out of the cage.

Once the trader had gone from sight and the sound of a closing door met Noble's ears, he turned to the women along the walls. Noble tried a smile, hoping it would calm the racing hearts pounding in his ears.

"I mean no harm to you," he said, holding up his hands.

The clinking of shackles sounded as the women backed away to the walls.

As Tabansi had instructed him, Noble kneeled to the wood plank floor of the cage to make himself less threatening to them. Turning his empty palms in front of him, he showed them he held no whip. "Do not be frightened. *Bā lua. Bā lua. Méndemo abië?*" he whispered. The clinking of chains stopped as he whispered again, "Are you Mende? *Bā lua. Méndemo abië?*"

The darkest of the women with large, frightened eyes took tiny steps forward and spoke, and he understood. "I am Mende; we are all Mende. You know our voice?"

Looking up at her, Noble nodded and, trying to not frighten the captive females, said, "A little ... *ga mero kru kru.*"

The woman turned to the group behind her, and whispers started moving throughout the cage.

"Can you understand me in English?"

Eyes narrowed around him, and the room fell silent. "I am seeking a woman called Siti?"

Women looked out from behind other women, but no one spoke.

"Siti? Please, I must find her," Noble tried again.

"There is no Siti here. Why are we here? Why?" asked the brave dark woman.

"Are you to set us free?" whispered another.

Unwilling to meet their eyes with unpleasant news, Noble looked to the floor. "*Sao* ... no. I'm sorry. I know not your fates; I can only guess. What I do know would not set your minds at ease."

The dark woman kneeled in front of Noble, surprising him as her eyes met his. "Why do you seek this woman when you are no man? In those eyes, you are a dark creature, but your voice is not."

"I must find her for my master; she is his wife and quite possibly the only thing keeping him from slaughtering the whole of this land." Sighing, Noble blinked and stood up, wishing he could take them all out of the horrible place and return them home. "I'm sorry. I must go, *bi lemungo le. Gĩ' I la.*"

Stepping out of the cage, Noble did not look back as the women called out to him in Mende, further questioning their future and begging for freedom.

As the slave trader stepped past him with his keys, Noble wondered what satisfaction he might get from giving in to the hunger gnawing away in his gut and killing the small, horrible man, if only to set the people caged around him free. He shook the thought from his head. Freeing them, but giving his soul to hell for eternity for the murders and death the creature he would become would surely set upon the world.

Noble left the building, mounted his horse, and set off to the next town's slave traders.

WARMTH FOUND

News of the sunken *Buscador De Alma* and her lost crew and cargo made its rounds through the coastal town and farther inland. The beach was crowded with carrion birds and other animals eating parts of corpses the sea tossed up on the shore.

Tabansi, holding a lantern, snuck past the innkeeper into the rented room late on the sixth evening of Noble's awakening. Walking over to the bed, Tabansi shook the sleeping white man.

Noble fought to open his eyes.

As Tabansi sat down on the mattress, his eyes did not hide his disappointment. "You look as if you have already died, No-bell Leencoln."

Struggling through the agony, Noble spoke. "It cannot come soon enough. My gut is swelling with pain, and it is most terrible. My limbs are stiff with cold." He paused, wiping the trails of bloody tears falling from his eyes. "I cannot stop this incessant bleeding from my eyes." Noble fell silent for a moment, looking toward the window. "Darkness keeps consuming my head; each time, I pray it is the last. But then I awaken again, still here."

Nodding, the African spoke. "Did you find anything at the slave market about Siti or my people?"

Noble shook his head. "I've spoken to many traders over the last few days but have learned nothing... There is no sign she was ever here."

Sitting silently, he looked at the white man before speaking. "Your God has not answered you?"

Noble's teeth chattered from the cold running through his body. "No, but soon enough, death will take me, and every question I have ever wanted answered will be so."

"You put great faith in a man you cannot see, No-bell Leencoln."

Searching the eyes of his maker, Noble asked, "Do your people have no God?"

"We have Ngewo. Instead of kneeling before a statue or reading from a book, we ask our ancestors and Nga-fa to help us to speak to him. But I do not think he hears me. When I find my infant son in the fire, I ask my ancestors why. No answer. When Diallo dies to the men with the spears that throw fire, I *demand* to know why. Still no answer. When Siti tells me to run away, I think in my heart that Ngewo must speak through her to me. But then she is also gone from me. After the Asasabonsam put the spirit of the winged beast in my soul, I know Ngewo is not there anymore, only Siti. She is my God. She is the only one to tell me why I must live." He pointed to his temple. "I know in here she has gone from the earth with my sons." He placed his hand on Noble's chest. "But I know in here if I give up looking for her, I will have no God at all."

Noble looked into the Tabansi's black eyes. "You put your faith in someone you believe already dead."

Tabansi shrugged. "But I also put my faith in a man who wants to die but still searches for Siti for me."

Noble tried to smile, but it faltered. "Then, by definition, I'm still a holy man, for I am helping a man find his God."

Tabansi laughed. "I believe you are right."

Trying to laugh, Noble coughed hard until blood spilled from his mouth and ran down his chin.

"You are running out of my blood, and you will leave me alone in a world that is not mine, Holy Man."

Fighting to keep his eyes open, Noble responded, "When the winged beast entered your soul, you stopped belonging to the whole of this world, Tabansi. Just as I have." Noble's eyelids fluttered for a moment until he forced them open again. "I now believe *you* were right... I am a lost man of God."

"Yes. It appears you are right. You are lost to the world. I have seen your woman with the golden hair and sky eyes dressed in black and mourning for you at the place of many stones."

Alarmed by the thought of Tabansi following Elizabeth, while he lay so ill and unable to protect her, Noble tried to sit up. "You've seen her?"

"A wood cross sits amongst many stones on the hill near your home. She cried on her knees there in the early morning rain. You should go to her, No-bell Leencoln."

"No, no, I can't. I fear I would kill Elizabeth to abate this pain. I feel as though I am not myself. I can hear so many hearts beating, even ones so far away they are barely a whisper in my ears. I've shackled myself to the bed to keep from leaving. I fear all of this blood pulsing around me is driving me into madness."

Tabansi pulled back the blankets and saw the rusted iron shackles Noble had secreted in his bags from the ship cutting into his ankles and wrists. Necrotic skin surrounded bloody gaping wounds as if he had been desperately fighting to release himself, making even Tabansi grimace and shake his head. Looking into the white man's dying eyes, Tabansi spoke. "You will sleep now, Holy Man."

The African stood up, and Noble's eyes closed.

Noble awakened to the hoots of an owl. Instead of the dank-smelling darkness of the seaside inn room, fresh, cool air and stars filled the sky above him. He felt strangely better. Looking toward the trees, he rubbed his eyes and smiled at the large golden-eyed rouser as it spread its wings and flew away. Noble raised his hands above his face and found the shackles gone. Alarmed, he looked around, finding himself on the balcony of his home. The light came from behind the curtains. Trying to find his feet, but weakened by the death six days coming, he fell against the windows, knocking against them hard, and slid down to his knees.

Footsteps ran toward him, and the windows opened into the room. "No, stay away," he demanded as his eyes met hers and he fell back against the railing. "Elizabeth, no, you must run away. I am no longer the man you married. Please, Elizabeth, leave me."

Elizabeth's hands grabbed at his collar, keeping him from falling. "Noble... My Noble. We believed you dead. We heard the ship in the harbor was yours, and they said they found no one alive."

Noble collapsed, and Elizabeth dropped to her knees and pulled him into her lap. His wife cradled his head in her arms. "My poor husband," said Elizabeth.

For Noble, her words were all but drowned out by the sounds of her heart beating and the blood flowing through her veins. Pushing her arm away, he said, "Please, no... You mustn't."

"You're hurt. My poor husband, let me get Joseph to help you inside."

Fighting to regain his feet and flee, he pulled away from her; his stomach felt as if it was collapsing on itself. His lips started to feel pinched by his descending fangs. "No, Elizabeth, please leave me here. You must stay away from me. I am not myself."

"Your eyes, what's wrong, my Lord Lincoln? Why do you act so strangely?"

"You must let me go. I bring death."

A baby started crying in the room, and Elizabeth looked into the room. "I am coming, my sweet Silas," she called out to her child. "Let me get Joseph to help you inside so I can get the baby."

"No, Elizabeth, don't..."

Noble's head felt as though it was spinning, and he could not get enough air. He tried taking deep breaths; his stomach lurched, and he reached for the rail and released the contents into the grass below before collapsing again and blacking out.

Noble awakened in the candlelit room. A cold towel wet his forehead and cheeks. The soft, down-filled mattress beneath him felt familiar. Worried blue eyes looked down at him. A thin smile played upon her lips. "Hello, my love. I'm trying to bring the color back to your cheeks. You were chilled to the bone. I was worried you were dying," she said, laying her hand on his. "I put the bed warmer beneath the blankets to chase away the cold. Joseph said you were like ice when he carried you in."

Candlelight gave her skin a light honey color, and the flame's reflection sparkled in her eyes. He had missed her. Elizabeth placed her hand on his cheek and smiled, and Noble felt like he had awakened from a nightmare. The sounds of heartbeats had gone silent. His wounds were gone, and Elizabeth gave no notice to the blood that had rained down his face. *Had it all been a dream? Had he never left home? Was this a dream now? No horror like that could ever be real.*

Raising his hand to her cheek and touching her to assure himself she was real, he responded, "I've slept with the worst nightmares and awakened in the most beautiful dream."

Elizabeth smiled down at him. "I've lived the worst of my days these last few months until now. There are no words for the happiness I feel for your return." Leaning down, she kissed his lips gently.

Her breath was warm on his mouth, and her lips soft and giving. A long stray curl fell upon his cheek, tickling him. Pulling her closer until she was almost on top of him, he longed for the feel of her. As he lay beneath her, she started to unlace his shirt, pushing her warm hands beneath the cotton. "You're cold, my love. Let me warm you," she whispered into his ear.

Nodding his response, he kissed her. His tongue found hers between deep, hot breaths, exploring hands pushing away the robe over her nightgown.

Reaching to the top of the delicately embroidered neckline of her white dressing gown, he started to pull the lacing loose until the fabric slid down her shoulder, then arm, exposing the top of a pale breast. He slowly pulled the other shoulder down until she was nude to the waist. His hands reacquainted themselves with her body, his mouth to her mouth, as hearts quickened and their breathing hastened. She unlaced his trousers while he pulled his shirt over his head, letting it fall from the bed before meeting her lips once again. Running her fingers lightly down his chest, she kissed his neck as he pushed down his trousers and pulled her entirely on top of him.

Looking at her golden skin, completely naked in the candlelit room, he was in awe. The softness of her beneath his fingers and the love in her eyes could never paint a prettier picture. He sat up, meeting her lips. With both hands on either side of her face, he pulled her down until her breasts brushed his chest. She felt the fullness of him brushing against her inner thighs, meeting the inviting warmth of her. Unable to wait any longer, he grabbed onto her hips, directing her until he pushed inside of her and heard the low moan she released in his ear as she wrapped her arms around his neck. She moved gently against him as his hands held on to her hips, setting the rhythm of their lovemaking and seemingly the flicker of the candles about the room.

Afterward, he lay with her upon his chest, feeling the rise and fall of her slumbering breath against his side. Slowly, he ran his fingers through the long golden curls of her hair. "Please, God, make this the heaven I have prayed for," he whispered as his eyes fell closed.

Scratching sounds above had him squinting to see in the darkness. Exhausted and half-asleep, his slowly opening eyes just made out something large and black looming as he closed his eyes again, slipping further into his dreams.

He lifted her from the floor as the music played in the ballroom. She smiled down at him as her feet met the hardwood again, then she circled him and moved down the line of men in the bright candlelit room. The new girl in front of him curtsied, and he bowed, but his eyes did not leave Elizabeth as hers sparkled and caught his glance.

"Feed from her," was whispered in his ear.

Laughing, Elizabeth fell to the bed beneath him, still wearing her wedding veil. "Will you place a babe in my womb this night, my husband?" she asked as he unlaced the front of her gown.

"If it is your wish, my dear wife."

She smiled and placed her hand on his cheek. "I love you, my Lord Lincoln."

"No, I love her," he whispered to the nightmare as he rolled to his side in his sleep.

They ran through the yard, chasing a small boy running for a swing hanging from a tree. The child looked back, giggling. "Father, push me so that I can fly as high as the geese!"

"Push him carefully, Father," warned the ever-protective mother.

He pushed the boy gently with one hand while his other arm held his wife close, and he kissed her lips.

"You should be careful; you will give Yancy a brother or sister before we're ready."

He smiled at her. "I should think he would like a playmate or you a little girl to dress up."

"She will wake next to a rotting corpse if you do not," whispered the nightmare.

The housemaid held his young daughter while Yancy clutched tightly to Elizabeth's skirts. They stood on the dock at the ship as men carried things past them onto the schooner. Her golden curls fell around her face as her worried eyes searched his.

"Can't your uncle take care of your parents' last wishes?"

Noble looked into her begging eyes. "I will be back before our child arrives, I promise. I must go now, Elizabeth." He kissed her quivering lips. Tears slid down her cheeks.

"Take care of my family, Jenny," he told the house slave.

"Yes, sir, Master Lincoln." Noble walked onto the ramp and stepped down onto the ship's main deck.

"I would rather be a corpse than a killer... Let me alone," he whispered forcefully.

Noble rolled again to his other side as the nightmare continued. Flashes of memories, bloody teeth gnashing, screaming and moaning as lightning crashed, illuminating the black beast that turned to him.

"Denying the beast will only cause your death," whispered the grave voice.

Waving her handkerchief in the coastal breeze, she called out, "Return to me quickly, my love!"

Seeing the creature raise its claws, Noble begged for death. "Kill me, and let me suffer no more, demon!" he called out.

He smelled the foulness of the creature, and wet warmth poured over his body. The pain vanished, but the strong smell of copper met his nose as he rolled toward the occupied side of the bed. His hand rested on something warm and sticky.

Noble woke, sitting up in his bed, breathing heavily. He tasted a wet, coppery warmth in his mouth and felt the same on his lips and chin. The slowing of a beating heart met his ears. All but one candle had gone out, and the fireplace had gone dark. As his eyes focused on the light, he saw her and cried out, "No, Elizabeth, my Elizabeth!"

She lay on her back, her glassy eyes staring upward. Red painted the once cream-colored sheets around her, staining her golden hair and pale skin.

Putting his fingers to his lips, he pulled back the same red. "No!"

Overwrought, he pulled her into his arms, holding her as the pulsing blood in her veins fell still. He rocked her as he sobbed into her hair and kissed her brow. "I prayed not to become this beast," he shouted, looking up. "I wanted to die! Why didn't you take me? Take me and save her..."

Footsteps pounded against the wood floors of the servant's rooms above as the doors leading to the balcony burst open.

Tabansi stood outside. "You must come; they cannot see you."

Noble shook his head as tears continued down his face. "I will not run from what I have done."

A child's voice called out in the hallway outside of the locked doors. "Mother! Mother, are you alright?" Small fists pounded on the door when there was no response and the door handle refused to turn. "Mother!"

The African's dark eyes met those of Noble. "Do you want to have to kill your children or let them see you like this?"

"I must be punished, Tabansi, for I am evil."

"Do you believe the beast that did this will allow itself to be punished by mortal men?" Tabansi asked, motioning to the woman Noble clutched in his arms. "You would only kill them."

Kissing her brow again and again, he rocked her as voices outside the door begged for her to answer.

"Mister Lincoln, Missus Lincoln," called out Joseph frantically. "Are you alright? Do you need help?"

"Go gets the keys from downstairs," demanded a woman's voice.

"Mother, please, open the door," called out a smaller voice from the hallway.

"Missus Lincoln, we're trying to get in," called out the familiar voice of Jenny, the kitchen servant.

Footsteps ran from the door as Joseph headed for the first floor.

Remaining silent, Noble looked at the man standing on the balcony.

"Holy Man, we must go. Now," pressed Tabansi, his fangs descending and his eyes glowing red. "Do not force me to kill what remains of your family."

Fearful of Tabansi's sobering words, Noble looked down at the face of his wife as tears of blood fell onto her cheeks from his eyes. "I'm so sorry I did not return your husband and that I allowed this beast I've become to murder you. My heart meant you no harm, but a demon has consumed my soul, and I cannot control it." He covered her body with a blanket and kissed her lips. Laying her on the bed, he gathered his clothes and shoes.

Pulling on his pants, he heard Joseph returning, the keys jingling as they fell, hitting the floorboards. "Gimme the keys, Mister Joseph."

As the lock disengaged and the doors flew open, Noble's feet hit the grass below. "I'm sorry, Elizabeth. There are no words for the sorrow I feel, little Yancy, my dear Mira, and Silas, my dear infant son, for taking your mother," he whispered to the windows above him.

Joseph ran to the balcony and looked around the grounds as a great winged beast flew past a bright full moon, carrying what seemed to be a man from its talons.

The house slave crossed himself as his master had taught him while a woman screamed and children cried out in terror.

AN ANGEL'S HAND

N oble fought for release from the hooked talons carrying him over an open field near the town. "Release me!" he called out to the beast.

The beast dropped him and flew over his head, landing just in front of him. It crouched down and smelled the air before its hair vanished, and it returned to human form. Tabansi stood up; his black skin turned gray in the moonlight. He looked puzzled by Noble's request. "Why have you stopped us?"

Caught off guard by Tabansi's question, he grew angry. "You put me there, on her balcony, knowing what would happen! Why? I demand to know!"

The stoic African did not speak. Instead, he glowered.

"Do you think after watching my wife die I would be happy to follow along as if it is all done... as if I have tied up the loose ends of my life?"

Tabansi flared his large, round nostrils. "Killing them all would have been tying loose ends. You are finished here. Your woman is dead, and we have many places left to look for Siti."

Running forward, he pushed Tabansi with all his strength, trying to topple him, but the African stood fast.

He dared not mention his children to a man so willing to kill anyone.

"You should have killed me on the ship. I don't want to be this monster, and I won't be your servant!"

Tabansi pushed back; Noble fell back to his elbows in the tall grass. "I need you to talk to these white men. I must find Siti. You will do this for me."

Jumping to his feet, Noble glared. "My wife is dead; my care is no longer with yours!"

Pounding on his substantial, muscular chest, wide-eyed and spitting between descending fangs, Tabansi ran at Noble again. "Siti is alive. You are going to give me back my wife. It is your people that took her! You will listen to me! You will give me what I lost."

Pushing back against Tabansi, he felt as the grass gave way under his feet; his boots dug into the dirt. His fangs came down, and his eyes glowed red. "What makes you believe that you deserve to get her back? You are not her husband anymore. You're a demon and a murderer, and you've made me one. No God forgives that."

The African grabbed the front of Noble's shirt and overcoat, picked him up above his head, and slammed him hard against the ground onto his back, knocking the wind from him. As the beast spoke, Tabansi leaned over into Noble's face with rancid, heavy breath and drool. "My God is forgiving."

"If I *were* God, I would send you straight to hell to burn for all eternity, never to see your family again," Noble scolded between clenched teeth. "Now, release me."

"You serve me, white man."

Seething, Noble responded, "I serve only *my* God."

Releasing Noble, the African growled at him, turned back into the beast, and flew into the moonlit night toward the coast.

Noble sat in the field, looking down at his hands as his claws returned to fingernails. Closing his eyes, he thought simply of her, the eyes so loving and the caress of a kiss so soft it faded like her dying eyes. Tears ran down his face as he looked at the sky. "I am sorry I have failed you."

Anger, fear, sadness, and hatred ran through him as he stumbled through the dark streets. Noble cried crimson tears that he wiped away, hoping to be unnoticed. The roads had a few stragglers who were headed toward their homes after late-night drinking had settled them. He counted them as his ears picked up their heartbeats and shuffling footsteps. Ignoring the sound of beating hearts that sent his stomach lurching and his mouth watering, he walked on, staring at the high steeple of his destination. His only thought was to rid himself of the demon possessing him.

He slowed as he reached the heavy wooden doors of the Bruton Parish Church. Wrapping his coat tight around him to hide the blood on his shirt, he pounded hard upon the oak. There was no response. He thought it was almost four in the morning, thus Father Benedict would be sleeping. He pounded again, desperate for someone to answer.

Footfalls hit the stone floor inside. Noble prayed he would not be turned away. A small door opened, and a woman in a black coif appeared, carrying a lantern. "What is it at this hour?"

"I need Father Benedict; I must speak to him."

Raising the lantern above her head, she looked at his face. She could not miss the crimson tears running down his cheeks. "Father Lincoln, is that you? It's been at least half a year since we've seen you. We thought you dead at sea."

"Sister, yes, it is me. I must see Father Benedict ... please?"

Closing the small door, she opened the large oak door and moved out of his way so he could enter. "Come in, Father. Are you hurt? There is blood on your face."

Before he could answer, someone holding a lantern at the front of the church moved toward them. "Sister Nan, what is it?"

"Henry," said Noble, moving toward the man in a black cassock, "I am in desperate need of your help."

The priest stepped toward him. "Noble? What's wrong? Where have you been? Elizabeth has been here every sunrise and sunset, praying for your safe return." The priest raised the lantern above his head, getting a better view of his old friend. "What's wrong with your eyes?"

Noble moved closer to his friend. "I did not return alone, Henry. Something terrible is inside of me, and I am most desperate to have it take its leave of me."

"I do not understand."

Noble sat down on the end of a pew, crying again. Henry kneeled next to him, studying his face. "Tell me, Noble, what is troubling you?"

Noble's eyes took a red glow for just a moment, looking up at the priest. The priest looked startled and grabbed the cross from his chest. "What demon is this?"

"Henry, the ship that was supposed to bring me home safe was taken over by a monster you can only imagine in your worst dreams. It cast a demon inside of me, a horrible, winged thing. The beast fed on the rest of the passengers. It also tried to make me eat them, but I fought it and escaped. I have never felt such fear. I am afraid I am no longer your friend, but something to cast back into hell. I am frightened, Brother. Please help me."

"What are you asking of me?"

"I need to have this demon gone. It has done something, something terrible," Noble said, opening his coat so his blood-covered shirt was visible. "I have sinned horribly. Please free me of this beast."

"What happened, Brother? Whose blood is that upon you?"

Noble covered his face with his hands and wept. "All I can recall is making love to her, and then she was in my arms just lying there, her eyes wide and her throat torn open--blood everywhere..." He paused, looking up at the priest. "Henry, you know me. I am no killer. But this beast inside of me. I think it murdered her using my hands. Her blood was on my lips when I awoke, but I do not recall doing it. I love Elizabeth so. This must be the work of Satan. Please free me, Brother." Bloody tears ran down his cheeks again, and the whites of his eyes glared red in the lantern light.

Father Benedict crossed himself. "Oh my God, Noble. Is Elizabeth dead? It makes no sense. You're a man of the cloth. What am I to do to help you?"

"Please, Brother, send this demon back to hell. I must be free of this beast, and then take me to the magistrate. I must pay for my crime. And please pray for my wife's soul so that she may go to the heaven she deserves. She and my newborn child, they must meet God."

"Oh, Noble. I'm without words."

"I'm losing my soul. I am damned. You must rid the earth of this creature, Henry."

"You're asking for an exorcism?"

Taking the priest's hands in his own, Noble looked into his eyes. "If you don't, I don't know what I will do, what this beast will have me do. I am so afraid of this demon. I have never feared anything like this before."

Father Benedict nodded. "I warn you, I've not done this before. If I could have more time, I could call upon the bishop to come."

"I don't know how much time I have. Please, Henry, I beg of you. Free me from this monster."

"Alright, Noble."

The priest looked up at the nun holding the lantern near the door. "Sister Nan, I need your assistance. We need to gather some things for an exorcism."

The nun crossed herself. "Yes, Father."

Noble stood up and walked to the east wing of the church. Carved into the marble was a baptismal pool. The water was pure and clear. At all points was a marble bench bearing a cross. Noble kneeled before the cross on the wall above the water and crossed himself. *Had I not abandoned God for the love of a woman and the lusting of her flesh, would I not be inhabited by this demon? Was this God's punishment for leaving the church?*

Sister Nan lit candles about the pool, casting light on the walls. Pulling off his coat, he slowly unbuttoned his shirt, his mind settling on a memory.

Bishop Timms looked at him in shock. "You wish to leave the church for this woman?"

Feeling as though he were begging, Noble pressed on. "I do not feel like a man deserving of this cassock or this great church. My flesh is weak, and I cannot stop wanting her."

The bishop let out a deep breath and leaned forward, folding his hands on his desk. "Have you committed carnal sin, Father Lincoln?"

"No... No, of course not. I am still pure. But I fear I cannot remain so. I have prayed long and hard, trying to rid myself of these thoughts. No manner of prayer has given me an answer."

"Then you must pray harder, Father Lincoln."

"I'm done praying. God has no resolution for me. To me, it is a sign that he understands. I want to be free of this binding. I want to marry this woman and do something else with my life."

"This woman has bewitched you. Can you not see it? The evil carried upon a methodically lifted bosom and a poisoned tongue that whispers sweetly in your ear, meant to fill your head with impure thoughts."

Noble smiled for a moment, thinking happily of her. "She has bewitched me, but I do not see evil in her or her ways. I am taken with her. I feel as though every breath she takes is also mine. As if without her, I would suffocate and wither away into dust."

"I don't understand. You were one of the strongest of God's servants. How can you have fallen so easily into this sin?"

"If you only understood this amazing warmth in my heart, the love I feel, more so than that which I feel for God. Maybe I was never meant to be here."

Bishop Timms got up from his chair, walked to a pedestal, and opened a large wooden box. He pulled from it a cloth-covered package and turned to Noble. "Pray with blood upon your back; beg forgiveness, and he will answer you."

Noble accepted Timm's answer and looked into his friend's old, tired eyes. "Will he, Steven?"

The older man let out a groan. "If he does not answer you by the time you return to your feet when the sun rises, then go. But know, although you have taken this punishment in stride, it may not be the only suffering that will befall you for such flagrant abandonment, Noble."

"Yes, Bishop. I will do as you instruct. I only pray it is an acceptable step in what lies ahead for me, if it is with her or here with you and the church."

Kneeling before the altar in his room, naked, with tears running down his face, he prayed to the cross while the separate leather strips from the cat-o'-nine-tails hit his back over either shoulder with traumatic force.

The kisses later laid upon his wounds took away the misery of his decision as Elizabeth gently pulled the blanket wrapped around his shoulders.

Tears fell as she whispered, "I'm so sorry, Noble," with each gentle touch of her lips.

He looked up as a hand was placed on his shoulder, returning him to reality. Henry smiled down at him. "I will do my best, old friend."

Nodding, he picked up the manacles attached to the stone floor by iron hooks. He attached one to his left wrist and ankle, immediately noticing the burning against his skin. Looking at the links, he saw each was engraved with a cross. Ignoring the pain, he stepped carefully to the southernmost stone altar. Pulling himself upon it, he swung his legs up on the cold granite. Henry pulled up the other manacles and placed them around his friend's remaining ankle and wrist.

"Henry, make sure to pull the chains tight. I do not want this beast loose nor the deaths of more people I care about laid upon my conscience."

The priest nodded. "I will be careful. With you helping me with your faith, I have no doubt of our success, Brother Lincoln," he said, laying down his Bible, a silver cup, and a large iron cross on the altar next to Noble.

The nun picked up his bloodied clothes and took them from the room.

"I will do my best, Henry."

"Are you ready?" asked the priest as the nun returned.

Although he looked worried, Noble nodded. "Yes."

Sister Nan pulled a lever in the floor, and the altar began to spin slowly, the chains pulling tighter as they pulled into the iron track surrounding the platform. Henry held his shoulders tight so that he would lie down gently.

As Noble's back touched the bottom of the cross on the altar, he started screaming. Smoke filled the air, and flesh burned.

"Stop the chains, Sister," said Henry.

As the nun reached for the lever, Noble shouted, "No, keep going, don't stop! It's the demon."

Henry cringed as the smell of his friend's burning flesh filled the air, and Noble's shoulders finally rested on the altar.

Holding back screams, he arched his back as his elongated fangs descended, and he reached for the priest with sharp claws and glaring red eyes. The irons clanked and squealed as the monster took shape. Henry raised his cross and started reading from his Bible, shouting the words to hide his fear:

"*Crux sancta sit mihi lux!*

Non draco sit mihi dux!

Vade retro satana!

Numquam suade mihi vana.

Sunt mala quae libas.

Ipse venena bibas."

Sister Nan stepped up next to the altar, crossing herself and praying with Father Benedict in a whisper:

"Let the Holy Cross be my light.

Let not the dragon be my guide.

Return to which you came, Satan!

Never tempt me with vain things.

What you offer me is evil.

You drink the poison yourself."

Father Benedict watched the creature bow its back repeatedly as flesh burned on the cross beneath it. *"Vade retro satana!* Tell me who you are, demon! *Crux sancta sit mihi lux!"*

It pulled hard at the chains but remained trapped and unwilling to answer.

"Who are you? Tell me your name so that I may return you to hell!"

Sister Nan shook her head and continued to pray quietly as the priest picked up his silver cup and dipped it into the pool. Praying over the water, he took his place back at the altar and demanded again, "Tell me your name, demon!"

With no response, the father started splashing the holy water over the beast. It screamed in pain, and its widened, glowing eyes glared. Its skin burned, and more smoke rose. The stench of it was unbearable. But still, it did not speak.

The priest refilled the cup. "I shall baptize the demon from him," he said, looking at Sister Nan. She nodded, holding tight to the silver cross on her chest, and continued her prayers.

He stepped up to the altar and started the baptism. Reaching down, he poured the water onto his friend's forehead. An inhuman shrieking filled the room. One of the creature's clawed hands pulled hard against the chains. Benedict continued shouting prayers of baptism and pouring water until the chain snapped. The creature grabbed on to his cassock, throwing him against the wall. Benedict slid down until he slumped on the floor. The beast screamed again, trying to free its other hand.

Suddenly, a brilliant light filled the room, brighter than the sun. The creature recoiled, covering its eyes until the claws shrank back down into human nails and fangs receded into his gums, leaving no trace of the beast. His eyes took back their ocean color, and he lay silent on the altar as the light vanished.

Moving his hand away from his eyes, he looked up into the glowing green eyes of a young woman hovering above him. Her robes of white shone light, and her skin glowed gold. She moved toward him. Brightly shining wings silently moved up and down as if to keep her in flight.

Noble began to speak, but she placed a finger on his lips, silencing him.

Her voice echoed while her lips remained unmoving. "We need not hear your prayers. We know what they are, Noble Lincoln. We've come with a message you must hear. The beast you seek to be free of is no more a demon than you are. It is a creature you have become, a Lamia. It is only as good or evil as you allow it to be, for it is you. The night is now your day, the blood of man is now your water, the cross is now your damnation, but soon your salvation."

Unable to move or speak, he stared at her with frightened eyes. She placed one hand around his throat while the other reached into her robes and pulled out a large silver cross. "Be still, and know through the pain, you shall live."

She pushed the cross into the bare skin of his chest. Noble screamed as the metal melted away his skin, exposing the underlying muscle and, finally, his ribs. Beneath the cage of bone, his black lungs inhaled and exhaled quickly and his black heart raced. The silver turned bright gold as it melted, spilling over his sternum and ribs while winding swirls of metallic liquid carved words into the bone. Gold dropped down between his ribs and began encasing his heart, which beat faster yet against the walls of gold starting to surround it.

Trying to escape, he tried grabbing for her hand but found his hand slipped through as if she wasn't there.

As his muscles and skin healed over the gold cross-covered bone, the angel ran her hand down his chest, outlining the underlying words so they etched in the newly grown skin. The intense burning sent blood-laden tears from his eyes as she released him.

Her words rang in his head. "You will walk the world as the beast you have become. But you will not kill the innocent. In turn, you cannot be killed by any manner of man or beast that walks the earth or those blessed by heaven or cursed by hell. The metal encasing your heart is God's shield and sword. Should you harm those he watches over, you will die from a crushed heart and your soul given to the lowest level of hell, worse than any hell you have ever imagined."

Noble found his voice. "What hope have I of finding mercy and a place amongst the heavens?"

"You must find the soul of your woman upon her return to earth. She must love you as she did when she died, and you must ask her forgiveness for letting evil take her. She must see what you truly are and accept it, love it, and forgive you. Only then will the gates open and allow you entry into the eternal light. Until that day, your soul is damned to this suffering plane."

"Elizabeth will return. When? When can I see her?"

"When your heart is ready and your soul is clear."

"When will that be? I'll do anything to have her back."

Closing the shackle back around his free wrist, the angel suddenly moved down toward his feet until she stood upon the floor at the end of the altar and transformed into the middle-aged nun, Sister Nan.

Wide-eyed, he stared at her. "You're... you're..."

She put a finger to her lips, shushing him again. "Ambriel," she whispered without her lips moving. Then she ran to aid Father Benedict.

Shaking him gently, he awakened, grabbing his head. "What happened?"

"You've done it, Father. The demon left him and returned to the fire," she said, motioning to the candles around the pool.

Still a bit off-balance, the priest stood and quickly moved to the altar. "Brother Noble, you're alright now?"

"Yes, Father. I am free," he lied as his eyes fell upon the nun again.

Benedict and Sister Nan moved around the altar, releasing his wrists and ankles.

After looking at his chest, he was confused. "What is this?" he asked, running his fingers over Noble's chest. "This scarring that wasn't here before ... and it looks like writing, but I cannot read it."

Nan looked into the priest's eyes. "God heard you and placed a prayer upon him to thwart the demon's return. Now he must go free."

Noble looked up at his friend. "Thank you, Henry. Now call the magistrate so that I may receive punishment for this horrible crime."

Confused, Henry nodded. "I am sorry you believe you must pay for the crimes of a demon. I do not feel right sending you to pay for the murder of dear Elizabeth when you could not have done it in your right mind."

Shaking his head, Noble replied, "Most men are pure of heart, yet they are weak to temptation and will give in to things we would find damning."

"They will put you to death, Noble."

"I know."

"Then why turn yourself in?" Henry looked deep in thought. "Let's find you something to put on." The priest walked through the church, and Noble followed until they reached his private room. He gave Noble a white shirt. "I have an idea."

"What is it?"

Looking into Noble's eyes in the candlelight, he took a deep breath. "I will not let the blame lay upon the kind sister. I'm doing this because I cannot see you die for the wrongs of a demon. I know of a ship sailing to England. The first mate came to us for Bibles and blessings for a safe journey. Go home, Noble. Return to the church. Bishop Timms will welcome you back with open arms if you do not repeat this grave tale to him. Serve the people again, serve the church. It would be a way to repay God for his kindness, and no one will know the better of it."

"I cannot, in good faith, return to the bishop, and I will not leave my children orphaned."

"I cannot, in good faith, watch a good man murdered for something he did not do, Noble. You loved Elizabeth more than God; you could not have killed her. I cannot for one moment believe you did this terrible thing after having heard you profess your love to her in my church when I married you both. You are pure of heart, and I will not let man's authority tear that asunder for the work of Satan. You are free of the demon, Noble. Do not let men finish the job that thing began. Get on the ship and go. I will watch over your children. They'll want for nothing. Maybe Yancy will follow in the steps of his father and become a priest."

"Henry, your words fall upon most glad ears, but I cannot."

"I will not hand you over to the magistrate. I will not kill God's lamb. For that would put my soul in jeopardy. Please, Noble, see reason."

Noble sank into a chair, looking at his friend. "I will do as you ask. My only request is that you tell my children every day how much their mother and I loved them."

"They will know they are loved. The ship is leaving soon; I'll make the arrangements. Stay here in the church until then."

Nodding, Noble watched his friend leave the room. *What will Tabansi do here without me?*

A MONSTER
MOST GRAND

J ust before dawn, Father Benedict collected Noble's things from the inn and brought him enough food and drink for a few days. He also gave him a cassock to wear.

Noble felt strange donning the clothes that represented something he had shunned.

Unable to leave because of morning services, Benedict saw Noble to the church's doors. "I will miss you, old friend," he said, resting his hand on Noble's shoulder.

"I will miss you as well. God bless you for taking care of my children."

"I pray God sees you safely back to London and back into the bosom of the church. You've fought a great battle and lost so much. There is only good left to come to you, Noble."

"I will not forget your kindness in freeing me and not seeing me as something evil."

Henry smiled, though his eyes looked sad. "You'd better be off; the ship leaves at dawn."

Noble nodded. "Goodbye, Henry."

As the doors closed behind Noble, men rode toward him on horseback at a fast gallop, stopping in front of the church. It was the magistrate and his deputies. "Father, we require your aid. It seems we have had an animal attack outside of town, and a woman has died," said the magistrate, dismounting.

Trying to keep his composure, he met the man's bloodshot eyes. "You'll need Father Benedict. I am on my way home to London; my church is there."

"Oh, I'm sorry, Father."

"I'm sorry to hear about the poor lost soul."

"Yes, it is a shame. She lost her husband on the ship that burned and sank off the coast just a few days ago."

Noble nodded. "I will pray for her."

The magistrate nodded. "I'm sure the family would appreciate it." Turning, the lawman pounded on the large doors. "Father Benedict!"

Walking down the cobbled road toward the docks, Noble pulled his coat high on his shoulders. A few meters from the shipyard, Noble heard the familiar metallic scraping of claws.

The beast descended from the roof of a closed fishmonger's shop. "Where are you going, Holy Man?"

Keeping his pace, with Tabansi following behind him, Noble replied, "I'm returning to the home of my birth now that you have made me a murderer."

"You are staying here," said Tabansi as he put his hand on Noble's chest, stopping him in his tracks.

Noble stepped around him in a blur and moved on. "I am taking my leave of you. You cannot keep me here. I am now what you are, and with that power, I will kill you before I allow you to stop me."

Tabansi was in front of him again. "I am the master here, white man."

Staring into the glowering red eyes of the African, he stood his ground. "You are no one's master if you seek a God to tell you what to do."

The purple and orange hues of the sky shimmered, causing Noble to worry about being left behind by the leaving schooner. He picked up his pace and ran onto the docks filled with men either saying goodbye to loved ones or carrying the last of the needed supplies for the crossing of the ocean. Tabansi kept behind him until Noble stepped upon the dock and ran up the ramp to the ship's deck. "Welcome aboard, Father. The sister said you'd be on time," said the captain. He turned and held up his hand in front of the African. "I don't take Africans. Step down."

"Thank you, Captain, and God bless you and this great ship," said Noble, crossing himself in front of the captain.

The rising sun and the large group kept Tabansi from attacking as Noble watched from the deck, still ready to fight if the African came upon the ship.

"I am with him," Tabansi yelled. But no one understood his foreign tongue.

Noble leaned in close to the captain standing at the top of the ramp, facing the glaring African. "He thinks he is with me."

The captain laughed and pushed Tabansi, who was pulled back by two other shipmen. "Priests don't keep slaves, African. Go back to your plantation and serve your master there, before the coppers arrest you or hang you for escaping."

Tabansi backed off onto the dock as the men kept pushing him away. "You would leave me here, Holy Man?" he yelled at Noble as he pounded his chest.

Refusing to respond, Noble stood watching him.

Pointing to the west, Tabansi shouted again. "I will kill the rest of your family. Then I will find you!"

Noble feared his words, but only for a moment, remembering that the angel protected Father Benedict, and Benedict would protect the children who would move from the house before sundown. He almost dared Tabansi to challenge Ambriel and survive.

Noble backed into the cabin as the sun came slowly over the horizon. Tabansi ran away into the city to escape the daylight. Once he was hidden away in the cargo hold, Noble cried for Elizabeth, her life stolen away, and the children he had abandoned.

January 25th 1713

Dearest Elizabeth,

Since we have both seen the heavens this night, my dearest love, anything else I write here is so that someday you may know my story when God brings us back together. I can share with you my life, as we promised before God. Today I went through my things and found my journals. I've always traveled with all of them. Within these volumes is the rise and fall of my life. Anything more I write is as this creature struggling to remain a man. I am learning the new limits set upon me by Tabansi, the angel Ambriel, and God.

My heart aches as night after night you visit me in my dreams. The sun is shining in a clear blue sky. Birds sing gaily, and there is a light, cool breeze on an otherwise warm day. You are alive and well, running through the orchard while I give chase. As we once did, you hide behind the trees, only to jump out and startle me, laughing and running farther still.

As I run ever closer to you and grab for your hand, dark clouds roll in, and thunder and lightning threaten our game. When I finally take your hand, you suddenly turn, and the once beautiful blue eyes sink back into their sockets, your face becomes gaunt, your soft hands turn bony and gray. Your mouth falls open in a silent scream as the skin desiccates before my eyes. Golden hair turns silver, and you finally fall to the ground. The once beautiful wedding gown is a mess of moth-eaten and blackened cloth, no longer resembling a dress. I cry out your name to the heavens, but the sky is red and black, and the once beautiful orchard around me lay parched and dead. I awaken with a start and realize my nightmares are a darker reality as I weep crimson tears.

I am lost without you.

The ship is eerily quiet when darkness falls, and for the first few nights, I waited for Tabansi to land upon the deck, demanding my return or carrying me back, but he did not. I pray in my heart that my children are well and will write to them and Henry as soon as I reach London in a few months.

The winter wind is harsh during the evenings, and the nights are long. I spend my nights on the deck, drowning out the hearts' pumping with the sounds of the ocean. The waves are challenging, and the winter sky is overcast most days.

Rats are my staple, but I only take a few a week, hoping they will last the trip. I tuck their blood-drained bodies in my pockets until I go to the deck after sunset and drop them over the side, hiding the evidence of my carnage upon the ship's four-legged populace. They are enough to sustain me for a time, but by the third day, the last day before I feed, the hearts of the crew and passengers beat so hard in my skull that I pray I make it without killing one of them.

Today, a boy was sent to the cargo deck with a bludgeon but came up empty. So, the captain believes a cat found its way onboard and is eating the rats. I put my food ration down with the cargo for the rats. The boy caught me feeding them, but I did as Tabansi does, looking him in the eye and telling him he has seen nothing. Afterward, he nodded and left me alone, returning to the deck. No one came to question me, so I assume whatever power the eyes hold is a tool I can use in the future. I have also found that my eyes see in the dark quite well. Everything is tinged in blues and grays as if there is a constant pale moonlight touching everything. I sit watching the rats travel about while my ears can hear their tiny claws scurrying on the planks of the deck and along the hull's ribs. I also listen for the small boy Captain Jones calls "Runt," who sneaks about the ship, ducking behind barrels, eavesdropping on the crew and passengers. "The Captain's Ears" is what the cabin boy should be named. Runt rarely speaks to me even though we share the same cabin. If he does look at me, his eyes are wide and his mouth is usually agape for no reason. I can only assume he hopes to appear simple-minded so people are not so secretive around him. As I listen to the voices on the ship, his feeblemindedness is disingenuous when he is spouting off his report to the captain.

February 9th 1713

Today, I was awakened in my hammock by the wide-eyed cabin boy and the stopping of a heart upon the ship. Runt stood silent, watching my eyes open in the light of his lantern. "A man is dying, and Captain Jones wants you to read his last rites before we dump him overboard."

I covered my head with a hooded cloak and stepped out on the deck in the early morning light. The burn of the sun was instant upon my hands, and I pulled them inside my cassock.

I was thankful to have explained that I was ill and could not be in the sun when I came aboard, so no one asked why my skin bubbled. I quickly read the last rites to the man wrapped in linen. When I finished, the captain covered me in a blanket and returned me below decks.

He looked at me oddly for a moment as I opened my bag, pulled out a salve, and rubbed it into the already healing skin that I hid from his sight. "Sorry to have caused you any discomfort, Father, but I won't have dead men on my ship. It's bad luck. Next time, I'll have the boys bring 'em below."

I nodded and thanked him.

Then he startled me. "I think something beastly is already on board."

"What is it?"

"That man you give last rites to… Well, he had strange marks on his neck, like small holes. One of the lads hit his head on the wall on the way up, cut him real bad, but there wasn't any blood. You've seen plenty of dead. What do you think it might be that causes something like that?"

"Perhaps he was bloodletting on himself and it went too far?"

"I don't right know, but something is not right."

He returned to the deck, and I listened intently for heart sounds that were not the same as the others. I heard nothing amiss. I do not believe I am the lone beast on this ship. Or maybe I am, and the creature within me has come to taking smaller bites.

February 17th 1713

Two otherwise healthy passengers have been given the last rites. I checked the wounds of both, and just as Captain Jones warned, they seem to be void of blood. Neither passengers' injuries matched the ferocity of my own and that of Tabansi. I have decided to find out what is causing these deaths since none match that of my medical training received before I left behind my titles and joined the church.

I have walked the entirety of ship at night except in the private rooms of a few I do not see because of my daytime limitations. What other evil rides upon the sea with me? The captain has his little ears perked as the boy sneaks about, listening and reporting, but the little spy has no answers or suspects.

The creature, more man than beast, came upon Noble in the night. A coldness about it awakened him as his eyes met its gaze. Those gold eyes, surrounded by dark circles, Noble likened to that of a wild wolf staring at him. His skin was pale, and his heartbeat was so slow it was almost silent. His clothing was that of a well-off gentleman, his dark hair long and tied back at the nape of his neck. His canines were longer than a man's, but not as evident as the fangs of Noble's master.

"What are you?" he asked with an accent from the very east of Europe.

"What are you?" Noble asked in return.

The stranger smiled ever so wickedly but did not answer, instead querying on about the man he stood over. "Your heartbeat is like a bell playing upon my ears. Your blood has a foulness about it that I can smell without tasting. Have you been eating ... the vermin?"

"Tell me what you are," Noble insisted, sitting up in his hammock.

The pale stranger looked at the priest as if considering his question. "You are not human," said the golden-eyed man, elegantly tucking a long handkerchief down his sleeve and leaning over the boy who shared the space in cargo.

Without thinking, Noble spoke up. "Do not harm him."

The stranger turned his head to the side, his brows furrowed. "What interest have you of human life?"

"He does not snore or stink of mead."

The pale-skinned man laughed and smiled. "Please tell me what you are. I must know."

"First, you. I am what you see before you, a man of God."

The pale creature laughed so loud that Noble thought he would awaken the boy, but the child did not move.

"Do you know how many monsters out there have made that claim before burning, beheading, or murdering man, woman, and child in some other manner of ungodly evil?" He paused, waiting for Noble to respond, but went on when he remained silent. "Look, rat-eater, we will only continue this verbal cat-and-mouse game. I am not human; you are not human. What are you? Have out with it."

"I have no other name for what I am other than a beast. An angel proclaimed me Lamia. A crafty, evil African called what made him Asasabonsam, and since he made me, I can only conclude I am, if not one, all of those things."

He looked upon Noble thoughtfully. "Lamia, is it? That means you are a vampire, just as I am a vampire. Why are you draining rats then, dear friend, when you have a bounteous ship of willing creatures to feed upon?"

Relieved to know they were the same but not, Noble responded, "I have been damned by God and cannot kill innocents."

"Aren't we all?" He laughed again. "I find you amusing. When we reach London, I would like it if you would accompany me. I do find winters dull in England, but the colonies have too much sunlight, so here I am again, on a ship headed home, or close to home, I should say. I am Dmitri. And you, Father, are?"

"Noble or Father Lincoln."

"You are a first, my friend. A vampire priest. Listen, good Father, I will leave your bunkmate alone and stick to the upper crust in the rooms above. Please, stop eating rats. You can feed on humans without killing them. Just do it slowly and listen for the heart to skip a beat and then stop."

"But you kill them."

Dmitri shrugged. "I have fed on them a few times. It's the ship's meals. They cause deficiencies in health, and the poor things keel over simply because of mal-nutrition." Moving within inches of Noble, Dmitri seemed to sniff at him, while his face took on an expression of illness. "You stink of those four-legged things. Drink from men, please. You can do it; I've been doing it for centuries."

"I have no control over what I am. To even try to feed on anyone would mean death to them, and I don't kill. Your bite and mine differ greatly."

The vampire placed his hands on Noble's shoulders and smiled. "Well, I can't make you eat better. Maybe once we reach London, you can show me what it is that you are. Maybe I can help."

"I am intrigued by your offer. Perhaps after I reach the church and settle in, we might meet?"

Nodding as he stepped back, Dmitri rubbed the wrinkles from his sleeves. "That will be fine. Until then, my strange friend," he said, bowing his head and leaving silently from the cargo deck.

Noble prayed the vampire was as kind as he seemed and could help him find another alternative for food. His current diet left him riddled with fleabites that were slow to heal.

March 1st 1713

Four more are dead, but I know the culprit. He steals away in the night; his slow heartbeat drowned out by the rushing of his awakened victims, who do not cry out. There is a grave silence about him, allowing him to pounce without awakening anyone he does not mean to. He's not been seen feeding except by me. I have watched him drink from them as I try to follow him about unseen.

More than not, I am caught crossing the deck and asked to pray for a passenger who cannot sleep or talk to the night watchman, who no longer feels safe on board.

Dmitri moves like a dancer upon the stage, each movement too graceful for a man. He is fast and fluid. I've not heard one of his footsteps. He is no more menacing than a dancing child; nothing is ugly about what he is. His fangs come down from the top, and there is nothing beastly about him. His gold eyes are the only discernible trait of what he is when he is otherwise mingling, and he hides them behind dark spectacles, only peeking over them ever so often to talk a meal into a dark corner.

Dmitri's smile is so captivating the ladies aboard fall over themselves to be at his side, even to the dismay of their husbands.

To his victims, he is a beautiful beast to behold, his bite a blessing they invite. At times, he takes the ladies in their beds while their husbands sleep. The gentlemen slumber through the vicious lovemaking as if it is not happening.

Dmitri is flawless in his killing. All the while, his lack of conscience is ever so close to art; I am in awe of it while feeling most ashamed.

March 23rd 1713

As I write, just before dawn, I sit watching the sea turn into the brackish river. It is the only refuge I have to escape the skittering of rats now overrunning the cargo deck below. I have no doubt it's from eating so well over the past three months, with my share of rations filling their fat brown and black bellies. The boy and I have hardly put a dent in them, but he receives copper for every twenty he can bring to Jones.

We came to the shores of England in the wee hours of the morning. Dmitri, or natural causes, has taken the lives of thirteen passengers or crew. I watched as the captain wrote each name in his log on the appropriate days of their demise, while I stated what I believed to be their cause of death. For Dmitri's kills, I chose diseases not contagious to the rest of the living so as to avoid panic.

The sails slap the air as the mast turns and the wind pulls them taut. Fog hides the land as the ship sails carefully up the Thames, the wood of the hull groans in the warmer waters, but the river is calmer than the sea. The ship creeps forward. The only break comes just after the bells ring, and the fog breaks at the bow of the other vessels, begging to be avoided. I sit enjoying the slow bobbing as deckhands ready the mooring lines.

I stood on the deck, seeking the church tower of my old home not so long ago visited to break through the mist. This time, I would not be greeted. The Noble who had a pulse has no family to speak of, except an uncle unvisited for ages who would not know him as to step upon him. This beast has no family, only an acquaintance who is nimble-footed, mostly unknown, and the abandoned monster back in Virginia.

Finally, across the way, I see it, the great stone cross of The Church of England peeking up through the thick fog, my beacon of hope, my sanctuary.

"Ah, London. We are home," said Dmitri, stepping out of his room below Noble's perch.

ENGLAND

The thick fog had not left the streets when Noble rushed toward the church, carrying his bags and praying silently for a slow sunrise. Dmitri had vanished from the docks; Noble knew not where. He was also happy to see the winter all but gone as he reached the doors of the stone church.

The doors opened to him while a twinge of something he could not put his finger on hit the center of his chest. Leaving his bags near the entrance, he bowed and crossed himself. He avoided the marble vessel of holy water, remembering the pain as it was poured over him months earlier.

Bowing his head, he said a prayer for his children and Father Benedict, and while it seemed odd, he also wished blessings upon Dmitri.

He walked down the left side of the church vestibule and into the halls leading to the living quarters of the bishop and the other clergy. A nun spotted him and ran up to him, smiling. "Oh, Father Lincoln, you've returned."

Noble stopped cautiously, looking into her eyes. When he did not respond, she stopped. "Are you alright, Father?"

While waiting for whatever lay beneath the habit of the nun to reveal itself, as had happened with the angel across the sea, he stood silent.

"Father? I thought you had long left us to live amongst the gentiles?"

He smiled for a moment when he realized nothing was happening; this was just a nun. "Yes, I did for a short time, but God gave me a sign, Sister, and I have returned. I'm sorry. It's been a long journey, and I am thoroughly exhausted."

"Oh, you've come back from the colonies, have you?"

"Yes."

"What of your wife and family?"

"I'm afraid she has passed, and my children have been taken in by Father Benedict. God sought to bring me home so that I may take my place amongst my brethren. Being a part of this place is my true calling, Sister Augustine."

"The bishop prays in the garden," she said, looking down the hallway toward a large oak door.

Nodding, Noble walked the hall and stepped out into the small walled-in garden, where the sun was still hidden away by the soup-thick fog.

The older man kneeled in front of a statue of the Holy Mother. His quiet prayers, barely a whisper, stopped, and he turned and looked at Noble. His pale lips pursed, and his eyes were steely. "You left here a pure man, and you return with a demon buried in your soul."

Noble swallowed. "I have no demon within me."

Jonathan, Timms's servant, ran out of a corner and helped the older man stand. Once upon his feet, Timms stepped closer to Noble. "A pure man does not leave his children orphaned and run back to the church in hopes of hiding. I can see what you are, Noble Lincoln."

"What is that, Bishop?"

"A coward who realizes this is where he should have stayed," he said, clapping his hand on Noble's shoulder as he stepped into the church hallway.

"I know things would be different had I not left. I am no coward. I'm only protecting those I care about, now in better hands."

The bishop turned to him. "I thought a humbler man would have returned to me."

Kneeling at the bishop's feet, Noble bowed his head. "I am most humble before you. But I am a man still trying to find his way. Forgive the weakness of this creature, and I beg you, allow my return to the pulpit so that I may help others find the true Father, Son, and Holy Spirit and cleanse their souls so that they may be better servants of God."

The bishop lay his hand on the back of Noble's head. "Rise and face me as a man."

Noble rose to his feet, and his eyes met Timms's.

The bishop clasped his hands together. "God's home is always open to his lambs, his arms wide open to forgiveness and his eyes to the truth. I received a letter from Priest Benedict, and he told me of your troubles with the demon. Your children are living as orphans at the church. He begged forgiveness for his use of exorcism and told me what happened."

Noble bowed his head. "I know, but I saw no alternative to ridding myself of the demon. I take responsibility. I begged him until he could not say no. I am the one that must be disciplined if anyone is to be."

"Have you repented?"

"I have prayed daily, begging God for his forgiveness."

Timms nodded. "As you should be, but I must say I was intrigued when Benedict told me of the marks left behind... The miracle, as he called it. I wish to see these marks left upon you, and then I shall decide if you stay. Let us step into the library, Father Lincoln, since the light is better."

Both men, followed by Jonathan, walked to the library. Once inside, Timms sent his servant away, closing the massive doors after him. Candles lit the room brightly while the clearing sky sent fractured light through the colorful stained-glass windows. "So, get on with it."

Nodding, Noble reached up and started unbuttoning his cassock. "I know not what the words say, Bishop."

"I shall read them, and we shall know."

Removing the cassock, he laid it over a chair and unlaced his undergarments until the silvery-symbol scars showed and Noble stood naked as the day of his birth.

Stepping closer, the bishop traced the large scar of the cross on the priest's chest with his index finger. Then he moved on to the symbols. Timms's eyes met Noble's with concern and fear.

"Thousands of souls have wished to be touched by God in such a manner. This may be his word spread across your body, as if you are the bearer of new commandments to us all. Knowing who you are and your past, I find it inequitable that better men are left on bended knee their entire lives, pleading for a sign that would eliminate any inkling of doubt from their minds. They die, never *really* knowing if their faith was for naught. Though these thoughts alone are a covetous sin I should not be feeling. I cannot help but believe this is a fallacious message left behind when the demon left your body. You may be marked by Satan, which would make better sense considering your sins."

Swallowing hard, Noble spoke up. "It was an angel who delivered the message. I swear to you, Bishop, this is not Satan's work."

The bishop walked away, leaving Noble naked in the middle of the library. Reaching across a table, the older man grabbed a book and sat down. "We shall see if angels have the answers, then."

For hours, chilled by the moist, cold English air, Noble stood still silently, thanking the glass cherubs above for blocking the rays of sunlight as Timms tried to decipher the words on his body.

Ink met paper as the old bishop copied the signs and compared them to the symbols in several books.

As the early evening came on, the angels above his head turned gray, and Timms finally looked up at him. "You may don your clothing, Father Lincoln."

The bishop picked up the books and parchment and left Noble standing alone in the library. Kneeling, he pulled the undergarments over his shoulders. Hunger pains caused his stomach to ache, while his ears were berated by the beating hearts about the church. Trying to ignore them, he drowned the noises out with prayers. He donned his cassock and finished buttoning it as a knock sounded on the door.

Jonathan opened it slightly, but he did not meet Noble's eyes, and his heart-beat hastened as if he was afraid. *What had Bishop Timms told him?* "Father Lincoln, the bishop has asked me to take you to your bedchamber and to offer a meal of bread and wine."

"Alright. Thank you, Jonathan," said Noble. He nodded at the boy and followed him.

When they reached a familiar oak plank door, the boy opened it and stepped out of Noble's path. It was the same simple room he had left behind years before. A small, plain desk sat in the corner with a Bible, a pen and inkpot, and blank parchment, and next to them was a plate of bread and a goblet of wine. A corked bottle of wine sat next to the mug. Across from the desk was a neatly made straw-stuffed mattress on a bed with a wooden cross over it. At the end of the bed were his things brought from Virginia.

A small wooden dresser stood against the wall next to the door. On it lay a plain pine box decorated with a simple carved cross and words in Latin, *Manus Dei*: God's hand.

"Thank you, Jonathan."

The boy nodded.

Expecting the boy to leave him alone, Noble walked over to the bed and pulled his bag with his journals from the floor. The door closed quietly, but when he turned to place the books on his desk, the boy stood staring at him in wide-eyed wonder.

Noble furrowed his brow. "Jonathan?"

The boy dropped to his knees, grabbing Noble's hands as tears started down his cheeks. "Please, sir... Please, Father Lincoln, I beg of you. I have prayed for so long."

"And God hears those prayers," said Noble, laying his hand on the young man's head.

Jonathan kissed the priest's iron cross ring, and tears welled in his eyes. "God has touched you; I heard Bishop Timms tell the archbishop. You have words cut into your body. It is God's wish that man sees this, just as the Ten Commandments were carved in stone so that Moses could see proof of God's will. You are his messenger. I beg you, allow me to lay my eyes upon the miracle. Please, Father, it would forever bless my mind and soul. I'll tell no one."

Noble was caught off guard and could do nothing but stand silent while he thought to himself. *He does not know what he wishes to see is laid upon a beast so ungodly. It is no message, but a warning of what is to come if I kill God's protected children.*

"It would not be proper, Jonathan," said Noble, lifting the boy's chin until he met his eyes. "Thank you for assisting me in my room and getting my things. You should return to the bishop before he misses you."

The boy nodded nervously and kissed Noble's ring again. "Yes, Father Lincoln."

Jonathan left the room quietly, and Noble stood for a moment before looking skyward. "Make me not something grand when I am a sinister beast at best. I do not wish to be bowed to by men when I am no man and nothing godly resides within me."

Noble tried sipping the wine but found it soured his empty stomach, and the bread sat untouched. Reading by candlelight, Noble waited for the bishop as the moon rose in the sky and his stomach rumbled on.

Sometime after the candle died, the oak door opened, and the bishop entered. Noble stood up, lighting another candle on his desk, and turned to face his old friend and teacher. "Bishop."

The bishop nodded. "Father." The old man closed the door behind him. "I've come with the translation, and I am quite confused."

Noble watched as the old man furrowed his brow and handed him a parchment. He read it carefully.

> Upon his chest, as if scarred from below the surface of the skin and is smooth as the backside of a babe, are lines of symbols whose language matches ancient characters in old scripture. The characters seem burned from inside his skin, although there are no scars that point to this being possible. The symbols appear to run around his rib cage, each one written to follow the bone. The father states when the angel opened him up, the words were written in liquid gold upon each rib he could see, and when the skin healed over it, the words burned the underside of his hide. On Father Lincoln's back, a long cross runs from the neck down almost the entire length of his spine. Again, the burn seems impossible.

After many hours of research, I have found the words to say the following:

"God has made this man a martyr; he shall sing the songs of Christ and be the most prominent man amongst men. Father Lincoln will be protected, for the angels have begged it, and he will return as a man for every death until the end of all time. Lesser men will bow to him, and you shall call him the savior of humanity. He is to be forever cleansed of sin, and he will stand before God first and speak the wickedness of man. When God deems the Earth unfit, its men unseemly, his word will stand alone. To heaven or hell with souls, he is the one who will lead them unto damnation."

"It means you have died and risen again ... like Jesus of Nazareth..." The bishop's tired eyes looked up into Noble's. "I don't know what that means to the church. Have you wronged someone so important that God would place upon this earth something other than prayers or commandments to all men?"

Pulling out a chair, he motioned to the bishop. "Please sit; you look exhausted."

"I do not wish to stay. I won't keep you. I would write the archbishop about this, but I do not know what I would say of this miracle. I'm afraid, Noble. I've always known you to be a faithful and good man of God. But from the hand of God to your flesh. I don't know what to make of all of this. According to these words, you are damned to earth forever. How is that possible?"

"I do not know, Bishop. I would agree it is not wise to speak of this outside of these walls. I do not mean to make a mockery of God or these words upon my body. I can only follow them as truth. I swear to you, Bishop, I am faithful, and I will share that faith with our parishioners as God and the church would have it. Please, let me stay and do what I am meant to do."

"But if they found out, the people would make a spectacle of you. These marks would make even heretics believe. And the people need that so much right now. You are a walking miracle, Noble, and I do not know what to do with you. God placed them below your clothes for you alone, and I am afraid I would only use them for my agenda. What if God sees me as a sinner for exploiting his words?" the old man said. His eyes watered, and his hands were shaking. "I fear for my soul. I've no idea why, but I do. You must go, Noble. You must walk the earth as God's silent messenger."

"Where am I to go, Bishop?"

"I do not have those answers; they do not lie upon your body. Please take your leave. I'm sorry that I must send you away." The bishop suddenly turned from Noble and left the room, almost slamming the door behind him.

Noble listened to the bishop speaking to someone as he packed his journals back into his bags.

"You will gather his things and set him outside. No man on earth can sit higher than Christ, and no clergyman can sit higher than the King. If the archbishop asks again, I will state the miracle is false and that I sent him away for his lies and heresy. I do not wish to see him dead. That is what Pope Clement XI would have done to him if anyone in Rome found out. Our souls would certainly be damned if he were killed." Timms coughed and fell silent.

"This does not seem wise a choice, putting him out."

"I know, but what else can we do? Banishing him seems the only way to keep him safe. I wish I had never seen what lay upon his chest." The bishop coughed and then continued. "Be kind, but do not speak to him; he must not know any of this."

"Yes, Bishop."

Heavy footsteps moved down the corridor, and a knock sounded at the door.

"Yes, come in."

Jonathan opened the large door, picked up the remaining bag from the floor, and walked out. Following closely behind the boy, Noble was led, with great haste, toward the front doors of the great chapel.

The boy pushed the doors open, walked toward the street, where he deposited the bag, and then ran back to the building, leaving Noble in the darkness.

Picking up his bags, he started toward the high street, hoping to find an inn with a light still burning inside.

"So, the Church now throws out priests in the middle of the night?" asked a familiar voice from behind Noble.

Turning, Noble looked into the golden eyes of Dmitri. "The bishop knew a cursed man when he saw one and asked me to take my leave."

"Oh, what a shame. So now that you are not settling here, what will you do?"

Noble turned and continued walking. "Find an inn. Tomorrow, I will go about finding my uncle so I can hopefully regain my home."

"For a nightwalker, you certainly cling to the man you are no longer, my friend."

Stopping in his tracks, he turned back to the vampire. "What am I to do? Stalk young women, talk them into my bed, and hope my soul does not end up in hell?"

"What is it: your care of heaven or hell? We are to live, drink, and love for all eternity. Women are most like violins if you know how to play them, and they do so love to frolic in the sheets."

"Women are not instruments, Dmitri, nor are they lambs with no other purpose than to be slaughtered by beasts of hell."

Dmitri smiled wickedly. "You are a priest. What do you know of women?"

"I would rather not share my story with a monster that has little understanding of my life."

"Why are you always so difficult, Father?"

Shaking his head, Noble started down the cobblestone street. Without warning, Dmitri stood in front of Noble, his yellow eyes looking straight into Noble's soul. "You will come with me to my inn and room for the night. You will ask no questions, and you shall do as I tell you."

Noble started to speak but found himself unable as he felt himself go completely numb. He fought to take a step and could not.

No longer in control of his body or actions, Noble nodded and followed the vampire through the streets. When they reached a small inn, Dmitri walked in to find a man standing behind the counter holding a flintlock pointed toward the door.

Dmitri held up his hand. "You should go to sleep now, friend, but first, send that daughter of yours up to my room."

The innkeeper put the gun down and walked through a doorway behind the counter.

Within minutes of entering the room they would sleep in, Dmitri turned to Noble. "Put the bags down, Father." Noble complied.

A knock came at the door a minute later. Opening it, Dmitri smiled. "Ah, Mary, how nice it is to see you again. Come in."

The girl walked in and stood next to Noble, her eyes filled with confusion at having strangers call her to their room, until Dmitri whispered in her ear. She was thin, but not without the curves of a woman. Ratted brown hair fell about her shoulders, and her dingy clothes hung on her like a larger woman once wore them. Her dull gray eyes stared at nothing, and her mouth hung open enough to show she had her teeth. Her pallor was milky yellow.

Dmitri pulled off his gloves and laid them down as he looked at the people standing in his room. "I do not wish to treat one of my own like a puppet, but I see no other way to teach you. This faith you have in God is becoming most tiresome. Mary, some light, please."

He sat back in a tattered armchair in a dark corner, flinging one of his legs over one of the arms of the seat as the girl lit a candle near the bed as instructed.

"Mary, if you would, please undress for my friend. He's not seen a woman without clothes for quite a while, if at all. And you, Father, may speak once again," he said with a sly grin.

"Why are you doing this? She is but a girl," said Noble between gritted teeth.

"Mary, show my friend you are not a child."

The girl slowly undressed in front of Noble, who looked into her vacant eyes, trying his best to avoid looking at her naked figure.

Walking up to him, she rammed her lips against his.

"Go on, Father, kiss her."

Noble glared at Dmitri.

"You will do as I command. Kiss the girl!"

The girl's breath was heavy and hot on his face as her lips met his.

Standing up, Dmitri stepped up behind Mary and laid his hand on her shoulder. Pulling away from Noble, the girl stood without expression as she waited for her next command. "See, that wasn't so terrible." Dmitri pulled a dagger from his boot and set it down on the table next to the bed.

"Mary, take that knife, and stick your wrist with it," said Dmitri.

The girl took the knife from next to the bed and stabbed her wrist without a thought. She moaned as blood ran down the length of the metal. Dmitri took it from her and licked down the long shaft of it before speaking. "Very nice, Mary. Now put your wrist to his lips."

The girl's wrist met Noble's mouth, and he awakened from the trance with the smell of blood. Noble's eyes scanned the room until they settled on the golden eyes of Dmitri.

Dmitri's clasped fingers held the knife in front of his nose as if the remnants of blood left upon it were a flower he enjoyed. "So, your mind is your own again, or is it only your conscience?"

"I cannot move."

"Ah, your conscience is powerful, but your will is not." Dmitri stood and stepped toward them. "I know you are starving; your eyes tell me so. They turn red just smelling her."

"I would not kill for my master ... and I will not kill for you."

"Who said you have to kill anyone? I've been drinking from this one since she was but an infant feeding at her mother's breast. I did kill her mother, but this one, she tastes like a fine wine, meant to be enjoyed until the grapes sour. You should try her. Don't let this go to waste." Dmitri motioned at the blood dripping down his chin.

"I am not your toy, Dmitri."

The vampire laughed as he pulled the girl's long hair back from her neck. "I offer you a wonderful meal, a place to sleep, and you speak to me this way? Do you not have manners?"

"I'm no murderer."

"I am no murderer either, Father. I am a connoisseur of love. And of the beautiful red wine that spills from the veins of mankind. This girl is a wine bottle that refills itself for my pleasure, allows me to be drunk at my leisure. The sooner you see things my way, the less pain you will suffer, my friend. Now drink from her."

Noble pulled her wrist to his mouth. "I am so sorry, Mary," he whispered as his growing fangs cut through her skin then and the vessel walls, freeing what the beast within him sought to survive. Mary's warm blood slowly filled Noble's mouth as tears ran down his face, dripping down from his chin and fusing with the blood already soaking into clothing. The small taste caused a frenzy within him, and his fangs tore into her like a rabid dog, causing her to bleed faster still. She started moaning and crying as Dmitri sank his teeth into her neck.

Wrapping his arms around her, the older vampire fondled her breasts with one hand while his other hand slid down between her legs. He paused to smile up at Noble. "Do you feel it?"

The priest's red eyes met his as he continued to feed against his will.

"Do you feel that sheltered soul of yours slipping ever so much closer to hell, Father?"

Instead of responding, Noble closed his eyes, his ears filled with the sounds of the girl's beating heart as her blood passed through his lips and down his throat. He felt stronger, though. His mind felt more lucid, and his senses heightened. Dmitri's slow heartbeat pounded in his head loudly. Noble could hear Dmitri's fingers finding the girl's wet womanhood while the vampire's other hand fondled her breasts again. Her moans crashed upon his ears like the ocean beating against rocks. The sound of the burning flame on the candle's wick sounded like a bonfire snapping as the breeze outside poured through the cracks in the mortar, threatening to extinguish it. The sound of blood dripping upon his already-soaked cassock sounded like rain on a pond. His heart started to ache, and his chest tightened as a hand pushed him away, first gently with mumbled words, then forcefully as Dmitri shouted, "Stop, you're killing her!"

Noble released the girl and backed away, suddenly conscious of what was happening. The pain in his chest made him fall back onto the bed, grabbing at the buttons as he cried out.

Dmitri fed the girl from his wrist and looked on the bed at the priest. Strange light emanated from beneath his black cassock. Intrigued, the vampire jumped onto the bed and pulled open the priest's clothing, causing a spray of buttons to scatter. Dmitri shaded his eyes as the cross in the middle of Noble's chest lit up like the flames of fire, and the words surrounding it bathed the walls in golden light.

The girl on the floor moved, trying to make sense of her surroundings as the vampire blood in her veins started healing her.

The vampire's laugh filled the room as the glowing symbols and the cross disappeared. The girl screamed, and Noble blacked out.

THE SAINT

Noble woke but found himself no longer in the room of the inn. He lay upon a slab of stone. Lit candles sitting in sconces on either side of the small room allowed him to look around. Sitting up, he realized he lay upon the lid of a sarcophagus in a family mausoleum. On the other side of the room lay Dmitri asleep on another. Smithe was the name carved on the wall, followed by the Lord's Prayer.

Remembering the intensity of the pain felt before passing out, he grabbed for his chest and was relieved the pain had passed. Noble was no longer in his cassock but a gentleman's suit. The room was cold, and the iron doors sealed them away from the outside world.

Moving to the entrance, he pushed against the iron.

"I would not do that if I were you," said Dmitri, not opening his eyes.

"I find it difficult to stay with someone willing to take me so close to death... making me act against my will and my conscience."

"You may leave when you like, but I don't see you surviving out there in the sunlight or amongst the wolves."

"I find the worst of beasts lies across this grave from me already."

Without opening his eyes, Dmitri smiled.

"Think what you will, dear Noble. You are better off with your own kind."

Noble knew he was right. Feeling trapped and claustrophobic, he demanded answers. "What time is it? Where are we? Why are we here?"

"You have so many questions. Thankfully, we have a few hours before the sun sets to answer them."

"Then do so."

Dmitri sat up and looked at Noble, annoyed that he was awake. "We are in Bunhill. It's the only cemetery not consecrated. Therefore, it is a safe place to rest. As you have already read, these are the Smithes, and I come to spend the day sometimes if the sun threatens to rise before I have finished my excursions of the night. Sometimes, I bring those excursions here. When I am alone, I usually bed down with John Bunyan, but since there are two of us, I did not want to crowd the old boy out."

"This is what it means to be a vampire? Hiding all day and sleeping with the dead?"

"You are not just a vampire, my friend," said Dmitri with a smile. "You are so much more."

"I don't know what it is you speak of."

"You are filled with the light of the heavens, yet drink the blood of men. I admit I am greatly confused, but extremely interested in how you came to be this way."

"I do not wish to share that with someone who almost killed me."

"How was I to know you can die so easily? Look at me. I have been shot, strangled, dropped down a well, and dumped from the cliffs of Dover. That is just in the last half-century. You drink from one girl and nearly drop dead. I have no idea what to make of it. So, tell me, Father, what are you really?"

"I am a creature removed from his church ... and his clothes," he said, patting down the front of the jacket he now wore, "and have lost my patience for games. Where is my bag?"

Dmitri motioned to the corner. "There."

Ignoring the golden-eyed monster, Noble kneeled next to his bag and started searching through it. He noted his cassock was missing.

"Alright, so you won't tell me."

"No."

"Then this is going to be a long, boring eternity for you. Just so happens, I could read what that writing says there on your chest."

"How? It took hours for a bishop to decipher."

"I would wager he read it wrong. There's not a book within the library of the Church of England that can decipher that. I'm older than the church that sent you away. That writing is even older than this city. It's a kind of curse. You must have angered someone to receive such a—"

"So, what does it say if you know so much?"

Dmitri jumped upon the stone on the other side of the room and sat down with his back against the stone wall. "No weapon fashioned against you shall succeed, and you shall confute every tongue that rises against you in judgment, save one. God's word is a sharp two-edged sword that discerns the thoughts and intentions of the heart and stands absolute. Lest she, whose life was taken by evil, rises and speaks forgiveness for your sins against her, only then will the sword break open the gates of heaven to you.'

"'You shall not fell an innocent lamb of God, but you may live from its blood. If a lamb falls to your hunger, the sword of God shall crush the heart it guards. From now until heaven or hell takes you, you shall walk the earth until its end.'" Dmitri smiled. "It seems you are damned several times over: by God, by an angel, and by this master of yours... What did you say he called himself?"

"Asasabonsam."

"Yes."

"How do I know you're not telling me falsehoods?"

Jumping down from the lid of Lady Smithe's stone coffin, Dmitri walked over to him and pulled back his coat sleeve, exposing a pale wrist. "After nine hundred years of this, what reason have I to fabricate falsehoods? Taste from me and know my tale. The blood does not lie, Father."

Noble looked at the pale arm of the vampire, recalling those same words spoken by Tabansi.

Dmitri held his wrist up higher. "Go on and see. I speak the truth."

Grabbing Dmitri's arm with both hands, Noble bit into his wrist. The cold blood ran into his mouth, and his eyes closed.

The man reached through the small hole in the door, touching the hand of the man inside. "I will give you freedom as you have given me Christ, brother, with no fear."

"Your father sought to kill me, but was unable. Your brother may well finish me. Pray for my soul, but beg not for my life, Enravota. For if I die with the love of Christ in my heart, he will see me in heaven. I shall be martyred and remembered forever as a man who died for his beliefs, whereas the Khan will find eternal burning. No one will remember him."

Footsteps sounded in the stone halls. "Go now, brother, before you are discovered."

"I will see you set free. I will talk to Malamir and make him see Christ is not false."

The man ran for the doors and saw the sun shining through the trees, wishing his friend and teacher in the dungeons could see it as well.

In his chamber room, Enravota knelt before a cross he had drawn on the stone and prayed for mercy for the tortured man screaming below in the dungeons.

The sounds of armor clinking brought Enravota to his feet. Then the noise stopped behind him. He rubbed at the cross on the wall as tears rained down his face.

"The Khan has ordered your arrest and orders you before him for the reading of your charges, Prince Enravota."

The prince turned to the men carrying spears. "Jesus Christ is my savior. I am his servant, and he will rise and judge you all."

The men grabbed him, causing him great pain, and his Bible fell to the ground. Reaching for the book, he yelled, "Jesus Christ is my savior! I am his servant; death cannot kill belief in him, he is eternal, he is everywhere, he is the only true son of God!" as they dragged him away to the throne room.

Malamir stood up, staring down at his brother before seating himself. A Khan at twenty, he sat up straight and proud, as their father once did. His light beard was barely filled in, while his fair hair was long to his jaw and accented his pale skin. His blue eyes—shared with his mother and brother—seemed more steely than blue. He waved at a servant who brought him wine, took a sip, then handed back the cup before speaking. "I once was proud to call you brother, Enravota, proud to watch you return from war with tales of heroic deeds. Now I see you are no better than the sheep in the fields, ready to follow lesser men into foolish dreams of man-gods. You are nothing to me now but another head to fall to the executioner's axe."

Thrown down at his brother's feet, he fell on his knees. Looking up into the angry eyes of Malamir, he reached out to touch his brother's feet. "After all I have given to our people, including my blood in war and a leader they can cheer on the battlefields, you sit on the throne in my place because Father saw you more fit because of my beliefs. I am humble before you and beg the release of the Byzantine man Father imprisoned. I shall take his place, and he has promised to go far from here, never to return."

A tall, dark-haired man Enravota did not know leaned to the smaller man on the throne and whispered in his ear.

The young man looked down at his brother. "I freed him once for you, and you allowed him, a slave, to further twist your mind into believing in a false God, one not of our father. You threaten my people with your Christianity. There will be no one freed. You will join your brothers of false beliefs in the dungeons. There, you will await your execution unless you renounce this man-god. I will not allow an easy death with the loss of your head. I want you run through. It is a slow death you have coming to you. You will bleed out like the gutted sheep you have become."

"Brother, I beg of you, there is no crime we've committed. Release the Christians, or I fear your soul shall perish!" he shouted as two guards hooked his arms and half-carried him to the dungeons.

Enravota sat in the dungeon, shackled to the wall. A skittering in the darkness startled him.

"You are the brother of the Khan?"

"Who is speaking to me?"

Movement close to his feet startled him. "I am one that believes in the old ways. I was taken prisoner in these dungeons ages ago. They tortured me, even cut off my hands and my nose and ears for a confession. Then the wars took them all away, and I was left alone here. Left with no face to be remembered, no hands to grab at freedom. Therefore, forgotten. But no one wants me dead. The voices tell me you are going to meet your end come the morn."

"My brother has ordered my execution unless I renounce my Christianity. I will not, for I would deny the one true god's son."

"What if I said I could save you from death?"

"How could you—a handless, faceless man, as you claim—save me? There is little anyone can do when someone's run through with a pike."

Laughter sounded in the darkness. "For most, that is true. But I can save you."

"How, unless you were to take my place at the execution?"

"Your father robbed me of my freedom before you were born, boy. I swore off the gods and damned them every day that I was told 'On the morrow, you will die' and death did not come. I even killed a guard, hoping they would lay me open, but alas, here I am. These forty-five years buried away, and I still exist. He has fallen, the mighty Khan Omurtag, and his child has taken the throne. His other son is meant to die, caged with me. Still, death eludes me."

"How does that knowledge save my life? My brother will not forget me. He feels I have wronged our father and endangered the minds of our people, believing in something he does not."

Ignoring the prince, the voice in the darkness talked on as if speaking to no one. "Then the priest came, chained like you. Told me to forgive and forget what happened to me. He paid for his words. I stabbed him and damned his soul to the seven hells. Then God made me pay in the most grievous of ways. He made bread poison and water feel like nothing upon my lips. My soul belongs to hell, just as the priest said as I stabbed him over and over and over again. Ate him, I did. No matter if they come now and swear death to me as they have in the past. I have killed myself over and over, and still, here I sit in the darkness, talking to you."

"You've gone mad. No one can kill themselves repeatedly."

The stranger growled. "I will not deny that I hear things and see things that may not be there, but I know what I am."

"Begone from me. I will take death with honor and become a martyr to those who believe as I do." Sweat was forming on his forehead.

"Pretentious boy! I offer you a life beyond death. You spit on it like I have offered poison."

"To live on forever after death is blasphemy. Even Christ died, and he was the son of God."

"I am beyond God; I am the darkness. His blood is my water. I drink from men as you drink from goblets."

"You are greatly troubled in your mind, friend."

"I'm mad, yes, but I will outlive you, your brother, whatever family takes the title Khan, and all that follows them."

Skittering on the stone ceiling overhead and the echo of the stranger in the dark scared him enough to cause him to call out, "Guards!"

Laughter filled the darkness again. "Yes, yes, call them... I am ravenous." Something scampered away in the pitch-black room.

Keys jingled in the locks, and light entered the dungeon. Enravota's eyes scanned the room, looking for the voice in the darkness. The corners, still hidden in shadow, found no light with the torch as a young man ran to the prince's side. "What is it, Prince?"

"Someone is here with us."

"No, no one has been in here in years."

"He says he has been here for ages, before my birth."

"No one has been here. Your imaginings must be brought on by fever. Look at the sweat on your brow. That will not matter come morning."

The door to his cell closed, driving out most of the light. The guard pulled his sword and walked toward the doorway, holding up his torch. "Show yourself."

The laughter came low at first, building louder as it echoed in the halls.

"I say, show yourself!" the guard shouted as he backed toward Enravota.

Sudden silence. The only sounds were the labored breathing of the guard and the same scampering overhead. Both men looked upward in alarm as the guard raised the fire toward the ceiling. Then gold eyes lit up, and something batted the torch to the ground, setting the straw on the floor ablaze.

The bright light filling the room showed Enravota what had been in the darkness. The creature had no hands; only stumps remained. It was almost skeletal, with long stringy hair and a thin beard. Its nose was gone, leaving two gaping holes in the middle of its face. The mouth of the creature was filled with teeth like a dog. It moved on all fours on the ceiling as if it were the floor.

Enravota watched with wide eyes as the golden-eyed creature pulled the guard to the ceiling, where it pulled off his armor with ease, tossing it to the floor with a loud clank. Its arms held tight to its squirming treasure as it sank long teeth into the screaming young man and fed off his blood with a voracious hunger, its eyes ever staring at the young prince chained to the wall.

As if the gold eyes held him in a trance, he did not move as the flames burned closer to the door, and he did not cry out as other guards rushed the door shouting, "Fire!" He did nothing but stare at the eyes of the thing on the ceiling. As it finished, it tossed the now limp body to the floor and smiled with a wickedness Enravota had never seen.

"Fire!" shouted a guard, looking into the cell through the window in the door. Smoke swirled around the room as the creature landed in front of the prisoner. "Live forever, son of Khan Omurtag." The creature grabbed him, snatching him with so much strength it snapped the chains. Biting into the prince's neck, Enravota screamed out in pain. As the creature fed, it carried him to the back of the cell until they could not be seen by the men breaking down the door.

Enravota felt as if his head were floating as his heart began to slow. Blood ran down his body and into the mouth of the darkness clutching him. "I die in the name of Christ," said Enravota in a whisper.

The creature released his prey and looked into his heavy-lidded eyes. "You will not die, boy. I have other plans for you," he said, biting open a stump where a hand used to be as the men broke through the door and started dumping pails of water on the flames. He pulled open Enravota's mouth and let the blood fall in until the boy coughed, choking on it. The ugly creature's face fell into a morbid grin as the prisoner drank the blood.

"More water," shouted the guard, tossing water on the fire, trying to close in on the people in the back.

Smoke filled the space, and Enravota blacked out.

The prince was doused with water, and he sat up with a start.

"Wake up. I don't want your eyes closed when you meet your end. What kind of executioner would I be?"

Enravota coughed up the water, tasting smoke in his mouth and feeling the heaviness of it in his chest. "Where is it? Where is the monster?"

The man laughed aloud. "You were trying to off yourself. It didn't work, young prince. Your brother is not happy. So much so, he has ordered your death at first light."

"I did no such thing. It was that thing with no hands and eyes of the wolf. It attacked and killed the guard and set the fire. Then it attacked me." He touched his hands to his neck and found it unharmed. Confused, he looked at his hands. Though smoke-blackened, there was no blood on them, only water.

"You were the only one in the cell other than the guard you killed trying to escape."

"How did I break the chains? I swear I have done nothing but watch a man die to something I have never seen in the ugliest days of battle."

"Well. I guess you won't be seeing it again since this is the last of those days."

The executioner walked away from the prince, who was once again chained, this time to a wooden post.

Crossing himself, he began to pray. "I shall fall today, and unlike those who will still walk the earth, I will follow you into the valley of death. The sun will meet me on the other side, and life, unlike this suffering, shall be led in your name, in your peace, and your love, for all the days to come. May you not hold shadows over the heads of men who will see my end. Raise them in your love for allowing me to meet you sooner than I would in natural death. Amen."

As the colors of the sky started changing, Enravota watched it with hope and fear. People began filling the yard. Some looked up at him with blank stares, while others shouted at him, "Blasphemer!" Some threw fruit at him. The noise of marching men filled Enravota with dread.

Carried in on a wooden throne, his brother waved to his people, who cheered his presence at the execution of his brother.

The marching men stopped, and Enravota bowed before his brother.

"Are you ready to renounce this Christian religion as false, foreign, and not of your father or your Khan?"

"I will not."

"I order you! Renounce this false faith and find that of your father and your Khan."

"I refuse."

"Then you shall perish. Any last words, prisoner?"

Enravota stood, looking at his brother.

"This faith, which I now die for, will spread and increase across the whole Bulgarian land, although you may wish to oppress it with my death. In any case, the Sign of Christ will establish itself, and churches of God will be built everywhere. Pure priests will serve the pure God and will deliver 'sacrifice of praise and confession' to the invigorating Trinity. Idols, and priests as well, and their ungodly temples will crumble and will turn into nothing as if they had not existed. Besides, you alone, after many years, will cast away your ungodly soul without receiving anything in reward for your cruelty."

A priest walked up to him and placed a wreath of flowers on his bowed head.

"Enough." Malamir nodded at the executioner. "Run him through."

The executioner rammed hard on the pike, and it pierced the gut of the chained man, who dropped to his knees as blood poured from his belly. The executioner ran the pike through him again. Enravota fell forward as a thin smile formed on his brother's face. Pain and blood loss pulled the prince into darkness.

As if surfacing for breath in water, Enravota rose to a sitting position, breathing in deeply. Linen covered his face, and he could not see. He pulled the thin cotton *from his face and looked around a small torch-lit room that he recognized from his father's burial.*

How do I live? *He looked down at the linen wrapping his body and felt a strange peace. Getting up from the stone on which his body was laid to rest, he walked to the door of the temple and looked upon familiar symbols on the stone door. He ran his fingers over them and looked back into the tomb at his father's burial box. "Goodbye, Father. I will not be joining you in hell."*

Pushing the door aside, he stepped out into the night and realized he could see in the darkness. He could also smell everything, hear everything, and feel everything. "What am I? Am I now brother to God's son?" he asked the starless sky.

Dmitri pulled his arm away and looked into Noble's eyes. "I tell the truth."

Noble blinked at him. "Yes, you do, except your name. It is not Dmitri... And your past. They are both familiar to me." Thinking for a moment, he looked into the yellow eyes of the man from his dream. "You are a saint," he said, kneeling before Dmitri.

"Please do not bow before me. I am no longer that man, and I have not been him for nine hundred years."

The vampire saint returned to his stone lid and lay down upon it. "Now that we have that out of the way, we sleep until sunset. Then you can either accompany me and learn something or go your own way."

Sitting upon his stone, he looked over at the vampire with closing eyes. "You once loved God, and now you deny him. Why?"

"I did everything to find him, to prove his existence. I fought in his name. I died in the name of his Son, and never once did he allow me to know of him as you have. He denied me death, even as I walked the earth murdering his people, and he has refused to end me. You can see where my faith would falter until, finally, I almost came to deny his existence. You will learn this, Father Lincoln. Evil is real. It is everywhere. It is the plague that steals children and robs babes of breath. It makes creatures like us strip further the humanity of their lives. It sends famine unto the fields and leads the people working so hard only to starvation. Evil brings men to their knees without understanding or reason. It takes and takes, and yet no one stops it. You will find God less evident. He sits back, watching all of it, and does nothing. He hides like a scared child, demanding faith while ignoring men in the time of their greatest need."

"Do you believe again, now that you've seen my marks?"

"I believe as I have always believed. God may exist, but my belief that he has abandoned these weak men, leaving the devil as our caretaker, is stronger still. Nothing since my death so long ago has proven different. Maybe someday I will look upon your marks without further hating God for abandoning me when I needed him most."

After several moments of silence, Dmitri looked over at Noble. "So, what of you. Will you set out on your own, or join me?"

Noble met his eyes. "My home is gone. My church has abandoned me as a false prophet. God has placed a curse upon me, and I have nowhere to call home. I can think of nowhere else I must be."

The vampire smiled and closed his eyes. "Good."

CONTROL

July 14th 1718

For years, I have followed Dmitri and learned the creature he is. By day, we sleep in Bunhill. By night, we frequent the inns and pubs of the high street. Dmitri says the best meals can be obtained from the local whores. They ask few questions, and not one can say no to him. He whispers in their ears and their hearts.

I am taking to human blood, although I still find the thought of it ill. Control is slow to come. Dmitri and God's warning in my chest are the only things standing between myself and eternal hell.

The whores smile and offer a wrist for little more than a coin. Dmitri has tried to push me into their beds. He says there is no grander sensation than fornicating while feeding. I decline each time, for in my heart, I am still wed to Elizabeth. Each time I touch a woman to meet her wrist or throat, a pang of guilt strikes me, and Elizabeth's face enters my mind. Then I am haunted by the words of the angel, telling me of her return.

I have not shared my story with Dmitri, and he does not press for it. I do not ask any more from him, for I have seen his pain.

I often wonder as I look upon the ladies surrounding him if there was once someone for him. He has such a way with them.

When we do not share in meals, I often walk the streets alone, listening to those behind closed doors of houses. I hear dinner conversations, children playing, families sitting around crackling fires.

My favorite is the voice of a young mother who tucks her children in with stories each night. I find myself jumping to her rooftop and sitting out of sight of the street below to hear the tales so much like the ones Elizabeth once told our children, filled with magic, whimsy, and wonder that would have Yancy and Mira wide-eyed instead of slumbering. The same was true for the children beneath the rooftop on which I perched. They whispered and giggled long after their mother had snuffed out the candlelight.

It's been a few years since the light in Elizabeth's eyes extinguished, but it feels like a lifetime ago, though my heart feels all the more for her. I find myself daydreaming about her. Closing my eyes as I touch the arm of another woman just before feeding, imagining it is her arm, I run my fingers down. Sometimes even after opening my eyes, the illusion remains but changes as I plunge my teeth into a wrist, but it is not her lively face I see; it is the one that stared unseeing, skyward. I close my eyes and remember what has happened and that the dream is gone—for now.

I have no idea how long the wait will be or where and when to start looking for her. Perhaps I should share my story with Dmitri; maybe he can help me.

Noble placed his journal back in his bag with the rest as the sun sank below the horizon and a full moon rose.

Straightening his clothing, Dmitri rose from his slumber. He smiled at his friend.

"Another night of hunting?" asked Noble.

"Ah, yes, but tonight we have a party to attend, and I think I have found a more suitable home."

"No more cobwebs or spiders crawling over my face as I sleep?"

"No, my friend, we shall have down pillows and feather-stuffed mattresses hidden behind heavy curtains. But first, to the ball of Duke Dumas. There are always women about him. I usually pick off a few for myself. And those royal bloodline ladies taste like nothing you've ever had. They are quite scandalous, and though they claim purity, there is nothing so pure about them. You can have them again and again, and they always claim to be virgins. I shall introduce you to my lady of choice, Margaret Luveatu. She loves to be on the brink of death when I take her, and her blood tastes of honey and lusting."

"I shall follow you to the party, but only for the promise of a comfortable bed."

"So, we go," said Dmitri, pushing open the mausoleum doors.

The ball was a costume party for Duke Dumas. The music was grand, and the number of guests—with beating hearts so loud they almost drowned out the violins—had Noble's stomach begging to be fed. After talking two men out of their masks, Dmitri handed Noble one, along with a glass of wine from a servant's tray. "Do you hear that, Noble?"

Noble replied, "What?"

"The sound of one hundred dinner bells calling our names," he said, walking down the steps to the ballroom below.

Nodding, Noble followed, holding up his mask.

Like moths to a flame, the ladies flocked around Dmitri.

A brunette beauty smiled as she pulled down his mask and looked into his yellow eyes hidden behind dark lenses. "Oh, Lord Addleton, wherever have you been? I was telling my sister it has been some time since the kind lord has been to one of our parties. I have no doubt you were charming your way under the skirts of many a lady across the channel in Spain or France?"

Dmitri took and kissed the hand she held out. "I was dreaming of you, Catherine, and your sister, and how fiery your tongues are. How I missed them so."

The lady took his arm. "When will you make an honest lady out of either of us? I've waited so long, and I have said no to many suitors awaiting your offer."

Dmitri pulled his glasses down for a moment, looking into her dark eyes. "I would make brides out of both of you if the King would allow a man more than one wife, but alas, he will not. I cannot, in my heart, choose just one of you."

Catherine giggled and looked upon Noble. "Who is your friend? Is he a worthy suitor, perhaps for Louisa? I would so love to have you all to myself."

Noble pulled back his mask and took her offered hand, kissing it. "I am Noble Lincoln. It is wonderful meeting a friend of Dmitri."

"Oh, the wonders. I am Catherine Rippringham. Are you by chance related to the late Lord and Lady Lincoln, the brother of the Queen's physician?"

"No."

Holding up her mask to hide her embarrassment, she went on. "Oh, of course not. I think Lord Lincoln became a priest. A priest would not be at a gathering such as this. I am sorry for the confusion. I saw him once at the home of Lady DeMaris, and he was as kind to the eyes as you, although he always seemed nervous around her niece, Elizabeth Darby. Come to think of it, Elizabeth moved to the colonies across the ocean. She always fell in love with men she could not have. I think she fancied that priest and moved away in shame."

Annoyed by her presumptuous chatter, Noble again covered his face with his mask. "I am enamored with your story, but alas, I have seen where the wine sits. May I bring you some?"

Dmitri smiled. "I think that is a grand idea. A little wine to change the subject. Although I love gossip, my friend is more interested in meeting that sister of yours."

Catherine smiled and giggled. "I'm so sorry; I tend to rattle on when no one stops me. Wine sounds divine, and I should go and fetch Louisa. Lord Addleton, Mr. Lincoln," she said, curtsying quickly before disappearing into the crowd.

Dmitri leaned in close to Noble. "So is Elizabeth the woman mentioned in your curse?" he whispered.

"I would rather keep those questions for another day."

"Oh, but now I am most intrigued. A priest falls for a woman, perhaps out of his reach?"

"Now is not the time."

He gave a slight nod and looked out on the crowd. "Forbidden love is a story better told away from crowds. It is also nice to know you were a man of titles. Although with these great crowds, I would change your name to avoid drawing unwanted attention, Lord Lincoln."

"Lord Lincoln is no more and gone, as is Father Lincoln, the priest."

"And I thought I was the only one with a history worth hiding."

Another lady wandered up, offering out her hand. "Ah, my dear Lord Addleton, I am ever so pleased to see you. It has been so long."

Dmitri bowed and kissed her hand. "You are still ever beautiful, Sophia. There is no better reason to return to London than to lay my eyes upon the prettiest of maidens. Your eyes set my heart racing and me, well..."

Putting her fingers to her lips as her cheeks blushed red, the raven-haired girl curtsied before taking his arm. "And what of you, dear lord? I have missed you so—though my body has missed you more," she whispered in his ear behind a lace-gloved hand.

"My lips have missed your thighs and your..." He paused, teasing her.

"My what?" she asked, with a wicked smile.

"We are amongst a gentle crowd, and those words are better meant to keep private. I would be abhorred to have your reputation tainted by my wicked words."

"You would not need to keep such things between us if you would ask to marry me, Lord Addleton. I am so taken with you. There is no other lord here with your ability to please me. If it pleases you, of course."

"When have you failed to please me, Lady Sophia?"

The girl giggled under her mask. "I would be pleased if you would meet me later, upstairs."

"Nothing would please me more," he leaned in and whispered.

Sophia waved and walked through the crowd.

Noble returned with two goblets of wine. "It sounds as if your dance card is filling rapidly."

Dmitri looked around the room. "I am only just beginning to fill it."

"For a saint, you certainly have no scruples."

"Yes, that sums it up well. I have gone from saint to sinner. Although I must say, the sinning is much more enjoyable while adding warmth to my bed and smiles to all of their pretty faces."

"And not one of them is wiser to another?"

"A simple thought placed in their pretty heads lets them believe they alone are my only pursuit. Who am I to break their hearts? You should try it sometime instead of wandering through all those terrible memories of being alive. You're dead. Live a little," he said, walking toward a fiery redhead with a thin, mischievous smile playing on her lips.

Noble smiled and shook his head as he eavesdropped on the whispers Dmitri left in the lady's ear.

A faint-looking gentleman biting into an olive walked up to Noble. "It is disconcerting how he alone controls the room. They flock to him like that thing between his legs is covered in jewels worthy of the crown, and he won't marry one of them."

Taking a sip of his wine, Noble nodded. "Then he is most lucky."

"Lucky? I think not. He is a traitor to his country, and he hides here under the skirts of ladies. Lord Addleton—more like Lord Idle Tongue. That's what the ladies call him, you know, when he's not listening. If I were you, I would steer clear of him. He will have your lady as he has had mine."

"I have no lady."

"Well, don't expect to find one here. All of these ladies have one name in mind for courting: his."

Watching as Dmitri led a girl through the crowd toward him, he smiled. "Ah, well, I hope that is not your lady he has there by the hand."

"No, not this time. I'll take my leave. I find Lord Idle Tongue's company lacking."

"Stanwyk, are you leaving so soon?" called out Dmitri with a wide grin.

"I'm off to find Caroline. Good evening to you, Lord Addleton, and you, sir. I dare say; I did not get your name."

Shaking Stanwyk's hand, Noble replied, "Noble Lincoln. It was an interesting chat. I hope you do find your lady."

Stanwyk refused to look at Dmitri as he walked away. The vampire walked up to his friend. "Noble Lincoln, I would like to introduce you to my very good friend, Margaret Luveatu."

The blonde looked at him with an air of confidence as she held out her hand to Noble. Leaning down as he met her eyes, he pressed his lips gently to her hand. "You are the beauty Dmitri told me so much about."

"Mr. Lincoln, I know you."

"No, I don't think so."

"I am sure I do. Your uncle is the physician to the Queen. You and I danced once, and my father offered me to your father as a betrothal to you. Your father said yes, but you were in medical school at the time."

"I hope it did not cause you issue with finding a husband of your liking?"

Noble remembered the conversation with his father.

The tall, thin man smiled at his son as they sat in front of the fire in the library. Noble was reading a thick book when his father coughed to get his attention. "I've come to speak to you about the match I've made."

"Not this again, Father?"

"Noble, you will need a wife, and she is quite striking. Her father is Duke Luveatu, and he has the title of many lands. She can give you many sons and daughters. She is seventeen and a talented musician and has been educated in the ways being of a good wife."

"Father, I've told you I have no interest in marriage. This bartering system of selling daughters..." Noble shook his head. "It's as if these women are cows to be bred and sold to the richest man."

The white-headed man looked at him with teary eyes. "You can insult the old ways all you like, but if you do not accept this match, my name dies with you, and I greatly fear that. I've already heard you are thinking of leaving medicine for the church."

"I am."

"Why? Lincolns have been physicians for generations."

"Lincolns have also been butchers for generations, Father. I believed I would be helping ease the suffering of men, but I've found it more akin to butchering sheep."

"Then don't practice. I can accept that much easier than you never marrying and having children. Your mother has been waiting for the day there would be little ones running around the house and her son would find happiness."

"The church will make me happy. Marrying some stranger to propagate a bloodline is not my idea of happiness."

"*My father matched your mother and me, and we grew to love one another enough to bear an ungrateful son.*"

Noble furrowed his brow. "It is not that I am ungrateful, Father. I wish to be left to make my choices for the future. I have done everything you've asked until now. I cannot bear the idea that I must follow protocol to be a good son."

"*A fitting marriage would settle the hearts of your mother and me both. That's all we're asking. You can have all the mistresses you like if the maiden Luveatu does not make you happy.*"

"*Father, I won't marry to have mistresses. If I did wish to marry, it would be for love and a love of my choosing, not something forced upon the young daughter of a duke who wishes to farther expand his lands. I will not accept this way of things. I do not know this girl. It's not that I think she is so terrible. I'm sure she is quite lovely, but the church forbids it.*"

"*So, you've made up your mind?*"

"*Yes, I have.*"

"*Noble, you will be stripped of your titles and lands.*"

"*There are no bishops with lord titles, Father, and for that, I am most happy.*"

"*I don't know what to say.*"

Placing his hands on his father's shoulders, he looked into his eyes. "Say you'll come to church when I am a priest and that you will honor the wishes of God and myself. I cannot apologize enough for not being the son you wish I was, but I must find my own way."

Noble shook away the memory as Margaret continued. "I have never married. My father is not happy, of course, but I know someday someone will wish to have me as a wife. I have become used to the life of a lady always waiting. I am the oldest of them all, but I now watch myself accordingly. I will say I kept track of you for some time in hopes you would honor the match. My brother went to university with you. He said you were quite gifted, so much so the queen wished you to be her sole physician. Instead, after graduating, you left school and joined the seminary. Why would you decline such an esteemed position?"

"There is more butchery in medicine than actual medicine."

"I don't understand."

"Let's just say I was turned off by the bureaucracy of it all and the lack of true science. I was chosen for my name and as a favor to my uncle. I refused to do procedures he deemed fit, for I do not carve holes in living men for no other reason than idle interest."

"Ah, an honest doctor as well as a clergyman," said Dmitri, kissing his lady's hand.

"I see no cassock. Have you left the church, Lord Lincoln?"

"I have, and my father's name died with him since my uncle has no sons and I am the only remaining Lincoln. I left the church to marry and have children as it was the wish of my father to propagate the family line."

"How noble, Lord Lincoln. Have you set a wife?"

"I did, but she died quite suddenly in the colonies across the sea."

"How dreadful for you. I'm sure any lady here would be willing to help ... console you. You do have such a respected family name. That is better than I can say for my dear Dmitri," she said, looking up at Dmitri. "He is ever the rogue and spoiler of maidens." Margaret's eyes shone amber for a moment before taking back their dark blue color, catching Noble by surprise.

"My dear Margaret, it is my duty to assure future husbands a pleasant experience in the marriage bed."

Margaret looked upon Dmitri with adoring eyes. "You are a wolf amongst sheep, Dmitri, but I am also a wolf, and I will not tolerate this behavior. You will find my bed, the only one you need to enter tonight. Bring your friend. My sister is starving for attention, and this one seems as if he can handle it."

"Ah, I am afraid my friend is not really over the loss of his wife."

"I'm sure Maleficent can change your mind. If all you wish to do is feed, she is fine with that."

Caught off guard, Noble watched her smile as he looked alarmed. She leaned into him and whispered in his ear, "Do not be alarmed, Lord. I know what you are."

"I..." said Noble as she took his hand. He felt as enamored with her as he had been with Elizabeth. The twinkle in her eyes, the sound of her voice as she laughed, and the simple movement of her as she outlined Dmitri's lips with a long red fingernail.

"We should go. I am bored, and my sister has probably already found her way to the carriage. She gets tired of these things so easily."

"Yes, as do I," said Noble, following Dmitri and Margaret as they climbed the stairs and left the great house.

At the Luveatu home, they drank wine and consumed small plums and grapes in front of a large fireplace.

Maleficent was even more beautiful than her sister, and three years younger. She looked deep into Noble's eyes as he kissed her hand. "It is wonderful to meet such a kind soul, considering the company you keep, Lord Lincoln."

"I keep hearing that I should find a new friend."

"I agree," said the girl as she took his hand.

"The wine has me a little drunk," said Noble as he followed the girl through the house. "I almost don't feel myself."

Maleficent smiled back at him as she led him. "I will find you a room to settle in for the night."

"You are so kind. What of your parents?"

"They are in Rome. Father's affairs keep him there most of the time."

"Oh?"

They climbed the stone steps until they reached the second floor. "I wish I had known you before all of those horrible things happened to you."

"What horrible things do you speak of?" he asked, his mind growing cloudy.

Noble did not remember how he ended up on the bed, nude from the waist down, beneath the writhing hips of the Lady Maleficent. "Please, I beg of you, stop this. I have a wife…" He was startled when his limbs were too heavy to move. "How?"

She placed a finger upon his lips. "Shh … there's no need to speak."

Noble lay quiet as she leaned back. She took his arm and leaned closer and bit him. Feeling powerless to stop her, he watched. "What are you doing?"

Her blue eyes shone gold like Dmitri's. "You are quite something. Such a haunted soul. It's beautiful how sad you are inside."

"You're a vampire…"

She smiled, her mouth red with his blood. "No, I am human … mostly. I recognize melancholy because I am a pathetic woman who lets Dmitri drain me until I am sad and cold. A woman he promised to make beautiful forever, share life with for all eternity. He favors my sister. But I can't say no to him." She pulled the scarf from her neck. The skin beneath was the gray color of a rotting corpse, thin and hole-ridden.

Noble could not believe what he was seeing. "Dmitri did this?"

Maleficent nodded with a thin smile that wavered. "Long ago and ever since."

"Your parents are not away, are they?"

"They are. Our mother and father have gone to Rome, along with our brother. They are seeking a cure for this terrible malady laid upon my sister and me by your friend. Of course, they are ancient now."

"Oh."

"Let's talk no more of my family. My interest lies with you and your interest in me."

"I'm not myself at the moment. I feel odd."

"Oh, that's the dead blood in the wine," she said with a hint of wickedness.

"Dead blood?"

"Yes, so I can control you. You see, Dmitri has promised us immortality for so long now, and I don't wish to wait any longer. You are drunk on the dead. You can't enamor me with your eyes or your voice; you are powerless over me. You can hardly move for the weight of it in your veins." She reached under the pillow and pulled out a wooden stake. "Now, you will turn me completely, or you will die."

"Trust me, you don't want this, and I wouldn't know how to turn you if I could."

Maleficent raised the stake over her head for a moment and brought it down in front of his face. "I want to be beautiful forever, live forever, love forever."

"I am very sorry this has happened to you, but I cannot help you."

"You may not know, but I do, and you can help me. I swear I won't hurt you if you do this for me. Give me your blood freely, and take mine until you leave me just at the precipice. Only then may I become immortal." She pulled his shirt open and ran the point of the stake across the skin on his chest.

"You don't want to be this thing I am. It is most terrible."

"What are these funny marks? I've never seen them on Dmitri."

"It is a curse... I am not what Dmitri is. I am much worse."

She leaned into him and pushed the stake into his skin until it scratched against his sternum. A small amount of blood pooled around the tip of the stake. He groaned under the pain as she leaned down upon it, resting her chin on her hands. She looked deep into his eyes.

"You are a vampire; that's all you need to be. You drink blood to live. You can look into the eyes of maidens and make them love you, satiate you even. You are pale; even your eyes are so light blue they remind me of a beautiful early spring morning sky. You are cold to the touch and inside of me. I know you can hear my heart beating in your ears."

As she sat straight up again, Noble reached up clumsily—for his arms were like lead—and put his hand over hers on the shaft of the stake. "I would rather see death than see you become this thing. You are beautiful and young, and you deserve real love, not lies from a creature who wishes nothing from you but a short, painful feeding. Maleficent, you deserve a life, and this is no life. If you were this thing I am, you could never look upon a sunrise, never feel the warmth on your skin, or truly love anyone, because when you look at them, all you see is a meal, and all they see is a monster."

"Did you know Dmitri is over nine hundred years old?"

Noble responded, "Yes."

"How can someone so old be so beautiful, yet heartless? He is everything to me, everything I've ever wanted. He whispers love in my ear and then denies me what I want in return. I give him everything." Tears fell down her cheeks. "Please do these things I ask. Feed me, feed on me, and kill me."

"I will not kill you."

Her eyes fell upon the table next to the bed. Noble looked over and saw the dagger. Maleficent dropped the stake and reached for the knife.

Smiling down at him, she placed the knife at his throat. Noble lay staring up at her. Her tears fell on his chest as she leaned close to his neck. Her living breath warmed his face as Maleficent kissed him deeply. "All I want is to be loved forever," she whispered. "You will give me that."

Before he could respond, she slit his throat. Blood gurgled out, and she was on him, lapping it up.

Maleficent's heart raced as she sat up and smiled, her face covered in blood, while her eyes wept. Noble struggled beneath her, his hands shaking as he felt himself bleeding out. With great effort, he raised a hand to his throat. His fangs and nails grew as his body fought to survive. His hand started turning black. Noble's top and bottom jaw jutted outward, and his lower fangs grew.

Maleficent screamed and moved off him as the creature's eyes turned blood red. He grabbed her wrist, pulling her to him. She fought, stabbing him again and again with the dagger, but he was upon her, his teeth scratching her throat as he whispered through his fangs, "I will not damn you as I have been damned, but I will drink from you to ease the pain you have caused."

The woman screamed again, "No!"

Biting into her throat, he pulled her to the apex of the high ceiling, where he clung, listening for her heart as Dmitri had taught him. The many holes she had stabbed into his chest healed as her warm blood poured down his throat. Dropping the dagger to the floor, Maleficent struggled, kicked, and hit him while his neck healed.

Loud footsteps outside the doors caught his attention, and he stopped feeding.

The doors burst open, and Dmitri stood looking up at him. There were even more footsteps running behind him. "You are an ugly thing, my friend. Still, we must flee..." The sound of a crossbow release sent the vampire reeling forward as a stake pierced his shoulder. Dmitri got to his feet in a blur, pulling the wood from his body. In less than a second, he was at the windows on the other side of the room.

"*Iuguolo monasteries*," shouted a voice from the hallway as two men entered the room. One stood taller than the other, his dark hair hidden beneath a brimmed hat while his dark eyes scanned the room. He held a crucifix out before him and shouted at Dmitri. "*Intereo malum bestia!*"

The other man, smaller, wearing a monk's robe, reloaded the crossbow as his companion shouted, "May *Deus* have *Misericordia in vestri animus.*"

Dmitri pushed open the windows and jumped onto the windowsill. "You are quite mistaken, my friend. God has no mercy to give."

The beast on the ceiling released the girl. The strangers stopped as she hit the floor and pointed their weapons up at him. As he jumped from the window, Dmitri shouted, "Run, Noble!"

The creature spread its wings as the crossbow shot another stake, striking him in the abdomen. The monster shrieked and flew through the window, leaving the men alone with the woman who tried to kill him.

Dmitri watched from a rooftop a few houses away as the dark-winged beast flew across the sky toward the cemetery. "You, my brother, are something quite special," he said aloud to no one.

The monk jumped out onto the rooftop beneath the window and started toward Dmitri with his reloaded crossbow. "*Subsisto bestia!*"

Far behind Dmitri, screams filled his ears before running footsteps jumped from the window of the Luveatu home. Dmitri listened past the racing hearts of the men chasing him for the familiar heartbeats of the Luveatu ladies, but could no longer hear them. *Damn you, Archers.*

He jumped across to another rooftop, and another, then started for a building far too high for the humans following to reach.

Leaping up to the next rooftop, he looked back just as the men fired upon him. He caught one stake midair, ducked out of the way of the other, and barred his fangs. "Zealots!"

"*Nos mos reperio vos quod ut nos operor nos mos transporto vos tergum ut abyssus, Lamia.*"

"Not if I find you first!" shouted Dmitri before running out of sight.

Noble dropped out of the sky onto several gravestones, breaking one. Landing on his hands and knees, he was a man again, out of breath and in pain. Noble reached down and tugged at the stake sticking out of his gut. As he pulled on the oak protruding from him, it scraped his spine, causing him to wince. He yanked again, and this time, it pulled free. Rolling off the stone onto the ground, Noble lay face up, staring at the sky, waiting to heal. Only then did he realize he was nude.

Someone leaned over him, blocking out the stars, and pointed a stake-loaded crossbow at his chest. The woman was tall and thin with a beautiful face and dark, glowering eyes. Placing the heel of her boot into the open wound, she raised an iron cross with her other hand as he groaned in pain.

"*Quam decet a Lamia in a cemetery. Iam vos intereo, occisor.*"

Yanking hard, he pulled the crossbow to his chest until the stake met his skin. "Do it. Kill me."

"You want to die so badly. Why?"

"I did not choose this, nor did I ask to be something so ungodly."

"I do not understand."

"Must you understand something before you kill it, though you already despise it so?"

"I do not kill things that ask for death."

"May I know the name of the woman who would not see me dead?"

"Lucia Archer."

Looking at her clothing, he noticed a crest on her coat. Two keys intersected with a crown between them. "So, the Pope sends 'light' to destroy me? You should kill me before I kill you."

The creature started emerging again.

Lucia suddenly looked nervous. "I will beg forgiveness from God for you." She crossed herself with the hand holding the cross. "May God have mercy on your soul." Noble lay still as she pulled the trigger. The stake shot through his sternum and hit the metal surrounding his heart below, stopping with a *clink*.

The symbols around the cross scar on his chest glowed in a golden light as the stake started to work its way out of Noble's chest.

Lucia crossed herself again. "*Quid* in God's *nomen*?"

The stake fell from his chest, and the hole it had made healed before her eyes. Then the symbols went dark. "God only has one name for what I am, and you know what that is... You cannot kill me, Lucia. I'm sorry. I wish you could."

She backed away slowly, holding out her cross. "What are you? I watched you fall from the sky after you changed from that thing. You may have wings, but you are no angel."

Noble rose to his feet in a blur and walked toward her carefully. "God sent an angel, and she set this upon me. I don't mean to be the monster I am. I was a priest once."

The woman stepped back into a tall monument. She froze. "Step back," she said, shoving the cross between them.

Moving closer to her, he pulled the crossbow from her hand and let it fall to the ground. His chest met the cross; it burned, and his skin blistered, but he did not back away. Mere inches from her face, their eyes met. Her eyes avoided his, knowing he would try to charm her. The marks on his chest and shoulders, lit by the moon, caught her attention.

"Why are you and your other crossbow-toting friends trying to kill me?"

"I will not answer the questions of a demon."

Pulling the cross out of her hand, he dropped it. "You will answer my questions," he said, his red eyes glowing.

Her eyes stared hard into his for a moment. Then Noble doubled over as she stabbed him in the gut with another stake pulled from beneath her coat. "I told you, I don't answer to you, strange demon."

"Damn it," he groaned. Lucia ran off, grabbing her weapon and the cross as she fled.

He listened as her racing heartbeat moved farther away before starting for the crypt of the Smithes.

Dmitri opened the door as Noble closed in; he was carrying Noble's bags. "I've finally lost them, but we've got to move. The sun is about to rise."

"What of the home with the feather beds and heavy curtains?"

Noble pulled out trousers and a shirt from the bag.

"You need to explain that thing I saw. You can fly. How do you do it?"

Pulling on the pants and then his shirt, Noble shook his head. "Take me to the home with feather beds hidden in darkness, and then you'll have my story."

A DEMON'S PRAYERS

J ust as the sun peeked over the horizon, Noble followed Dmitri into a large stone palace. It towered in size over the manor Noble had lived in as a child and young man. The stones were gray, with green moss covering the corners of the blocks. The entrance was large and looked more like the door to a dungeon rather than a large house. The wood was held together with iron slats, with protruding spikes pointing outward.

How perfect for the creatures that mean to make it home, doors that bite through the skin if you are to rap your knuckles on it, thought Noble.

Servants met them at the door, asking no questions and avoiding eye contact.

Noble craned his neck to the large stained glass that filled the second- and third-floor openings, as though the builder wished to live in a cathedral rather than a home.

After their bags and persons had been tucked into a sizeable upstairs room with wine and thick curtains, Dmitri smiled upon his friend in front of a large, fitful fire.

"So, what do you think of our new home?"

"I do not understand how this is our home."

Dmitri laughed. "Once, it was a lover's home. Her uncle left it to me conveniently upon her death."

"It seems all things are convenient for you. This is quite a large home for two."

A wicked grin played upon Dmitri's lips. "Yes, it is, but we can always fill it with willing women, and I know many."

"I am most assured you can. But I must know what you did to the Luveatu ladies. Maleficent's skin showed signs of necrosis."

"Oh, the willing do so find our sin enjoyable. I fed upon them time after time, to the edge of death. When the brain is robbed of blood, it lets you see things no amount of life can show you. That ledge over the precipice was like opium to them. It was never enough. They wanted this *gift,* no matter how much I told them what they were after were simply delusions of a dying mind and did not carry over to this life." He sat with an expression of satisfaction before continuing. "But if I had done it, could you imagine the destruction they would set upon the men of London, given our gifts? There would be so many torn-out throats. We would all fall into peril."

"Tell me, who were those people chasing you and then meeting me in the cemetery? What fate has befallen the Luveatus?"

Dmitri plucked the fingers of his gloves free from his fingers as he smiled at his friend. "So many questions, my dear Noble... One at a time, please."

"Alright."

Setting his gloves upon the mantle, Dmitri glanced at the embers. Annoyed, he pushed a stick into the dying fire, prodding a big log into them and causing the flames to pop back into life. "Those humans, my friend, are the Archers. They hunt us by a silent order of the Vatican's Knights of Malta. They are men who are sent forth to relieve the rest of the world of creatures like you and me in the name of God. They are why I left London. Every time I settled down anywhere, I would find a stake flung at my head or the house I resided in burned to the ground. So, I crossed the sea where they have no foothold. For centuries, I have run from them throughout Europe and, for a time, in China. I'm afraid Margaret and Maleficent probably saw their last sunsets this very evening. Giving one's self to a demon willingly is seen as a sin, and I'm sure the Archers ended them for it. They will see it as food deprivation, while I see it as a relief. I was growing bored with them and their incessant whining about becoming vampires."

Noble let out a breath of discontent. "Those poor wretches. "

Dmitri settled into the large twin armchair next to Noble. "Do not cry for them, Noble. Sin is sin, my friend, and they were connoisseurs."

Deep in thought, Noble looked over at Dmitri. "The Archers have chased you for centuries?"

"Yes, they are persistent annoyances. I believe they put an end to my maker as well. That faceless fool went for the throat of the King of Spain. Like I said before, the blood of royalty is wondrous on the palate, but he had no control. I think those forty-five years in the dungeons robbed him of his sanity. The Archers mean to return us to hell; little do they know, a great deal of hell is here upon the earth, as it is meant to be."

"Living nine hundred years has granted you vast experience and knowledge."

"Yes, but at the moment, my interest is with you. That black beast with wings was most magnificent indeed," he said with a wicked smile as he held out his hand to Noble. "Share with me your past, friend."

Noble held out his wrist before Dmitri, who smiled before biting into it. Groaning, Noble waited for the pain to pass as his friend drank his story.

After a few moments, Dmitri released him and shook his head as he wiped the blood from his mouth with a handkerchief. "I thought I was a tragedy. You, my friend, you're better and worse. That thing that made you, he was the one at the docks in Virginia?"

"Yes, that was Tabansi."

"I should find it a wonder if there are still living souls in the whole of the colonies once that thing unleashed its wrath."

"He is limited by daylight and the color of his skin for now. When he is able to speak English and charm people, he's sure to travel unhampered."

Dmitri was sitting in silence, staring at the flames, when Noble noticed tears of blood running down his cheeks.

"Are you alright, Dmitri?"

Turning to Noble with a smile and blood welling in his eyes, Dmitri nodded. "I know now my faith as a man was not wasted, and this thing I became is not without purpose. My brother was wrong. For you, Noble, have laid eyes upon God."

Shaking his head, he looked into Dmitri's hope-filled eyes. "It was an angel, not God."

Smiling, Dmitri shook his head. "No, God was most certainly there in the light of the angel, Noble. How did you not see it when I could? It was the most beautiful of anything I have laid eyes upon."

Noble thought back to that moment when the angel looked down upon him, but he could not recall what lay beyond her. "I do not know."

Dmitri watched the fire again like a child whose eyes had finally opened and discovered the realities of the world. "You are not cursed; you are blessed with love eternal. She will come back to you. God is out there, and he is watching over you."

Furrowing his brow, Noble looked at his friend, though Dmitri's eyes did not leave the flames. "Do you know something else I don't?"

"That I could only wish for what you have, for what you have seen."

Nothing else was said that night. The only noises filling the room were the fire flicking and popping and the wind at the top of the chimney.

October 31st 1718

I know not what to make of my companion. It has been six months since Dmitri drank of my past. With newfound faith, he has tried and failed many times to step into churches about the village and city proper. Each time, there seems to be an invisible wall at the entrance, and if he touches the doorway, he is burned as if a silver cross is set upon him.

When Dmitri found himself unable to enter churches, he turned to prayer, using the cross I once wore with a cassock when I was a priest. Although he cannot directly look at it or touch it in his hands, he still tries.

His hands leave blood, soaking the pages of my Bible, as touching it burns away his fingertips while he searches the pages almost frantically for something he seems unable to find.

More often than not, I find him praying on his knees in his room as if he is trying to speak to God. His mind is on little else.

Dmitri is no longer the self-assured creature I met on the ship who showed me how to live as this beast. He is now fearful of his life, having lived in sin, even though he has had no real pulse for well over nine hundred years.

He still feeds from the servants, refusing to leave the house. Unlike his past victims—left dead in pubs and inns—he leaves the servants alive but with no memory of being fed upon, for he heals them with his own blood afterward.

Dmitri tells me he feels alive again like he did before becoming a vampire, even going so far as to ask me to baptize him. Dmitri has also demanded that I call him by his given name, Enravota.

I fear baptism would kill him, so I have kindly declined. His begging persists, as does his growing anger at my denial. Again and again, he begs to see God, and I have given in, allowing him a moment at my wrist here and there only to calm him when he is overwrought with his existence.

I feel as though I am losing him to the same turmoil I felt before and just after I became this thing. His years of yammering about my emotions getting the best of me have become wasted on him. I believe he is so far gone from what he was that I am not *able to bring him back. He is not yet asking for death, but in my heart, I fear he soon will.*

To avoid these tiring, nightly occurrences, I usually traverse the streets of the small village, sometimes taking a chance in London to find my meals. So far, I have seen no sign of the Archers, but I feel as though they are still somewhere close, waiting to pounce. With Dmitri in his current state, I don't believe he would avoid his end if he were to face them again.

Tonight is All Hallows' Eve, and I have begged him to join me for a ball we've been invited to attend. I only hope that I can pry him from the house for a night away from praying and possibly alleviate some of his sufferings.

Noble burst into Dmitri's room with the chamber servant at his heels. Kneeled before the cross hanging on the wall, the vampire prayed.

"There will be no more of this tonight, Dmitri. We have a party to attend, and I will not leave you to this. This gathering is very important to me, and I want you there."

Dmitri looked up at him with dried blood and crimson tears raining down his pale cheeks from his gold eyes. "I must receive his forgiveness, Noble. I must be cleansed for centuries of sin and genocide upon mankind."

Kneeling before his friend, Noble took Dmitri's hands in his own. "Enravota, God does not see us as men any longer. He will not pluck us from the earth and allow us passage into heaven. You told me that."

"He allowed you to see him; he allowed you to become more than immortal. That is your blessing. Mine will be a clear conscience and a peaceful death."

"You are a vampire; you cannot turn back into a man. We are Satan's creatures; we are death's doormen. Just as swords wielded by soldiers' hands plunging into another man's chest are, we are meant to feed upon them. We don't have to do it happily, and we can feel remorse, but we cannot change what we are."

An urgency came over his voice, and tears started down his cheeks. "I must change, Noble."

"But you can't. And you cannot commit suicide, for that leads to *limbus patrum*, and there, you will never find God."

Dmitri sobbed and cried out in Noble's face. "I am surely lost."

"No, you don't have to be. Be as you once were, a proud and sinful beast who celebrated his existence and the demise of others."

"I cannot."

"You can, and you will."

Noble turned to the empty-eyed man standing in the corner of the room. "Servant, clean him up and ready him for the costume ball. I want him in the carriage and ready to take his leave in an hour."

"Yes, milord."

Snatching the cross from the wall, Noble left the room. Walking into his room, he flung the cross onto the bed. His chamberman stood behind in the doorway, waiting for commands.

"Tell the stable boy to ready the horses and carriage. And send the kitchen maid to my room."

"Yes, Milord Cross."

Noble stared at the *Bible* on his desk as his chamber servant helped him dress, hoping the party would awaken the old Dmitri.

After feeding on the young woman who worked in the kitchen cooking uneaten meals, Noble dressed for the ball.

"Tonight is important, John," Noble said to the servant, helping him dress.

"Yes, Lord Cross."

"Do you know why tonight is so important, John?"

"No, milord."

"Tonight, there is a very good chance I may see my wife again, my Elizabeth, in the flesh." Noble noticed his hands were shaking as he buttoned his shirt.

"Very exciting news, milord."

"Yes, it is. I've waited for so long for Elizabeth's return. There is no greater wish in my heart. She is everything to me. Wouldn't it be nice to have a lady about the house, John?"

"Yes, Lord Cross."

Noble took the invitation from the bed and reread it. Lord and Lady Darby, we wish your company to celebrate the birth of our granddaughter, Elizabeth Alford, to Thomas and Christine Alford.

Please God, I beg this be my love returned, he thought as he straightened his suit in the mirror.

The carriage set out upon the fog-covered roads in the early evening, just after dark. Noble watched Dmitri, who sat in silence, angry for having his praying interrupted.

"Dmitri, it is good that you've come out. I hear the most lordly of lords and their ladies are stepping out for this grand occasion, some of them your favorites. I know how you must miss them and their royal blood."

Through the dark of the carriage, Dmitri's gold eyes glowered at him. "I would rather be shedding my sins upon my knees, friend."

"Feeding is not a sin. If it were, all men who feed upon animals in the fields and woods would have their souls sent to hell. End this insanity already, Dmitri."

"You, the servant of God with *his* words carved upon your chest, chastise me for not wanting to be a demon? For years, I have listened to you tell me of my sin, and now that I've seen the truth, I am wrong in your eyes?"

"Dmitri, I mean no harm, but this path you tread upon will end you and not in a way that will have you heaven-bound. I want you to be as you were. You were my teacher, my companion in blood. Now you've become troubled in the head, much like the damned creature who made you."

Dmitri was suddenly in his face, his fangs bared and his eyes glaring. "You'll not compare me to that beast!"

"I will if I believe it to be so, Dmitri."

The vampire sat back in his seat and straightened his coat. "We'll speak no more of it. I will go to this ball you demand I attend, and you will leave me to do as I please afterward."

Noble nodded, and both remained quiet for the rest of the trip.

Dmitri sported a smile as he pulled on a wolf mask, but Noble knew it false. He pulled on his mask of a goat, and they both stepped up on the doorstep of Darby Manor.

The butler stood stoically, staring at them. "Your names, sirs?"

"Lord Dmitri Addleton and Lord Cross of London, kind sir." Noble bowed his head to the servant, and the servant bowed in return. "Very well, my lords."

The two walked in as their names were announced, "Lord Dmitri Addleton and Lord Cross of London."

Ladies turned their heads, hearing Dmitri's name.

Noble's mask allowed him to walk about the home he had been in many times. He remembered the first time he had come to Darby Manor with real purpose.

Holding tight to the brim of his hat, Noble stepped into the house. The butler took it from him, which left him feeling naked.

"Lord Darby has been waiting to see you, young Lord Lincoln."

Noble nodded. "Yes, sir."

He followed the butler back through the palatial home. Sitting in his solar, poring over maps, Lord Darby looked up at the two men as they entered. His still-thick hair, with more silver than brown, rested flat over eyebrows, making him look more like an owl than a man, with features softened by age. His deep-set eyes twinkled.

"Lord Noble Lincoln to see you, milord."

"Ah, yes, yes. Go and fetch us some wine, Grimms."

"Yes, milord."

Noble stood in place, unsure of what to do.

"Come in, young man, and rest a bit. We have much to talk about."

Bowing his head for a moment, he walked in and sat in the chair motioned to him by Lord Darby.

Sitting in silence, Noble watched the older man roll up a map and set it aside, all the while looking over his spectacles at the young man.

"You've come to talk to me about Elizabeth, have you?"

"Y-yes, my lord," he said nervously.

"Are you certain? You don't sound sure of yourself."

"Oh, Lord Darby, I am most certain of my want of your permission to court Elizabeth."

Lord Darby laughed. "Now, your tongue has loosened."

"Yes, Lord Darby."

"I have heard you were betrothed to Lady Luveatu at one point. Is that still so?"

"No, sir. I turned down that betrothal before I went to the seminary. And as a priest, I was not allowed to marry, so her father moved on to a different family."

"Are you still a priest?"

"No, Lord Darby, I've left the church, for the beauty of your daughter and the loveliness of her soul has left me believing my future with her stands above God."

"Will you say the same should you marry her before a priest? Men should not place women above God."

"I did not mean marrying her will be greater than God, sir, it's just... I feel that marrying her will serve a greater purpose for me as a man than serving God as a priest. God willing, he will bind us with faith as well as our hearts."

"So, you are courting her as a man already taken by her?"

"Yes, my Lord Darby. I am most taken by her. When I first laid eyes upon her, it was as if heaven shone a light upon her, and there was no greater light."

The older man smiled. "You are a man in love, Lord Lincoln."

"Yes, Lord Darby. What man would not be entranced by a lady such as Elizabeth?"

Lord Darby smiled and nodded. "Elizabeth is quite special and much like her namesake; she is just as headstrong. So much so that she has commanded my permission be given to you."

Noble felt nervous once more when Lord Darby took on a serious air. "Lord Lincoln, I have been told you are going to practice medicine in the new colonies across the sea, and you mean to take my daughter with you."

"My father means to go. He has purchased land in the Virginia Colony, and he wants me to go with him, but I will not go if Elizabeth cannot."

"I hear the sun shines so brightly there, and the air is so clear the sky is bluer than the oceans. It seems there is no better place for her. I don't think she would allow me to keep her here since her demands have been made clear. What kind of father would I be if I did not see it through and give her the happiness you promise her?"

"I don't know, Lord Darby."

"Your father and I have spoken at length, and he is fine with the match, as are my family and me."

Noble smiled. "You have done me a great service, sir, and there are no words to thank you enough."

"I will announce your engagement at the spring ball we are having in two weeks."

"Thank you, sir."

"No need to thank me, Noble. You make sure that Elizabeth is always smiling, for that attribute alone should always shine."

"Yes, Lord Darby. I promise it will."

A book suddenly fell from a stack sitting on a table near the rear door of the solar and hit the floor.

Lord Darby let out a sigh. "Dear daughter, you may come out of hiding and say hello to your future husband, and do stop sneaking about, knocking over my things."

Elizabeth smiled as she stepped into sight. "Hello, dear Lord Lincoln."

Her eyes sparkled in the sunlight coming through the windows, and her tied-back hair shone gold with the sun upon it.

"Hello, my Lady Elizabeth and soon wife."

She blushed, and there was not a more beautiful sight in his eyes.

Noble smiled at the memory of her as he and Dmitri stepped into the crowd of mask-adorned guests.

Making his way through the large house—after escaping the ladies who quickly surrounded Dmitri—Noble wandered down the halls of bed chambers, listening for the quick heartbeat of the child he had come to see.

Closing his eyes, he blocked out the hearts from the floors below and stood silent until he heard it. It was fast and dear. He walked down the halls quietly, hoping not to run into other guests, or worse, a Darby.

Opening a door at the far end of the west end of the house, Noble met the eyes of the child's wet nurse.

"This is a private room. Party guests are not allowed here, sir."

He walked in, looking straight into the eyes of the young woman, and removed his mask. "You need to fetch tea from the kitchen for yourself. The child is safe with me. I am her uncle."

The blank stare on her face let Noble know she had fallen into his trance as she went through the door, leaving him alone with the infant.

Once she was gone, he crept slowly toward the cradle as he had done with his children. He sucked in his breath and smiled upon the child. Blonde curls covered her head; her bright blue eyes looked up at him as he kneeled to get a closer look. He ran a finger down her chubby cheek. "You are the spitting image of your Aunt Elizabeth, tiny girl. My heart is most grateful. Do you know who I am, sweet child?" The infant cooed and shoved a dainty fist into her mouth.

A seventeen-year-old Elizabeth smiled as Noble bowed his head. From across the room, Duchess Anne swatted at the physicians attending her. "Go away, go away!"

She calmed herself and tried a kind smile as she spoke to a young woman in the room.

"Elizabeth, please send a messenger to your father. I think tonight I die. He must be here."

"I must apologize, my dearest Auntie Anne, Father has gone to Spain, and he will not arrive home in time."

"Send the messenger anyway. I will wait if I can, if death does not take me sooner."

"Yes, your grace."

She bowed to her aunt and left the room.

"Father Lincoln, read me my last rites; I believe I am close to death."

Noble nodded and opened his Bible before stepping up to her.

Frustrated by her indecision, she waved her hand at him. "No, wait, not yet. Tell the bishop I am on death's doorstep and I should like to have him read me last rites, for he baptized me."

He did not argue. "Yes, your grace, right away."

Leaving the room with a bow, Noble walked down the hall toward the steps leading to the kitchen.

There, hidden in the dark stairwell, he clutched his Bible to his chest and held tight to the cross hanging from his neck as he looked to the sky. "God, you have placed an angel upon the earth, and for this sign, I am most thankful."

"Father, you've seen an angel?" asked a voice on the steps below him.

Startled, Noble stood up straight and dropped his arms to his sides. "I meant it symbolically. It is a prayer for Duchess Anne."

Elizabeth took the stairs until she stood in front of him, her blue eyes gazing into his. "My aunt finds comfort in your kind words and prayers."

"Your aunt?"

"Yes, oh, I am very sorry. My aunt does not always introduce people, so caught up with her illness. I am Elizabeth Darby."

"I am Father Noble Lincoln of The Church of England," he said, holding out his hand.

She took it for a moment and curtsied. "I am honored to meet you, Father. And I want to thank you on behalf of our family."

He did not release her hand right away. The softness of her skin and the blue of her eyes captured him as he stood staring at her without realizing the passing time.

"I am doing what she asks and what God asks of me in this time of great illness and unrest."

"Elizabeth!" shouted her aunt from down the hall. "Elizabeth, come and save me from these infernal quacks!"

"I'm sorry," she said, releasing his hand. "My aunt needs me. Do know I am glad of your visits. They settle her so... And me, of course."

Smiling, he said, "I am glad that I can help ease your sorrow."

"I must go now," she said as her aunt shouted again.

Noble nodded. "God bless you and Duchess Anne."

"Thank you, Father."

He watched as she walked the hall and entered the doors of the great bedchamber.

Closing his eyes, he put his hand over his heart and whispered, "Why, God, do you put such unattainable beauty before me?"

"Who are you, and why are you in this room?" demanded a woman's voice.

Noble stood up, turning toward the woman.

"Noble, Noble Lincoln," she said, smiling. "Oh, dear brother. We feared the worst." She ran up to him and put her arms around him.

He pulled away from her. "Beautiful, Christina." She shared the blonde curls of her sister but had her father's green eyes.

"Are you here for the children?"

"Children?"

She looked puzzled. "Mira, Yancy... they were sent here from the colony in Virginia. And that is why you've come?"

"Who sent them here?"

"The church sent them to us after Father Benedict died. It was quite sudden."

Noble felt like the air had been knocked out of him. "Father Benedict is dead?"

"Yes, they arrived five years ago. We received word that your ship went down. Elizabeth wrote to me about it. She was going to bring the children here, and then I never heard from her again. We next received word she was killed by an animal and was buried next to you there. But now you're here. They are not orphans after all!" she said, hugging him again. Christina pulled out of the embrace; her eyes searched his for answers. "Where have you been, Noble? It's been six years."

"I will tell you the truth, but then I must take it from you, dear Christina."

"What do you mean, brother?"

"I am not the man your sister married, nor am I the children's father. I was until I stepped on that ship, but then something most terrible happened, and I lost my humanity."

"I do not understand," she said, looking at him with concerned eyes.

"I left the children with Father Benedict, for I feared I would do to them as I did their mother. She died in my arms, and I have felt no greater sadness."

"What are you saying, Noble?"

He looked into the eyes of his sister. "You will not remember my being here, for I am long dead in your mind. The children *are* orphans, but you will love them as your own and remind them how very much their parents loved them. Do you understand?"

"Yes."

Noble leaned over the cradle and kissed the forehead of the infant before putting his mask back on. "Goodbye, sweet child."

In a blur, he made it to the steps and out of the house's back entrance. He stood against a wall, breathing hard. His eyes were closed, deep in prayer, with the hope the child upstairs was his Elizabeth returned.

Dmitri appeared next to him, pulling off his mask. "Are we not a pathetic lot? Here we are, two demons, praying God hears us."

TO WISH
OF DEATH

November 4th 1719

The party and those since have not drawn my companion from his Bible. Dmitri now refuses to feed, and I can see the hollowness of his faded, gold eyes as though he is indeed dying. His prayers are desperate and tear-filled. His body has become gaunt as he slowly starves himself. His dark hair seems to be graying before my eyes. I watched him from a dark corner as he settled upon bleeding knees and begged God to forgive him for his thousands of murders of the innocent.

I patiently wait until I see it fit to interrupt and ask if he would like to accompany me out into the night to hunt.

He throws things at me and glares as lines of blood pour down his sunken face. "Go away, you foul beast. I must be here, waiting for God to answer me. Your presence only mocks him and drives him away from me."

Time seems to crawl as with the knowledge I have so much of it ahead of me. Looking in a mirror, I note no aging. I am as Dmitri was before seeing God, a perpetual youth, although I am older at twenty-eight.

I wonder how I might capture the heart of the child when she is grown as I lay on the roof outside her window, listening to the sounds of the people inside sleeping. I think of how I might fall in love again and how she might come to love me in return.

Everything about me has changed, except what is seen on the outside. I know this, for my heart no longer seeks God, and my soul is no longer my own.

How can love as pure as Elizabeth's be for a monster?

In the early evenings, just before allowing myself that bit of peace as close to her as I dare, I find myself in a pub on the high street. Mr. Golding, the barkeep, allows me, for a few coins, to take his ladies for the night. Something about his eyes and demeanor has me believing he knows I am not what I seem and that I will do no harm to them. Dmitri also knows I do not bed them as most men would. A simple nod and I am in a room feeding on whatever lady he sends to me. He never delivers the same one twice. I ask no questions, pay, and leave them sleeping peacefully with a little less blood in their veins.

I am embracing the monster if only to pass the time while I await Elizabeth's return and the end of this curse.

Still, I question the time it will take for Dmitri to awaken from this unfortunate dream, and will I be loved soon for the man I am no longer?

Noble stepped into the pub and nodded to Mr. Golding behind the bar before passing people headed up or down the stairs. Walking down the hall, he stopped at each door until he found one with no heartbeat hidden behind it.

He placed his hat on the dressing table, walked to the window, and waited.

It was not long before there was a knock at the door. A young woman, maybe fifteen, with blonde hair and shy eyes stepped in; she had difficulty looking at him. Her heart rate was elevated as he stepped toward her. He stopped as she stepped back.

"Mr. Golding said you were looking for a bit of company. Said to ask if I might be alright for the night?"

"A dove?"

Looking up at him uncomfortably, she shook her head. "Not a bird."

"Mr. Golding sent me a dove."

Realizing she did not understand, Noble explained, "I mean to say, someone who has never done this before... a true innocent."

Her heartbeat hastened. "No... I've done lots of things with men like yourself."

Noble raised a finger under her chin until her eyes met his. "Your heart gives away the lies of your tongue. But I understand." Putting his hand in his pocket, he pulled out a few coins.

"Tell Mr. Golding I'll not have a dove, but thank him most kindly for the thought."

The girl's bottom lip quivered, and her eyes welled up. "He'll be so angry with me, sir. I can do it, I swear. I have to do it; my mum's sick, and we need the money."

Noble placed the coins in her hand and closed her fingers over it. "You are a pretty girl; you should have a proper suitor to offer yourself to only upon the marriage bed, not strange men who will do horrible things and make empty promises for a look up your skirts and a chance at taking your innocence."

Her eyes filled with confusion, but she nodded. "Yes, sir."

"Now, leave me and this place. I've given you enough money to take care for a while. Do not set foot here again..."

His eyes glowed for a moment, and she nodded.

The girl shut the door behind her just as shouting outside the room started, and a familiar voice called out his name, "Lord Cross."

Stepping out of the room, he looked down at the bar. The young carriage driver from the manor stood there, sweating with blood on his shirt. "Lord Cross, you must come home. It's Lord Addleton."

Descending the stairs, Noble tossed coins toward Mr. Golding. "This is to pay for the girl you will sack." Running outside, he followed the driver.

The frightened driver opened the carriage door outside the public house and looked at Noble. "I was going to fetch a doctor, but Miss Rebecca told me not to and that I should find you."

"What has happened, Mr. Greer?"

"I think Lord Addleton is dying, milord."

"Drive us home, Markus."

Mr. Marcus Greer closed the carriage door and climbed into his seat. Seconds later, the carriage took off.

Noble entered the bedchamber of his friend and was shocked to see the state of him. Dmitri had withered. He lay in the fetal position, his bloodied knees covered in deep wounds, and his face and hands so bony and gray; he looked like a corpse six months in the grave.

Kneeling next to his companion, Noble tried to take a curled dry hand, but stopped short, finding it brittle as flesh fell away. Dmitri could barely meet his eyes.

"What have you done, dear friend?"

"I wait to die, but I can't," whispered the corpse-like man.

"Dmitri, you must feed."

"No, I shall not kill another man, woman, or child. God will damn me."

"We are all damned; praying is not repentance enough for creatures like us."

"Show me God again, Noble."

"I've not fed this evening. My blood would only make you worse."

"Please, I beg of you, friend."

"Let me call the chambermaid or the cook..."

Angered by his offer, Dmitri shouted loudly, even in his weakened state. "I want to die, Noble! Can you not get it through that thick skull of yours? All I ask of you is this simple vision to settle me."

"You are a vampire; you can't starve to death. That's the damning part of our existence. We cannot simply wish to die."

"I'll have death."

"Suicide leads to limbo, not heaven. I'll show you no God."

Noble stood up and walked toward the doors.

"Noble, do not leave me alone."

Turning, Noble looked upon Dmitri. "If it is a coffin you want, I will arrange it. Maybe after some time away in a box, you might come to your senses."

Slamming the large doors behind him, Noble walked away with a single crimson tear spilling down his face.

BURYING
A FRIEND

November 5th 1719

According to Dmitri, although we are damned to immortal life when driven to it, we can face a painful and lingering death if we wish it.

I have watched Dmitri fade into a mere shadow of himself, and it is most terrible to witness. His gold eyes have faded to the color with which he was born. They are a deep green with flecks of blue and brown. The once pale-cream complexion is now gray. The skin is so thin you can see what is left of the muscle fibers and small black veins beneath it. His bones are more prominent, so much so that his ribs are quite evident. As I hold him, I can feel his vertebrae and how light he has become.

I feel as though he could be taken away by the wind whipping around outside as late fall makes its presence known.

Sadness has overtaken me, and I wonder when it might end. Can Dmitri truly meet death? Will all his prayers and begging for forgiveness deliver him to God, or will hell swallow his soul?

I weep for his freedom. He has suffered long enough.

The simple pine coffin was delivered in the afternoon, and the carriage driver knocked on the door. Noble sat on the floor of Dmitri's room with his friend's head in his lap, watching the last of his strength leave him. The old vampire's skin had shriveled and grayed. His muscles had atrophied. He lay in the fetal position, arms across his chest, with his curled hands upon his shoulders. His fingernails had fallen out, as had his hair. His half-closed eyes had a waxy look about them. Noble had wrapped him up in the bed linens.

"Come in," Noble called out.

The man opened the door far enough to look inside. "It's arrived, sir."

Noble nodded. "Thank you."

The servant closed the doors, leaving Noble and Dmitri alone.

"I never wanted to share my shame with you. And had I known what you would see, I would not have."

Dmitri struggled to speak. "No man ... has ever been so lucky ... to have seen his creator. I know now ... it takes a demon to see it clearly. And for that, I am most glad ... and settled in my head," said Dmitri, his voice raspy.

"I do not want to do this, Dmitri. It is like burying you alive."

Dmitri coughed, and his laugh sputtered. "I should've been buried centuries ago."

"When you can speak no more, I will do this for you."

"Say a prayer for me, dear Noble. When it is done, do not look back. See the world and its wonders. Taste life and be not sad for me."

Noble nodded as Dmitri's head turned more prone, and he fell quiet.

Sitting in silence, Noble watched the light around the curtains fade into darkness.

His heart was heavy; he covered and lifted Dmitri's stiffened body from the floor. Carrying him through the house, he walked past several servants who bowed their heads and moved against the wall, out of his way. A few crossed themselves and whispered kind words.

Dmitri's coffin was carried behind the manor in the cover of darkness to an already dug grave.

In the light of torches lit by servants, Noble nodded as the carriage boy and the housemaster lowered the box into the hole. Noble stood dressed in his cassock. Backing away, he opened his Bible and began to pray.

"Dear God, find it in your heart to forgive this wretch, his sins in life and death. When he breathed, he loved your Son so much so that his life was taken from him. Afterward, he only acted upon the instincts of the creature forced upon him, and that is no sin. Hold his cleansed soul close, and let him see the gates of heaven and be accepted as the man who worshiped you without question or doubt for a lifetime and died in your name. Amen."

Noble tucked away his Bible. Sending away the servants, Noble started burying the box in the ground.

Settling into bed, Noble stared at the ceiling, wondering what fate lay ahead without Dmitri.

Several evenings later, after attending a ball, Noble walked the fields until he came upon the mound covering his friend. "You've no idea how badly I wished you home last evening. It is an odd and lonely existence amongst the largest of crowds. No one else hears the beating of hearts or fears ending them as I do. I can speak to no one of our adventures, for who would believe them?"

Listening intently for a response from beneath the earth, Noble heard nothing fall upon his ears other than the winds of early November and the fluttering of dried leaves in the forest.

He headed home before the rise of the sun.

The streets at night did little to settle him. Whores offered wrists and throats with little charming required, and he fell into a sort of ritual. Waking with the sunset, Noble walked the house until the darkness took the sky, hoping to find Dmitri returned. When he failed to find his friend, he had the carriage driver take him to the city, where Noble found comfort in the words not spoken to him but around him, as mortals' lives carried on. Just after midnight, with a full belly and a settled mind, Noble walked home in the relative silence of the night, wishing he was not alone. In his sadness, Noble all but forgot the small, growing child under the roof of Darby Manor and, for a time, Elizabeth.

ALONE

January 2nd 1720

I have always been one to doubt everything. When I was a physician, it was medicine; when I was a priest, it was my place in the church; and after having fallen in love with Elizabeth, it was whether I was a worthy husband and father.

The one thing I have never questioned nor doubted was my absolute adoration for my wife, and I beg God for her return every night. It seems I shall have to pray harder still.

The sad news was carried to the ears of my coachman as he drove the maids around London to shop. Christina Darby's young daughter was taken in the night by scarlet fever.

I later watched from the edge of the woods as two men buried the small box in which she lay, long after her parents had gone away, sobbing. One girl stood still at the foot of the grave, somehow familiar to me. Dark hair was pulled back, most of it under a hat. I could hear her crying as she said goodbye to the young cousin raised as her little sister. The girl's eyes kept to the ground until a young man with a lantern walked up behind her. I heard his voice. "Come on now, Mira. She's gone, and you have to let her go."

"What if I don't want to, Yancy? Aren't you at all tired of all the death we've seen?"

"I am," I said quietly to myself. "I am sorry for leaving you without a mother, father ... without your home."

As though they could hear me, the children turned and looked in the direction of my hiding place. Yancy was my spitting image, save the golden hair and the eyes of his mother. Mira's blue eyes, so like mine, welled up as she cried into her gloved hands. She is both of us, Elizabeth and me.

I stood silent and unmoving, afraid they might see and know me.

A bird flew above my head, and my children turned and left the cemetery.

Yancy and Mira are alive and well, and no longer are they babes.

I was filled with dread and sadness, knowing that I had abandoned them and left them alone in the world after murdering their mother in our marriage bed. I, too, began to sob. My life, though over in the eyes of my family, haunts me as they walk alive in the sun, with unknown fates and the world open before them. I am alone, dead, forgotten, left to a future of bloodletting and the screams of those I choose to feed on.

Noble settled into a bottle of wine in a dark, quiet corner of a pub. As he drank, he thought back to his life before it was all taken from him.

Jumping down from his horse, Noble handed his bag down to the stable boy. "Please take this to the house for me, and might you know where your mistress is?"

The young man nodded. "She's in the garden, milord," he said, pointing to the house.

"Thank you, Alex."

Walking down the garden path, he spotted her.

Elizabeth smiled up at him from the garden. She swatted at a gnat and wiped her cheek with a dirty hand. Rising to her feet, she ran to him, jumping into his open arms.

"Oh, dear husband, you're home."

"I could not bear being away another day," he said, kissing her.

"I've news, my dear sweet Lord Lincoln," she said, smiling into his eyes and then looking downward at her midsection.

Noble grinned. "Really, already?"

Biting her lip, she nodded. "Yes."

"Why, Lady Lincoln, you've grown plump already."

"I'm not plump yet," she scoffed.

He kissed her again, and she wrapped her arms around his neck. "I will be, but you can never tell me so."

"So, dear wife, what am I to say?"

"You can say, 'You are as radiant as the day I met you.'"

"But you were only thirteen, not at all near the woman you are now, milady."

Settling back on her feet, she looked thoughtfully at him. "Alright then, milord, you may say, 'You're as radiant as the day we married.'"

"Well, now, I don't remember this dirt on your face the day we married," he said, wiping it away with his thumb.

"No, but I was planting the flowers I had promised you before we wed."

Elizabeth laughed and took his hand as they walked toward their home.

"I'm truly happy, Elizabeth. Our family is starting; the house is finished; I want nothing else for this life."

"And I am hopeful that we will have a son, the first of many children that will fill our home."

Shaking off the memory that caused his chest to ache even more, Noble stared at the empty bottles that filled the table. Heartbeats filled his head like drums, continually pounding.

One of the whores of the house came up to him. Looking up at her, her hair long and golden, he hoped it was Elizabeth. The name even escaped his lips.

"No, but you can call me that if you like."

Waving her off, Noble said, "No, I am most sorry. I would like to remain alone for the evening, drowning my sorrow in this mug, miss."

After consuming several more mugs of wine and mead, Noble was talked into an upstairs room by a young prostitute, where he passed out on the bed, still clothed. He did not stop her hands from sorting through his pockets, robbing him of the remaining coins he carried as he passed out.

As a second woman started going over him to see if her friend had missed anything, she found the gold locket hanging from a cord around his neck.

"Oh, look, Bess, you missed this. I'm sure it's worth a crown or two," she said, tugging at it.

A final tug broke the cord, but as she looked closer at the locket, the passed-out man grabbed her arm with glowing red eyes and flared nostrils. "You shall not have my wife."

Bess screamed, dropping the locket, and tried to pull away from him. Her friend started beating on his chest. "Let 'er go!"

A large man flung open the door to the room, ready for a fight.

"You there, let the lady go."

Noble released her arm and picked the locket from the floor as he got to his feet, still drunk. "Ladies do not rob men of their memories or their coin. These women, if you would like to call them that, are whores."

"He don't got any coin, John," said Bess.

"Then out 'e goes," said the large barkeep, grabbing Noble by his collar.

The door opened in the otherwise empty bar, and the sun poured in. Noble cried out as the barman threw him into the street.

"What's wrong with 'im?" asked one of the women as smoke rose from Noble's burning face.

"Don't know, don't care," said John, slamming the doors shut.

Noble scrambled to his feet, groaning in pain. Ducking into a shaded doorway, he tried to gather his thoughts.

Looking around the street, he tried to get his bearings as his skin healed.

The sun had risen, full and bright in a clear blue sky.

Noble slid down until he was sitting on the stoop of the house, his only protection from the sun, as the street started filling with people heading to jobs or selling wares and services.

He sat unnoticed until the front door of the house behind him opened.

"What are you doing here?"

"I... I'm sorry," said Noble, getting to his feet. Looking into the man's eyes, Noble spoke. "I command you to allow me shelter in your home."

The man shook his head. "I'm sorry, *milord,* but you ain't staying in my house, and you're about the sorriest I ever have seen."

Blinking, Noble tried again. "You will do as I say."

"Piss off. Move on 'fore I call the constable on ya!" shouted the man, pulling on his cap.

Noble moved his hand into the light of day slowly, but otherwise stood just out of the sun.

"I said bugger off, man," the stranger said, shoving Noble off his stoop.

His skin burned and bubbled as Noble pulled his coat over his head and ran down the street, shoving past people until he found another place to hide from the light.

Ducked into yet another doorway, this one boarded up, Noble sat, pulling his coat over his head. Looking down at his hands, he groaned in pain. The skin looked melted. Though it fought to heal, his occasional feedings over the last few weeks slowed it.

Sitting back in the corner as deep as he could go, he watched the sunlight slowly push back the shade, ever so much closer to his shoes.

Pulling his charred hands to his chest, he watched the people passing by. No one looked in his direction as he pulled his knees up to his chest and wrapped his coat around him. Exhaustion and hunger had taken his power from him.

Now I shall meet my maker's dark son, he thought, as he closed his eyes and dreamed.

Noble stood in the grass, watching her hold her hat on her head as the sea air blew her skirts and hat brim. The sun shone, and she looked out at the ocean.

"Elizabeth, could you be fairer?" he asked as she turned.

"Noble, you've come home!" she cried out, running to him.

Her boots sank into the sand, but she seemed oblivious, smiling still. Noble moved toward her quickly, but she looked farther away.

"Elizabeth!"

He ran faster still as the sand rose to her knees, her smile wide and sparkling eyes holding no fear. "Come to me, my love."

The sand rose to her hips, and she released her hat. The wind gusted, blowing it into the sky where it floated like a bird riding the gusts, to and fro.

Just as the sand sucked her down farther until all that he could see of her was from the chest up, he finally felt himself begin to move toward her.

She raised her hands above her head, and his eyes met hers. The sounds of gulls and wind faded, and everything around them darkened until he could barely make out the shape of her.

He reached for her, and suddenly he was above her, hanging upside down. A candle was lit, and he saw the hand he now offered her was black. Claws had replaced his fingers.

She lay on a bed beneath him. Instead of the dress she was wearing at the beach, she now wore a nightgown.

Smiling, she remained oblivious to the danger reaching out to her; she raised a hand until they barely touched fingertips.

"My love, come to me," she whispered, her eyes filled with the adoration always shown to him. "I have missed you so, Noble."

He tried to speak, but the only sound that came from him was the screech of the creature as he dropped onto her, his hunger taking over. Attacking her throat, he felt nothing meet his lips as she sank into the mattress until she vanished, and all that was left were bedsheets soaked in blood. Screaming filled the room, and he looked up to see his children, young again. Tears poured down their faces. The sounds faded, and the children vanished in a swirl of fog. When it cleared, he stood once again as a man, the house in Virginia white and anew in front of him. The gardens bloomed, birds sang in trees, and his happy children ran across the yard, neither seeing him.

"*Are you ready to go home, No-bell Leencoln?*" asked a voice next to him. He turned, and there stood Tabansi with a wide smile.

"*Tabansi?*"

"*I release you, lost man of God.*"

Looking past Tabansi, Noble saw his wife Siti, who carried her infant son. Holding her other hand was Diallo, grinning and carrying his spear.

Meeting Tabansi's eyes, Noble said, "*You've found them... Without me, you have found your family.*"

"*I ask Ngewo, and he told me where to find them.*"

Noble looked back at the house, and the front door opened. Elizabeth smiled as she stepped out onto the porch, holding his infant son. "*Noble, children, it's time to come home,*" she called.

The children stopped playing and ran toward the house. A bright light from behind her flashed as each child ran past her through the door.

"*Noble, come home.*"

Running toward the door, Noble found his feet were sinking into the dirt with every step; he descended farther still until he reached the porch and plunged into the ground up to his chest. Reaching out his hand, he grabbed the wood slat of the first step.

The door behind Elizabeth started to close. "*Hurry, Noble.*"

The ground sank farther still beneath his feet as he struggled to climb out.

"*Death comes, and I fear it not,*" he whispered.

"Lord Cross?"

Noble looked up and met the eyes of the carriage driver from the house. "Mr. Greer?"

"Yes, sir. I've come to take you home. Ms. Harris said you might have lost your way since you hadn't made it home. She sent me to find you, and here you are. You look dreadful, milord."

The young man covered Noble with his cloak and helped him to his feet and quickly into the dark carriage.

Closing the door, Thomas jumped up into his seat, and the carriage started home.

Once home, Noble was rushed into his rooms. A woman, dressed neatly, with her hair in braids that circled her fair-haired head, worked quickly to rub salve on and wrap his heavily burned hands without speaking.

"Ms. Harris? Will you not tell me how you knew where Mr. Greer would find me?"

Her silence had Noble trying to look into her eyes, even reaching out a bandaged hand to her, imploring her to respond as she pulled the blankets up over him in his dark room. But her gentle eyes did not meet his as she worked.

"Have we met, Ms. Harris?" he asked the woman, whom he did not remember hiring.

She looked at him for a moment, and he saw halos of light in her light blue eyes as she put her finger to her lips, shushing him. He fell silent as he met a familiar gaze. Her name did not pass his lips, but he knew it: Ambriel.

The woman stood and turned, opened the bedchamber door, and looked upon him for a moment before leaving him alone in the dark.

Looking upward, Noble crossed himself. "You are a most confounding God, sending your angels to save a lowly monster from death. I beseech you. Why? Why is this terrible, wretched thing worth saving when more deserving creatures cry out to you, ever suffering yet ever faithful?"

No answer came as exhaustion took him into a dreamless slumber.

BLOOD BATHS AND BURNING HOUSES

January 21st 1722

My years of melancholy ended tonight. I do not know what brought Dmitri back last evening. I only know I awoke to him standing, wrapped in a dirty, rotting bed sheet over me as I lay in my bed. He smiled wickedly, and his gold eyes flashed as bright as I have ever seen them.

"God rained blood upon my hallowed ground, and I am reborn. I am forgiven in the eyes of God and raised once more!" he shouted before running out of my bedchamber.

Before I was even in my clothes, Dmitri had gone from the manor, hunting.

Noble lit a torch and headed out into the field where Dmitri's grave had been. The dirt had sunken in where Dmitri had escaped his coffin. The scent of copper hit Noble's nose. Kneeling, he searched for the source. Something sticking up out of the dirt at the center caught his attention. Reaching down, he shifted the soil about, unburying it. They were fingers. Grabbing on to the unburied hand, Noble pulled upward until he stood with a dead boy dangling from his grasp. Then he saw another hand and then another until he uncovered eight bodies. Lying the corpses on the ground, Noble looked them over. They were all children; Noble guessed not of the small village since this many missing would have been known to him. He found all their throats and wrists slashed.

A strange mark on one of the children's wrists caught Noble's attention. Wiping away the bloodied mud, he saw a cross he had not seen in years. The pope's cross was tattooed on the skin of the boy, who was maybe six. One by one, Noble pushed bodies back into the hole and buried them with his hands.

Crossing himself, Noble spoke over the mass grave. "May you see these innocent children reach the gates of heaven and take them into your arms with love and never-ending peace. Amen."

January 25th 1722

There is no doubt in my mind the children's blood, mixed with last night's rain, seeped through the ground, awakening Dmitri. Who would murder them, and why there? I cannot say that the thought has not crossed my mind; someone intentionally killed these innocent souls over the grave of my desiccated friend. What of their marks? Had they been orphaned and under the watch of a church when they were murdered? I know of no church that would sacrifice children in such a manner.

Whatever the reason for such a horrific deed, the proud monster has returned, and I am no longer alone.

I was awakened just before sunset by screams and pounding at my bedchamber doors.

I do not know whether to be overjoyed that the chambermaid came to me, fearful and sobbing after discovering the body of a young woman in Dmitri's room, or troubled by his reckless actions. I banished the memory from the maid and sent her home for the day.

Upon entering his room, I understood why she had been so frightened. A nude girl hung by her feet, upside-down from the chandelier, over a chamber pot that collected blood dripping from her ripped-open throat. Small splashes surrounded it like tiny red children dancing in a circle.

Dmitri lay in blood-soaked sheets. Wine glasses lay broken on the floor, surrounded by bloody footprints and scattered clothing.

I pulled the blanket from him and saw there were, in fact, two fatalities in his bedchamber. The other was a young maid with a large red wig falling off her head as she lay splayed out and naked between his legs. Her eyes glazed with death, and her blood filled the mattress.

He rose in a blur and rammed me against the wall, breaking the stone. "Why are you here, Noble? I'll have no more of religious rhetoric. I'm no longer praying! You should celebrate since you wanted this so badly."

I pushed against him until he backed away. "I've said nothing. I was going to offer a hand getting this mess cleaned up. I've already sent the chambermaid away before she reports us as murderers."

"Are we not killers, dear Noble? Are we not blasphemous in the eyes of God? Are we not monsters? We feed on the living like gluttonous fools at a feast! They bleed for one reason, my dear friend: to feed us, to sustain us until the next vein is ripped open."

I stood unable to reply while Dmitri stood in silence, naked, covered in blood, and seething at me through his fangs.

After the fall of darkness, we snuck the bodies from home and into the woods. After burying them without speaking or even looking in my direction, Dmitri threw the shovel at me and was gone.

I only hope tomorrow is not met with the same end. Dmitri's sudden shift troubles me greatly.

He is angry with me, and I have no idea why. When he does speak to me, it is with a wicked tongue.

Noble stood looking out of the clear panes of glass on the first floor as Dmitri wandered toward the house with two girls. Laughter and slurred speech told the tale of the evening as the doors opened, and in stumbled the vampire with guests. He smiled at his housemate. "Dear Noble, meet my friends, this one..." Dmitri said, pointing to an intoxicated brunette with mussed hair and smudged lip stain, who smiled and giggled as she downed more wine from a bottle.

Looking up at Noble, she grinned. "Oh, ain't he a pretty one. I'm Gretel, and you look like a nice time." She walked toward him, running a finger up the collar of his coat as she stumbled in a drunken circle around him.

"Meet Gretel, Noble, my good friend. The other beautiful girl is…" he said, looking the mousey-haired girl in the eyes.

"Izabelle," she said, smiling meekly.

Dmitri took the bottle of wine from Gretel and gave it to Izabelle. "Drink up, girl, and then we will play games. Do you like games?"

"I love games," said Gretel, walking back to Dmitri. She placed her hands on his shoulders as she stared at the still-silent Noble. "I like games of chance, do you? And what of your friend, the serious one?"

"He can be fun, but these days, he is a wretched creature to be around. You see, his love is years in the ground, and his only other hope was still a babe of three years, last I knew."

He had not told Dmitri of the child's death, and with his mood and company, Noble ignored them. Instead, he watched, silently measuring up the women for the unmarked forest graves he would have to dig later.

"Sounds ill, those thoughts in his head," said Gretel, slurring uncomfortably.

Dmitri tousled a curl of the woman's hair in his fingers as he looked at Noble, his gold eyes glowing. "Oh, do not believe he has ill intentions, for our friend here is a man of God. He will wait to pounce when she is seventeen again, in celebration of the year she first became his love. I only hope that she does not recall the rather messy end he set upon her the first time she was his."

Gretel walked up and placed her long-fingered hands on Noble's long coat. "Seems since she's still a babe, we might play games. Seventeen years is a long time to pine away at something you can't yet have, sir," said the mousy girl with a grin. "Play with us, sir," Gretel said, looking up into his eyes.

Noble removed her hands from his coat, annoyed. Looking up at Dmitri, he replied, "I'm afraid I will not be joining you in your games. I've somewhere I need to be. I assure you, my dear Dmitri can play enough for the two of us. I just ask that you don't make such a large mess this time, friend."

Nodding, Dmitri rolled his eyes. "Go, Noble, go and peep upon your infant child and fall asleep on her rooftop, wishing she could grow quicker."

Bowing, Noble ignored the spiteful tongue of Dmitri. "I bid you all good night."

Glaring at his housemate, Noble took his hat and coat from the butler on his way through the front doors, hoping he would not have to clean up another gluttonous mess.

Noble walked through the snow-covered field between his home and the village without noticing the black horse-drawn carriage headed to the manor behind him.

Sauntering down the streets of the village, he listened to the homes of families, supping and chatting in the early winter's eve. When he met the edge of the village, he ran behind the church and then into the cemetery, where he tucked his clothes into a raised marble coffin box. Nude, he ducked behind a mausoleum and transformed into the beast, then took to the sky.

Flying to London and into Bunhill Cemetery, Noble landed and quickly retrieved his stashed clothes and dressed.

London was busier in the evenings than the village he lived in. Children threw snowballs at each other by the street's lamplights. People hurried about, trying to either get home or to other places after a busy workday. Noble walked until he was in White Chapel, Dmitri's favorite hunting grounds.

Closing his eyes, he stood unmoving in the street, his ears listening. The chatter of the people on the roads and in buildings surrounded him like a coat. For a few moments, he picked out voices, finding interest in what they were saying.

"Rumor is prostitutes are going missing. Ruby vanished just the other night. Not a sign of her. Of course, she was in debt to quite a few people."

"She probably went home, hoping people forget."

"I don't know, she ain't never gone anywhere. Her mum is caring for them bastards she left with her."

Turning his head, he listened carefully.

"How long's Lizzie been gone now? This gent wants a room, and he can pay."

"Whores don't pay. Give it to 'em, Morris'll clear the rubbish she left behind."

Noble opened his eyes and sighed. Dmitri's house guests were being missed.

Continuing down the street, he wandered toward the Darby home. He did not sit on the roof but hid amongst the trees after jumping the wall surrounding the house. Most nights, Christina could be heard playing the piano in the lovely way Elizabeth always admired. He listened to his children talking, trying to catch up on their lives. Yancy and Mira talked to their grandfather and aunt, and Noble pretended they spoke to him, but he could not answer.

When the house finally fell silent for the night, Noble returned to the streets, seeking a meal. Entering a high street pub, he found a table in a dark corner and waited to be served by the mindful barkeep, who nodded to one of the girls leaning against the rail of the second floor.

The buxom brunette picked up a mug from the bar and carried it toward Noble. Setting it down on the table, she raised her skirt a little, showing him the top of her hosiery. "You lookin' for a little comp'nee, milord?"

"I am seeking the company of a lady. Would you be the lady I'm looking for?" he asked, pushing the mug aside.

She smiled toward the barkeep as she took the seat next to the gentleman. "So, what's your name, love?"

Slyly smiling, he looked into her eyes. "My name is of little consequence. I would like to smell the perfume at the nape of your neck."

"I'm not wearing no perfume," she said, giggling but stopped short as his eyes gleamed red for a moment. "You can smell me, though, iffen you want."

Leaning in toward him, he listened to her heart and spotted the raised vein almost hidden by her mussed hair. The smell of her was not wholly unpleasant: sweat, mead, and a hint of onions from a stew eaten earlier in the evening, most likely in this same pub.

"Closer," he whispered in her ear.

She leaned in closer. "Is that alright now, milord?"

His lips brushed her neck. "Yes."

Noble held back her hair as he repeatedly kissed her neck while the eyes of the barkeep pried from across the room. He listened to the hastening of her heartbeat as her body reacted to his attention.

Her breathing picked up. "What say we go up to my room, milord?"

"I would very much like to go with you."

Without pausing, she stood up and curtsied to the barkeep as she led her companion up the stairs.

She led him into a small room with a bed and a chest with a few lit candles sitting upon it. Without any other discussion, she started for the buttons of his shirt. "It's nice to have a clean lord to lie with. Been dirty blokes and shipmen most the day."

Noble nodded as he lay his hands upon her fingers, stopping her from undressing him. "Someone is coming."

A knock came at the door. "Paulina, he's got to pay now."

Noble opened the door and placed four coins in the barkeep's hand. "She'll be seeing no one else tonight, and I do hope you will keep that in mind before you knock again."

"You are paying this much for 'er, you can take 'er home and keep 'er," laughed the barkeep, walking away and shaking his coins.

Closing the door, he turned back to her, and she went back to his buttons.

He stopped her again, placing his hands on hers. "I do not wish to lie with you. I mean to talk and kiss you a little."

The woman looked a little put out as she backed away from him. Her hips met the edge of the bed, and she sat. She pulled at the shoulder of her dress, lowering it. "You sure you don't want a little…"

"No," he said, stopping her short. "There is only one woman I wish to lie with, but she is long dead."

Resting her hand on her shoulder, she sighed. "I'm sorry, milord."

Noble lowered his eyes to the floor for a moment before looking into hers. "You are not at fault."

"Well, you paid good money. What ya want to talk about, sir?"

In a blur, he was next to her, his eyes burning bright red. It startled her, and as she started to scream, his hand clapped over her mouth. Her heart raced.

"You will not scream. You will make no sounds that might bring someone in, and you will remember none of this. I promise you will have a peace-filled sleep."

The woman stared into his eyes, and her heart started to slow as she nodded.

He moved to her throat, his fingers running down from behind her ear, following the carotid as it pulsed.

"I only feed because I must, kind woman. I mean you no harm, and I shall be as gentle as a babe upon the breast."

In one fluid movement, he was upon her, his fangs piercing her skin and the wall of the artery beneath it. Noble fed on her, his ears listening for the telltale sounds from her heart telling him he could take no more. After wiping his mouth, he laid her back on the pillow. Her eyes shut as she passed out from blood loss.

Just before exiting the room, he tucked several coins into her hand and kissed her forehead. "Thank you, dear lady."

Walking down the stairs, he nodded at the barkeep, who nodded in return as usual and then spoke. "I know you come from that direction and all. I hope you ain't staying in the Rutherford Manor; the coppers say it's gone up in flames it has."

Damn, thought Noble.

"I thank you for your services once again, Mr. Golding."

Noble dashed into the street and started past the few street people still out at the late hour.

Running north, Noble headed home. Once beyond the small village, he saw the rising flames of the manor as it burned. In a blur, he stood in front of the doors as they blew open from the built-up heat within the stone building. Noble flew backward but landed on his feet.

"Dmitri!" Shading his eyes from the flames, he ran around small fires where the furniture had been only hours before.

"Dmitri!" he shouted as he ran. "Dmitri!"

Climbing the stairs, he heard the burning beams start complaining about the weight of the roof as it began to sag. Noble knew everything above him was about to collapse, but he fought his way to the bedchamber of his housemate. The doors were open. "Dmitri, where are you?" The fire was so intense he felt as though his skin was burning. "Dmitri!"

Through the flames and the stench of burning wood, hot stones, and something else familiar, Noble made out the shape of a human body lying on the burning bed. Dashing over, Noble looked down at the blackened body and suddenly understood the destruction surrounding him. Firmly planted in the chest of the burning corpse was a stake in the shape of a cross, just like the one Lucia had used to stab him. The Archers were responsible for the burning of his home and the death of his friend.

Not yet ready to mourn, Noble ran for his room. The doors burned his hands as he pushed them open and flames rolled out around him. Forcing his way through, he started for his desk, where he kept his only picture of Elizabeth. It was already consumed and collapsed. Running over to it, he picked through the flames, searching for her locket until he found it. Tucking it to his chest, he saw the fire starting to consume his clothes. He cried out in pain and began running through the high flames. He jumped, shattering the glass window, and landed in the courtyard of the manor. Colored shards of glass rained around him.

Crawling away slowly, his body stiffened by flames, he saw the walls start to fall apart. Noble cried out as small stones dug into his chest and blackened clothes pulled away scorched skin, leaving a trail of bloodied, burned fabric behind. His body was already regenerating the lost flesh. He rolled over on his back and extinguished the fire that was still burning. He then inched to the grass, where he was far enough away to avoid being crushed by the falling walls.

He lay listening to the sounds of the fire burning away the manor; no one tried to put out the flames as they would have in the village, for no one was supposed to be living there. The Archers who had set it aflame were gone, likely drinking to their triumphant destruction of an almost-millennium-old vampire. Noble wondered if Lucia had been amongst them, and he grew angry.

Noble looked at the sky, which was starting to show the colors of sunrise, and got to his feet. His clothes, now almost ash, fell away from his new skin. After retrieving a horse blanket from the barn, he made his way toward Bunhill Cemetery, his home away from home.

Sitting on the stone sarcophagus of Mr. Smithe, Noble sat back with his journals, kept hidden away in the old tomb out of the sight of the help.

He suddenly felt as Tabansi must have: alone and questioning. He would find them, the ones who had left him alone and hiding once more in Bunhill.

HUNTING

The new moon left the streets black, silent, and empty. Noble walked them, listening to the world sleeping around him. All safe and sound behind closed doors, tucked into beds, with only embers glowing in the fireplaces.

Loss and hunger caused both his heart and stomach to ache. The hunger would have to wait. Noble followed the tracks of carriage wheels from the burned-out shell of his old home to the village. After searching the village, he moved on to London. One after another, Noble stopped outside of inns, listening for something that might point him to the Archers.

With no sign of them, Noble headed farther south, listening to the wind for any trace of them.

It was not until almost dawn that Noble came across a camp far south of London. A carriage and four horses were beneath a tree while a campfire kept a group of six warm as they talked. They each wore black cloaks, embroidered with the Pope's cross, wrapped about them.

"We have once again done God's work. Three devils are back in hell where they belong."

The men cheered and emptied their mugs.

Noble kneeled silently on a hill and looked skyward. "I must admit wrath is very much on my mind, though I have never felt any ill will to man in all the days of my life. But as this creature, it is almost impossible to act as I once did, with goodwill and calm regard."

Deep in prayer, Noble did not notice someone behind him until something sharp pierced through his chest from his back. He cried out in pain as he fell back onto the frozen grass, and the stake exited just right of his heart, burst through his chest wall, breaking a rib. Looking down on him was the girl who had stabbed him before. He groaned, trying to grab the stake to remove it.

"You can't pull it out that way; it is a Papal stake," she said with a sly smile.

Kneeling next to him, she got a closer look at his face.

"Not you again. What are you doing here? Thinking of killing my father for killing your demon whores?"

Rolling to his side, he tried to pull the stake out of his back. "They were not my whores, but the man you murdered was my friend, and I feel the need to avenge him," Noble said between gritted teeth.

She cautiously walked around him while he fought to remove the stake from his back without luck. In one fluid movement, she pulled another stake from her belt and struck, pinning his hand to the ground. She laughed as he cried out in pain.

"If I stake you to the ground, the sun will finish you, foul beast."

"No, it won't," he said, grabbing for the stake in his other hand.

She was on him at once, grabbing his free hand and pinned it over his head to the ground with a third stake.

Flinching, Noble fought the urge to kill her for both the pain she was causing him and Dmitri.

Lucia stood over him, her eyes narrowed. "Why do you not fight back, demon?"

"I will not harm a woman sent by Papal order to destroy me. It would be a sin against God and all I stand for."

"Who are you?"

"I am as you see me, a beast, but one who loves God and simply seeks freedom from a curse I did not ask for. Why do you torture me?"

"You beasts have trickster's tongues, but I will not fall for your deceptions."

"I have no tricks for you, Lucia."

"It is commanded that I must kill you. Your soul is black, as is your heart. But how do I end you?" she asked, kneeling as she pulled the edge of a silver blade down his cheek, leaving a streak of his blood behind. Even as the metal broke the skin, the wound healed.

"You cannot."

"The last time I saw you, I saw strange markings on your skin. I want to see what is written upon your hide." Lucia placed the blade beneath the top button of his shirt and yanked it, sending the button flying. She did this all the way to his trousers. Pulling back the shirt, she ran her warm fingers over his skin. "Who did this to you?"

"The angel Ambriel."

"Lucia," called out a man's voice from the camp. "Lucia, where are you?"

"Angels do not write on the hides of demons," she said, holding the lantern closer to his chest. "I cannot read most of it, except for these symbols. I know them..."

Her face turned ashen, and she blinked rapidly. "*O Maria, gratia plena, ignosces,*" she said, crossing herself as she backed away from him, eyes wide.

"Why do you beg forgiveness?" Noble asked, trying to meet her gaze.

Shaking her head, she stood up and ripped the stake from his back. He groaned and almost screamed.

"Shh, they will hear you."

He gritted his teeth as she took the stakes from his hands. Looking into his eyes, she whispered, "Run."

"Why should I run? What does it say?"

"Lucia!" shouted several voices, getting closer.

"It says I cannot kill you, and you should run because my father will be coming for you, and he will try."

"Lucia, answer me!"

"*Ego sum omnibus iure,*" she called out to her father.

Her heart rate picked up as she repeated forcefully, "Run."

"Thank you, Lucia," said Noble, disappearing in a blur into the woods.

Lucia's father ran to her. "What are you doing?" he asked, looking down at the blood on the browned grass.

"Nothing. I told you, I'm fine. Do not worry, Father. There was an injured deer, and it ran into the woods."

"And you didn't catch it?" he asked in a suspicious tone.

"No," she said, looking toward the woods.

As Lucia and her fellow hunters returned to the fire, something in a blur ran into the camp. All of them jumped at the ready as one of the Papal brother's heads, loose from its body, flew into the high flames of the campfire. Arrows flew.

When another head flew past the flames, Lucia's father turned to her. "*Currere,* Lucia!"

Loading her crossbow, she raised it. "*Currere modo!*" her father shouted. Then his head flew toward her, torn from him.

"No!" screamed Lucia, looking down at her father's severed head as it rolled to rest at her feet.

Hearing the scream, Noble stopped and turned in the direction of the camp he'd run from only moments before. Another cry sounded as he ran toward the camp.

Turning to the woods, Lucia ran as her father had commanded while the blur killed the remaining Papal brothers and started for her. Firing her weapon toward it, she turned and continued into the dark woods. She dropped the crossbow, unable to reload.

Running as fast as she could, she wove back and forth through the trees, trying to put distance between her and her pursuer. She knew the monster was playing with her.

Then Lucia tripped. As she looked behind her, the blur became solid and landed on her back. Turning her over, she saw the gold eyes she had seen a night earlier.

"Ah, Lucia, how sad it is that you should meet your end where you have found your greatest pleasure: beneath me."

"*Transite ad inferos*, Dmitri," she said, spitting in his face.

He laughed, wiping his face on his sleeve. "What do you say to one last moment of passion before I tear your throat out?" he asked with an evil grin. "Don't worry... I didn't tell Anigo you and I were *intimo* as I removed his head. Such a fool to believe you are pure."

Angered, Lucia spit in his face again. "You charmed me with that tongue of yours! *Transite ad inferos*!"

"I will only go to hell if you promise to join me, Lucia."

Dmitri tore into her throat, feeding his ravenous appetite.

Struggling to get to her belt as she felt death coming upon her, Lucia pulled her gun and fired it into Dmitri's side, causing him to cry out, releasing her throat. He backed away as the silver burned in his gut. Holding pressure on her neck wound, she raised her pistol again. Dmitri was seething, ready to pounce again.

Pulling back on the hammer, Lucia pulled the trigger as Noble landed on his feet between her and Dmitri and caught the silver ball with the Papal cross engraved upon its surface. Dropping the projectile to the ground, he looked at Lucia and shook his head. "No more."

Dmitri started toward her, but Noble jumped in front of him. "Stop, Dmitri. Let her go."

The old vampire's gold eyes glared at his friend. "I will kill her, Noble."

Noble met Dmitri's eyes as his hand lay upon his chest. "Not tonight, friend. I owe her a day of freedom for releasing me."

"You owe her nothing."

Shaking his head, Noble motioned through the trees to the eastern sky. "The sun peeks over the horizon, and we must find a place to wait out the day. Do not die for one woman."

Looking to the east, Dmitri saw the glint of early morning light. Turning to the girl who held her hands to her throat, he scoffed and growled through his fangs. "Fine. When I happen upon you again, I will see you dead, Lucia Archer," he threatened. Then, in a blur, Dmitri fled north.

In an instant, Noble was next to the woman on the ground. Biting into his wrist, he drew blood and placed the open wound to her mouth. "Drink, or you will die."

Tears fell as she felt life slipping away. "I would rather die than have the blood of a demon flowing through me."

"I would rather you live."

Her eyes showed her obstinacy as she pushed his arm away. "I will not."

Noble's red glowing eyes met hers. "You will drink of me and heal, for I command it."

Her dark eyes lost their stubbornness, and she accepted his blood to her lips. Noble watched the terrible wound heal as she drank.

When it closed completely, he pulled his arm away. "I must go. You should bury your dead and get as far away from here as possible. Dmitri means to kill you. You can mourn your father when you are safely within the city of Rome."

Lucia nodded. "I will... Thank you."

Able to stand again, Lucia watched the monster who saved her life look to the east. "God protects you, and I understand why."

Turning to her, he said, "I try not to interpret God's plans for me. This curse laid upon me and why it is so remains a mystery, and I don't believe I am meant to solve it."

"I hope you find your woman, noble beast," she said, walking away toward her dead family.

The orange light illuminated the horizon, and Noble moved to the north with haste, meeting Dmitri within the tomb of the Smithes just as the sun shone whole in the sky.

Noble groaned as his wounds healed, and he looked upon his friend through the darkness.

Pushing his fingers into the hole in his gut, Dmitri moaned in pain. He dug around to retrieve the ball of burning silver. Finally finding it, he pushed until he was able to grip it solidly and pull it out. Dropping it to the floor, Dmitri leaned back against the stone wall, staring at the projectile as it rolled across the floor and slipped behind the sarcophagus, out of sight. "I hate silver."

Noble sighed in agreement. "I am most glad you are alive. I thought you dead at the manor."

Dmitri groaned as he dug another projectile out of a hole in his belly and let it fall to the floor. "The Archers attacked soon after you left. They killed the chambermaid and my whores and set the whole place ablaze when they were unable to catch me."

Noble nodded. "And still, we live to fight them another day."

Dmitri shook his head. "So, we do … without servants and a home to speak of," he said, annoyed by their plight. "I quite liked my bed. I will kill Lucia for destroying it."

"I am almost certain you will, friend."

Dmitri nodded. "She will return to the Brotherhood of Archers, and they will send more after us for killing the others."

"Yes, I know."

"It looks as though we have no choice but to cross the sea once again, friend."

Even though Noble dreaded coming across the beast left behind in the colonies years before, he knew Dmitri was right. The Archers would return, and they meant to end them both.

CROSSING A DARK SEA

May 14th 1722

After months of gathering clothes and collecting money from various victims, we again said goodbye to London. We climbed aboard the Ventis Validus just before dawn and settled into a dark cabin.

The smell of the salty air during the day sends my past after me while I slumber. When I close my eyes, Tabansi hunts me inside the ship's hull. He is silent as he chases me, save the sounds of his claws cutting through the planks. I run from him, unable to turn into his equal.

I am human again. Children, my children, scream from somewhere far away. As I run, looking forward, I see the ghost of my wife. While I run from the hell behind me, I find myself desperately giving chase to her. She leads me again and again into danger, in circles until Tabansi's claws stab into me, and I awake, crying out.

As the ship glides, pushed by fair winds, I can only pray he does not find me once we reach the American colonies. Although I am a man of God, I hope somehow he has been dispatched. He is the only thing I fear as we head toward the colonies. One saving grace is the ship on which we've taken passage is en route to Nouvelle-Orléans.

Dmitri thought it a better place to set sail after overhearing sailors talking about the women who walk the streets at night and the many people of society made rich in the new world.

I have decided to stick with rats for the duration of the trip since two of us feeding on the crew and passengers might draw unwanted attention.

Dmitri, of course, will complain about the smell and my lack of energy, but only until sunset when he seeks out food and leaves me alone.

Dmitri brought a woman into his bed late in the evening as Noble lay quietly listening to the sea, trying to drown out the heart sounds all around him.

The drunken girl giggled as she fell over her own feet. She was a homely thing, but Dmitri would take anything with breasts and, so far from civilization, anything with a pulse.

Noble covered his ears as the woman moaned and her heart raced.

"Noble," whispered Dmitri from across the way.

"What?"

"Have a bit. She's a large girl, lots of blood to spare."

"I will stick with my rats, dear friend."

There was a pause. "I beg of you, Noble, please. The smell of dead rats has become too much for my senses."

Noble turned to look at the nude girl lying partway on the floor. Her pulse called to him as she reached out her hand. "Help me, sir. I feel so ill and weak. I did not earlier..."

Stepping onto the floor, Noble kneeled before her outreaching hand. Taking her wrist in his hands, he bit into it in a flash, his hunger overtaking his senses.

Dmitri listened carefully to her heart, and just as it started to taper off, he pushed Noble away. Biting into his wrist, he shoved it into the girl's open mouth, allowing the dark sanguine fluid to flow down her throat, healing her wounds and giving her strength.

Sitting back and wiping his mouth, Noble closed his eyes, feeling much better.

Dmitri rushed the girl back to her room and returned with two bottles and two mugs. "Drink, my friend," he said, passing a cup to Noble.

Noble downed the mead and closed his eyes again. "She was drunk... completely off. I feel it in my veins."

"You can't dine on rats for months and not expect to feel something when you return to a proper diet," Dmitri grinned. "After all those months I spent beneath the earth, I drank from a man so far gone on opium that I saw fairies. It was the most beautiful drink I've ever downed. The fairies were so small and beautiful. They would make your Elizabeth the foulest looking of creatures. They kept flying off and back, fluttering in front of my eyes, dumping wine down my shirt from tiny goblets of gold each time."

"I'm drunk already, and you bring me more alcohol, friend?"

"If it settles your mind and I don't have to hear you scream in your sleep, I will do it every night."

Looking down in his mug, Noble said, "I am so very sorry."

"What is it you dream of?"

"Tabansi, the creature that made me. I was turned on a ship headed to the colonies. He hunts me when I close my eyes, and there is nowhere to run."

"A monster, dreaming of a monster. The great irony."

Noble sighed. "Yes, I only hope we don't find that monster when we reach *Nouvelle-Orléans*."

"I pray you are not stolen away by your maker. You've become a loyal companion, Noble, my friend."

"And you, Dmitri, have been quite a preceptor in the ways of this existence."

Dmitri looked into his friend's eyes. "Drink, my friend, and find peaceful sleep."

Noble drank his mead and closed his eyes.

July 1st 1722

Between the inebriated passengers and the mead, I have remained in a drunken stupor most of the way to Louisiana. The nightmares have stopped, leaving behind nothing but the darkness behind my eyelids.

Dmitri brings passengers into his bed with the flicker of his eyes and tongue, and I gladly take from them.

I have made few trips to the deck, except to throw dead rats over the side. This captain, Captain Vicinni, has no cabin boy.

He keeps a girl, young and pretty, at his side. Vicinni calls her Mella, though I doubt that is her name given at birth. Her skin is a glowing brown, and her eyes are light green. She is mute, save the grunts and moans she releases when Dmitri takes her to his bed. It takes no charming to bring her below. I've watched her run her fingers through his hair as she arches her back while he feeds betwixt her thighs.

Mella's heart races whenever we go to the deck and she lays eyes upon him. More than once, she has been caught by the captain staring at Dmitri. The captain glares at Dmitri with disdain, while my friend's smirks in return only drive the hatred building up within him. Vicinni grabs her up by her arm and, believing no one else can hear, whispers, "You're mine. I bought you. Don't think to be anyone else's. I feed you, and one day, I'll fuck you. I won't have you sullied by some Bulgarian bastard."

More than once after hearing this have I smiled as I looked out over the dark sea. Little does Vicinni know his property has been sullied many times, and there is still a month more at sea for Dmitri to sully her even more.

She sneaks below just after dark when the captain has settled back in his bunk. Dmitri says she puts some powder in his rum, and he sleeps the whole of the night.

Dmitri returns her to her small bunk in the captain's quarters each night after healing her wounds from his feeding.

I do not take from her because she is frightened of me. This beast has so many more teeth than her lover.

If this woman fears me so, what will my Elizabeth make of me when I must show her what I am?

Six days out from Louisiana, Noble woke to the sound of a pistol being cocked. "Wake up, you bastards!"

A pistol was pressed to Dmitri's forehead while two crewmen held the girl by her arms and hair. She grunted and struggled against them.

Another of the captain's lackeys held a gun to Noble's face.

Dmitri met Noble's eyes and nodded.

Noble shook his head slowly.

"You don't move, or I'll put a hole through that pretty face," the captain said through a rotting grin.

Noble held up his hands as he sat up in his bunk.

"Captain Vicinni, good morning," said Dmitri with a sly smile.

"Stop with the pleasantries, you evil shit. You've sullied my wife."

"Your wife? You bought her, and she is a mere child who will do nothing more than hate you."

The captain grinned as he grabbed the jaw of a frightened young woman, forcing her mouth open. "She stopped spouting her hate years ago... You see, I cut out her tongue."

Unphased, Dmitri responded, "Still, Captain, you bought her like a man buys a sheep. I have not sullied your wife; I've sullied a sheep. And she does bleat as such when I mount her."

The captain flipped his French cavalry gun, catching it by the barrel, and bashed Dmitri in the face with the butt of the weapon while the woman struggled with her captors and glared at her lover.

Dmitri's long hair fell in his face, and his glasses flew from his eyes. Wiping the blood from his lips, he looked up at the captain, grinning while his gold eyes glowed menacingly.

Vicinni stepped back, shaken. "*Mostro?*"

"You've not seen a monster like me, Captain."

Anger replaced fear as Vicinni pushed his pistol under the chin of the golden-eyed beast. "Get these things off my ship."

Without warning, but in his usual yet fluid grace, Dmitri moved so quickly only Noble could follow his careful steps, each one done with purpose. The old monster pulled back the head of the captain. As if in slow motion, the weapon fell from the fingers of the sea-worn man to the floorboards as the vampire ripped into his throat, draining him of blood and leaving him close to the final dark precipice.

The other frightened men, with no time to respond to the attack, screamed as Dmitri ripped into them. After Dmitri threw the sailor who held a gun to Noble's head to the floor, he started for the men holding the girl.

Noble's hunger took over as his jaws elongated, and he tore into the man's throat as he lay on the floor.

Screams filled the room as the lackeys holding the girl tried to run. Neither got anywhere as Dmitri's eyes glowed, and he commanded, "Stop."

Both men stopped, staring at Dmitri as he walked up to the trembling girl who stood between them. "You caused me to hurt them when I did not need to."

Noble pushed away from the man, who fell on top of the captain. Blood ran down Noble's chin as his jaw returned to its human size. Wiping his mouth, he watched Dmitri.

"Save the captain and clear his memory of this, and then tend to his friend, Noble."

Kneeling, Noble lifted the head of the captain; his dying eyes blinked as his breathing slowed. Biting into his wrist, Noble fed the man with his blood until his wounds healed. Red eyes met the frightened eyes of Vicinni. "You will remember nothing of this day. You will return to your cabin and sleep."

Dmitri stepped over the captain and straddled him. "You do not have a wife. You did, but she drowned after falling overboard. You are mourning her passing. So sad you will be in the days ahead, dear Captain. I am very sorry for your loss."

Noble looked up at the girl, who cried, her feet unable to carry her.

Dmitri helped the man Noble had fed from off the floor. "This one dies, and those two."

"Three missing shipmen and a girl?"

"I'm famished. I've been kind, having almost starved myself in the process. I will not put us in danger by weakening myself to save a few sailors." Nodding at the girl, Dmitri continued, "And she, she is a slave to Vicinni. She will know nothing else. I consider it a blessing that she be taken from this terrible life."

She sobbed quietly.

"Can you not spare her?"

"I've told her master she is dead. I will not reconsider. I will, however, let the rest live if it plagues your mind so, dear friend. You can pray for her soul."

Moving in a blur between Dmitri and the girl, Noble looked into the golden eyes of the old vampire. "Her life is terrible, yes, but is only made worse by awaiting a death she does not deserve."

"We beasts are gods amongst men, Noble. One way or another, God will see her dead."

Dmitri moved around Noble, who closed his eyes, unwilling to watch Dmitri end her.

Swallowing hard, Noble found himself begging. "Please, Dmitri, reconsider."

"Try and stop me, Noble, and I will kill you, friend or not."

Noble knew stopping Dmitri was not possible and the girl would die. Leaving the room, Noble made his way to the cargo hold. Falling to his knees between the crates and barrels, he started praying for the girl, whose neck was broken with a swift swipe of Dmitri's hand. Noble sat, unable to block the sound of her body falling to the floor, her eyes ever open but unseeing.

The two men wrapped the dead girl in a sheet and carried her out of the hold. The captain nodded to them as he left the cabin, leaving the two monsters he meant to end only moments earlier.

Noble kneeled and grasped the cross he wore, tied in a small pouch around his neck.

"Though she fell under the spell of a beast, please God, grant her entry into heaven. I believe she did the best with what you gave her. Please forgive her and the beast that saw her dead. Help me to fear not Dmitri, for this child was lost to my cowardice," he whispered.

The sound of a body hitting the side of the ship startled Noble out of his prayers.

Noble sat in the darkness below decks as the sun set.

Dmitri stepped into the cargo hold and looked down at his friend, who sat with drying streams of blood running from his eyes.

"You are the saddest of monsters, my friend. I have never seen a beast who so hates his own kind."

Looking up at his friend, Noble shook his head. "Someone has to beg forgiveness for all of our trespasses, and one of us has to have a conscience... I find both are the consequences of befriending a demon who lacks both the ability and the heart."

Kneeling in front of Noble, Dmitri met his friend's eyes. "You keep that conscience, Noble, and you will forever beg forgiveness. I shall seek none." Dmitri kneeled and clasped his long-fingered hands together. "I do pray for something, dear friend."

"And what may that be?"

"I pray that time will take your conscience, that you will no longer feel the need for repentance for what you are, and that you will cry no more for what we do. Only then will you find this world an easier place to exist," Dmitri said with a thin smile.

"I am not you, Dmitri. I can't simply abandon my heart and my faith. I will never accept this curse as the gift you believe it to be."

The old vampire laughed aloud as he disappeared from the cargo hold.

August 19th 1722

The moon sits high and full in the sky as Dmitri takes another woman below decks. More have died in this sail upon the sea than the first voyage from the colonies. I believe he does it to further my suffering and his amusement. The captain doesn't even write the dates of those lost in his log. The only acknowledgments of their deaths are the crossed-out names on the ship's passenger list and their internment in the sea. Captain Vicinni is quickly running out of passengers. I am most thankful this sail is almost at its end.

In all, Dmitri has killed five sailors and eighteen passengers.

The sea changes Dmitri, and getting caught by the captain has left him with a bloated ego. I have watched him attack passengers in front of the frightened man's eyes. Vicinni cowers or runs to his cabin. Dmitri has charmed his way through the whole of the people on this ship. He says the ones who make it will reach Louisiana and not remember a thing. Every morning, they seem oblivious to the dance of death ending in screams that carry on at night. I hear them chatting about how they have never had a better sail upon the sea as large waves slap the sides of the ship and the rains pour upon the deck in the blackest of skies.

I have returned to my rats since Dmitri has full run of the ship, and though he cares not who sees him feed, I am but the shy beast hiding in the shadows, praying those lost souls whose bodies are flung into the sea find peace.

Even this feels longer and more terrible than traveling the Atlantic with Tabansi in an ocean of rotting corpses.

Standing on the deck staring at the moon, Noble listened to the sounds of the sea, his eyes scanning the horizon for land that would spell freedom and possibly return Dmitri to his more bearable self.

"Ah, brother, you should not brood as you do. It will... Oh, never mind, I sometimes forget men of God *are* already miserable, suffering souls," Dmitri mused as he leaned on the rail, mesmerized for a moment by the moon's reflection in the water.

"My only misery is you, dear Dmitri."

"I am but a calm and happy monster, simply enjoying these people as they do the cherries that pass their lips. You could be doing the same. Instead, you are desiccating the vermin population and hiding below decks as if you are one and the same. You tell me which is more miserable?"

Noble did not look at Dmitri, although he could feel the glaring of his gold eyes. "I do what I must to remain alive, such as it is."

Dmitri laid a hand on Noble's arm, but the vampire's gaze remained on the sea. "Brother, do not hate me for being what I am, for you and I are the same."

"I do not kill innocent people for simple game and pleasure."

"And that is your failing; you're wasting what you've been given. These so-called people's lives end eventually, no matter the way of death. I bring it along a little sooner, just as they do sows. And like sows, they are food and amusement, Noble. The sooner you realize that, the happier and more content you will be."

Noble turned to the monster. "I do not have to be the monster, Dmitri. I can fight it."

"You did not fight it when you fed on the sailor in our room."

Returning his gaze to the ocean, Noble thought aloud, "This is what life will be, a war between my moral mind and the hunger of a demon."

Leaning in, Dmitri whispered into his friend's ear, "The demon always wins, Noble."

"I won't let it," Noble whispered, more to himself than his companion.

FOUR-LEGGED
BEASTS

September 19th 1722

The rain has been unrelenting since our arrival in Nouvelle-Orléans a week ago. It turns out, the rumors of this city's grandeur were vastly exaggerated. There are few buildings of noteworthiness, and the streets are barely passable. Flies and other insects dine on the excrement-filled mudways that are the thoroughfares of Nouvelle-Orléans. The mosquito population here is robust competition for two vampires, one being most gluttonous. The streets are filled with traders, thieves, whores, scaley beasts, and serpents unafraid to cross the paths of men.

By night, the ship landed. The remains of the crew and passengers departing the vessel seem unaware of the happenings upon the sea.

Dmitri has found a bevy of young women he happily brings to our rooms. He usually sends one to me in the night, and while I do not send them away, they leave my room alive.

Creole whores waste no time in showing their knowledge of pleasuring men. They are so numerous you would think there is not a virtuous woman in the whole of the city come nightfall. Laughing and drinking, they feed grapes to Dmitri as he tells

them tales of the women he has conquered; all the while, he mea-
sures them up for his next night of storytelling.

Dmitri beds them, feeds on them until they die, robs them of
their valuables, and vanishes them into the night.

No one seems to miss these women selling the wares betwixt
their legs.

My companion is as calm and calculating as ever.

Although tonight, I believe he may have met his match.

When she walked in, Dmitri stood at the bar of a Creole tavern, downing whiskey to curb his hunger. She was something Noble had never laid eyes on. Her delicate form and the fall of the dress upon her body had all eyes falling on her. Her complexion was dark, but not African. Long, straight ebony hair told of her native background. Her eyes were startling and spoke of something dark as she glanced toward Noble. For a moment, her eyes flashed an impossible silver color. Then she turned her gaze to the barkeep. The room fell into silence as she unpinned her hat and set it on the bar.

"*Barman, un drink, whiskey,*" she said in French, pulling off her gloves.

Instead of pouring her drink, the barman stood mesmerized, staring at her.

"*Whiskey, maintenant,*" she said in precise French, keeping a calm tongue, though she seemed in a hurry.

"The Creoles are a slow people," said Dmitri, stepping up next to her. The tavern's noise returned as he tossed a coin on the bar, and the barkeep seemed to awaken, pushing a filled glass in front of the woman.

"*Merci,*" she said, holding up the glass to the barman before downing all the amber liquid in one gulp.

She turned to Dmitri and slapped him in the face. "You should watch your tongue, *monsieur.*"

A thin, sly smile played upon his smug face as he ran his hand over his cheek. "I never thought I would see you again, Nalini. What a pleasure. In that dress, though? Have you embraced the ways of the white man finally?"

"I meld into the town so as not to stand out like you and your companion."

Dmitri grinned. "Tell me you are happy to see me, Nalini."

She glared at him. "I'll be happy to see you leave. I had hoped never to lay eyes on you again, Enravota."

Noble turned, hearing the ancient name no longer used by his friend.

"I always turn up again, no matter the hope. I pride myself on consistency."

"Who is your friend?" she asked, nodding toward Noble.

"Ah, this is Noble Lincoln, the saddest and most miserable creature of God; who hates what he is."

Her eyes studied Noble. "He's not like you."

"No, and I feel sorry for him."

Noble ignored Dmitri's chiding and stepped between his companion and Nalini, taking her hand. He gently kissed it and looked up into her unusual eyes. "It is a pleasure to meet you, miss."

"Your eyes, they're strange," she said, meeting his gaze. "What are you, besides English?"

Noble swallowed hard, ready to answer, but found himself interrupted.

"English, yes, and enchanted, I'm certain," said Dmitri. "Let's keep things civil here. I thought you were avoiding town." He leaned closer to her, speaking quietly. "All of the hatred of the natives must be affecting your hunt?"

"I find my hunt unaffected. Men see me as a charming lady; their interest is more with the heave of my breasts. Few care about the color of *my* skin. And besides, I don't hunt humans. A few dead deer in the woods are hardly gossip-worthy."

Dmitri's eyebrows rose, surprised by her answer. "So, you have this territory staked out. What of your brothers?"

She fell silent and nodded to the barkeep, who refilled her glass. Downing it, she picked up her hat and walked toward the door.

Dmitri tossed another coin on the counter to pay for her drink and followed Nalini out. Noble stayed behind, watching the room. He listened to Dmitri's voice outside.

"Nalini, what has happened?"

"You should not have come. It's not safe here. My brothers were fools, and it got them killed."

"Who killed them? The town's people?"

"No, it was Father. They let the beast overtake common sense. Killing foolishly, in the open. They betrayed us. Father believes you are why my brothers started ignoring the spirits and him, leaving them focused on killing the white man. They believed themselves more powerful than the spirits. Mikah murdered the sheriff in the street two weeks ago. People know we're here. Enravota, you and your friend need to leave this town. You'll be killed. If not by my father, it will be by the people who already know you're here."

"No one knows what we are."

"They've taken the curtains from the windows of all the inns, save your rooms," she said, nodding to the inn across the way.

Shrugging it off, Dmitri tried to calm her. "Like you, I have found the hunt unaffected. The whores have been plentiful."

Nalini turned to Dmitri, her expression one of confusion. "Are you certain you've been at the throats of whores?"

Dmitri's face mirrored her confusion. "I..." he said before falling silent.

The Indian looked past Dmitri to Noble, who met them as they stopped. "Has he?"

"I believed them to be whores. They were ready to bed him..."

"Where did you find them?"

"I charmed the innkeeper into sending them to me," said Dmitri, looking toward the inn.

"Louie Delane is the innkeeper of your rooms?"

"Names are so trivial... I never asked."

She stood quietly, as if deep in thought. "What did you tell Delane exactly?"

Thinking for a moment, Dmitri furrowed his brow. "'Send me a beautiful woman every night, ready and willing to please me, or I'll kill you.'"

"How many has he sent you?"

"Four or five, maybe six?"

Shaking her head, she walked quickly toward the inn where Dmitri and Noble were taking their lodging.

"What is it, Nalini?"

"He's been sending his daughters. He has six."

"If you have killed them, he'll send his wife, and you don't want her coming for you."

"I don't understand," he called out behind her.

An arrow sailed past his head, striking Noble in the shoulder. Groaning, Noble pulled the arrow out and gazed toward the inn. A woman in a cloak on the porch was reloading a crossbow.

Nalini was at her throat in a second. She paused for a moment, her fangs bared.

"Don't stop me, Nalini. They killed my children," sputtered the woman as her weapon fell to the porch.

"I know of their crimes, Agnes. I'm sorry, my friend. We are a dying race, and I can lose no more brothers, guilty or not."

Nalini bit into the woman's throat, and Agnes screamed.

Suddenly, Dmitri was behind Nalini, pulling her away from the woman. A whore screamed from the porch of a tavern.

Dmitri's gold eyes met those of his would-be assassin as he pressed his bitten wrist into her mouth. "You know nothing of daughters or monsters. You are a simple, innkeeper's wife. Do you understand?"

The woman nodded and walked back into her home.

Noble followed suit, charming the witnesses of the attack.

"Let us take our leave of this town," said Dmitri, annoyed.

The trio moved to the outskirts of *Nouvelle-Orléans*.

Dmitri glared at the native woman as she wiped the blood from her mouth. "You have much to explain, dear Nalini."

Taking a deep breath, still angry, Nalini responded, "To them, we are no longer things of nightmares. We can die as easily as deer. You should return to your home across the sea."

"Why would your brothers attack mortals?"

Her silver eyes glared back at her old friend. "Archers came. The game has changed. Hunting us is no longer enough. They must spread the word in the churches here as they have in Rome. They are training those who have come to the colonies. They are taught to look for the signs."

Noble looked startled. "Archers are here?"

Nalini nodded. "Yes, even now. They teach the women and children how to defend themselves from the demons of the night. They are the ones you need fear, Enravota."

"Tell me where they are," said Dmitri with a sly smile. "I'll rid us of them. I did not cross the ocean to be driven out of the colonies by the bastards of Rome."

Nalini's eyes met Dmitri's. "Your world is closing in on you, Enravota. But I'll see no more dead."

"They must have reason to let you live, Nalini."

"The bishop wishes to talk sense into Father. He will allow us to live in the wilds while these pale-skins take over our land, as long as we do not attack the colonists."

"The Archers would have nothing over the Rougarou. Your tribe could wipe them out without blinking," said Dmitri, nodding. "You are not limited by the sun as we are."

Noble asked, "Rougarou?"

"What are you?" she asked once more, meeting Noble's eyes.

"I might have the same query for you, miss."

Instead of answering, Nalini moved within an inch of Noble's nose, stared into his eyes, and sniffed at him for a moment.

Startled, Noble took a step back away from her.

"You *are not* what Enravota is." She paused, stepping away from him but looking him up and down. "Made or trueborn?" she asked, pressing him for answers.

"Made ... I guess."

"From what?"

Grabbing onto her arm, Dmitri turned her toward him. "There is no time for queries. Where are they?"

"I can't tell you, Enravota."

"Why?"

"I can't tell you that either."

Dmitri grabbed her by the throat, his eyes searching hers for answers. "You will tell me, Nalini."

Noble's brows furrowed. "What is a Rougarou?"

Ignoring Noble, Nalini glared back at Dmitri. "I couldn't even if I knew."

Dmitri was not relenting. "I don't want to play games. They mean to chase us all to the ends of the earth, don't they?"

"The church does not allow monsters outside of their walls they cannot control. Men are supposed to fear their God and God alone. Those simple fools," she said with flashing eyes.

Grabbing tighter still to her throat, he lifted her so her feet came off the ground. She grabbed onto his hand with her fingers, struggling to loose her throat from his grasp. "You mean to help them in hopes they'll leave you and your people be?"

"I just saved you and your friend, and you dare question me?" She coughed. "This is a war your kind brought on; we had nothing to do with it. So many of you are running from across the sea, thinking this is your haven. You're wrong."

"While you parade about the town like a queen? I assure you, dear Nalini, they will thrust oak stakes through your hearts and cut off your heads just as they will ours. If there is anything I know of Rome, there is no trusting them. The Pope spews hope to the people in God's name while he drives daggers into the backs of those he promises exculpation. You are as much a part of this war as we are."

Seizing his hand, she pierced his wrist with long claws. "Release me, you bastard," she growled at him as her eyes turned to the shiniest of silvers.

As if reading each other's minds, both let down their fangs, ready to end one another.

Laying his hand on Dmitri's shoulder, Noble looked at his companion. "She has saved us. It is only right to free her. Do we *all* not deserve a chance to flee?"

The corners of Nalini's mouth turned up into a sly smile. "You should listen to your friend, Enravota."

Dmitri gave a smug smile for a moment, then drew back his arm and threw her into a large tree. Slamming into it hard enough to knock the wind out of her and damage the bark, Nalini fell to her knees.

Once she found her breath again, she growled at Dmitri, her silver eyes glowing in the moonlight. As Noble watched, the Indian woman's skin sloughed away, leaving a thick coat of black hair. Her teeth bared as her face elongated, and a deep growl rose from the creature's throat as the last of the elegant woman fell away, leaving an animal Noble had never seen before. It stood larger than both he and Dmitri, with two bent, solid legs, the head of a wolf, and the body of a woman now covered in fur.

She dropped on all fours in a blur and turned, vanishing into the forest.

Dmitri cursed and glared at her. Turning to Noble, he grinned for a moment. "That, my friend, was a Rougarou."

Dashing off after her, Dmitri left Noble alone in the woods.

GOD'S MIGHTY STORM

Noble looked toward the sky as fingers of Spanish moss waved down from an old willow. A cold rain began to fall.

Footsteps came up somewhere behind him, joined by more. Turning, Noble saw bobbing lanterns and torches in the distance, moving toward him. Voices sounded.

"They came this way!" shouted a man.

"Be ready to take the monster down!" called out another.

Running in the direction Dmitri and Nalini had gone, Noble fled.

September 20th 1722

> The rain does not seem to end, and there is something odd about the air I cannot put my finger on.
>
> It may merely be the smells of the ripening cemetery I hide in by day as I await Dmitri's return from his chase.
>
> The blustery winds and the rain seeping into the crevices of my place of daytime slumber are daunting and threaten the lit candle that I write by.
>
> The smell of the man whose stone sarcophagus I've taken residence in has caused me to hastily and most unforgivingly place his remains within the grave of one Mr. Anthony Riviere. I am

annotating this so that I may set him back within his proper and final resting place once I no longer need it to ward off the sun.

I've avoided town at night save once, to return to the rooms we left to retrieve my things. The guards outside were easily swayed, allowing me to enter and then take my leave. My gut is screaming for food while I hide. I thought to quell the angry rumblings within my stomach by taking down a deer or some other creature, only to find the woods at night filled with men looking for us. A few wear the robes of Rome and carry crossbows. I know what they seek. As Dmitri predicted, it seems we are being pursued to the ends of the earth.

For days, I have heard nothing from my companion, and all I can think is Dmitri has met his end already, either by the hands of Rome or the wolf-like creature he gave chase.

Maybe Lucia will have her revenge after all if she has not already.

The winds churned, and rain poured down so thick it was as if the sky was falling. Ocean waves beat against the buildings of *Nouvelle-Orléans*, sending people dashing about like ants looking for a haven. Buildings washed away from their foundations and began to collapse. The winds and rain drowned out screams.

Noble tried coughing without relief. His chest felt heavy and full as he opened his eyes, seeing and suddenly feeling the water he was submerged in. Taking a deep, water-filled breath, he pushed hard against the lid of his coffin. It did not budge.

Overwhelmed by the sense of drowning, Noble struggled. His panicked heartbeat filled his ears as his head became light. His arms lost their strength, and his body fell limp as darkness overtook him.

He felt shaken hard, and his eyes fluttered between open and closed. He coughed hard, expelling the weight from his chest. Looking up, Noble's eyes met the familiar gold of Dmitri's. His eyes fell closed again.

In the starless night, Dmitri smiled for a moment and flung Noble high above the trees and into the air. Suddenly awakened, Noble's body found gravity, and he plummeted toward a tree. Fear gave him wings and black skin as he landed gently on a large branch. Dmitri jumped up to him as Noble, the man, settled with soaked, shredded clothing.

Looking out across the expanse, Noble sat in awe. The ocean had consumed the land. The lights of *Nouvelle-Orléans* had been snuffed out and the buildings drowned.

"How does the sea swallow so much of the land like this? Do you believe it is the end of days?"

Dmitri smiled up at him. "Not the end of ours."

"How did you find me, Dmitri?"

"Over the howls of churning winds, I heard the tinkling bell in your chest that has haunted my ears for all these years suddenly stop. Only it restarted again. I followed it until it stopped here. Alas, here was my friend, hiding away and drowning over and over again in a flooded grave, about to float away into forgotten oblivion upon the hungry sea."

"Thank you, Dmitri."

Handing up the bag Noble kept with him, Dmitri smiled. "Oh, and I found these. I figured, since you were willing to run into flames matching that of hell after these, you would most likely dive to the greatest depths for them—your books."

"You have my gratitude," said Noble.

Hugging his bag to his chest, he looked into the eyes of his friend. "The woman you gave chase. Did you catch her?"

"No, I'm afraid four legs are faster than my two, even on my best day."

Noble nodded to the east as the sun lit up their side of the world. "What do we do now, Dmitri?"

His gold eyes looked north for a moment, and then Dmitri turned to Noble. "We go to higher ground and find somewhere to spend the day out of the sun. Those remaining people down there will be punished for following the Archers tonight. I shall return the favor of hunting them." He paused, his eyes meeting Noble's. "Your conscience can spend the day deciding whether to join me."

WHITE SPIRIT
WALKER

September 22nd 1722

I followed Dmitri into what was left of the city. We found the Archers had either fled or perished in the storm. The remaining few citizens sat around fires and makeshift shelters built on the edge of the swamps. We were not the only predators. The gators were also on the hunt for easy prey as the waters receded, and waterlogged corpses spit out by the gulf started surfacing.

The mosquitos are thicker still, only adding to the suffering of the survivors.

As Dmitri was to pounce upon two gentlemen and a lady, mud-covered and whining about the lack of food, I was taken from behind.

Arrows rained down upon me in my hiding spot. I was struck by several, and as silver entered my veins, I felt weak. I did not even have time to send a warning to Dmitri as I struggled against the strong arms entangled about me. Arrows sailed by my head, and the creature that carried me wailed out as it was struck.

What was left of my strength was no match for whatever held me captive in its jaws, running through the woods.

After what seemed like a quarter-hour, we slowed until I was put on my feet. I turned to my kidnapper and met the eyes of Nalini. She turned from the huge wolf-like creature back into a human.

"Why have you taken me from my hunt? Dmitri will come for me. Why would you endanger yourself?" Noble asked bluntly.

The nude woman leaned against a tall, thin tree and started tugging at an arrow sticking out of her thigh. "The Archers were coming up on you, and I could not watch you die. You're not like Dmitri. There is something innocent about you. You smell different: sweet, not rotting like your old friend."

"I do appreciate you saving me, but my place is with him." Noble stepped toward her, seeing her difficulty with removing the arrow. "Let me help you."

"No, I've got it. You have your arrows to deal with."

Looking down at his chest, Noble stared at several arrowheads protruding from him, burning him with their silver tips and poisoning his blood. One at a time, and quite painfully, Noble pulled each of the arrows through, squelching his cries behind a clenched jaw.

The native woman sat looking down at the arrow through her thigh; it had gone through the bone and was not coming out easily. She looked over at Noble as he pulled the last arrow from his shoulder.

"You are so blinded by that gold-eyed beast."

"Sometimes, blindness is needed for self-preservation, and other times, it is simply called loyalty."

"You do not know what he is."

He watched as her blood-covered hands tried to grasp the arrowhead, only to have her fingers get burned by its silver tip.

"While it may call weakness to my character, I do know what he is. He is a most terrible creature, not so unlike myself." Touching her shoulder, Noble's eyes met hers. "I can get it out for you."

She nodded at him and leaned against the trunk of the tree, clenching her jaw.

Kneeling, he looked at the entry and exit wounds. "I hope you heal as quickly as I."

The girl nodded. "Do it."

Noble cringed for a moment as her blood poured over his fingers. Grasping the arrowhead, he tugged the arrow out fast.

Nalini screamed through gritted teeth. "Thank you," she said, trying to compose herself. "The bone is healing. When I can stand, we will go. I am sure we have drawn attention to our hiding spot."

Nodding, Noble dropped the arrow as shouting and lamps started moving somewhere in the woods behind them. "We need to move quickly."

Standing carefully, she looked to the west for what seemed like several minutes. "I cannot change form. They put silver dust on their arrows to make us easier prey, and it is still in the wound. We will have to run on foot and go to my village and warn them."

Running west, Noble followed, surprised by her speed and grace through the trees and swamp. Branches stabbed holes through his coat. With her pace, the voices and lights were gone in seconds.

Stopping suddenly, the woman kneeled and sniffed the air before taking off again. "We are being followed, but not by men."

"What is it?"

Nalini sped up instead of answering him.

The forest fell silent, and the wind stilled. Noble looked around. He could feel something watching, something quiet and foreboding.

"Something is here," whispered Noble.

In the distance, the sounds of gunfire erupted. The wind moved again high in the trees.

Nalini and Noble moved through the trees until they reached a clearing. Three huts stood there, made of mud and sticks. A small fire burned in front of one. Other than low dancing flames, the village was quiet.

Movement from the corner of Noble's eye turned his attention to the trees. A giant beast, much like the wolf-beast Nalini became, moved toward him, its steps making not a sound while its lips curled back, teeth bared.

It was suddenly joined by another and then another until they were surrounded. Nalini met each set of eyes, her hands raised before her. "He is not the enemy."

Noble stood outside of the hut, waiting. Surrounding him were several men, their faces painted red. The few still calling themselves Quinipissa were wary of white men or anyone not of their family, and their glaring black eyes glinting silver at Noble made that evident.

A woman of small stature carrying an infant walked out of a small hut, their eyes showing the same silver color, before moving to a log sitting by the fire.

He could hear the slow breath sounds of those around him and the voices of Nalini and the chief inside.

"There are so few of us left, and what is left has been scattered to the winds, and you bring a white demon here? Why should I not gut him and feed him to our people?"

"He is not like Enravota. He is something else. Something gentle and kind lies within him. There is a light surrounding him. You must see it. You must speak to him. He saved me from the white Roman's silver arrows."

"Nalini, you cannot tell me he means no harm when he keeps company with that demon, the creature that turned your brothers against his people so that I had to take their lives... With these hands, he forced me to kill my children. He stole away your sister and murdered her."

"Noble is not like him, Father. I feel there is a good spirit within him, one that will help us."

"I will hear nothing more about this, Nalini. Take him back to his people. Because you have brought him here, we must move again."

"Please, Father," Nalini begged.

There was a low growl from inside the hut, and Nalini came out.

Behind her, a tall, dark-skinned man ducked out of the hut and looked down at Noble.

"You align yourself with my enemy; your skin is the color of my people's greatest adversary. Tell me why I should not kill you, White Devil?"

Noble let out a slow breath before speaking. "I have never raised a sword to your people, nor have I ever thought to. We are the same: beasts hiding within men, trying not to allow these creatures to define our existence upon the earth or in the eyes of our gods."

"You speak wise words, but I have heard wise words before from Enravota before he stole away my daughter and killed her. Your words are meant to trick me. I know the power of your kind's tongue. I will not kill you this time, but I will not listen to the trickery of white demon tongues. I do what I have to protect my people."

"I understand." Noble stood his ground as the chief breathed heavily down on him. "I do not alter the will of men unless it is to survive. Trust that I mean no ill will, nor would I take any of your people. I was brought here," Noble looked at Nalini and then met her father's eyes again, "well... I don't know why I was brought here."

"I will kill you if you and I cross paths again, and if I ever see Enravota again, I swear I will destroy him." The old man glared at him, silver shining from his eyes as he bent forward and his skin sloughed off, leaving an enormous beast that ran into the trees.

Nalini started running after him. "Father."

The creature did not look back and vanished out of sight. Nalini stopped, standing stoic as the rest of her people turned toward her.

A howl from far away sounded, and the others changed into beasts and headed into the woods, each vanishing as if turning into trees, leaving Noble alone with the woman.

A howl sounded in the distance.

"Father is calling me."

"Then go. Thank you for saving my life, Nalini. Go with your people and protect them as you have me."

The Indian woman looked in the direction of the howls before looking back at Noble. "I understand why you keep the company you do. It is a lonely existence. But know Enravota leaves nothing but destruction in his wake. There is a dark shadow spirit within him. He will leave you in ruins and feel nothing for doing so."

"He is my friend, Nalini."

She continued as if Noble's words meant nothing. "Dmitri is no friend ... to anyone. If you ever thought of killing him, all the gods would forgive you, for he is truly evil. No manner of his death brought about by your hands would change the light within you."

"I cannot take another creature's life and consider myself a man of God. Your gods may be more forgiving of murder, but mine would surely punish me."

She stepped close to Noble, her silver eyes begging for understanding. "Evil is meant to be defeated by good, and within you is the brightest of lights. You can survive it, for you are immortal."

Before he could respond, her hand brushed his cheek for a moment. Then she whispered, "Be safe and ever blessed, White Spirit Walker."

Within a moment, the woman changed form and disappeared into the trees, leaving Noble alone in the abandoned village. Moving to the fire, he sat back on a log. His veins burned, and his mind was left to wonder what Dmitri had done.

NORTH

September 24th 1722

Dmitri found me hiding in an empty coffin inside a cemetery mausoleum that had not been destroyed by the floods. His eyes met mine as he pushed the lid from my resting place.

"Ah, there you are. I was rather put out by my having to slaughter those poor starving wretches alone. Oh, how they reeked of shit and the sea."

"Hello, Dmitri," I said, pulling myself out of the box.

"I smelled the bitch who took you. I rather thought she would try to eat you, but here you are."

I picked up my bag of journals and clutched them to my chest, not wanting to explain it was he they wanted dead and me to be the one to do it.

"I can only ponder a guess that I may have smelled too much like shit and the sea after floating about in the saltwater with corpses."

"Aye." Dmitri laughed for a moment before looking at the stars. "We must leave. There is not enough food to sustain us

160

here any longer, and I do not want to exsanguinate wild vermin or what's left of the livestock while waiting for more to arrive."

"Where are we to go?"

"North. I've heard following the coast will find us more than our fill of blood and money."

I nodded. "I only ask that we avoid Williamsburg."

"Of course, I would not want to meet your master if he is anything as monstrous as you... And lacking that conscience of yours or your control, well, that would be a frightening beast, indeed."

I, too, hoped never to lay eyes upon Tabansi again. There must be so much anger within him since I abandoned him. I do not feel safe traveling so near to him, but if I am ever to find Elizabeth again, I must move with Dmitri.

ABANDONED
AND BROKEN

January 9th 1723

Coming back to the colonies has changed me. I do not know whether it is the impending danger being so near to Tabansi or the nightmares reminding me I am a monster.

I also cannot deny being shaken by the words of the native chief and his daughter. There is so much I don't know about Dmitri.

We have made our way to Maryland, traveling only after darkness. Our trek has taken us from town to town as Dmitri tries to find a place to make a home for a while.

Many inns have welcomed us, though Dmitri spends his nights away from our rooms as he hunts different towns, seeking women of the night. I sit across drunken-men-filled rooms as he waggles his tongue in the ears of young women who believe him to be a great and rich man. And later still, I find myself sitting alone outside of our rooms while Dmitri takes these women, sometimes several at a time, into his bed. Rarely does he invite me to share his victims, as he has heard me tell him "no" all too often.

These women hold no interest for me, no matter how many times Dmitri tells me to see them as cherries on a tree, waiting to be plucked, that need to be plucked so that I might live. But alas, I feel no hunger, only numbness.

I have searched every face in the different pubs, shops, and other businesses, looking for the one face I only seem to see in slumber. Her face, the only face that makes my heartache and sadness overtake me.

While Dmitri was out hunting, I found myself, without even thinking, on the land that was once mine. The house I had proudly shown to my bride was now abandoned and broken. The grand entry doors were smashed.

I walked inside quietly as things skittered along the floors above me; animals were the only living things residing there.

Stepping into the sitting room, I stood for a moment, staring at the painting on the wall above the dark, dingy fireplace. Untouched by the dust and spider webs around the rest of the house, there she was, still and ever so beautiful. She sat in her quiet grace. I imagined her eyes meeting mine and not that of the artist whose careful eye and brush had captured what he could of her beauty.

Flourishes of an artist's implement are all I have of her, I thought, running my fingers over the melted locket I keep in my waistcoat pocket, though the painting inside it was lost to the fire in London.

Elizabeth had been abandoned on the wall; perhaps the looters of our home felt she alone had to remain since everything else was taken or destroyed. She was the only reminder that this once palatial home was filled with life and something beautiful, that was so loved as to be captured in a painting, forever frozen in time. So, I stole it away. Yanking the portrait down, I set it on the floor and kneeled before it in the dust. Running my fingers down her painted cheek, I closed my eyes as crimson tears trickled down my own.

Noble paused in his writing as he stared at the painting. A thin smile played upon his lips as he remembered that day.

Holbeck's dark eyes darted between Elizabeth and the canvas as she sat blushing at me and laughing at my anecdotes when she was supposed to be completely still. The otherwise messy room had large doors looking out upon a waterway of Venice. It was a bright day, much too beautiful to be trapped inside, but Elizabeth's father *had paid greatly for the work. It was a gift for our wedding. And she'd asked me to come to help pass the time.*

I sat across the room, every so often peeking over the top of a book I wasn't reading. Smiling at my love for a moment, I raised the book once more.

She craned her neck, trying to look at me behind my medical procedural book.

"Lady Darby, you must remain still if I am to capture your likeness pleasingly," said Holbeck yet again.

"I'm so sorry, Sir Holbeck. I will try harder."

There was a moment of silence as Holbeck returned to his canvas.

Lowering the book, I made faces at her. She laughed and then tried to cover her mouth to hide it.

"Lady Darby, I beg you, please," said Holbeck, getting more and more annoyed.

"So sorry, sir."

Smiling, I sat back, taking her in as she sat straight-faced, her eyes only stopping to peek at me for a moment. She is to be mine forever, *I thought.*

"I believe you are blushing, Lady Darby," I said, taunting her.

"It is only because you are looking at me like that."

"And how is that?"

She smiled and turned to me. "You know the look I speak of, dear Noble. The one that says you can hardly wait to marry me."

"Really? And how does one illicit such an expression, may I ask?"

Working hard to contort her face, she only made herself laugh, and I joined her. That was the final straw.

Holbeck stood and turned to me, his face red with frustration. "You there, you must leave, sir! I cannot paint her with such an expression as this! If I paint her that red, she will look like a harlot, and I will look like a fool!"

I stared at him until one of his eyebrows rose so high upon his forehead that I thought it might take over where his hairline had failed. "Pardon, sir?" I asked.

He threw up his arms and walked toward me, holding out his paintbrush. "I cannot work under these conditions! If you want her painted, then you do it or leave so that I can finish."

I understood suddenly. "I am so sorry, Sir Holbeck. I shall take my leave."

Noble sighed as he continued to write about his day.

Leaving the painting in the sitting room, I wandered the rest of the house until I reached our bedchamber. The elements, thieves, and small furry occupants had each left their mark, and it no longer resembled our home. The bedframe sat alone, a dried-out wooden skeleton. Dirty remnants of the curtains and bedding lay strewn about the floor, tattered. I fell to my knees next to the bed once shared with my Elizabeth. It was our marriage bed, the bed we had made love in. The wood she had grasped hard to when she had birthed our children was now splintered by the beast that had taken her life. The pain, knowing that creature was me, only sent my mind back to that night. I shook it off.

Returning to the sitting room, I carefully took the painting from its frame, rolled it up, and tucking my wife under my arm, I walked out of my home.

Sitting outside under the oak Yancy used to swing from, I built a fire. Looking up at the house, I no longer wanted to think about it, standing there abandoned and broken.

Lifting out a fiery stick, I walked the rooms, down the halls, and even into the attic where Jenny and Joseph had roomed, burning away the pain I'd left behind. Then I just stood there in the sitting room, watching the fire blacken the shattered frame from the portrait of Elizabeth.

Everything we had built together as a family was gone, while the shell of it all burned away. The children I orphaned were in England, my wife in the ground. Tears fell down my face as I sank to my knees, surrounded by flames.

For the first time, I feared not the fire, nor death, nor that which would certainly follow it if I could finally be extinguished. To cause and suffer no more pain, to feel no shame, no guilt for this thing inside of me, I silently begged for death as the ceiling came down around me. The burning home bellowed at me in wails, creaks, and snapping as it slowly burned into ash and splinters.

The smoke grew thick until it was the only thing I could see other than flames. It moved ever closer to me, and I welcomed it as I sat unmoving.

"What are you doing?!" a man's voice shouted, startling me. I sat up and wiped away my tears on my sleeves. I looked over as a man covering his face moved carefully toward me, stepping over the damaged, burning bits of my world.

He grabbed me, pulling me up.

"No, leave me," I begged. A beam fell toward us as the stranger shoved me out of the front doors and followed behind me, coughing and hacking out the smoke that filled his lungs.

Having fallen forward in my grief, I was turned over quickly. I met the eyes of Joseph, and he looked afraid. "Master Lincoln. What are you doing here?"

"Seeking finality … death. Why are you here, old friend?"

"Live in a shack a ways in the woods, me an' Jenny. I was out walking when I saw someone was around the old house. Seen you come in here." He shook his head at me, confused. "We thought you were dead already. Thought I saw a ghost. But here you are. Why you burning down the house?"

"It haunts me, and I desperately want it to stop."

"Ain't my business what you do wit' your house, but seem a shame. The missus really liked it."

"You cleaned the painting?"

Joseph shrugged. "Only thing I can do these days for Missus Elizabeth. Now you have gone and destroyed that, too."

"No, I saved her," I said, motioning toward the tree. "Thank you, Joseph, for taking care of her for me."

The black man nodded as his eyes returned to the burning building he once called home. He stared at it as if mesmerized, but he was remembering. I knew this as soon as he spoke.

"I knew you didn't come back right at all. I saw it, even felt it when I lifted you off that balcony. Smelt like a dead pig I fount on the edge of the woods once, all cold too. Then I saw them eyes a yours when you fading in and out, they all red like demon eyes. I warned the missus something wasn't right. She love you too much to see it. You come out that water from that ship, and you ain't you no more. Then I saw what you done to her, and then that thing that carried you off. I thought it was taking you off to hell." He paused, rocking on his heels before looking me in the eyes. "Why you back? Ain't nothing left except Jenny and me, and I warn ya, Master Lincoln, I'll fight ya off if you dare go after Miss Jenny like you did Missus Elizabeth, as God as my witness. I don't want to hurt nobody, but you ain't my master no mo', and I ain't going to lie down for you to kill me, whatever you are."

I sat up in the tall overgrown grass and watched the fire. "I would not blame you for doing so, Joseph. But I assure you, as I did not with her: I mean you no harm. I don't know what I am anymore. Am I a man, or am I a monster? Why am I haunted by this life long gone?"

"Men sometimes do things no one understands, not even God above. But you ain't a man no more. And I'm not the man to be talking about none of that. God might give you an answer, but I wouldn't expect him to forgive you, because I don't. Neither do them chillins you let see they momma that way. You might be better off talking to the one down below. Sound like what he do."

"I'm sorry, Joseph." It was all I could say. He wasn't my children or my wife, but he had been a part of what my family was.

He looked at me with real anger flashing in his eyes and then sadness. "You should leave before the constable come up here and start asking questions you can't answer, and before I stop actin' like a righteous Christian man and start actin' more like what you is."

When I finally arrived back in Maryland, Dmitri informed me we were to leave the next night.

"Why are we leaving so soon after our arrival?" I asked as I watched him pack his trunk.

"You are miserable here. Why do you smell like you've been set ablaze?"

"I burned down my home. I could not bear to see it standing, lifeless and empty."

"You cling to the life you no longer have. It was just a house, dear friend," he said, pushing my trunk at me. "Time to leave it all behind. I hear Boston is frightfully dreary this time of year."

NO MORE PATIENCE

May 1st 1731

We reached Boston at the end of winter almost eight years ago. It was so like the London I left behind, save the manner of the people who seem to be in various states of drunkenness. The public houses were nearly full at night. Dmitri took that as an omen that the city is where we should settle down. And settle we did.

The women here seem a little reluctant, making bedding them much more a game than with the women Dmitri has met thus far in our travels. Most easily fell into bed with the worst of men if there was a chance they might be swept away to a more luxurious or adventurous life. Dmitri offers no better future to them other than a night they will never forget.

These Boston women move away from him when he tries getting close. It's as if they know evil is near.

He has always been one to toy with his victims, but I find it harder to be around him when he hunts.

Last evening, I sat in silence over a mug of wine and ignored the slippery tongue of my golden-eyed friend as he ran his lips down the arm of a plain-looking, auburn-haired woman selling the wares he sought.

Searching the eyes of the people around me, I seek what I always have: Elizabeth alive and well, the chance to fall in love again, and the end of this curse.

Almost twenty years of loneliness have left me feeling hollow, and I am no longer weary of death. On more than one occasion during the last week, I have had Dmitri crashing through my bedchamber door to stop me from taking a life as I feed just as voraciously as he does until a heart is just about to stop. The pum——pum——pum———pum sings to me as if a sad melody is calling me to end it. Dmitri has pushed me away from the necks of whores at the last possible moment, just when my chest becomes fiery with warning and my heart throbs in pain from almost being crushed. His teeth sink into their throats, and he finishes them so that I cannot.

I have reached the threshold of his patience. As he dropped the body of a blonde woman on the wood plank floor of my room and dropped to his knees before me, he pulled my hair back until I was forced to look into his gold eyes. Out of breath and half-naked, his mouth bloodied by that of mine and his whores, he spoke. "What are you doing, my friend? What are you doing?"

I glowered at him, anger filling me. "I want to die, just as you did once."

"And you tried to stop me, for a good reason. Why am I suddenly the one who must be the sophist, Noble?"

"I don't want to think anymore; my conscience tears at my very core. I look at this life I must lead, and I grieve my existence upon the world, on that woman lying there. In my mind, I am not a monster! In my soul, I am still a man, the same man I was born. But I am a monster. I leave death in my wake, and I am cold to the warmth of the world. I am dead. My wife is dead, my heart that beat for her is dead, and yet I live," I sobbed.

"I am the murderer of men here. Stop being a fool. You will never find your Elizabeth in death, Noble. Stop this foolishness before you damn both of your souls to hell," he said to me, letting go of my hair and my gaze fell to my knees. Dmitri left the room shaking his head as he left me to my thoughts. I fell back against the wall.

I have no more patience for this life.
I have no more hope.

THE COMPANY YOU KEEP

December 4th 1732

Not long after our arrival, Dmitri had all of Boston's royalty believing he was someone of importance and, therefore, worthy of their celebrations.

Politics bores him, but the wives of aristocrats are not to be wasted on their fat, boisterous-mouthed husbands who would rather go on all night about how the colonies should be run and the goings-on of colonial leadership.

I find myself watching him mingle and wrap the attention of these women about him like a cocoon. They pay little attention to me and me them. Dmitri drinks from them in quiet corners, and of course, they love him for it because he makes them love him.

His bed is rarely empty, and they lavish him with gifts, those who have not made husbands of the colonial men. Dmitri even talked his way into a home for us, a large house that overlooks the sea. The woman who was so kind as to give up her home spends most of her time in a trance-like state as she willingly feeds him. Her eyes are empty, and she does not see me. I am always quick to move out of her way as she opens the drapes after darkness has fallen. She does not question when he leaves her alone in the house as he pursues other women and brings them into his bed.

Her name is Rebekah Vanderhorn, and she is a widow whose husband fell in battle. She is elegant and graceful in her ways. He met her at a party, and I watched the dance of the black widow in all its glory. Though she the widow, he is the spider.

He walked up to her after having overheard her name and the casual mention of other party guests in whispers about her great wealth and an empty bed. He held out his hand as his gold eyes found hers over top of the dark lenses of his spectacles. I listened intently to my friend as he spoke to her, taking her hand.

"I saw you from across the room, and I am ... captivated by your eyes and how they make me feel."

She shook her head and tried to pull her hand back, having been startled by the stranger's attention.

"I don't know you."

"Isn't that how all of the great love stories begin?"

"I don't know," she said, blushing, then sipped from her glass.

"I have never seen a greater beauty so full of sadness. What will make the lady smile again, dear Miss Vanderhorn?"

Finally meeting his gaze, her mouth fell open a little, and she was trapped as he spun her into his web.

What strange power is this?

Noble leaned against a column out of the way of the other partygoers, watching Dmitri carrying on with his ritual in the home of Nathan Covington, a rich man who was "feeding the whole of the colonies" with his fishing boats. The old vampire drew the Covington's charmed, wigged wife to a corner, which of course, with her laughter, attracted the attention of more women desperate to be amused.

An older gentleman stepped up next to Noble, puffing on a pipe. With a thick accent Noble could not place, he spoke. "Ah, to be young and able to woo... Or ancient and cursed with dashing looks and the tongue of a snake."

Turning to him for a moment, Noble looked at the pale old man with a strikingly long nose, deep-set black eyes, and an old powdered wig. His red cloak and red coat were embroidered with a Papal gold cross; time and arthritis battered his hands.

"Is this where the ancient Archers send their holy soldiers to retire?" asked Noble, unshaken.

"I still own a quill and a stake or two. I'm sure Pope Pius would love to know the colonies are rife with vampires."

"He would kill you before you've dipped your pen in an inkpot, sir."

"I suppose he could, but what of you? You stand here alone, watching your master. I suppose he throws you his scraps every so often."

"He is not my master."

"I suppose not. You are not of the same beast. No gold eyes. But you are a monster of some sort. No human keeps company with vampires."

"What is it you want, old man?"

"I seek peace in the home of Lord Covington and the head of your friend."

"I bid you luck in your endeavors, though I fear your confidence will be the end of you."

"I don't think so," the old man said, motioning to Dmitri. "He is the one hunting in a forest that is thick with wolves baring their sharp teeth."

"I will be sure to tell him of your concern."

The old man laughed until he coughed. Wiping his mouth, he responded, "It is not a concern I convey. I am simply enjoying the thrill of the hunt. He has been running from me for a time. I almost had him in Maryland."

"Ah."

"He and I have a long history, and I would like to see his finality written before this world is done with me."

Noble laughed. "Dmitri fears nothing."

A sharp burning pain hit Noble in his back, causing him to groan and fall, unable to move. The old man caught him before he fell forward. "He is mad. I'm sure you know that, just as I know you are a vampire of sorts. You see, my friend, that pain and your sudden inability to move comes from a silver stake, covered in the blood of a dead man, that I've shoved into your back," the old man whispered in his ear.

Sucking in his breath in pain, Noble struggled but spoke. "Dmitri will surely kill you now."

The old man laughed out loud as several people walked past. "My friend does not know how to hold his drink."

When they were alone again, the old man tugged at Noble until he stood somewhat upright. "I do not fear Enravota. Now, let's go elsewhere to chat," he said, pulling his cloak around Noble.

Another man, taller and much younger, joined the old man and helped carry Noble out of the house. They dragged him toward the woods.

Pleased with his catch, the old man said, "Enravota is here. This is his companion."

"I knew you would find him, Father."

"Let's find out what kind of creature is guarding him these days."

They moved quickly through the trees until they reached a road on the other side of the woods.

A covered wagon waited, its driver concealed in a dark cloak. The two men dragged Noble to the open end of the wagon.

The younger man pulled back the flaps, and a woman leaned out, holding up a lantern. "Oh, Father, you've found him?"

The young girl with dark hair hanging in her face raised Noble's head with a finger under his chin, and her expression was not happy. "This is not him."

"No, Carissa, but his companion will have to do for now. Enravota is at the party."

They pushed him into the wagon on his side. The girl lifted another shining silver stake and dipped it into a jar. In a fluid movement, she stabbed Noble in his chest, just missing his heart. Tugging out the stake in his back, she let him fall back.

"He doesn't have gold eyes. We don't know what he is?" asked the girl.

"No, though he does react like a vampire to silver and blood of the dead," said the old man, picking up a book as the girl leaned over Noble's face.

"What are you?" she asked, her warm breath hitting his cheek.

"What are you? You, your father, and brother are much too quick to be human," said Noble through clenched teeth.

He was ignored.

"Upir, maybe?" asked the young man.

"I don't think so. He has been hiding from the sun with Enravota and only comes out at night. And he's English, not Russian. True Upir are born."

The old man flipped through the pages of a tattered old book.

"When are we going to get Enravota?" the young man asked.

"Calm down, Darro. We will kill him soon."

"Let's kill this thing and grab the monster when he leaves the party," said Darro, his dark eyes staring at Noble.

"Release me," said Noble, staring back into the young man's eyes.

Darro jumped up, pointing down at Noble. "Do you see what he's doing? He's trying to charm me. Let's kill him, Father."

"Respect our ways. We do not rush to kill. We kill for God, but we do not kill monsters that are not evil. It comes back to us," said the older man, the children called 'Father.'

Darro nodded. "Like Mother said."

"Yes, like Mother said," added the girl.

The father continued through his book, stopping every so often to look closer at his captive.

"Darro, I want you and Carissa to go back to the house. Be sure you are not seen and follow him home carefully. I want to know where he hides from the day."

"Yes, Father," said Darro.

Carissa nodded. "Of course, Father."

Leaving the wagon, the two children did not make a sound as they returned to the house.

Noble looked up at the old man sitting over him, who started coughing into a tattered rag.

The old man coughed harder. Pulling it away from his mouth, he did not look at it. But Noble could smell the blood.

"You are not long for this world, Archer. You are dying of consumption. Your lungs are slowly filling with blood, and you will drown in it."

The old man laughed, and it caused him to cough even more. When he finally stopped, he shook his head at Noble. "I am no Archer. I hate them. I stole these clothes off one I killed." He coughed again, holding his rag over his mouth. "What do you know of death, short of being its cause?"

"I do not kill. As a man, I was both a clergyman and a physician. Trust that I can recognize a man who is looking on his final days. I can see the desperation to fulfill what you believe to be your destiny."

He ignored the monster on the wagon floor and picked up a stake, setting its point on Noble's chest. "What you see in my eyes is your death. Now, what are you, monster? I demand to know what I am about to kill."

"I am a man who means no harm and a creature who cannot kill."

"I don't believe you. I have killed so many of Enravota's past companions. You cannot lie to me, monster."

The canvas door of the wagon flew up, and a smiling Dmitri stood at the end of the wagon, his eyes gleaming. "He cannot lie to you, Vincent. He doesn't kill. But as you know, I do."

Vincent stood and backed up against the crates at the other end of the wagon. He pulled a large crucifix from his belt. "Enravota, where are my children?"

Dmitri wiped the blood from his lips and looked down at Noble. He smiled. "Why do I spend so much of my time saving you?" he asked, pulling the stake from Noble's chest.

"Why must I be the target of those you have made enemies of, dear friend?"

"I have not a clue." Holding the bloody silver stake close to his nose, Dmitri shook his head with disdain. "Blood of a dead man? You know, Vincent, this means we cannot simply take our leave. My friend will need blood to heal. So, I guess we wait for your spawn to return," he said, throwing the stake into the trees.

A WARRIOR'S PROTECTION

The old man shook. "Not my children. You promised, Enravota."

"And you swore never to seek me out again, yet here you are, holding my companion prisoner," said Dmitri, annoyed.

The old man white-knuckled the crucifix and pulled another stake from his coat. "I want to leave this world knowing you are no longer a part of it."

"And I want you to die in horrible pain, having suffered this sad and pathetic life. Whom do you believe will get their wish first?"

The old man stood silent.

Noble tried to pull himself up as blood poured from the wound in his chest, and he fell back again. "Damn."

Vincent coughed hard and stepped forward, holding up his cross. He pushed Noble toward the golden-eyed vampire. "Take him and go. Just leave my children alone."

Dmitri stepped back out of the wagon. Noble pushed through the pain and moved over to sit precariously on the edge of the wagon.

Two blurs appeared on the edge of the woods, darting to the wagon. Darro and Carissa were both holding stakes.

"Father, are you alright?" Darro called.

The old man stood in the wagon. "I'm no worse than usual."

Darro yelled as he moved toward the old vampire with a raised stake in one hand and a knife in the other.

"No, Darro!" shouted the old man. He coughed hard, and blood spilled from his mouth.

"Father!" cried Carissa, running to him.

In a flash, Dmitri struck Darro hard in the face, knocking him onto his back on the ground. Blood spurted from his nose and he cried out.

"Boy, I will end you," Dmitri said, shaking his head.

"I will not let you kill my father," shouted Darro, getting to his feet more quickly than the vampire expected.

Dmitri kicked the young man's legs from under him, knocking him to the ground again.

The old man moved toward Dmitri, his weapon drawn.

Noble caught him by the arm and knocked the silver blade from his hand. "Dmitri will kill you if you don't stop this foolishness."

"I am already dying. What does it matter?" asked the old man, going slack in Noble's arms. Noble kneeled, allowing the old man to slide down to the ground.

"And that, Vincent, is why I do not respect you," said Dmitri, grabbing Darro. "You've always been this sniveling, weak fool, incapable of living up to your full potential. You could have been so much more."

Darro held tight to Dmitri's arm, trying to keep the vampire from crushing his throat as sweat and blood dripped down his face from his broken nose.

"Not my son. Kill me, Enravota, but leave my son."

Dmitri gave the man a look of disdain. "He does seem a more capable killer than you. He comes at me with strength and determination. How many has he taken down all on his own?"

"Thirty-five," croaked Darro, struggling. "Thirty-six if I get the chance."

The golden-eyed vampire laughed. "I'm sure it would be, but not in this lifetime. Your father should have taught you to respect your elders. Family does not hunt family. It always comes back to haunt you. Just ask your mother, who decided to put a stake through the heart of my last companion." Dmitri laughed. "Oh, I forgot, you can't, because I turned her, then snapped her neck and set her aflame. I watched as you tried to save her. She kept healing while her body burned, only to feel the flames again as nerves burned and healed again and again. She screamed for hours, and there was nothing you could do. Poor, poor Christina."

Tears fell down both Vincent's face and the girl's.

Moving the boy toward Noble, Dmitri's claws sliced the boy's throat, and he rained blood down on his companion and Vincent. "Drink, my friend, and be healed."

Darro struggled to cover his throat frantically, but he was weakening fast.

"No, Darro!" screamed the girl as she rushed at Dmitri. A stake was in one hand and a silver-coated blade in the other. The vampire knocked her away quickly, and she fell back.

"Not my son!" Vincent cried out. Noble licked the blood from his lips and leaned his head back, catching more in his mouth.

Noble felt his strength returning as the dying boy's blood ran down his throat.

Carissa was on her feet again and ran toward Dmitri, only to be knocked back again.

"Oh, my girl, you are persistent," he said, dropping her brother on the ground.

"You won't kill any more of my family," she said, glowering at him.

"I am not my brother, Carissa. I only kill family in self-defense. Noble, if you are up to it, could you feed that stupid boy some of your blood before he dies?"

The girl stopped.

Looking for affirmation, Noble said, "I don't understand, Dmitri."

"You don't have to, but I cannot let him die, and I cannot give him my blood."

Confused by Dmitri's benevolence, Noble lay the sobbing old man on the ground and bit open his wrist for the young man.

Vincent grabbed Noble's arm. Noble looked into his strange amber eyes. "Now me, heal me."

"What are you?" asked Noble, confused by the old man who had gone from sobbing to sudden desperation.

Dmitri's expression was flat. "Do not heal him. He is dhampyre. *He* is the reason I kill the women I bed. Ever since he tore his way out of one of the few women I ever loved, killing her, I have been saddled with this curse of a child and his offspring."

"You abandoned me with my dead mother in a whorehouse," said Vincent, coughing between words.

Noble looked up at Dmitri. "He is your son?"

"Yes. Be glad you are celibate."

Shocked, Noble looked down at the old man's face and finally saw the resemblance. "Why would you hunt your father?"

"He is the demon who let me be born. He is an abomination of the earth as I am, always hunted by those who hunt him. Always hiding, never allowed peace, never living free."

"You should have let them kill you, Vincent. Death is freedom. Just ask my companion."

Noble raised his bleeding wrist to the old man's mouth, but in a flash, Dmitri took his arm. "Do not heal him. He is finally dying, finally freeing *me*."

The old man burst into another coughing fit as Noble moved away.

Carissa rushed toward Vincent.

She sat, pulling her father's head onto her lap. "Why won't you save your son?" she begged. The old man's mouth was coated in blood. She wiped his lips with a rag from her pocket.

"So he can hunt me longer? Vampire blood will kill him, and he knows that. That is why you are hunting me now," said Dmitri, kneeling in front of Vincent. "You are looking for an easy death, hoping I would kill you and your offspring would carry on your vengeance for all eternity. And you call me the monster?"

Carissa shouted at him with tears running down her cheeks, "You tell nothing but lies! You killed our mother. That's why we hunt you."

"Is that what he told you? He has always hunted me, and your mother killed Aponi."

"He said you were going to turn her."

"Vincent knew I couldn't because she was a Rougarou. Have you never loved?" Dmitri asked, looking into the girl's hazel eyes.

Instead of answering, Carissa looked down at her father.

Dmitri shook his head. "You haven't loved, have you? Either of you? You've always followed this fool's words your entire lives, never living for yourselves. Vincent, can't you see you've robbed your children of their lives? Release them."

"Do not listen to this silver-tongued beast," said Darro.

"My tongue is not the one that has trapped you and Carissa, for he uses the same poisoned tongue as I. You could both live happy, quiet lives in Bavaria. He only has death to look forward to. Do not be as foolish as this old bastard," said Dmitri, standing.

Darro got up, his wounds now healed. He moved to his father, sitting down near his sister.

They both looked down into the pale face of their father as he fell quiet.

"Leave them be," the old man said.

"Release them, tell them goodbye, and I will grant you the death you wish since you are much too weak to kill me. Release them, Vincent. Tell them to go home, to live happy lives. Tell them you have died and they are free."

With welling eyes, the man looked up at his children. "Darro, Carissa, you must go home and forget this old man and your mother, who hunted every waking hour of our lives, living only for vengeance. You have no such thing in your hearts. Return to Bavaria and live happy lives. I am sorry for all the wrongs I have done and all I have robbed you of. Now go," the old man said with tears in his amber eyes.

Darro and Carissa stood.

"Take the wagon and go," said Dmitri.

They both looked at the old vampire and nodded.

Noble stood as the wagon began to move down the road. "Do you wish me to feed him?"

Dmitri stood silent for a moment, staring down at the old man.

"Dmitri?" asked Noble.

Shaking his head, Dmitri responded, "No, dear friend. He is my son. Only the blood of the father who gave him life can take that life away. Just say a prayer for him if it pleases you."

Dmitri kneeled on the ground next to his son, who started coughing again. Reaching inside Vincent's coat, Dmitri pulled out a short blade. Turning it in his hand, he stared into Vincent's eyes. "You have tried to kill me many times with this blade. It was your mother, Juliana's knife. She kept it for the rough men she encountered. I was the last man she ever pleasured holding this knife. She held it to my throat as I thrust myself inside of her. I loved that about her. She never showed fear. In fact, she embraced the monster that I am, and she loved it so. She was licentious, but there has never been a more passionate creature than she. And here it is again, the blade that helped bring you about, Vincent. Half-human, half-vampire. I guess it is only fitting that it be your end."

The old man grabbed the hand of his father. "Let us be done with words and revenge," he said as blood dripped from the corner of his mouth, and his hand fell to his chest.

The golden-eyed monster cut his wrist and held it up to his son's lips. "May you find peace in hell, Vincent, my poor damned child."

Dmitri held the back of the old man's head and forced his wrist into his mouth. Vincent grabbed onto the wrist and began to drink. Blood of the beast fell into the man's mouth, and after a few minutes, his eyes closed, and his hands released the vampire's arm. Dmitri laid the dead man back on the ground and stood up while Noble crossed himself, completing his silent prayer.

Smashing the lantern, Dmitri let the oil fall over Vincent's body. Lighting a match, he flung it on the corpse. Slowly, it burned until the oil caught fire.

Noble laid his hand on Dmitri's shoulder as he watched flames consume the body of his son. "I have always questioned whether compassion was something you had within you. Now I know you were once a man, and you did love as a man. There is still hope for you, dear friend."

Dmitri looked hard at Noble. "Hope is for fools wishing for a light in the darkness."

"Light can show us the truth, dear friend," Noble responded.

"But only part of the truth. There are always shadows. When I was a soldier in the wars back home in Bulgaria, I killed this boy aged maybe six or seven years. After seeing me impale his father, he ran upon the battlefield shouting at me, damning me. His tiny legs carried him toward me, and he held out this tiny knife he could barely get his small, fat fingers around. A man with hope sees a child, but I did not. I saw a tiny man with a knife who meant to kill me, and I ran him through with my sword without another thought. As he met my blade, I stared into his eyes. They were wide and without fear as I pushed the blade through his chest. They were a man's eyes, a warrior's eyes.

Later that night, after we brothers-in-arms rode home victorious heroes, I did weep. But I wept not for that child. I wept for my brothers lost on the battlefield. At the same time, I drank and damned the bravery of my small enemy. Warriors in battle who wish to live see not age, only the impending danger that must be stopped. Vincent was nothing more than that small, vengeful boy I killed on the field that day, except I allowed him to grow, because, for a brief moment, he was my boy. But then he raised a sword before me, and I saw not my offspring but a man who meant to end your life. You see, dear Noble, I am and will always be a warrior protecting my people," he said, laying his hand on Noble's shoulder for a moment before walking back into the woods.

June 14th 1732

I look forward to the day that I might tell Nalini that Dmitri is not the monster she thinks him. Though time has hardened his heart, he did not kill her sister, Aponi. Dmitri told me the story as we walked through the trees toward home.

"She came out of the trees, teeth bared, ready to make a meal of me. I was not going to be easily taken, and I bared my fangs and claws. I fought this large wolf-beast for the better part of an hour." Realizing he could not feed on her because her blood was not human, he stopped fighting her, and then she stopped attacking him.

She was the very meaning of beauty. Her red-brown skin shone in the moonlight as she turned from a beast into a woman. High cheekbones looked exquisite, with large dark eyes. "Who are you, and why do you hunt in my forest?" she asked.

"It seems these trees hide more than human hunters. What are you?"

"I am Quinipissa, but the pale-skins call us Rougarou, and I hunt these forests with my brothers."

"Should I worry about them bursting from the trees?"

Caught off guard by his question, she stood silent, staring at him.

"We both stood there until just before sunrise, and I was forced to flee," Dmitri told me.

Over several months, Dmitri hunted the beautiful beast in the forest. They would meet, and after a time, she grew to trust him. They fell in love, and one night, Aponi lay with him beneath the trees. He told her of his travels and his life, and she told him of hers. They became lovers.

Then the Archers started moving into the colony. Wanting to take Aponi away from danger, he went to warn her and her people and ask her father's permission to take Aponi across the sea. Her father said no and that she needed to remain with her kind and Dmitri with his.

One night, when her father finally spoke of moving his people farther into the swamps, Aponi fled, meeting up with Dmitri, and they escaped by ship to Europe.

They traveled around the whole of the continent, killing and making love until one night, while walking hand in hand, a stake was shot from a crossbow into Aponi's heart, killing her. Dmitri wanted his revenge on Vincent's wife then, but he could hear the flutter of life in Christina's womb and would not kill his son's unborn child.

Foolishly, Dmitri returned to Aponi's family to leave her meager belongings and beg forgiveness for her death. After almost losing a battle to his lover's father, Dmitri was forced to flee the colonies, meeting a pathetic rat-eating beast returning home to London on a ship.

Not since I drank of his life have I seen Dmitri as a man. Though he was not a man when he lay with Vincent's mother, creating a sort of half-life, he passed his seed onto another without a drop of blood being spilled.

Dmitri has said nothing more about the death of his son, except that dhampyre are not meant to live. "They are abominations that have fallen through the cracks of creation. Man and beast cannot exist within the same body without there being consequences. One always consumes the other," he said as we walked home.

I expected him to be sullen, but he is the same dashing monster, drinking at the throats of aristocrats, acting as though their politics interest him so that he may have his way with their wives. He is cunning and unchanging.

Boston has proven a haven since the passing of Vincent and the departure of his children.

So, here is where we have made our home, for now.

The New England colonists care little for the rule of the Papacy from Rome. Dmitri believes the Archers will keep to the south since their redcoats are a more accepted dress there.

I only hope they do not force Tabansi north.

FEARING THE INNER BEAST

June 12th 1733

Boston is rife with rebellion these days. I note this as I quietly sit and watch smugglers bringing molasses barrels in on small boats from ships outside of the harbor, trying to avoid the tariffs set upon them by England.

It is strange to hear the gongs of church bells tolling the hour, for they are just noises that mean nothing more than one more hour of these miserable mortal lives is over, while my own remains unaltered. I quietly realized today is my birthday, and while my age from my actual birth would make me fifty, I also realize how long it has been since the death of Elizabeth. Over two decades have passed, and I have yet to set eyes upon her. Recent events have made me quite glad of it. I am not myself, therefore, fearful of what might occur if I did happen upon my love.

Resting on the roof of a warehouse, I write, hiding here from the women I know are running about the home I share with my companion. Their very presence reminds me of how close I have come to actual death. I must live if only to save Elizabeth from the purgatory she is to be born from.

Dmitri hunts in the taverns for his meals, while I have been feeding on deer when I can. My hunger at the throats of whores has become too much for me to control. Two months ago, I consumed my last human meal. She was pretty and walked into my bedchamber with little persuading on my part. Suddenly, out of nowhere, her heart pounded in my head so loudly I could not make out a word she was saying. I did not hear her until she screamed, and her heart started to race. The veins on her neck pulsed, and my control ended.

It was as if I became a passenger in my body, incapable of controlling my movements and the beast within. I felt my body change to that of the monster. She screamed again and ran for the door. The creature screeched at her, and she screamed again as the animal gave chase. Running down the hall, she lifted her skirts from her feet, taking the stairs two at a time.

Taking flight, the monster grabbed her up and carried her back to my rooms. Hanging from the ceiling, I was at once at her throat, feeding more ravenously than I ever had. Her blood poured down my throat as I bit deeply into her neck. I could feel the crushing and popping of the veins between my teeth. The ripping of muscle fibers in her neck just made my bite ever more profound. Suddenly, my heart stopped, and I could not breathe. My chest was ablaze in light burning through my coat. My head was light and pounding. I could not release her, though I wanted to, even with her heart so quiet I thought it stilled.

"Noble, stop, you're killing her," Dmitri shouted as he burst through the door and tried to separate me from her. He fought to take her from me, but the beast fought back. Claws ripped through his chest, tearing through his shirt. He seemed to ignore the pain, fighting for both the life of the woman and my own.

"Release her, Noble, release her now!"

The beast screamed as Dmitri tugged at the woman, trying to pull her from its grasp.

"I am sorry, my friend," he said, grabbing my bottom jaw and the top of my head, pulling them apart until my jaw broke from my face and was left hanging by muscle and skin. Blood poured from the wounds, and the bone was no longer connected. Dropping the girl, I fell from the ceiling into a pile on the floor, wings spread, and the beast cried out in pain.

Dmitri grabbed the girl and finished her. Dropping her body next to mine, he looked at me, his face filled with something I had never seen before: fear. "Why are you still the beast?"

I did not answer because I could not even if my jaw were intact. The room spun as I pushed my jaw back into place and began healing. I was back on my feet in a moment. Claws grabbed at Dmitri, and the scream of the monster sounded. They were my claws reaching for him. His face contorted, his fangs becoming more prominent as his claws pushed through his fingertips. "Noble, stop!" he shouted, moving away from me. The beast gave chase, flying through the high-ceilinged halls. Dmitri moved ahead with great speed, and I followed just as quickly.

Large wings knocked things about, and the sounds of shattering glass, porcelain, and wood shook Dmitri's patience. Finally, he made it to the front door. Throwing them open, he dashed out with the beast at his heels. Smashing through the doors, the loud crack of breaking bones left the creature screeching as it crashed to the ground with a broken wing.

Turning around, Dmitri started for the winged demon. It spread its wings repeatedly until it healed enough to gain altitude, then continued after the old vampire.

"Noble, you must end this chase!" he shouted.

The persistent beast grabbed for him, catching him by the shoulders. Dmitri tugged at the beast's talons as it started flying straight up in the fading night.

The air started thinning as the creature soared farther into the sky. Dmitri slashed at the beast's legs with his claws, but it kept on its course.

"Release me, Noble!"

All I could think was, I am going to fly us into the sun. The clouds thinned, and every star in the sky showed itself brighter than I had ever seen. The warmth of the earth stopped as we passed into the outer atmosphere. The cold froze my wings, and all at once, we started plummeting back to the world.

Dmitri snapped my ankles, freeing himself. I closed my eyes, screaming, and felt the beast melt away. I could control my body again, but all I could do was fall.

"Noble, you must become the beast again!" Dmitri shouted.

I opened my eyes and saw we were closing in on land.

Turning, I grabbed my friend and spread the wings of the beast wide.

When we finally landed gently on the grass of our home, Dmitri looked me in the eyes, questioning without words.

"What is happening to me?" I asked, falling to my knees on the grass.

"I do not know for certain, but I believe you are losing yourself, friend. I don't know how to help you."

I stood in the garden, watching and waiting for changes in my hands and my face in the mirrored fountain water, frightened of myself and what I could no longer control.

Without Dmitri around, I would indeed have met my fate in hell that night. He and I are both baffled by my sudden change.

CHAINED BEAST

July 14th 1733

I am now a chained beast, but no longer by the sun alone. During the day, Dmitri locks me away in the cellar in an iron cage. He fears this beast of mine will walk outside into the sun, so for my safety, he has taken to chaining me inside an iron cell.

It seems the sun might be my only reprieve, for it is not the sun that frightens me so, it is what I cannot remember.

I pray night after night for clarity of my plight. If I am forsaken, God, then please let me die. I have never had it in me to kill without conscience. Now I awaken to death more often than not.

I am most frightened. I am becoming that beast from the ship that carried me home from Africa. I am again the creature unable to recall murdering my dearest wife.

What am I to do, Holy Father?

Noble's hair hung sweaty and stringy over his face, his beard dripped blood, and his eyes glowed red as Dmitri grabbed his chin and forced him to look into his gold eyes. "What are you doing, Noble?" he demanded.

Shaking his head, Noble looked at him, his eyes confused. "Nothing, I was sleeping."

Dmitri moved aside from the armchair Noble sat in and shook his head. "I guess it would have been much worse had you been awake," he said, holding a lantern high over his head.

"No, no, I did not do this, I could not have done this..." Noble said, shaking his head as he looked past the light into the room.

Half a dozen corpses lay torn and broken, heads separated from bodies, on the glistening blood-bathed floor.

Looking at his hands, he saw them coated in blood, and his tattered clothing was thick with drying sanguine. Falling to his knees at the edge of the mess, he clasped his hands together and closed his eyes. "What challenges do you lay before me, God? Has your curse failed, or have you forsaken me for better men? I am bewildered that I kneel, still here, surrounded by bodies that would otherwise mean my end."

The room remained silent, as though both monsters listened for a reply.

Dmitri stepped next to him and surveyed the carnage. "God has no answers for this, Noble, though we do now require new servants, and you've killed the carpenter who did so well repair the entry doors again."

In the forest, they pulled body after body from the back of the wagon, dropping them into a mass grave dug just after nightfall.

Noble did not speak. Instead, he prayed as he threw the body of his chamberman on top of the rest.

While Dmitri headed out to hunt, Noble stood in his bedchamber in front of a mirror near a curtained window. Lighting candles, he watched the flames grow until the room was bright. Looking at his reflection, he pulled the tattered clothing from his body until he stood naked before the glass. Almost every inch of his skin was stained with blood. Noble started emptying a pitcher into a washbasin, letting the cold water fall over his other hand slowly. He watched the red cascade turn the basin water a murky brown color.

Picking up a sponge, he soaked up the water.

Rubbing away at the dried blood on his chest, he looked intently into the mirror at his skin.

"You are suffering greatly, lost man of God," said a familiar voice from behind him.

Noble's eyes met those of Tabansi's in the looking glass. The African, dressed in a gentleman's coat, leaned on a cane.

"Come to seek your revenge for my abandonment of you?"

"I think you suffer enough, No-bell Leencoln."

Noble continued to wipe away the blood, ignoring his master.

Tabansi spoke as he watched the white man clean himself. "I cannot say that my life has been easy since you left me on that dock in Virginia, but I am happy for your return to me."

Leaning in, Noble smiled for a moment, feeling a sense of relief, for under the blood he was cleaning from his skin were the symbols of God's curse. Noble met Tabansi's gaze in the mirror. "I have not returned to you, Tabansi. I did not seek you out. I abhor the mere idea of your existence upon the earth instead of the hell in which you should be burning."

Tabansi laughed. "You have lost your kindness, No-bell, lost man of God."

Continuing to bathe himself in the mirror, Noble ignored the remark.

The African walked around Noble's bedchamber, picking up his progeny's things before putting them back. "You will leave this pale beast you follow around and join me. We can carry on as we were. I have not yet found Siti or my sons."

Startled by his maker's words, Noble turned to him. "Have you truly gone mad, Tabansi?"

Shaking his head, Tabansi replied, "I am a simple man seeking out his lost family. The white man keeps them chained, working them to the very bone. Blood pours from their fingers, and he keeps after them with whips to keep them going."

"Your sons are dead. I saw them die when I drank of your blood. Blood cannot lie."

Suddenly, the African was upon him, eyes wide and red. Grabbing Noble by the throat, he stood mere centimeters from Noble's nose. "My sons live, they live. Siti is waiting to be found, and you will help me find them, and then you will take my family home," he said with spittle flying from his lips onto Noble's face.

Pushing back against his maker, Noble pulled free of Tabansi's grip. "No one can bring the dead back, Tabansi."

"You will get them back for me, I command you," the African said as blood welled in his eyes.

Noble walked to his bed and picked up his dressing gown. Pulling it on, he watched Tabansi standing in the middle of the room, holding his head in his hands.

"I have spent so many years fearing you and the retribution you might set upon me if we were to meet again. Instead, I find you a wretched, foolish creature."

Tabansi looked up, his eyes changed to that of the beast, and his face contorted as he transformed. "We will see who the fool is."

"If it is what you must do, then I will defend myself." Noble's jaw jutted forward and up, his human teeth pushed out of his jaw, filling in with the pointed teeth of the monster. His skin turned from its usual pale color to black.

Both transformed beasts stood facing one another, wings spread and claws at the ready.

Tabansi's claws ripped toward him, and Noble backed away, raising his own. Claws ripped into Noble.

Noble sat straight up, screaming. Breathing heavily, he looked down at his human hands. Closing his eyes for a moment, Noble enjoyed a rush of relief. Finding he was no different than he had been before falling asleep, his eyes searched the darkened room where only embers remained in the fireplace. Nothing was out of place, but unusual noises met his ears as he intently listened.

Taking a deep breath, he laid back down. The smell of copper hit him. He ran his hands down the sheet on either side of him. One of his hands found something sticky and cold.

Sitting up again, he pulled back the blankets. A young woman lay nude beneath the bedclothes. One hand rested across her chest, and her eyes stared unseeing at the canopy above. Her neck wound was so deep her head looked as if it could fall away. The pale skin of her breast was splayed open, having been shredded by claws.

Noble ran to the mirror and with shaking hands lit candles. Looking in the mirror, he saw the blood, staining his face and beard once again and having run down into his chest hair and in thin trails down his legs.

Why do I still live?

Pulling the sheets off the bed, he wrapped the girl's body. He paused to look down into her face. Blue eyes now glazed by death were deep-set, but she showed no sign of fear. Something he always told them not to. Blonde hair, matted with blood, hung about her face.

Gathering her clothes, he stuffed them within the linens as he tied them up.

Cleaning himself up quickly, he pulled the curtains back, looking for signs of the rising sun, but found it dark and misty.

Noble carried the body into the forest farther still than the bodies he had interred earlier. He buried her, all the while trying to remember even bringing her home. A deer ran through the trees somewhere to the west. He felt the pangs of hunger in his gut as he piled on the last shovelful of dirt and then ran west after the animal.

As Noble drank of the doe, he listened intently to its heart, waiting for the telltale sign to stop. Her heart raced, but she lay ever so still as he fed. After a few moments, he pulled away, his stomach content with its meal. Biting into his wrist, he let a little of his blood into her throat.

Afterward, he sat with the animal lying still on the ground, protecting her from other predators that might come upon her. Running his hand over her fur, he felt its coarseness on his skin. Taking it to memory, he closed his eyes, trying to recall anything before this. He could remember all of it since awakening, but nothing before.

"Perhaps I have gone mad," he said to no one as he continued petting the deer while she regained her strength.

Dmitri walked into Noble's bedchamber just after sunrise. Noble sat in an armchair before a blistering fire.

"I wanted to ensure you were home safe, Noble."

Noble stared at the flames and then raised his hands, looking down at them. "I am, though I am most unsettled. I do not recall ever having left, but I must have. I awoke with a woman dead beneath my sheets and my body covered in her blood."

The old vampire looked around the room and then noticed the bed sheets missing. "If it were not you and instead another fellow of our kind, I would simply say it is what you are. But alas, my poor cursed friend, I cannot."

"I have no more control of the beast. It seems to come at its leisure, leaving me to think each time I awaken if I will survive the next time it takes over. Why can I not satiate this thirst? When will God finally deliver his punishment upon me? I fear he has forsaken me, and possibly this is the true retribution I am to receive: to be abandoned by that I hold most dear since there is no longer my Elizabeth."

"I am sorry, friend, I can offer no comfort to you," said Dmitri, laying his hand upon Noble's shoulder. "Shall we settle you for the day?"

Nodding, Noble stood and followed Dmitri through the house to the dark cellar.

DREAMS OF HELL

July 29th 1733

*Tabansi has become all too frequent a visitor to my dreams.
He presses me to leave Dmitri and carry on with him, to search
for Siti. And every night, without fail, I find yet another body in
my bed. Whores and other women, drained to death, are filling
the forest with shallow unmarked graves. They number so many,
I fear those in the village are missing them. This fear was made
concrete by my companion tonight upon arriving home.*

Dmitri came home, dropping a stack of drawings of young women on the
table. These were women Noble had buried over the past few nights.

"Though I have in the past pushed the limits, feeding without thought or care,
I have never made the whole of a wall, papered in missing women's pictures, rile
a town into calling the magistrate to start a search and investigation. Women are
being told to avoid strangers and be in by sunset. Whores are no longer to be left
alone with customers, which has certainly put a damper on what I had hoped
would be a pleasant evening," he said, throwing down his coat.

"Oh..."

"'Oh,' you say. There must be three dozen or so missing notices plastered all
around the village and even more in Boston Common. The papers speak of a
serial murderer, and the watchmen there question everyone they pass in the

193

streets. Husbands, beaus, and pimps are searching the homes in the village. How long until they find their way here, to the home that is supposed to be empty?"

"This should not be happening. I do not recall partaking in the blood of any of these ladies," Noble said, pushing the drawings away.

"But you can recall burying them?"

"Of course, I've told you of them all."

Shaking his head, Dmitri sat in the chair opposite Noble. "If this carries on for much longer, we will have to leave. I am sure the Archers will be called upon if the local friar has not done so already, and we will be forced to flee again."

"I know, but can you imagine this on a ship?" Noble said, motioning at the paper pile. "We would be forced to sail the vessel ourselves within a month."

Nodding his head, Dmitri stared into the now-dark hearth. "It seems so, but what have we left to do?" Dmitri asked.

"For your safety, I can only suggest leaving me here alone. The Archers can come. I will gladly fall on my knees before them and pray they can end me, for I have become a beast worthy of death and hell."

"You have been a loyal—albeit annoying—companion, and I would rather not abandon you."

"I will get us both killed. You have lived so long, it would be a shame to see that fiery flame extinguished, and I would rather not have your death on my conscience, though it seems I've lost even that with my murder spree."

"I will leave if I sense danger is imminent, Noble, but not until I see the whites of our enemy's eyes."

How close those eyes are indeed, thought Noble.

Noble and Dmitri had stopped setting fires in the hearths and lighting candles in the night. Neither stepped into the village, and Dmitri had taken to leaving Noble caged throughout the night, but still, the dreams of Tabansi continued.

Lying in his cage, sleeping, Noble awakened. Someone was kicking the iron bars. "You must awaken, No-bell Leencoln." The African kneeled next to the bars, looking in at him.

"Tabansi, you are a plague in my mind. If I return to my slumber, will you vanish?"

The Asasabonsam ripped the door from the cage and kneeled in Noble's face. "We are not finished, lost man of God."

The beast attacked Noble's throat, ripping into him, blood spraying. Noble sat straight up in the cage and called out. Reaching for his throat, he found nothing amiss save the shackles torn from their anchor, a missing door, and the body of a young woman splayed out across his lap.

Out of nowhere, Dmitri appeared, having heard the commotion. His gold eyes widened at the sight of the girl.

Pounding on the large, heavy entry door echoed throughout the house.

"Seems danger is knocking at our door, bloody Englishmen," fumed Dmitri.

The pounding continued as Dmitri freed Noble's wrists and ankles. "Get only what is important. Gather every bit of money you have and meet me in the forest. Do not martyr yourself to save me. I don't do well alone," said Dmitri before vanishing from the cellar that was no longer Noble's dungeon.

Pushing the body from his lap, Noble moved out of the cage and up the stairs into his rooms. Pummeling the doors, the people outside screamed, "Murderer, we saw you enter here! Come out!"

Gathering his books and crowns, Noble packed them into a bag. Looking into the mirror, he sighed at the sight of his skin, again bathed in blood.

Running out of the open rear doors of the house, Noble dashed into the forest. Behind him, men carrying lanterns moved around the back of the house just in time to see Noble going toward the trees.

"Here! He's here!" shouted a man as he gave chase.

Pulling the long strap of the bag over his head, Noble moved faster. Tree branches tore into his skin as he raced into an unfamiliar part of the forest. Cuts healed as Noble stopped, listening for Dmitri. Instead, he heard men screaming and wailing far behind him.

"Dmitri, you suicidal fool," Noble said under his breath as he started back toward the house. Before he got a foot down, he was grabbed from behind. Turning on his heels, he met the red eyes of Tabansi.

"Lost man of God, it is good to see you again."

"Tabansi, how... You bastard!" Noble grabbed tight to his maker's throat, raising him off the ground. "You brought these men to my home."

Far away, the screams continued.

The African laughed for a moment before his eyes locked onto Noble's. "I have saved you from a true demon."

"I choose my companion. You do not."

"I am your master."

"I have no master!" Noble shouted as he held his maker over his head, and his skin turned black as he started to turn.

He threw the monster into the trees, then chased after him. Tabansi's heels dug into the leaf-covered ground. Fangs appeared, and both creatures shed their human skins and stood face to face, snarling and growling.

Claws came down as both beasts attacked. Red eyes gleamed in the darkness as the monsters ripped at each other and equaled each other's wounds. Suddenly flying up into the air, Noble grabbed tight with hooked feet to his maker's neck. Tabansi grabbed onto his progeny's legs, digging in deep with his claws. Both monsters spread their wings, fighting for control in the air. The two beasts rolled about in the sky. Noble finally released Tabansi, who started to drop but stopped short, his wings catching him mid-air.

Noble flew toward him, his talons grabbing onto the other's wings. He chewed into his throat, tearing away muscle and downing his blood.

Then the blood spoke in images and screams that further angered Noble.

As he drank more, seeking still more answers, Noble felt a tightening in his chest and watched as the symbols glowed their warning on his black skin.

He broke away from his maker's throat, seething through the pain of a crushing heart. Noble fought to free his legs from the beast.

Shaking Tabansi hard and moving still higher in the sky, the beast fell limp as his wings snapped. Dropping the African monster, Noble watched him plummet into the trees. The pain stopped, and the glowing symbols faded. He waited for a time, then started for the trees where he had left his bag. Landing, Noble saw no sign of Tabansi. He picked up his bag and again made for the skies. His red eyes searched over the forest. Seeing no sign that Tabansi had regained flight, Noble flew back toward the house.

SOUTH

Noble, once again a man, stepped down on the grass and into the carnage behind the house.

A dozen or so bodies lay strewn about the lawn, and in the middle of the massacre stood Dmitri. His gold eyes gleamed through the crimson mask of blood that covered him. He bared his teeth as he kneeled over a man who still breathed. "You think to bring death down upon me? You've failed. Take that message to Saint Peter at the gates so that he may send you to hell. You've failed your master." The man groaned, and Dmitri attacked his throat, draining him until his heart stopped.

Pulling at his victim's cloak, he yanked off a bit of it. Through the blood, he could see an embroidered papal cross wrapped in a red rose. "Archers now think they are worthy of a rose."

Noble stood near him, now covered in both the blood of the woman in the cellar and his master. "When does the running stop?"

Dmitri threw the swatch of fabric to the ground. "When we are dead, though I believe if we entered into hell, it would be a more peaceful an existence than this has been."

"I feared you would say that."

"Have you your crowns and books?"

"Yes. I am ready to leave."

"We need to clean up. Sunrise is almost upon us, and we must find passage across the sea. Your master is too close, and the Archers closer still. More will come when these fail to return."

July 30th 1733

I stood on the ship sailing to Virginia, wrapped in my cloak, holding tight to my bag, watching the horizon. It is a beautiful glow in my eyes as the gloaming fades to a deep-plum hue and then an orange-gold. That is all I can see of the day before my eyes start to burn and catch fire, causing considerable pain.

Once again, I was leaving Tabansi, though I felt nothing more than relief this time. We could have never been together, not like Dmitri and I. Tabansi and I are at our worst when in proximity and would have slaughtered everything around us. I realize this now and feel no more shame for abandoning him again. I want to kill him. He is the reason these past few months have been terrible. I saw it when I drank his blood. The murders committed and dropped all around me. I watched them all die again through his eyes, and it brought about great sadness and relief—relief that I was not a murderer and sadness at their loss for no other purpose than to drive me into madness, believing God would leave me. God has not forsaken me. He sought to protect me when I took Tabansi ever so close to death. His warning rang clear, and I saw the truth of it.

I am still cursed, and for that, I am most thankful. God is still there, which means I have not forever lost my Elizabeth. She will return to me.

Distance from Tabansi has calmed the beast within. Maybe everything that happened in Boston occurred so that we might end up moving back toward home. Though the house is no longer there, I feel almost relieved to return. Tucked in my bag is the painting of Elizabeth, my heart, my soul, and my only love.

August 10th 1733

I cannot explain it, but something draws me to stay, though Dmitri is most desperate to leave. Something floats in the air, giving me a sense of peace and familiarity as the butterfly does in a garden heavy with blooms.

Tonight, we fought, Dmitri and I. He wishes to sail for Europe, while I feel remaining in Williamsburg is vital.

"I am a vampire, not a hunter of deer and vermin," he shouted as we walked through a field late in the night away from town.

"I know, friend. But mustn't we strive for survival?"

"Not in this fashion. Merely surviving is draining a woman on the street. While my preference is a room with a bed and a whore. I can do without privacy in which to feed, but this chasing deer because some Puritan bastard sees whores as witches or sinners to be done away with? What creature tolerates a town without a bevy of whores? Not this creature. It isn't possible to even ask such a thing. That's what whores are for, feeding while finding pleasure. I find no pleasure here any longer. Let us return to Europe. Perhaps France this time. The French, their whores, are quite affable," he said with a smile.

"As pleasant a trip as that sounds, I believe I should stay here."

"Noble, you cannot be within your right mind. Is it the monster frightening you again? Is it causing you difficulty? Or do you wish to join your master once more?"

"No, Tabansi is a curse worse than that of hell. There's just something I must remain here for. I feel as though if I leave, I might miss something. Maybe Elizabeth is here somewhere in the colonies, waiting for me to find her."

"I doubt your master would allow her to live, given the circumstances."

"What do you mean by that?"

"Nothing, just please consider it. To walk the streets freely in the night and drink to our heart's content, does it not sound most prodigious after our latest adventures? Besides, this new land is rife with Archers and religious zealots alike, threatening our very lives."

"Though you bring about excellent points, I feel I must remain here, dear Dmitri. I do wish you good travels and bounteous feasts."

Dmitri turned to Noble. "Friend, I do not wish to leave you here alone. If I were not the heartless bastard, I would say I fear for your safety. Instead, I will tell you that this woman you seek is never to be found. She is merely a dream. All men would seek to dream if they believed it so. You're a fool, Noble."

"I know. I am a cretinous man who wishes to live as though the dream is real."

Though Dmitri tried to talk Noble onto the ship early in the morning some days later, he remained on the dock, waving to his friend as the vessel moved out into the fog.

DRAWN INTO THE WAR OF MAN

March 3rd 1758

It has been twenty-five years since I said goodbye to my companion and started my travels alone. Oh, how the colonies have changed. An almost constant war is being waged between the Indians and the Europeans, who hope to conquer the vast unexplored frontier. The Natives fight with the vigor of warriors; their simple weapons against guns and cannons seem hardly fair. But what they lack in arms, they make up for in persistence, stealthy attacks, and conviction to keep their lands.

I have avoided such wars, sticking closer to Virginia, preferring a quiet life, but the war has come to me.

One month ago, the smell of blood drew me to a battlefield. Instead of diving into what would most certainly be a feast, I looked at a field of bodies. Some writhed while others remained still. Stepping out from the edge of the wood, I kneeled next to a man. Tears fell down his face as he looked at me with hope, for someone had come back for him, and he thought me his brother-in-arms. His coat was covered in blood, while one side of his face was severely gashed and free-flowing. His slowing heartbeat berated my ears.

"Please, help me. I don't want to die," the soldier said, grabbing my coat. At that moment, the beast failed me, and instead of feeding, I lifted him off the ground and carried him to his camp, following other soldiers who were pulling comrades from the field. The colonial soldiers struggled to care for their fallen with little knowledge.

I have found a purpose other than that of a monster. I've again taken on the role of doctor, though it is only possible at night; that is when the camp is calm and the wounded are brought in under cover of darkness, while the sky, though still filled with a thick fog of gunpowder, is sometimes silent.

I am a volunteer on the side of the colonists Elizabeth and I adopted as our own. Their soldiers' wounds are terrible since they lack so much as a physician, festering all day long until I can attend to them. Other soldiers with lesser injuries hold bandages—most dirtied by the dead who have already used them—to try to stop the flow of blood from those newly brought in. I watched them as they entered the tent. I've taught them about tourniquets and do my best to stave off death with minimal supplies and prayers.

An aide to Colonel Braddock, known as George Washington, has demanded on more than one occasion during this month of fighting that I remain during the day to treat his men. He is reliable and steely-eyed indeed for someone so young. Dmitri would surely call him a warrior. His passions run deep, and his piety for his men seems more fervent than that of God. Upon arriving at the camp tonight, I was immediately taken to his tent by force, since I have yet to abide by his orders.

"Doctor Lincoln, how nice of you to return. I believe I had ordered you to remain just last evening."

"Yes, sir, but as I have explained, I have a physical reaction to sunlight that causes me horrible suffering and—"

Washington held up his hand, interrupting Noble. "You will stay and treat these men as I have ordered you to do."

"I assure you, sir, if it were possible, I would certainly do so."

"Then we agree. You will stay and ensure these soldiers live."

"The daylight makes it almost impossible."

"You are one man. They are many," he said, motioning around us at the injured men in his tent. "And the cries of wives and children over the bodies of fallen soldiers are a crushing blow to morale. You could have saved at least five this day. This day when you vanished, leaving them to die. I should like to hang you, Doctor. The preacher has taken to treating my men in your absence. But that absence is no longer acceptable in the wake of the coming days. We are moving forward and you with us, whether it be as a shackled prisoner awaiting trial before General Braddock for treason or a physician and patriot, treating my men."

Noble stood silent, wishing the room was not so full of soldiers so that he might charm Washington into understanding, but as always, he was surrounded.

He looked into Noble's eyes as he quietly fumed.

"Have we an accord, Doctor?"

Knowing this was not a question, Noble responded, "We do."

"Good. Then I would suggest you return to your tent and get my men back on their feet. We march tomorrow. Ives, Beaumont, go with him."

Finally released by his soldiers but being shadowed, Noble returned to his tent, dreading the sure rise of the morning sun.

Three days after Washington's warning, Noble stood up straight from his bent position over a patient as the familiar sound of an arrow's release caught his attention. The tent was dark, save the lanterns held up by Noble's assistants as he went from one soldier to another.

"Indians," said the man whose shoulder Noble was stitching up. The death cries of soldiers outside the tent surrounded them.

"Sounds like an ambush," said Noble, looking at the guards who stood watch, keeping him at his post.

They stood their duty, as ordered by their commander, but uncomfortably so.

"Your brothers are being killed just outside, and yet you stand here, holding your muskets as if nothing is happening. Help them!" Noble shouted.

The men ducked out of the tent, and Noble ran to his bag for his pistol. Tucking it into the hand of the injured soldier, Noble nodded down at him. "If you see the enemy, defend yourself."

The man nodded in return. "Thanks, Doc."

Noble pulled out his long black cloak and covered himself while he continued working.

The clash of weapons and cries from outside put Noble on edge as he looked around the tent, at the soldiers who lay suffering as they awaited his care.

Noble stared down at the mug one of his assistants had filled with water the night before, thinking long and hard. The pungent scent of copper and necrotic wounds was both putrid and enticing to the hungry beast within.

They deserve a fighting chance, he thought.

Pulling a knife from his bag, he dragged the blade across his hand swiftly and watched the free flow of blood as he held it over the water, turning the brownish liquid red. War continued outside as Noble went from soldier to soldier, making them drink from the cup. Their wounds healed, and some sat up, startled, no longer in pain and confused as their wounds closed up.

A young man, maybe eighteen, looked at the doctor as he forced the remaining liquid down the throat of another soldier. "You healed me, Doc?"

"Yes, but I am afraid you must take up arms and fight again."

"Yes, sir." The young man nodded.

War cries of Indians sounded as the tent canvas burst open. A lantern extinguished as it fell to the ground, leaving Noble and his patients in partial darkness.

"Act as though you are dead if you have to. I will pray for you," Noble whispered to the man on the table, whose wounds were closing.

"Thank you," whispered the man as he lay still.

Indian and French soldiers ripped into the tent and started to dispatch his patients, and the last lantern fell to the dirt as part of the tent collapsed.

A tall Indian ran at Noble, a knife at the ready. The dark eyes of the Indian met his, the Native man's face filled with malice as he slashed at Noble. Knowing he could not fight back without killing him, Noble let himself fall. His eyes lit red in the darkness, and his jaw jutted forward as his mouth filled with large pointed teeth, startling the Native man. The Indian yelped and screamed "Demon" in his native tongue, and pushed his way out of the tent.

Something large came in through the back of the tent, grabbing hold of Noble's legs as the remaining lantern light flickered out and screams filled the air. The doctor was dragged away into the fog.

Clawing at the ground, Noble fought his captor. For those few moments in the dense mist, he was afraid. The wails and musket fire faded as he was dragged farther and farther away. Noble tried turning to get a glimpse of what was taking him he knew not where, but he groaned as he slammed into rocks and over sharp sticks and rotting logs.

Angered at having been dragged so far, Noble became the beast. He drove his claws into the ground and kicked at the creature. It yelped as he pulled free.

The familiar scent and the yelp told him of his captor in an instant. It was a Rougarou.

Before he could see it, it vanished into the thick fog. Finally released from its grasp, Noble bared his fangs and screeched at the beast in the mist.

Deep growling sounded all around him.

Leathery wings flapped loudly as the beast took to the air. He followed the noises below from above, unable to see the creature through the thick mist. Suddenly, his ears were met with silence as it stopped somewhere below. Noble began to drop from the sky when the giant wolf jumped up out of the fog and grabbed his leg with its teeth, pulling him down into the mist.

Fighting the Rougarou, the creature clawed at its head as it clamped down on his leg hard enough for the bone to snap. The Asasabonsam wailed and bowed its back, trying to get its wings off the ground and back into the sky. The wolf-like beast pressed its front feet into the winged monster's chest, pushing it to the ground. Its growls seemed to turn into words as it stood atop the flying beast. Then its face became that of a woman, her silver eyes staring into his.

"Stop, stop fighting me, White Spirit Beast!"

The Asasabonsam melted away, leaving behind Noble. "Who are you, and why did you drag me off?" he growled at her in pain.

Noble's leg healed, and the discomfort disappeared quickly.

Her caramel-red skin was dirty, and feathers from her long, dark hair fell on her face. She was maybe in her late twenties and looked scared. "Nalini sent me to find you. I smelled your blood on the wind."

Noble looked up at her. "Nalini, where is she?"

The Indian girl got to her feet. "She's been taken prisoner by white warriors to the north. She said to find you, that you would help. Nalini also said to tell you your white woman is up there. The one you keep in your head."

Noble stood, his eyes filled with confusion. "How?"

"Your blood. Nalini saw her when she carried you off years ago to see her father, my grandfather. She did break the skin with her teeth. As I did just now."

He nodded and then furrowed his brow, remembering how Nalini's bite had poked many holes through his clothing so many years before. "Who are you?"

"I am Ayiana. The last time I saw you, I was but a cub. I remember when Nalini brought you to our camp. She told me you are the white spirit walker that darkness cannot consume. She said you were good."

"I don't know how to define myself these days."

She looked him up and down, her eyes sparkling. "Your spirit is filled with light. I see no shadows."

Gunfire sounded in the distance. "The troops are moving in this direction. We must go," said Noble. "They'll be looking for me."

The girl changed form and vanished into the trees. Noble followed behind her.

CROSSING LINES

March 29th 1758

I have been biding my time whilst my friend searches for her mother. We have wandered for so long that I feel as though I have most certainly missed Elizabeth by now. Still, Aiyana presses on as we go settlement to settlement or town to town. Some settlers prefer her to keep away whilst I am able to enter and search for Nalini, who would most certainly be a prisoner rather than allowed free rein to walk amongst these people. Soldiers walk around as if guarding the towns, and I feel their glares and paranoia.

We travel together but bed down apart.

By day, I bury myself in the earth or cellars of abandoned houses if I happen upon them.

At night, we run silently through the countryside, avoiding people as much as possible.

It seems we will never reach the north in time. War rages on between British troops, the French, and the Indians.

Both sides are taking prisoners, and we have run from musket fire more than once. I've dashed across battlefields, watching men fall to their enemies' flying musket rounds. I am the blur that knocks musket rounds from the air, interrupting their trajectory. In the darkness, men fire upon one another blindly. The air is heavy with gunpowder, and heavier eyelids try to meet their marks from the other side of a dark field or between trees. Captains and commanders shout "Fire!" as arrows and musket balls rain down from the sky.

Unlucky men fall where they stand, and other men are called to take their place. The rain of metal, stone, and bodies is all I see as I fly slowly overhead. Even through its hungry eyes, I see the pointless loss of life: man's petty fight over land that is not theirs.

I have had to start feeding on men once again as the constant firing of weapons has scared away the deer. I pull my compatriots from the lines and take them into the forest, far from the battlefield. I drink until their hearts start to skip a beat, and then in return, I give them just enough blood to keep them from death and heal them. They pass into a deep sleep.

Aiyana pulls men from the lines and drags them to the forest, past where even I stop. I hear them scream as she tears them apart, for she fears no death. She fills her belly and then comes to me as the beautiful Indian, silver eyes gleaming, her face painted in the blood of her victim. It is her people's way to respect the dead until she downs another man. I have watched her from the trees. She goes for the throat to ensure they suffer little. I say a prayer for them as their hearts stop.

She kills only to eat what she needs to live, the rest she buries.

Men see her as a monster, but I see a beautiful beast that only takes what it needs and gives the rest back to the earth. I don't know when I stopped seeing these soldiers as my fellow men. I feel as though I am jaded to mankind for its cruelness and its many weaknesses. Am I losing my humanity? Am I becoming Dmitri?

The Indian walked out of the woods and looked upon me, having finished her meal. "Shall we go north now, White Spirit Walker?"

I look skyward, searching for the North Star as Captain Allsopp taught me on my last voyage as a man.

As we start north, her large padded paws and my worn shoes running across the earth, I feel myself more and more at ease, knowing the end of my journey will bring Elizabeth back to me.

Weary of running through the trees of the unknown forest north of Pennsylvania, Noble walked through the wooded expanse, looking up at the stars. Aiyana, who usually traveled ahead, had come back and started walking next to him. Sloughing off the wolf, she stepped forward as they reached a creek bed. "What will you do when you find your woman?"

"I don't know. I hope Elizabeth recognizes me and remembers how much I love her."

"Ah. And what if this woman doesn't?"

"I've not even thought that far ahead. I do not know what Elizabeth knows about her past life, if anything. But I feel drawn to her even now; I can feel she has returned. I hope that she feels drawn to me as well."

"I hope she knows you, White Spirit Walker."

Setting out again, the duo continued traveling north, following whatever it was inside of Noble that pulled him closer to the woman who could free him.

Please know me, Noble prayed.

June 13th, 1758

I dreamed of Elizabeth tonight. It was not the same dream that makes me damn myself upon awakening: the nightmare of her death. It was worse.

Her blonde curls were tied back, and her hands and skirts covered in blood not her own as she ran toward me down the side of a hill. Her arms opened as she reached the bottom, though her face showed no emotion. Still, she ran until she caught me.

Reaching her hand up to my cheek, she ran her fingers down my face, her eyes searching mine for what I can only guess was recognition.

"Elizabeth, my heart has ached so long to see you again."

Her eyes seemed hollow. "You killed me. Why did you kill me, Noble? Did you enjoy tearing out my throat with those monstrous fangs? Did you not love the gnashing of tooth and bones as you tore me apart, caring not for me, not for your children?"

"I did not mean to kill you, Elizabeth. I was not a strong beast; I lacked control. I know there is no forgiving that. But I promise you with all that I am, I am changed."

Shaking her head slowly, she backed away. Her head fell to the side, and her throat split open, blood spraying from the wound in a crimson fountain. Her eyes melted from their sockets, and her skin dried, hugging her skull as the underlying tissues disintegrated and ran through holes poked through by worms. Falling to her bony knees, she collapsed under the weight of death. I stood there in shock of her loss once more. I tried to move toward her but could not.

I cried out as I dug my way out of the dark soil under the trees. Looking skyward, my eyes were met by the full moon above, and I screamed.

Aiyana ran to me from wherever she had spent her day. As the silver canine, she whined at me as I pulled myself out of the dirt. I shook off the nightmare and looked at her. The wolf melted away, and I looked into concern-filled silver eyes.

She kneeled in front of me. "Why do you scream, White Spirit Walker?"

Noble shook his head and dusted off his clothes. "Do not worry. I am fine. It was just a nightmare."

"You suffer many nightmares."

Noble smiled for a moment. "A man is not a man if his dark deeds do not haunt him. I am thankful to God for allowing me such deserved suffering."

Aiyana looked at Noble, her face filled with confusion. "You thank your God for giving you pain?"

"Of course. He is God, and I prefer it to being forsaken."

Still confused, she stood and looked to the east. "We are very close to Nalini. I have caught her scent in the air."

In the early evening, just after sunset, Noble and Aiyana reached Fort Carillon. Noble walked to the front gates, his hands in the air. "*Je suis le médecin de l'armée britannique et je me rends!*" he shouted, trying to get in.

The soldiers standing on the walls looked down upon him, their gold-and-blue coat lapels blowing about in the wind.

"*Je suis britannique et je surprendre.* I am a regular and I surrender!" Noble called out again. "Take me as your prisoner."

One of the guards raised his weapon, pointing it at him. "*Pourquoi devrions-nous vous faire prisonnier si je peux juste vous tirer dessus où vous vous situez, vous lâche britannique!*"

"*Je suis un médecin, pourquoi voudriez-vous tuer quelqu'un prêt à vous aider? Les Britanniques sont à venir, vous aurez besoin de moi!* I am a doctor offering aid," Noble said, raising his bag over his head.

"*Pourquoi voudrions-nous un renégat?*" asked the other soldier, raising his gun.

"I assure you, I am no turncoat. I am simply a man who wishes to join you in the war against the British. I was forced to join them, for they lacked a proper physician, but with the help of an Indian woman, I escaped."

The soldier laughed and motioned to his friend. "*Je pense peut-être qu'il est un espion britannique, Louie.*"

"I am no spy," Noble called out.

"*Je pense que nous devrions tirer de cet espion britannique et en finir avec cela, François,*" said Louie, laughing as he pulled the trigger of his weapon.

François fired his gun near Noble's feet simultaneously, but Noble stood still, hands above his head. "I am no spy, and I fear not your guns or those of the British. I only wish to help your men."

An officer joined them at the wall, having heard the musket fire.

The officer, his gold buttons shining under the lantern light, stared at Noble with a sneer. "*Je pense peut-être qu'il ne comprend pas, nous ne voulons pas des chiens britanniques dans notre armée. Tuez-le, François.*"

"*Oui, commandant.*" Louie quickly loaded his weapon and raised it until Noble could see the black end of the barrel directly at eye level. Still, he did not move.

"We have a foolish British dog before us. Why don't you run away, little British dog?" asked the officer, laughing.

"I am no coward, and I know you are not stupid. I am a doctor, and I know the losses of this war have been great. They are greater still, with no physicians to speak of here. I know you have the wives of your men acting as nurses to your wounded and two medicine men from the Shawnee and Iroquois tribes. But still, your men continue to die."

The commander fell silent, squinting at the stranger outside his gates. "*Que proposez-vous que mes Indiens ne le fassent pas?*"

"I offer them a chance to live. Indians know nothing about treating malaria or scarlet fever. They have never seen it. Waving burning sage above those who are ill and chanting does not save lives. And you cannot win a war without your soldiers."

For several minutes, it was as though the commander was sizing Noble up. His eyes narrowed. "*Prenez-le, prenez-le maintenant!*"

Dropping his arms to his sides, Noble watched as the gates opened and six men poured out, all with guns raised. One grabbed his bag and emptied it on the ground. Journals, the painting of Elizabeth, various medicines, and pens and ink spilled out on the worn road. The Frenchman picked through Noble's belongings in the dirt. Reaching for the painting, he stood as it unfurled.

"What is that you have there?" asked the commander as he stepped out of the gates

"*Une chienne britannique, digne de la baise,*" Francois said, as he raised a lantern toward the painting.

Noble started for the soldier who picked up the rolled-up painting. "Not that, please. It is only a portrait of my wife."

Shoving him back into the circle of men, musket barrels aimed at his head, Noble fell silent. The commander raised his pistol and pressed the barrel to his forehead. "Where is your bitch, Doctor?"

Noble swallowed and closed his eyes as the commander cocked the pistol. "She is dead... That painting is all I have left of her."

The commander snatched the canvas from his soldier's hand and looked at it for a moment before shoving it at Noble. His eyes narrowed. "*Si tu me mens, je vais brûler vous et le chien qui vous a suivi sur la route. Vous me comprenez, docteur?*"

"I understand," said Noble, looking back to the trees as he grabbed onto the painting pushed against his chest.

The commander holstered his pistol and walked back through the gates of Carillon. "*Enfermez-le vers le bas avec les autres prisonniers jusqu'à ce que je puisse comprendre quoi faire avec lui. Envoyer Garone à moi, je vais lui envoyer pour voir si ce médecin est qui il dit qu'il est et si elle est en fait un espion,*" the commander whispered into Louie's ear as he passed him.

Sending a spy to see if I am a spy, thought Noble, as he watched the commander disappear inside the gates.

The soldiers grabbed up Noble's belongings from the ground and threw them back in his bag. They shoved it at him as they walked him into the fort and down into the prison.

Aiyana watched from the trees, her silver eyes gleaming as she changed form.

THE MAN OF MIRACLES

May 30th 1758

I have become a prisoner of the French. Colonel François-Charles de Bourlamaque. He is a tall man, thin and capable. His face is a scowl, and his eyes small and deep-set, made smaller yet by the length and height of his nose. He is ill-tempered. And just as Washington was, he is always surrounded by guards. They bring me up from the dungeons only when I am needed to treat soldiers.

Though I am dragged to the other side of the fort every night, I have yet to lay eyes on Nalini or my wife. I hear the howls of Aiyana just after dark as she cries out, waiting for a response that never comes.

Carillon is ripe with disease in the heat of summer, and the air is heavy with human waste and death. Dysentery is over-taking them by the dozens. Malaria is running rampant, and not a night goes by that I am not shown a fresh corpse and beaten.

Bourlamaque is a hard man. He loves to have his men take a whip to me. They laugh and drink to my screams, frequently calling me "Charlatan meurtre, murdering quack." Still, every night, I am dragged up from the cage I now call home to treat these men with so few medicines or supplies to speak of.

Their doctor is doing little better than I. He is a thin man of short stature, named Charles Dubourdieu. He whispers under

his breath how much he despises me, though I do not know him.
He pushes me aside when he feels he is the superior physician.

"Get out of my way, turncoat," said Dubourdieu, shoving Noble as he passed.

Last night, after the death of another soldier to dysentery, Dubourdieu looked at Noble, his eyes full of hate as Bourlamaque stood covering his face with a handkerchief and asking, "Another dead, why?"

"How are we to save anyone here? We have no supplies, save these bandages," Dubourdieu said, his face turning red as he tossed a box of bandages to the floor. "I cannot treat these illnesses with bandages! And why must I work with this British prisoner and these savages constantly chanting words I cannot even understand? All I ever hear is the clinking of his shackles and their singing! I want them out." Pointing to Noble, he proclaimed, "And shoot him and get him out of my way or free his hands. This way," he grabbed Noble's shackles, "he is all but useless to me."

Bourlamaque's nostrils flared. "You complain if there is no one, and you complain when you have many hands. Why should I not shoot you? I beat that British dog, and yet he does not complain."

Glaring, the doctor stood his ground. "I am well respected. The king sent me himself to help you so that you might stand a chance of winning this war. The king will have your head if you murder me."

"The king is in France, and we are here. I assure you, he knows of your failings, and I am sure he will not see you in the light he once did when I beg him for more soldiers."

The doctor stood silent, his shoulders drooped in defeat, but he did not hide the anger on his face. "Then do it; kill me. I would rather die than watch more men die because you are so pigheaded."

The colonel pulled his pistol from its holster and placed the end of its barrel against the doctor's forehead and there they stood, patients groaning and moaning around them. Noble smelled the fear in the room. It was as thick as mist on the Thames in winter.

"It is too easy to end your whining," said Bourlamaque, fuming.

"You are damning all these men to certain death."

"They die at your hands, or they die at his. What does it matter?" the colonel said, looking at Noble.

"If we work together, I believe we might better the situation of these men," Noble said, stepping forward. "Shooting him helps no one. If we could get some cinchona bark, we might better treat the malaria that is killing your soldiers."

"The British dog speaks, asking that I spare your life, with a real answer to our problem. And you ask that I shoot him," muttered Bourlamaque with a sneer as he lowered his pistol to his side.

Dubourdieu's heart raced in Noble's ears, and sweat dripped down the side of his face. "Kill me..."

Bourlamaque pulled the trigger, and the doctor's blood splattered on Noble's face as his body fell to the floor.

"You will have your cinchona, British dog." Turning to his men, he grunted. "Get this bastard out of the clinic and unshackle our new doctor."

The sound of manacles hitting the floor filled Noble with one part relief and another part fear. Bourlamaque whispered into Noble's ear, who was rubbing the skin now free of the heavy irons, "Do not make me regret my choice. I want these men up and ready to fight your British brothers. When the cinchona reaches here, I want you to treat my malady as well. If I am not cured, I will shoot you and replace you with Indians."

Noble nodded. "Yes, Colonel. Until then, I suggest the men find a fresh spring to drink from, something far from the fort not teeming with bacteria. The water here is causing dysentery. You need fresh water and plenty of it if you are to survive until the medicine arrives," Noble whispered back.

His eyes met Noble's. "Anything else?"

The doctor's eyes shone red as he took his only chance to charm him. "Get these Indians out of here. Dubourdieu was right. They serve no use. I wish to remain in my cell during the day instead of housing above ground."

"It will be so, Doctor."

Noble asked nothing more of him for fear his men might grow suspicious.

As the soldiers carried the dead man from the room, Noble licked the dead man's blood from his lips, and his stomach grumbled while the heartbeats of the men around him filled his head like a thousand beating drums.

"There are no more medicine men in here," announced Bourlamaque as he stepped out behind the men dragging away Noble's deceased colleague.

Now I can be a doctor.

July 5th 1758

Mixing my blood with wine has cured many of the soldiers of Carillon, but not all. I have let a few who are too far gone pass on so as not to bring attention to myself. Too many miraculous recoveries of those brought back from the brink of death will inevitably cause issues. After curing Bourlamaque of what I learned was syphilis, he started calling me l'homme de miracle: the man of miracles.

I disagree. I just see the pain and want to help end it.

That was the only wish I had when I decided to become a physician: to end the suffering of men. So many times have I lost my way, and now I see that the blood of this beast has brought me back. No matter the evil within me, I am still Noble Lincoln, the man who has danced with God, the devil, and my own indecision.

My allegiance has changed again and again, once with God, then without. I have tried to shun him, but my faith falters not. I have grown from the young man with stars in his eyes and love in his heart, never using his head. If only I could find Elizabeth. My mind would be settled and my soul clear of this thing that bleeds into wine glasses to heal men while sipping their blood at the same time.

I have traded my red coat for French colors. Bourlamaque has even made me an officer, replacing the one he shot. Though I reside with prisoners, I am free to traverse the fort freely at night. I have searched every corner of the Carillon and have found nothing that I seek. There is no sign of Nalini or Elizabeth.

I hung the painting of my wife on the wall of my cell. As in life, Elizabeth's beauty draws the eyes of the soldiers here, yet no one seems to know her. It begs the question, was she ever here?

I have asked the Indians living alongside us if they know Nalini. Not one has heard of her either. I remain confused as to why I am here.

I think more than not that something is amiss with the wolf beast that carried me off and promised my love was here.

THE WARS OF MEN AND BEASTS

July 5th 1758

Bourlamaque, my friend and captor, has returned. He has been ordered to retreat by a commander who means to win the attack of the British himself.

I stood quietly in the hospital full of men; some I would lose for lack of blood and hands. So many are running about me, trying to quiet the pained cries of our soldiers carried back from the battlefield.

Bourlamaque wrung his hands, and sweat dripped from his brow. "I did not want to leave them, but Montcalm demanded it of me. The British are coming in great numbers. Thousands are crossing the lake as we speak, soon to make land. Do you have any knowledge that might allow us the upper hand? I fear that, without help, we will surely be lost," he whispered in my ear as I pulled a musket ball from the leg of a soldier.

"I know little of the workings of war, save the plucking of lead from bodies. I am truly sorry, François," I said, shaking my head and wiping my bloodied hands on my apron.

François's dark eyes met mine, and I could not ignore the concern they reflected. "Get as many as you can on their feet. We will need every man. When it starts, you will be required on the wall as well."

Nodding, I responded quietly, "I understand."

Campfires were seen in the distance, and the French scouts returned to the fort. They were called to the walls to prepare for battle. Noble followed the soldiers to the wall. Ammunition was plentiful. Musket fire sounded as French soldiers pushed into the British camps in the distance.

Howls sounded from the forest, and Noble stood up and turned his head until he heard dozens of paws running through the underbrush toward the wall. His eyes searched the edge of the trees as other soldiers loaded their weapons and watched for the regulars, usually sent in before the red-coated enemy.

Just under the low branches of the trees, Noble saw the movement of shadows. His eyes, able to see in hues of blue in complete darkness, made out the shape of two giant wolves and something else farther down the tree line.

Looking around, he saw no one watching him for the first time in a great while. Without a sound, Noble jumped from the wall and entered the forest farther down from the other beasts. The smell of copper in the air startled him as the woods fell silent.

He moved quickly through the trees toward the creatures. A moment later, he stopped as the two giant wolves bared their canines at him. He had interrupted their feeding on a soldier. One wolf was silvery gray while the other was black, its silver eyes familiar to him.

"Nalini?"

"Blue is not your color, monster," said a familiar voice behind him, followed by the sound of a cocking pistol.

The wolves backed away, teeth bared, and silver eyes glowed as they growled through blood-covered muzzles.

Noble turned and was immediately upon his hunter.

Darkness could not hide the eyes of gold.

"Dmitri?"

His old friend, dressed as a British soldier, stood with his gold eyes gleaming.

"Noble, it is good to see you, but your friends, I think not," he said, pointing the gun at the wolves.

"There is no need to shoot them. And since when do you use guns?"

Dmitri shrugged, smirking. "I like the weight of it, and I do not wish to soil my beautiful red coat. As for killing them, dear friend, I beg to differ. I have grown tired of being the rabbit in their hunt. And you might change your mind after I tell you of your great love's rebirth and the silver-haired beast that lay open her throat."

Looking down at the four-legged creatures, Noble understood.

The wolves turned and ran as a cannon sounded in the distance.

Dmitri's fangs protruded from his gums as he ran through the woods after them.

Noble followed closely behind, steering through the trees as if he had run through them a thousand times, his anger giving him focus.

More howling sounded from the west as the vampires gave chase.

The golden-eyed monster stopped at the clearing when the sound of footfalls fell silent. Noble joined him.

"Why?"

"Fools easily follow beauty, and she wanted you to stay here so she could hunt me across the sea. She charmed you, and her cub gave you hope, the thing you have been so desperate to find. Rougarou are nothing more than wolves. And wolves kill. They separated us to make it an easier hunt, but no more, brother beast."

"Why would she kill my wife when she begged me to kill you?"

"We, Lamia, are not the only lonely beasts out there. And these bitches are vengeful indeed. Let us find them, and perhaps you might have your answers."

Anger grew within Noble, then jutting jaws turned upward as he changed from man to beast. His nose twitched as his wings spread. Taking in the fresh scents of the forest, the Asasabonsam hunted. The smells of forest soil, moss, trees, and animals filled his nose. And something familiar. His long ears perked up as he listened, and his friend smiled.

British soldiers poured into the forest behind them, muskets at the ready. Dmitri took off running as the Asasabonsam flew straight up into the air. The beast's red eyes searched the woods as he flew over the trees.

The war of men raged in the distance while the silent battle of creatures started. The great-winged beast dove into the trees, having spotted his prey.

The wolves scattered, and Noble flew after a black animal that was running across the forest floor.

With claws spread wide, he struck, knocking the animal into a tree. Though it did not fall, it yelped out in pain and continued a winding course.

In the opposite direction, Dmitri chased the other beast as he sprinted through the trees.

The black wolf burst out of the forest near the fort with the Asasabonsam on its tail. Slapping at it again, the winged creature knocked it across the field and into the high stone wall of Carillon.

Musket fire filled the air, striking him in the chest. The beast screeched at the men on the wall as his attention turned to the French.

He flew toward them, and they again fired upon him. Flying low over the wall, the Asasabonsam grabbed the two men who had fired upon him and dropped them on the ground inside the fort. Then he soared back toward the wall as soldiers scattered, screaming "*Démon!*"

Cannons fired. As the winged demon flew out of the fort, it noticed the wolf was gone and again started its hunt. One howl sounded in the distance, deep in the forest. The black, flying beast headed toward it as his brothers-in-arms fired upon him.

Landing in the trees far from the wall, Noble's eyes searched the forest floor. Soldiers ran through the trees on the forest floor below him. Their commander was shouting out orders as they moved closer to the fort. The unseen beast in the trees watched in silence.

Without warning, several dozen wolves lunged through the trees, attacking the redcoats. Noble searched the attacking silver-eyed pack below. None of them were the wolves he sought.

The pungent scent of copper and gunpowder invaded the air as muskets fired on wolves, and claws and teeth gnashed and tore at soldiers.

Flying up into the air again, his long ears perked up, and he listened to the rustling of leaves and branches. Another howl sounded to the west. In it was desperation as it sounded again and then waited for a reply. None came.

Across the sky, he flew until a familiar scent met his nose. He landed in a tall oak. Hanging upside down high in the tree, silent and unmoving, the creature waited.

Loud rustling sounded below. Dmitri appeared below him, looking up, clutching his now human-looking catch around the neck. "I guess Nalini escaped you, friend?"

The Asasabonsam snarled at the old vampire as he dropped to the forest floor, and the monster melted away into a man.

Grinning, Dmitri let Aiyana fall from his grasp and onto the ground. Her head fell at an odd angle, and a large branch stuck out of her chest. Her body was broken, but she fought to heal. Noble kneeled next to the barely breathing Indian woman and took her blood-covered hand. Her silver eyes blinked a few times before meeting his.

Noble swallowed hard before he spoke. "Why did you lie to me, Aiyana?"

Tears welled up in her pained eyes. "I did as I was told."

Letting out a long breath, Noble shook his head. "But why?"

Aiyana's other hand grasped the branch protruding from her chest and pulled it out a little, allowing her to breathe a little easier. "You cannot die, and Nalini did not want to fight you. She wants you safe, for your destiny means peace for us all."

"I don't understand."

A tear fell down the side of her face. "My mother sees the future, and you will free all men. You are the light in the darkness."

"I am a monster. I'm no savior."

"You will be."

"Did Nalini kill my wife?"

The Indian struggled, trying to pull the branch out of her chest, her bloody hands sliding over the gray wood. Dmitri placed his foot on her chest, just below the branch. "Answer him so I may end you, evil bitch."

Aiyana coughed, her lungs filling with blood, and she fought to speak. "She told me that woman was not the one you needed to find. You will see your woman again, but she will also die." The Indian woman coughed, and blood sputtered from her lips.

"This is not what God promised me," Noble said, his brows furrowed. "Tell me when. When will Elizabeth return?"

The girl's eyes glazed over, and she fought to breathe. "When your heart is ready and your soul is clear, the woman with golden hair will find you," she whispered as her eyes closed, and her heart stopped.

Noble pushed Dmitri back. The golden-eyed vampire caught his footing and stood back, watching as his friend yanked the wood from Aiyana's chest. Dropping to his knees, Noble bit deep into his wrist. Pulling the Indian woman's head into his lap, he let his blood flow into her open mouth.

"Noble, stop. She's dead. Your blood won't cure her. She is Rougarou. Just as their blood is poison to us in great amounts, ours is to them."

Leaning his head back, Noble closed his eyes and prayed as the war of men carried on in the distance.

Dmitri placed his hands on his old friend's shoulders. "Noble, she's gone. And we still need to find Nalini."

Wolves howled, crying at the loss of their sister. Her death hung heavy in the air.

Noble's red eyes looked up at his friend as he let Aiyana's head fall from his lap. "Though I am at odds with God and my conscience, I ask no favors of you. But if Nalini were to fall, I would feel no ill will toward you, friend. I fear my moral compass is thrown awry, since wishing death upon her might also bring about my damnation."

Dmitri's eyes gleamed, and he smirked. "I'm sure my vengeance far outweighs yours in the eyes of God."

ACCEPTING LIFE AS A MONSTER

August 19th 1787

I found myself reading some of my older journals as I desperately prayed for a small clue that might lead me back to her, perhaps in my own words. Some odd bit or mentioning.

It has been almost thirty years since we crossed the sea together after Nalini escaped us one final time.

The last I saw of her anger-filled eyes, I grabbed her, my claws piercing her flesh, my fangs glaring in the moonlight. She cried out and changed form just as I was rushed upon by more Indians with hatchets and knives. It was then that time slowed, and I watched her slip through my fingers, and the British ran headlong into battle in the forest around us.

I fought with my brothers until the threat of sunrise was upon us, when I could no longer stand with them. Many a familiar French face looked upon me, not realizing who I was, and those who did expressed betrayal, fighting all the harder against me. Dmitri stood beside me, doing what I could not. We drank from the French with little notice. Swords flailed, muskets fired, and cannonballs flew in the thick, gunpowder-filled air. Death cries and falling bodies did not stop as soldiers stepped over their countrymen in hopes of defeating those foes who felled their brothers.

As the skies started to lighten, Dmitri smiled, his face spattered with blood and his gold eyes shining as his wounds healed. He is a warrior through and through. I saw no fear in him, only the fight of a man who could take on the whole of the armies around us if it did not threaten our anonymity.

We are again brothers, companion beasts; I, the conscience, and he, the shameless murderer.

Once again in London, we have settled quietly back into our lives. We have found a home in the English countryside to spend our days far from prying eyes.

Of course, Dmitri still has his moods, and I, my moments of melancholy and despair, having not found my love.

Day after day, Elizabeth visits me in my dreams, though few are pleasant. I am glad of them. I still feel everything I've always felt for her: love and adoration. The nightmares are my punishment; her demise in them, my hell. I try not to think of the past in my waking hours as I wander London and the surrounding villages to avoid notice or question. All the while, I search the faces of those around me, seeking that one face that will bring about my happiness.

We have seen little sign of the Archers. Still, there are whispers in the whorehouses of missing girls, though much fewer.

Dmitri is reconciled to be a quiet monster, and of that, I am much relieved. He usually beds them, drinks of them, and sends them on their way mostly unscathed. Those Dmitri does kill, he does not share with me. Afterward, I can hear him as he takes their bodies from the house to the surrounding forests to bury alone.

He still drags me to parties and has his way with women of substance. Every so often, he takes a gentleman down a peg by feeding on him in a quiet, dark corner.

Dmitri is still ever graceful, so much so, I feel as if I alone am the audience, attending a ballet of blood and fangs. I watch in awe as lady after lady tries to talk him into marriage. He, the lord every woman wants, while I am the silent, unnoticed beast in the corner, covering my ears, trying to muffle the sounds of hearts beating all around me. They are so loud even Mozart cannot drown them out.

At the end of the night, as I watch the sky start to change from darkness to light, I ask God, how much longer must I wait?

Across the sea, the colonies are becoming states; the new world is changing. All the while, London stays the same old town I've always known. Gritty, dirty, filled with beggars and disease.

This is where I feed; dark alleyways keep my secret. Dark eyes stare at me as I walk quietly between the buildings. I can hear the rise in the pulse of those who wish to attack a well-dressed stranger for whatever might be of value in my pockets. The sound makes my own dark heart beat a little faster as fangs descend from my gums, and I become the attacker.

I leave those I drink from with a few shillings for services they have no idea they have provided. Then I return to whatever home we have taken residence in.

Our lives have become reticent and safe for the first time since I was made the Asasabonsam. It is an odd existence, and I know not what to make of it.

I am a monster living out eternity with another monster in the quiet outskirts of London.

WHAT WAS LOST IS FOUND

February 9th 1799

For the longest time, I stepped away from my journals, lacking things worthy of writing. That is no longer the case.

Tonight, I walked the cobbled high street of the village in the early winter night with nothing more on my mind than a simple dinner at an inn that has become commonplace to me.

While at times I believe there is real evil in the heart Tabansi placed in my chest, suddenly, as if it were my own, I swear it stopped beating tonight as a pub door opened. It illuminated the young woman walking toward me, and then past me, until she was once again hidden by nightfall.

I stood, my words unwilling or unable to do me service, in shock. At that moment, an old memory came back to haunt me.

I was back at the church, lying on the cold stone, demanding answers from the winged creature floating above me and the Indian woman below me on the forest floor. "Elizabeth will return? When... when can I see her?"

The angel's and Aiyana's words repeated in my head: "When your heart is ready and your soul is clear."

I now know my heart is ready and my soul is clear, for I have found her.

February 20th 1799

I almost called out Elizabeth's name when I saw her again in the village a fortnight ago. She was buying a coffin so she could lay her father to rest. A woman, who must be a relative, pushed her into a carriage and took her away. I followed until the carriage turned a corner, losing it in the street bustling with even more carriages.

There is now hope in my heart.

I have decided to tell Dmitri our time together will soon come to an end.

An odd look of disdain took over his features, with a brow having been raised, as he looked down his nose at Noble. "Do not allow this woman you do not know to cloud your mind. For we may be creatures of great power, but the allure of beauty makes us as weak as the men we hunt."

Noble smiled, unshaken by Dmitri's words. "I can only hope she makes me so weak that I might find my way into her heart without harming her."

Dmitri shook his head. "A monster in love is still a monster, my dear Noble. But know it is not true love, for the beast only hears the heart that pumps blood through her veins, and it will drive us to it, no matter what our stilled hearts want."

"There is nothing within me that wishes to drink from her. I feel alive, and my black heart aches no more. You will not ruin that small spark of joy, Dmitri. For now, there is hope. The hope of leaving this life you find akin to the grandest of celebrations."

Turning to Noble from the fire, Dmitri looked sad for a moment. It caught Noble off guard. "You would leave me alone after all these years of being my companion?"

Noble moved toward him and leaned upon the mantle, looking into the face of his companion. "My joy is not meant to bring you pain or loneliness, friend. It is just... I find no joy in spilling blood. I never have."

"That is your failing and that of God's curse upon you, dear friend."

"There is more to it than just blood, Dmitri. I miss the sun upon my face, the warmth of summer. Watching my children play on early spring mornings."

"Death has no seasons, no joy, no children, save the ones that fall at its feet cold and forever stilled." He paused, closing the book he held and set it on the mantle. "Noble, you have become death and brought many ever so close to its door. This delusion that you are once again a man, it's an impossible dream. And believing this woman can bring you life again, I grieve for you, and her when the unavoidable truth of you finally tears at her throat."

"The words upon my chest laid there by God tell me that it is so. I so love him as you once did and will not deny myself a chance at being who I was."

Dmitri shook his head. "I'll not waste my time arguing semantics, Noble. I only fear for you the fate I see."

"What fate is that?"

"The one where this woman sees the monster and denies you what you seek."

Noble stared at the flames. "If it is not to be or if only for a little while, I still may share her company, fall in love, and be filled with the warmth it brings. I have hope and God on my side. Why would he challenge me in such a way yet allow prolonged suffering?"

Picking up his glass of wine and sipping it for a moment, Dmitri turned to Noble. "You have been so blinded by your faith that you cannot see the suffering of men. Have I not proven it time and time again taking lives?"

"As man consumes the beasts laid out before him by God, you must take from those put out before you."

A thin smile appeared on Dmitri's face as he grasped the shoulder of his friend. "God doesn't care, Noble, not of men, not of monsters. I will tell you that a monster in love is a blind beast indeed and be done with it."

February 27th 1799

She was in the street again, this time alone.

I watched as she spent some time smelling the flowers drying in the window of a shop. In the reflection in the glass, I watched a tear fall down her cheek; perhaps a memory came to her or the realization of how alone she is. I know not, and to speculate her loneliness, I know it is only my own wished thoughts to fill the void in her life. I am overwhelmed at the mere idea that I might return the brightness to her eyes, to touch her, to feel what I have missed for so long, while at the same time, controlling the beast within me that would only mean to harm her.

I followed her carefully, only stopping when she did. Sadly, she never looked back.

I could not help but stare at her as people shoved past me on their way home or to the public houses and shops. After only a few moments, I found I was as oblivious of them as she seemed of my watching her.

I returned to the same spot every night until I saw her again. Her name is not Elizabeth, for I called it out, surprising even myself, and she did not turn.

Her name, I know not, but I will know it soon enough.

My heart aches at the sight of her, just as it did all those years ago in her aunt's home when I was a priest and could not have her. Just as before, what I am stops me. Although I am no man of God forbidden to love, I am a demon who has already brought death upon her once.

March 16th 1799

It was quite by accident that I came across her again. Walking the high street of the village, I saw a woman stumble and fall into the road ahead of a speeding carriage. Pushing herself up, she slid on the ice and fell again. Her heart raced, as did the hooves of oncoming danger.

Running, I caught her by her shoulders and pulled her out of the way. She cried out as I grabbed onto her, her face turning to me. I was caught off guard. Her eyes did not quite meet mine.

"I'm sorry to have startled you," Noble said.

"It's quite alright, sir," she said, straightening herself. She kneeled, her hands searching the ground for something.

Looking around, Noble saw what she was looking for in the barely lit street: a cane of oak with an owl carved on the top.

He handed it to her carefully. "I've found your walking stick, miss."

As he held her arm to help steady her, she stood up, reaching out, grasping air a few times until he placed the stick in her hand. "Thank you, kind sir."

"You must be careful, miss. There are many dangers in the darkness."

Her gaze did not meet his as she turned back in the direction she had been going.

She smiled for just a moment. "My whole life has been but darkness, sir."

"You have indeed brought light to this soul this night," Noble said.

"Thank you again, kind sir. Good eve to you."

It was so dark that he was sure she didn't see him clearly as he stood there, still unable to take his eyes from her as she walked away, quietly cursing herself for being so clumsy.

March 20th 1799

I followed her to her home secretly. It is barely a hovel, deep in the woods outside the village, and she lives there alone, her father having fallen victim to the consumption.

I peeked into her windows and was startled to see her looking directly at me but showing no sign of seeing me there. I now understood her words, noting her eyes held no expression as she felt around the table beneath the sill. I realized then why she did not see me; the maiden is as blind as the spine of the book she placed her hand upon.

I was filled with sudden sadness, and then happiness quickly overtook it, for I knew she would never see the monster I had become.

My only question now is how to approach the girl who unknowingly holds steadfast to my heart.

I watched her throughout the night, for she does not draw the curtains nor light a candle. The only light comes from the fireplace.

At times, it seems as though she is perfectly capable of seeing as she moves through the small house. Tucking her father's things away in a trunk at the end of his bed with little trouble, filling a mug with water, and eating bits of bread in the silence and the dark, I see no err in her movements.

The yearning to enter her home and tell her of my love is, at times, overwhelming, but knowing I am but a stranger to her keeps me from it.

Night after night, Noble vanished into the forest, waiting for the perfect moment to tell the woman of his presence.

Then he remembered the flowers.

Flying into the woodlands, the creature landed in a tree, listening to the stillness below for her voice.

Noble pulled the clothes he had stashed out of the hollow of a tree in the woods and put them on as he listened for the voice that played like music upon his ears.

"Father, who art in heaven, I pray all things kind and gentle be with thee. You have given me hope, for flowers appeared on my doorstep. Frozen buds of roses to make my heavy heart feel as though it is flying and giving me sweet dreams of the one who left them in secret."

Landing on the ground, Noble returned, kneeling before her window as he watched her. The woman ran her fingers across the cover of a book and then touched the rose blooms, now fading in the warmth. Her long golden hair fell about her shoulders. The curls were mussed, but the color remained the same. Blue eyes looked around but never fell upon anything. He smiled, watching as petals fell, wilted. She picked them up from the table, bringing them to her nose. She closed her eyes for a moment, taking in the scent.

A fire burned, sending smoke up the small chimney. Something cooked in a pot over the fire, and she looked toward the flames as if they enamored her, but Noble knew she could not see them.

Noble stepped in through her door and closed it behind him.

She stood. "Who is there?" Her heart rate increased as she picked up the wood-carved cane leaning against the table.

Standing still, making no sound, he realized how foolish he was being. "I am quite sorry to come into your home. I'll go."

"Who are you? Why are you here?"

"I mean you no harm. I only came to see you are well after the terrible incident in the village."

Lowering her cane, she stepped close to the table. "You're the man who pulled me out of the street when I fell?"

"Yes, and I left the flowers at your door."

"What is your name, kind stranger? And why did you leave me flowers?"

"Noble, Noble Cross. I saw you smelling the dried flowers in the village and thought you would like them."

"That is quite a lordly name, sir. I thank you for them ... and for helping me, saving me from being crushed by the horses."

"How do you know about the horses?"

"I could hear them, and Missus Carnegie told me."

Noble nodded. "Ah. Well, I am most glad to see you well and unscathed."

"How did you find my home, sir? No one comes here, few know of it."

"I must admit I followed you last evening. But I'll be going now. I'm sorry to have startled you."

Silence fell between them as he turned to the door and opened it.

"The roses are probably as beautiful as they smell. Tell me what they look like. What color are they?" she called out, stopping him in his tracks. "Mother always told me the color of a rose tells you its meaning."

Turning back, he saw her picking up a wilting bloom from the table. More petals fell.

Noble smiled. "They are red as fire is hot. They look like tiny, balled-up infant's fists, but they are wilted from the cold, for I feared to knock on your door when I brought them."

"Oh." She smiled in his direction, and his heart ached.

They are as beautiful now as you were in the village, Noble wanted to say but didn't. "I must question how you lost your sight?"

"It was never there, therefore never lost, kind sir. My mother used to tell me I was born this way because God did not wish me to witness the cruelty of this world."

"There is so much wisdom in those words. Your mother must have been very astute."

The girl nodded. "She was."

"You are alone now?"

Looking nervous, she backed up and raised her cane again. "What do you wish of me? Why are you here? I warn you, I will not be taken easily."

Noble took a step toward her, his hand outstretched, but stopped short. "I mean you no harm. I only wished to see you, to talk to you. To take away the loneliness, both yours and my own."

"What do you know about loneliness?"

"I know the deafening sounds of silence in an empty home where no heart-beat meets your ears but your own, further reminding you that you are alone. I have felt the ache in my heart when I experience something wonderful and wish so much to share it with another but find myself secluded. The coolness of an empty bed in the middle of the night is no stranger to me."

The woman lowered her weapon and looked as if she might cry. "You are also without someone?"

"I have been alone for some time. I had a love once, but she died and left me wishing I had met death with her."

She stood looking somber. "I am very sorry for your loss."

"And I yours. I was in the village when I overheard someone speak of the passing of your father."

"He was quite ill. I just never thought he would go before me."

"One so young should not believe death will take them so easily."

"Death has taken everyone from me... my sisters, my parents, and my grandparents. I am the only one who remains. I was the weakest of them all, and yet, I am the one alive, shunned by even death."

Noble fell silent. "We should not allow all who have fallen before us to remain before us. Those who loved us would want us to look past loss with open hearts and hope. And you are no longer alone."

"You are a stranger with such kind words ... but I must admit, I find some things do not seem right about you. I cannot hear your breathing, nor the footsteps I always hear when others come to my home. Are you a ghost?"

"Those who knew me long ago might believe it so, but I assure you, I'm no apparition. I am but a lost soul, simply seeking companionship to alleviate the loneliness of my heart."

She settled her blind eyes on the floor.

Noble stepped forward, making sure his boots alerted her he was real. "I understand your hesitancy, but I assure you, I will never harm you. May I know your name?"

"My name is Rosemary."

Noble sighed in relief and pleasure of a mystery solved. "A name so sweet passes my lips, only to become a gift upon my ears."

"I don't know whether I should be happy you are here or afraid, kind sir."

"Be not afraid, Rosemary."

He looked at the book on the table. "Would you like me to read to you?"

Running her fingers along the table, she found the book and picked it up, holding it to her chest. "It has been quite a long time since I've heard the words from this book. I should like to hear them again, but I won't take you from your travels. I know it is late, and you probably wish to go home."

Noble stepped in front of her, touching the book in her hands. "I would rather be here with you."

Rosemary's fingers met his on the book's cover. She ran her fingers up to his wrist; he pulled away, startled.

"You should let me tend to the fire, for you are quite cold, sir."

"You need not do it, for I am soon to be warmed just being here."

"I cannot let you freeze when there is plenty of firewood. My cousin cuts it for me."

Noble looked down at the pile near the fireplace as she released the book in his hands. Turning it over, he looked at the cover. "*The Iliad* is quite an undertaking for a lady."

Years of taking care of herself showed as she grabbed the wood and set it on fire. "My father was reading it to me. This fable was so beautiful in his voice. Homer made gods so much like men when they should not be. Gods should never feel things so beneath them. In these words, you are left to believe they are more like kings, queens, and princes. Flawed, yet filled with enough power to destroy humanity, playing with a man as you would the pieces on a chessboard. I would not think gods would waste such time acting like children."

Noble smiled. "Gods cannot be so unlike man."

She stood up and turned to him. "I could never imagine a god such as that, creating the world with such beauty, even for someone who cannot see it. Such flaws do not exist in creation; only through the eyes of men are there defects."

"What of demons?"

"Demons are man's creation. Men create their own hell; God does not. He is the purest being in existence."

"For someone blind unto the cruelness of the world, you certainly make up for it with intellect."

"Lack of sight has left my other senses my only way to get on here. I have spent my life listening to men, their writings, and their religions. The Bible is my favorite, for it makes mere men abide by the will of God, who behaves like a god. I especially love the creation of man ... and woman from man and the error of both, given limits only to break them and be punished."

"Then you are most mistaken. Adam bent to the whims of Eve in taking the apple. I believe when God took Adam's rib, with it, he took away some of his strength, for women have so much power over men."

"I don't perceive it that way. Only with a woman is the man once again complete, for God took from him skin and bone, making his match to ensure he would never be lonely, never want for another. I believe when Eve gave him that apple ... that is when man and woman first felt love for one another, proving love is not without challenges, Mr. Cross. It was the first real test of mankind, to bend to another's heart and suffer the consequences of it. Also, it proves man inferior to God. Was that not the point?"

Shaking his head in wonder of her, Noble smiled. "I believe you to be correct, Lady Rosemary."

A shy smile appeared on her lips for a moment, only to falter to the reality of her being. "I'm no lady, sir. I am but a simple, broken woman with plenty of time for idle thought."

"There is nothing idle about thinking, and though you do not believe it so, you are a lady in my eyes."

March 21st 1799

As the Galanthus nivalis, or snowdrops, have started sending their white blossoms toward the gray, clouded skies, I realize spring is returning, and with it, longer sunlit evenings and less time with her.

Rosemary often smiles upon me as I read or we speak of things that interest her. I am a most agreeable companion.

I have taken to bringing her food and keeping her fire burning with wood I cut behind the house after sunset.

She asks where I spend my days. I have told her I see to my businesses in London, and she seems content with that answer. I feel terrible lying to her, but she must not yet know that a demon in sheep's clothing has worked its way into her home and become a trusted friend.

Tonight, we settled before the fire. Venison stew bubbling over the flames filled the whole of the cottage, and she closed her eyes as if the scent was heavenly. I watched her as the corners of her mouth turned up. This is a happy time.

I often wonder how long it will take for her feelings to match my own. When will I become her heart's desire and no longer her friend?

With Elizabeth, the glances, the meaningless words meant to be other words, went on for years without conveying our true feelings for one another. Here I am, doing it again, but with a woman who has nothing more than a platonic air about her.

Conversations of poetry, music, and the Bible go on for hours. When I query Rosemary about her life, she says it is uninteresting and so limited it would be a mere few sentences not worth writing.

So many times I have come ever so close to her that I might touch her cheek or take her hand, but something within me stops me short, and I move away, back to the chair before the fire with an aching heart. Unseen tears fall down my face. I am so close, yet so far from her. I feel at times overwhelmed by the sounds of our hearts almost beating in unison.

LOVE'S LIGHT WINGS

April 20th 1799

Last night we sat, she, smiling and laughing over a hot meal, of what I cannot recall; I watched, enamored as always.

After weeks of praying for some sign that she might see me as more than a companion to whom she argues her politics and religious views with such vigor, it came.

Her arm, lying on the table—her ever motioning to some thought or proof—finally settled for a moment, and then without warning, she moved her hand on the table until her fingers found my own. The warmth that filled me was greater still. I fought the urge to take her in my arms, to feel so close once more. I thought much of it but decided it was better to be cautious since she is so like a deer in the woods: ever wary, ever listening, and invariably ready to flee.

To my wonder, she did not pull away as I took her hand in mine and placed it ever so near my lips, pausing. I then kissed the soft pale skin of her hand and watched as she blushed and smiled sweetly. It went no further, but at once, the air was light, the girl happy and the monster at ease, filled with hope and comfortable just being a man.

I've decided tonight. I shall tell Rosemary that I love her. I will tell her I want to take her forever from her loneliness and ask her to marry. I am a frightened beast wrapped in love's light wings.

Noble woke before sunset and smiled as he readied himself for another evening with Rosemary while a boy in the stable prepared his master's horses and carriage.

Dmitri knocked and stepped into Noble's room. "Good evening, Noble."

"Dmitri." Noble nodded.

Leaning against the doorframe, the older vampire watched as Noble pulled on his riding gloves. "I had hoped you might hunt with me tonight. You are looking paler than normal."

"No, thank you, Dmitri. I have set plans for the night. There is a show at the theater tonight, and I am taking Rosemary."

"The blind girl? Have you not tired of her?"

Smiling, Noble shook his head. "No, and why would I? She is so different than my Elizabeth, but still, I am quite taken with her. We talk for hours about things that I have never found a woman willing to speak of."

Dmitri walked close and took hold of Noble's chin until their eyes met. "I have no care of this woman that keeps you from me. But your eyes... You're starving yourself, Noble. Do you think it wise to put yourself in such close quarters with hundreds of beating hearts and your ravenous hunger?"

Pulling away from Dmitri, Noble turned. "When and how often I choose to feed is my business, dear Dmitri, as you made quite clear in the past when I did worry so on your behalf."

Dmitri laughed and shook his head. "Acting as though you are once again a man? Eating their food, drinking their wine, watching their plays. None of it changes what you are."

Noble picked up his hat and tipped it to his friend. "You and I can differ in our opinions. Maybe I no longer crave the blood of man." Noble smiled as he stepped into the hall. "I bid you good evening, friend."

Suddenly, Dmitri stood in front of Noble, his gold eyes staring straight into Noble's red and bloodshot eyes. "Your eyes are as red as babe's blood. You cannot hide your hunger from me. I am not blind like that foolish girl in the woods. I still see the black beast with wings who has shared his fair share of men and women with me. What makes this one so special to you?"

Noble glared. "You know what she means to me, what she has the power to do."

Dmitri looked into Noble's eyes. "You will stay with me tonight and forget that girl in the forest."

Blinking, Noble smirked, and his jaws elongated for a moment before settling back into his human face. "You no longer hold that kind of power over me,

Enravota. I am no more the young monster, unable to ignore your vile, blood-tinged words, and *you* are not my master."

With a sly smile, Dmitri seethed. "I may not be your master, but I am older and wiser to the ways of the world, and what it is to be what they out there fear most ... a bringer of death, a plague on their quiet lackluster lives. And you, Noble ... beast ... are not one of them! No matter how much you pretend."

Noble stood unmoving and silent for several minutes before saying, "Let me take my leave, Dmitri."

Dmitri fumed quietly before moving out of Noble's way, allowing him to pass.

May 5th 1799

I sat next to her as the actors on the stage played their parts. Her smile filled me with warmth. Her laughter was the only laughter I could hear as the rest of the room faded so far into the background. There were no other sounds. No hearts berated my ears, and even the actors fell silent to me.

Afterward, we walked the streets, her holding my arm while Thomas drove the carriage slightly behind us.

"Did you enjoy the show, Rosemary?"

Rosemary smiled. "It was wonderful to hear a story played out that way. I should like to hear all stories that way if I could wish it so."

"If I could give you anything in the world, it would be a theater constantly playing to your heart's desire."

"You are so kind to me and without reason. You make my mother's view of the world seem so far from what she told me. There is so much good in it when you are here with me."

"I am most glad you feel that way, Rosemary."

Noble let go of her hand and stopped in the street, unable to contain himself as he kneeled in front of her.

Having lost her grip on his arm, she reached out for him. "Noble?"

He took her hand and held it. "I am here. Dear Rosemary, you've been the light in the darkness of my days, made my aching heart feel warmth and love again. There is nothing more I could wish for than you to be my wife."

Her blind eyes fell toward him, her smile vanished, and her expression was taken over by confusion and sadness. "Nothing would bring me more joy, but alas, I am undeserving. I am but a blind woman, poor and wretched still."

Noble sighed, hearing her words. "You are the very opposite of wretched. If only I could describe your beauty to you in a way you could understand. My dearest Rosemary, your name would be the only word I would speak if asked the very definition of it."

Rosemary smiled for a moment. "Your words are ever so kind, Noble, but there are so many other ladies out there more deserving of your request and your love."

"Not for me, Rosemary."

"I know nothing of marriage, nothing of being a wife."

"I will teach you."

She stood in silence, unknowingly punishing Noble for a time until he felt his heart might break.

"Please," he begged her.

"I don't know what to say..."

"Say yes."

She nodded and smiled. "Yes."

Rosemary and Noble spent the rest of the night walking the streets arm in arm, talking. Thomas followed behind until the sun started peeking over the horizon, and they ducked into the carriage and drove to her home.

A CONTENTED BEAST

May 16th 1799

Sitting before the fire, I read to her. She faced the flames, and her eyes closed as the rain beat down upon the roof.

Turning to me as I reached the end of a page, she reached out toward me. "May I know the face of the man who means to marry me?"

"I do not understand, my love. Shall I describe myself?"

She stood and felt her way closer to me until her hands found the book and my fingers. "Your words would mean little, but my fingers will speak volumes to me."

I took her hand and lay it on my cheek while her other hand met the other side of my face. Her small delicate fingers ran over my face gently, yet thoroughly. "You have strong features, dear Noble. Your nose is long and straight."

Her thumbs ran over my closed eyelids. "Your eyes, what color are they?"

"Well, blue, like yours, on a warm, cloudless day in the colonies."

She smiled for a moment, pondering my words. "High cheek-bones and a beard. Short but groomed?"

"Yes."

"What color is your hair?" she asked, running her fingers through my chin-length hair, tied back out of my face.

"Dark brown, almost black, really," I said. "I would say more the color of your hanging cook pot lit by embers."

She laughed. "I don't think that translates to anything as well as hot and cold do."

Realizing the truth in her words, I laughed with her.

Rosemary smiled. "I do believe you are quite handsome, my dear Noble."

I grinned and fell silent.

"Are you blushing, my love?" she asked, giggling.

I laughed. "I may be."

Noble sat on the roof of the manor, writing in his journal under the light of the moon, when Dmitri climbed atop the eaves, joining him.

"So, here you are."

"Yes, and you, back from the hunt, I see, with the smell of whores and blood wafting about you."

Dmitri smiled slyly. "It is a pungent sweetness you lack, my friend."

"I have no need of whores, Dmitri, only this pen, inkpot, paper, and the moon in which to write."

"What of the hunger rumbling from your midsection? Do your paper, quill, and the love you write of quell it?"

Noble sighed. "Soon enough, I will be as I was, and that question will no longer come from your lips. I've asked Rosemary to marry."

Dmitri shook his head. "And she has accepted the proposal of a blood-drinking monster?"

Noble fell silent and dropped his eyes to the half-written page, unwilling to meet the burning gaze of his companion.

Dmitri laughed.

"She does not know that part of me."

Dmitri shook his head again. "What will she do when she finds a winged beast in her bed, covered in the blood of the whores and gentlemen it hunts?"

"That beast will never enter her bed."

"It will when you drive it to starvation, and your love is not strong enough to protect her from the death that is sure to come when it strikes, taking her from you ... again."

"I am stronger now, and I can control it better than I ever have before. I am not the monster, and the monster is not me, Dmitri."

"No, I must admit you seem less a monster than I. But to what end? It's still in there, its heart beating in your chest. It still takes men to the precipice of death when it's not stopped. It is a large part of you that you can only ignore for so long."

"And soon, the monster will be gone, leaving the man who will have his wife and a long and happy life until I am old and gray."

At once, Dmitri was at Noble's ear. "If you do become human again, dear Noble, do not think yourself safe from the other monsters of the world, for we are many and have no qualms about taking your life if it fills our bellies."

Noble stiffened. "I fear no beasts, Dmitri. If you or another were to take our lives, we would pass on together to heaven. There is no greater gift than eternal love in a place of light, no longer haunted by this curse and the memories brought about by it."

Moving away, Dmitri looked down into the forest in quiet contemplation while Noble finished his entry.

My hope will not be shaken, even by Dmitri, for I am a contented beast.

TO LIVE A HAPPY LIFE

June 1st 1799

> *I watch her as she sets her hands on the satins and silks of the dresses I have purchased her. She seems to enjoy the feel of them against her skin as she rubs the fabrics on her cheek. To further her education of the finer things, I have gone out each night, gathering fragrant flowers to surround her in her small home. She pauses to smell them often and speaks to her aunt, a woman named Ursula, who has suddenly found her to be more interesting now that a wealthy suitor has taken to her niece.*

The day before their small wedding, Noble sat in front of the fire in his room, awaiting the setting sun.

In the forest, his servants and Ursula helped pack up the few meager belongings of Rosemary's. After her aunt had climbed into the carriage, Rosemary's new maid, Miss Stone, helped her in and sat down across from her as the men climbed into the wagon that was to follow behind them.

"Are you alright, Miss Rosemary? Did you forget anything?" Miss Stone asked the young woman, who looked as if she might cry.

Clutching her favorite book to her chest, she sighed. "No, I'm fine. It's just that I have never left my home. I feel as though I have fallen into a dream, a frightening, wonderful dream, with an uncertain future in a strange place, amongst even more strange things."

The maid leaned forward and patted the girl's knee. "Lord Cross is most happy you are coming home, and you'll get used to us all, miss."

The girl smiled for a moment. "I am most happy to be joining Noble... I mean, Lord Cross."

"You will soon be a lady, dearest Rosemary," whispered her aunt in her ear.

"I think that's what frightens me most," she whispered back.

Noble stood next to his chair in the dining hall, watching her, her hand clutched to her maid's as she was led to her chair.

"Good evening, milady," said Noble.

She smiled. "Dear Lord Cross. I must thank you for the rooms you have given me. They are large compared to my home. I don't know how I will ever get around without knocking things about."

"The whole of my home is yours to traverse, dear Rosemary, and Miss Stone will help you. Please, sit."

"Thank you," she said shyly.

Miss Stone pulled out her chair and helped Rosemary sit. Taking Rosemary's hand, Miss Stone lay it near the plate of food before the girl and watched her fingers find the rim of the plate before backing up to the wall.

"Have you everything you need, and your aunt as well?" Noble asked, sitting down in his chair.

"Yes, thank you. Everything we would ever need is here, and I think Aunt Ursula is taken by your friend. He is quite kind. We met him tonight just before we sat down."

Noble picked up his glass and sipped from it. "*My* friend?"

"Yes," said Dmitri, appearing in the doorway. "You know of whom she speaks, dear Noble."

Noble glared at him. "I don't recall inviting you this evening, Dmitri."

"Oh, but your beautiful bride-to-be did. Dear Ursula and I did tell her no at first, and then I thought about how rude I had been, so here I am. I'm afraid I've left Ursula tired in her room. She asks that we dine without her."

"It is nice of you to come, Lord Addleton," said Rosemary, smiling and offering her hand as she had been taught by her aunt.

Dmitri looked to the corner where Miss Stone stood and winked as he shot across the room, taking Rosemary's hand. The servant's complexion went white, and her face was filled with fear and disbelief. Noble stood, his nostrils flared.

"Miss Rosemary, don't," Miss Stone spouted, warning her charge.

Both men shot her a look, but Dmitri spoke first. "Miss Stone, what is wrong?"

She stood straight and still, fear silencing her.

"Miss Stone, have I done something wrong?" asked Rosemary, turning in her chair in the direction of her maid.

Dmitri released Rosemary's hand and, in a blink, stood on the toes of the maid with his forefinger on her lips as his gold eyes shone over the top of his dark spectacles. "Miss Stone thought you picked up your fork before a guest was seated. Do not worry your precious head. She was mistaken."

"Oh, I'm sorry, Miss Stone," said Rosemary, turning to the end of the table.

Noble watched Dmitri closely, who was running his fingers down the side of the servant's throat. Noble ordered, "Miss Stone, leave us. You can wait in your room until we are finished."

The woman nodded, but her eyes did not leave the eyes of the monster in front of her.

"I'm quite taken with your throat and the beating of your heart. I would love to have a pluck at both," he whispered into the frightened woman's ear. "Mind your master and your lady."

"Yes, milord," she whispered back, shaking.

"What's wrong...? Miss Stone?" asked Rosemary.

Putting a finger to her lips, Dmitri moved away from the servant slowly as a sly smile played upon his lips.

"Miss Stone, are you alright?" she repeated, her face filling with concern.

"Miss Stone is fine, Rosemary. I think the long, exciting day has gotten the better of her. She only needs rest."

Rosemary nodded.

The servant walked quickly from the room, and Dmitri turned to his friend. "It's hard to find good servants these days. But I would love to hire her on if she doesn't work out for you and your missus."

"I think she does a satisfactory service," said Rosemary. "I'm glad you've come to join us, Lord Addleton."

"You are as kind as you are beautiful," said Dmitri once again, taking her hand and kissing it. "Noble was quite right about you, dear Miss Rosemary."

She smiled. "He reminds me often, though I do not feel deserving of such compliments."

"I never give compliments to those who are undeserving," said Noble, observing his friend.

Releasing her hand, Dmitri circled her and grabbed on to the chair. "Please, sit, Miss Rosemary."

"Thank you, Lord Addleton," said the girl, sitting back in her chair and allowing him to move her closer to the table.

Dmitri seated himself at the table, pulling grapes from a bowl of fruit on the table. Resting his leg over one arm of the chair, he sat back, watching her as if enamored.

"What brings you to this side of London, dear Dmitri?" asked Noble, trying to draw the old vampire's eyes from Rosemary.

Dmitri looked toward Noble for a moment, gold eyes shining. "As one of your oldest friends, I thought I might come to share in stories of old so that Miss Rosemary might know what she is getting herself into, accepting your marriage proposal and moving here."

Rosemary smiled as her hands found the quail breast upon the plate, and she tasted it. "I love stories and the idea I may learn something about you, Noble. That most certainly interests me."

"I've told you everything of interest. Trust me; there is little more to tell."

"I must disagree, dear Noble," said Dmitri. "I think she has much to learn."

"Oh, do tell me, Lord Addleton," Rosemary replied, turning her head in the direction of his voice.

"Did my friend tell you that he has seen God or that he was once a priest for the Church of England?"

"No, he didn't," she said before biting into more quail meat. "Tell me all about it."

Glaring at Dmitri, Noble almost growled, and his eyes shone red for a moment. "I do not speak of the past since I do not wish to return to it, nor can I change it."

Dmitri sipped from his wine and then smiled at Noble. "No one can, but hiding your purity from this woman who believes you so worldly? It would be a shame."

Rosemary turned back in the direction she knew Noble sat. "Why would you leave the church, Noble?"

"Oh, let me tell it," Dmitri said, holding up his hand.

Noble interrupted. "It was not to my liking at the time."

"Don't lie to the woman. It was because, and I quote, 'Dmitri, I have fallen for the most beautiful of angels, and she knows not what she is, for she is blind unto the world of corrupted evil around her. I must save her, and I cannot do so in this cassock or as a pure man of God.'"

"Oh, Noble," said Rosemary, bringing her hand to her chest.

"I never spoke such words. Lord Addleton is both melodramatic and toying with you," said Noble.

"Oh, I assure you I am, but he did, if not to me, then to God himself, hiding on the staircase after seeing her. So Noble goes to the church and tells his bishop he can no longer serve God because he wants to be free to marry. In fact, he told the old codger, 'God sent me a message, and I must follow his instructions.'"

"I said no such thing," said Noble, losing his patience with Dmitri's behavior.

"Why would you leave God for a woman?" she asked.

"Because God told him to," said Dmitri.

"Please, Dmitri, stop. I did leave the church, but God had nothing to do with it."

"Then what was it, Noble?" asked Rosemary.

"My love for a woman outweighed my love of serving God in the church," said Noble, looking at Rosemary.

Rosemary nodded. "So, Dmitri is right. You left God for me?"

"No, it was long ago and someone else, and I said nothing to him about it," Noble said, shaking his head.

Swirling the wine in his glass, Dmitri faced Noble, enjoying the many expressions of irritation and anger he was causing. "The woman you lost? Elizabeth, correct?"

"Yes."

The room fell silent, and Noble fumed at Dmitri.

Dmitri grinned at Noble. "Did Noble tell you how she died?"

"No. How did she die?" asked Rosemary, shaking her head.

"What was it, Noble, a savage animal attack?" said Dmitri, further toying with Noble.

Noble swallowed hard and closed his eyes as Elizabeth's dead eyes and ravaged body flashed in his memory. "Yes."

Dmitri guffawed, "He was lying on the bed with her when it happened. It dove at her like a starving beast. Tore her throat out, did it not, Noble?"

Closing his eyes, trying to control his building anger, Noble exhaled.

Taken aback, Rosemary's eyes welled with tears. "Noble, I'm so sorry."

Noble looked over at his fiancé. "You need not be. It was long ago. I have let it settle in my heart, and I would rather look upon the happy times to come."

"But still, how devastating for you. And to come into another marriage. Are you certain you are ready?" asked Dmitri, mocking his friend.

"I am ready, and I believe I hear the sound of your carriage arriving, old friend," said Noble, hoping Dmitri would take the hint.

Rosemary sat silently in her chair, having pushed her plate away.

"Oh, I think not. I hear nothing from out of doors. That's the thing with these old manors, always creaking like carriage wheels. Don't you agree, Miss Rosemary?"

"I have heard no such noises, sir," she said, her attention elsewhere.

"I should like to stay to see you married, Miss Rosemary, for a blushing bride is a gentle sight indeed... A blessing upon one's eyes. I believe you will be the most beautiful of brides I may see to the end of my days," said Dmitri, smiling.

Rosemary blushed and smiled shyly. "I hope that my husband sees me in such a way."

"There is no comparing you to a rose, for you are the most beautiful and gentlest of flowers placed upon the earth by God," said Noble, his eyes fixed on her.

"I'm sure your fiancé sees you as a second chance, or perhaps something more." Dmitri sipped wine and looked over at Rosemary. "Since ... you are a maiden about to let blood upon your wedding sheets; that is if Noble would allow such a thing to go to waste. Myself ... I would be lapping it up."

Rosemary stood up, her cheeks blushing, her heart racing, and her lips unable to speak.

Noble stood, his eyes glowing red and his teeth bared. "You've said enough, Dmitri, and I beg you, take your leave before I am forced to throw you out."

A sly smile played upon Dmitri's lips. "Oh, dear Noble, I am just toying with you. We have been friends long enough for you to know that. What's it been, eighty years or so?"

Rosemary turned in Dmitri's direction, her face filled with confusion and her eyes welling with tears. "Why are you so horrible to us?"

"Please stop with this disturbing play. It only makes you look foolish, and you're upsetting Rosemary. Charles!"

The thin butler stepped into the room.

"Charles, please gather Lord Addleton's things and call for the carriage to see him home."

The thin man nodded and said, "Yes, milord" as he left the room.

Dmitri smiled for a moment before standing and bowing to his friend. "I apologize for my behavior. The wine is strong and my tongue idle."

Rosemary nodded but said nothing.

Noble was at his side in a moment, his eyes flashing angrily and his claws digging into the vampire's arm.

Dmitri pulled his dark spectacles down to conceal his gold eyes as he walked toward the door.

"Rosemary, I shall see our dear Dmitri to the door. Stay, sit, and eat... Please, my love."

The girl nodded and sat slowly, trying to force a look of calm.

Dmitri stood outside of Noble's home, awaiting his carriage.

"When will you learn to curb your outbursts and control yourself, old friend? Are the days of hiding what we are from mortals that far gone?" asked Noble, fuming.

"I would consider the slaughter of dozens of Archers affords me the freedom of being myself, no matter the company I keep, old friend."

"You are foolhardy, Dmitri."

"Who is more of a fool, Noble, the beast who wants the impossible, to be a man again, or the monster who embraces what he is? When will your fiancée know she is marrying a monster? When will you realize you are doing nothing more than trying to live a human dream to which there is no happy ending?"

Noble watched as the carriage started toward them from behind the house. "Unlike you, I have not forgotten what I was all those years ago. I remember what it is to feel as that man did. The love and the overwhelming loss that was mine and for those I most cared for; all that pain is still here. I have a chance to have it fade away a little when I am once again human. Rosemary will help me, and she will understand what she has given back to me once I am returned to what I was. It is what I most want to be for her, unburdened by this black heart and the darkness: to be alive and hold her in the sun."

"But for how long, Noble? Why must you be mortal to have her? Her life is so brief, a moment in time; it cannot possibly make all that you have suffered vanish away."

"When will you understand I have and will always be the *man* and not the monster? I did not want this. I did not ask for it."

As the carriage pulled up, Dmitri shook his head and placed a gloved hand on Noble's shoulder. "You're a fool, and that girl you so mistakingly believe will forgive you your lies and deception is no more your savior than the God we once prayed to. You see, dear Noble, we monsters do not love. We destroy and consume all that is around us. But if we are careful not to think about it, we can do so without conscience or even shedding a tear for their fleeting lives."

"I do not believe as you do, old friend. I believe you can shake and even topple the foundation of all evil with one word: hope. And with that same word, we can make it into something more fitting and joyous yet. I have *always* prayed to God, no matter my status. He has torn my foundation asunder! Even as this beast, I am free to look at the world with new eyes and a heart that runneth over. And though you are incapable of seeing it, Rosemary is my salvation, for she will lead me from this ill-fated doom and into the light shone upon the world every day, by God's will. While you hide away in the dark, lost and forgotten."

The coachman jumped down from his perch and opened the door to the carriage. "Milord Addleton."

Dmitri nodded to the coachman and then took a step toward Noble, whispering in his ear, "I believe she will die, and you will return to me. To once again hide away in the dark while she rots and is forgotten, for we are God's monsters. Just as the light dawns upon the world, it *always* fades away into the darkness, bringing their throats ever so close to our hungering mouths for all time."

Backing away, Dmitri smiled as he climbed into the carriage, closing the door behind him. "I would bid you farewell, friend, but our time apart will seem so cursory, I don't see it a fitting gesture." Slapping the top of the carriage, Dmitri sat back out of sight as the coach started down the road.

Noble was shaken by Dmitri's words but stood stoic, trying to hide his fear, until the carriage drove out of sight.

Walking into the dining room again, Noble found Rosemary still seated, but she seemed uneasy.

"I do apologize for Dmitri; he tends to let the drink get to his head and foulness to escape his lips."

Rosemary nodded, her fingers fidgeting in her lap. "Is Miss Stone alright?"

"I'm sure she is quite alright."

Noble stepped up to his fiancée and kneeled on the floor in front of her chair. "Are you alright, my love?"

Turning in the direction of his voice as he reached for her hand, she nodded again. "I am fine. I think I should like to go to bed now if that is alright with you. I think the quail has not quite settled."

He kissed her hand and then walked with her to her bedchamber. Miss Stone stood just inside but avoided meeting his gaze as he spoke. "Rosemary wishes to ready herself for bed. Please assist her, Miss Stone."

"Yes, milord," she said, taking the girl's hand.

"Oh, and Miss Stone, I apologize for my friend. He is a scoundrel of the worst kind, and he did not mean any harm."

"Yes, milord."

Noble closed the door and returned to his seat before the fire in his bedchamber. Holding the old, melted locket in front of his face, he opened it and tried to remember Elizabeth's portrait. "She has gone from a brave woman to a meek creature who seems fearful. She is not you, but I care deeply for her still, though no love shall ever equal what I felt for you, dearest Elizabeth."

Whispers filled the air, and Noble turned his head, intently listening.

"Charles, I am so afraid."

"What of, Miss Stone?"

"Lord Cross has let a demon into the house. That man was this close to me, and his breath smelled like an old corpse. His hands were as cold as winter ice."

"I think you've been into the master's wine. Lord Cross has been my master for years, and he's always been good to us. Lord Addleton has always been kind."

"That demon moves faster than you can see, and the way he looks at Miss Rosemary... Why does the master allow it?"

"Because, like the rest of us, he sees what's real."

"I saw it. I smelled it, and I felt it!" said Miss Stone, angered by Charles's doubt.

"Shush, keep quiet. You're ranting like a loon, woman. If the lady or the master hears you, you'll be thrown out into the streets."

"I'll keep quiet for the lady. Miss Rosemary is innocent, and I fear for her safety."

"You should not worry past your duties to the lady, Rosemary. And you should not bring up such nonsense again in my presence, or I'll be forced to speak to Lord Cross," threatened the butler.

"He saw that demon plain as I did. I could see it in his eyes. I think it'll return and do us all in," Miss Stone persisted.

"Yes, yes, we are all doomed." Charles groaned. "I'm off to bed, and I suggest the same for you, Miss Stone. Maybe a good night's rest will chase away the imagined evils in your head."

Noble listened to the old butler shuffle away down the long hall to his room, and then he heard sobbing as Miss Stone moved toward her room.

After hearing the maid's door close, Noble was down the hall, ducking into Ursula's room. The room was dark, save one dying candle. He looked at the bed and saw someone lying there. Listening intently, he heard her breathing, though her heartbeat was weak. Noble made his way quickly to the bed.

Ursula lay on her back, naked, with her hands resting on her slowly rising and falling chest. Placing his hand gently on her cheek, he waited for her to respond, but she did not. Noble did notice how cool she was to the touch. Slowly, he turned her head, exposing her neck. Small familiar holes had scabbed over.

Shaking his head, Noble pulled the blankets over her and left her alone.

DANCING
AROUND FLAMES

After dressing for the wedding, Noble looked in on his bride. Without a sound, he smiled, watching her as she sat alone in her room, waiting for her maid to return. Her gown was the lightest of blues, matching her eyes. Holding tight to her book, she got up and walked toward a covered window and felt the material of the heavy velvet. Rosemary pulled the curtain back, allowing the sun in. Noble moved out of the doorway. Fumbling with the window, she opened it, letting in the fresh air.

He watched as she closed her eyes and leaned her head back until the sun bathed her face. Then, quietly, she spoke. "If you can hear me up there, I beg thee, God; please let me not fear my husband or his dark friend who makes my cheeks rosy and causes me to fear them both. I wish to be a true and considerate wife. Help me be what I am to be in your eyes."

A hand grabbed Noble's shoulder, startling him. He turned and looked into the eyes of Ursula. Her face was pale, but her words quiet and stern. "A groom must not see his bride before they are joined before God. It's bad luck."

Noble nodded. "I'm sorry. I just missed her today."

Miss Stone walked toward them both in the hall, beaming. The night before, Noble had taken her fear and made her a happy servant with his mesmerizing eyes and careful speech. She held no memory of Dmitri's vile tongue or threats.

"Well, off with you, then, milord..." Looking startled by her own words and Noble's lack of response, she continued, "Of course, I mean that in the kindest of ways."

"Is someone there?" asked Rosemary, turning to the door.

Nodding, Noble stepped away from the doorway and started back to his rooms.

"It's just us chatting on about how pretty you are, Miss Rosemary," said Miss Stone.

So beautiful and so frightened, thought Noble, angry at himself for ever allowing Dmitri to meet her.

Outside of the manor, under the trees and a full moon, surrounded by torches, the servants, and what little family and friends they had, Noble and Rosemary said their vows.

Servants cheered and made merry as they watched their master dancing with his bride. Noble held her close as Dmitri entered the ballroom, Ursula on his arm.

Her pallor lighter still, she held tight to the monster as if she could not take a step without him.

"Dance with me, Ursula," ordered Dmitri, giving the lady no chance to argue. As if in a trance, she curtsied to him, then he bowed to her. Before she moved into his arms, Noble could see the hollowness of her eyes surrounded in dark circles.

Rosemary turned toward the sound of her aunt's name being spoken. "Oh, Aunt Ursula, I hope tonight for you has been as wondrous as it has been for me."

"Yes, tell her, my love. Tell her she was lovelier still than the bride you'll make for me," said Dmitri, with a taunting smile.

Noble watched the woman in the monster's arms, barely able to dance, being flung about like a rag doll by Dmitri. Her mouth opened. "So, lovely, I cannot compare."

Rosemary stopped dancing and stepped away from Noble. "Aunt Ursula, what are you saying?"

"I am to be married, Rosemary. I am to be a wife, finally, after all of these years."

The bride reached out to her aunt. "Please, you must accept my sincerest wishes of happiness for you."

Ursula reached out to her niece, but both women were cut short by Dmitri. "Let us dance and celebrate our future joy, my love," said Dmitri, his gold eyes sparkling in the surrounding candlelight.

Noble stood next to his wife, watching his old friend's graceful steps on the wood floor, while Ursula was barely able to stand up, her feet dragging across the dark oak.

Rosemary leaned in close to her husband. "Your friend shall be your uncle as well," she whispered, her tone more afraid than happy.

Dmitri smiled, his eyes falling upon Rosemary. "Oh, yes, dear Rosemary, I will become your uncle."

Rosemary was noticeably startled by his words, believing she could not have been heard.

"I must congratulate you, Dmitri ... Ursula..." said Noble, moving toward his friend, who stopped dancing long enough to walk to the table, leaving his fiancée standing alone and silent in the middle of the dance floor.

"What is it that you are doing, Dmitri?" demanded Noble in a whisper.

"Are you the only beast that deserves to be happy, dear Noble?"

"Happy? You? You do not love her. You drain her and make her confess such love, though she does not mean it. You do not mean it."

Dmitri chortled. "That old spinster would marry a rock if it asked her. Thankfully for her, I am much more dashing a man than she would ever have a chance at, given her status."

"I believed myself accustomed to your many cruelties, but this... This is something I do not understand. And to bleed Ursula almost dry on her niece's wedding day? Her heartbeat is so faint, I would almost believe her dead."

"Your kitchen maid didn't have my usual fare on the menu, so I had to make do. You understand."

"Don't kill her, Dmitri. I beg of you, do not kill Ursula."

Picking up a glass of wine, Dmitri smiled for a moment, his eyes meeting those of his friend. "Begging does not become you, dear Noble. What of your bride? She looks and smells delectable, and I know you're starving. Your eyes are giving you away."

"I would never do such a thing."

"You have, and as hungry as that black beast within you is right now ... your wife has no idea how close she dances to flames that are ready to destroy her."

"I am in control," said Noble, walking away.

BE NOT AFRAID

A storm rained down, and intermittent lightning flashed just outside the walls as Noble stood on the other side of his bed in his sleeping gown. His eyes fell upon his wife in her gown. She stood silently, though her heart raced.

Walking around the bed, he set his hand on her shoulder, trying to settle her nerves. "Be not frightened, wife."

Placing her hand on his, she nodded. "What if I disappoint you? What if I am not able to please you? What will become of me...?" she started until Noble placed his finger on her lips.

"Worry not, dearest Rosemary."

Stepping behind her, he leaned into her tied-up hair, taking in her scent. Faint rose perfume filled his nose. Reaching for the ribbon wound through her hair, he pulled it, letting loose her blonde curls to fall upon her shoulders and down her back.

Rosemary's body shuddered as Noble's hand pushed her hair back away from her neck, and he leaned in, his cold breath blowing on her skin.

She started to turn to him, but stopped when his lips pressed against her throat. He kissed her gently, his lips brushing down her throat until he reached her nightgown. He slowly pushed it down one shoulder until it dropped down to her elbow. She grabbed tight to the fabric, trying to cover herself.

Noble moved back in front of his wife; her blind eyes faced forward. Taking her hand that clutched hastily to her gown, he spoke. "Please, my wife, do not fear my touch, for it is meant to be gentle and loving."

She relaxed some as he took her hand and laid it on his chest inside the opening of his nightgown.

"You feel so cold."

"I do not mean to be cold."

Leaning in, he kissed her lips. Slowly she started to respond, her heart beating slower as fear began to fade.

His body warmed as the fire started to heat the room. Noble placed her hands at the top tie of his shirt. Rosemary stood unmoving, confused.

"It's alright, my love," Noble said, placing the lace of his shirt in her hand.

She pulled the tie of his shirt, and the fabric fell away. Reaching up, she placed her hands on his chest. Stepping up on her toes, she moved closer. He met her lips again as their breathing hastened, and he pulled her closer to the bed.

He stopped kissing her and pressed his forehead to hers. "May I see you as only a husband is allowed to see his wife?"

There was a pause as she nodded. Her heart rate picked up once again and her breathing hastened as she met his lips again.

He slowly pulled at the ribbons keeping her gown closed but did not open it.

She stood still in front of him, looking sad for a moment. "I wish I could see my husband as only a wife can."

"I will do my best to share myself with you."

Noble untied his gown and let it fall the rest of the way to the floor until he was completely naked before her. He stood in silence as she reached out to him. "Noble?"

Taking her hands, he smiled at her childlike innocence. "I'm here, my love."

He raised her hands to his face. "You touch me, and I will tell you what you are touching."

"Alright," she said as her fingers started over him.

Beginning at his forehead, she explored his face.

"You cannot feel it, but in there is the mind that looks forward to many a night of passionate discussions and debates."

She nodded. "And there will be many, dear Noble."

Her fingers ran through his long chin-length hair that framed his face.

"My hair... it will always be there."

She laughed aloud and found his ears.

"Those are the ears that will always hear your philosophical challenges and any other words you might convey."

Closing his eyes as she ran her soft fingers over the lids and eyelashes, he went on. "These are the eyes that will always look upon you with adoration and love and see the world for you when you cannot touch it, so I can tell you of its beauty."

She reached his nose, smiling, and he smiled in return. "This is the nose that will always want to smell the rose perfume of you."

Searching down farther, she reached his lips, and he kissed her fingers. "These are the lips that will kiss you and always speak kindly, with the same adoration and love I see you with."

Moving farther still, her hands fell to his shoulders.

"These are the shoulders that will carry the weight of my life and now yours," Noble said, taking her wrist and leading her fingertips over his skin.

"They are strong shoulders, indeed."

"They will be for you."

Dragging her fingers down his arms, he watched her face as she waited.

"These are the arms that will lift my wife into our bed every night and out every morning."

Looking nervous for a moment, she nodded as he took her hands in his.

"These are the hands that will pull you into my arms and always touch you with gentleness and with love."

Happy with his words, she allowed him to continue with the exploration of his body. Her fingers ran down to his waist, pausing where the hair became coarser. Her smile vanished as her cloudy eyes stared forward.

"It's alright, I understand," he said, taking her hands in his again. "Be not afraid, for it is only what God gave all men so that they might become one with their wives and help bring children unto the world."

She swallowed hard and nodded, pulling her hands from his and reaching down once more. "I'm not afraid."

His body responded as her fingers touched him. He sucked in his breath and closed his eyes for a moment, having not been stirred intimately by someone he loved for so long.

He furrowed his brow as Rosemary stepped back from him a few steps and stood silent. "Rosemary, are you alright?"

She nodded. "Yes."

In the warm golden light of the fire, she let her gown fall.

Noble looked at her in silent awe.

Rosemary's pale skin turned honey in the light at her back. Her blonde curls looked flaxen on her shoulders, raining down upon her golden breasts and on the soft rise below her waist.

Startled by the long silence, she reached out. "Noble, please tell me..."

He took hold of her hand and smiled. "You are the most magnificent thing I have seen in this life. You are truly the most beautiful of flowers, dearest Rosemary."

Blushing, she smiled. "Thank you, and though my eyes do not allow me to see you, my hands find you beautiful. It only makes me wish all the more that I could lay seeing eyes upon you."

Leading her to the bed, he laid her down beneath him, kissing her until their lips parted and her arms wrapped around his neck. Moving between her thighs, he looked down into her eyes, wishing the clouds would part and she could see him.

A log fell from the top of the fire and popped, causing the flames to roar over the wind outside.

"Are you alright?" he asked, moving closer until he could feel the warmth waiting between her thighs.

She nodded. "Yes."

Noble slowly pushed inside of her, and her breath caught for a moment.

He moved rhythmically, and her body responded. Small, slender fingers pressed into his back, and her legs intertwined around his waist as he moved between them.

The fire crackled, and the wind whipped as the two lovers moved together in a golden light, their shadows making love on the wall.

Moans from her lips hastened him to climax as she cried out. Her body quivered beneath him as beads of sweat fell from her brow and a tear fell down her cheek.

Noble moved onto the bed next to her, and she rested a hand on his chest.

"Aunt Ursula told me this would make me a lady," she whispered.

"You were always a lady. But now you are a consummate wife. My wife, to be forever loved and adored."

Pulling her into his arms, she laid her head on his chest and faced the warmth of the fire.

"There is no greater love than mine for you, Noble," she said, kissing his arm.

TO REMAIN A MONSTER

R osemary awakened in her bed, alone. Her hands ran across the mattress, seeking out her husband, when her fingers ran across the soft petals of a rose. She plucked one up, bringing it to her nose. The sweet smell warmed her.

"Noble?"

The door opened, and he walked in, freshly clothed and ready, with a tray of bread and tea. Setting it on a table, he sat down on the bed next to Rosemary as she pulled the sheets up to cover herself.

"Noble?"

He leaned down to kiss her lips. "Good morning, my love."

"Good morning, dearest Noble." She beamed. "I thought you had gone."

"No, I am here ... but I must go."

"Oh, I had rather hoped we could ride into town or walk through the gardens."

The pangs of guilt from his lies weighed heavily upon him. "I wish it could be so. But I must attend to my business. Maybe tomorrow. You and I have much to discuss."

Rosemary nodded. "Alright, tomorrow, then. We can talk when you return."

"Yes, I look quite forward to it," he said, leaning down, kissing again, wishing he never had to leave her.

Soon.

Noble left the bedchamber of his wife and saw Miss Stone waiting outside. "Miss Stone, please take care of Rosemary for me. I am going out to tend to my work. Be sure that she gets outside to walk in the gardens in the sunshine. I want her smiling when I return."

258

"Yes, milord."

Continuing down the hall to his room, he found Charles. "Charles, as always, take my carriage to the city for the day and return at sundown. If anyone asks, I am tending to my business as always," Noble said, his eyes glowing red for a moment.

"Yes, milord."

Noble locked the doors to his rooms and settled in with his journal and pen in the darkness.

August 27th 1799

It has been almost three months since I wed my beautiful Rosemary, and I am so filled with love for this woman. I am sure she is just as in love with me.

My heart tells me to enjoy the simple life of being this limited mate to her, while my mind begs me to ask her what I need of her so that I can freely walk with her in the sun and hide no more in our home or with these terrible untruths.

I can hear her even now as Miss Stone chats with her. The shy, scared girl hiding in the forest that she was is now the married lady of a house she never thought possible. I can hear her laughing at something Miss Stone is telling her, and it is a beautiful sound.

Whether it is jealousy or the thought of once again being alone to wander the world, Dmitri is pressing to be closer to Rosemary, sometimes even reaching her side before I awaken as the sun sets. He's told us that Ursula has gone off on holiday to her own aunt's home while she makes plans for the wedding. He talks to Rosemary often about how wonderful it will be to become her uncle. He brings her flowers, telling her that her aunt would want her to have them.

I do not know what it is he seeks from her, but I cannot deny, I am filled with dread hearing his voice within my home, night after night. I've even heard pacing outside of Rosemary's bedchamber as we made love, even after having seen him off for the evening.

I fear that if I am made man again soon, that I may be presenting us both as easy meals to him. So, for now, I must remain the monster hiding within a man. I fear for Rosemary's safety and cannot face the possible loss of her.

I must know what Dmitri is doing.

STARVING THE BEAST

Before Noble even awakened, Dmitri was walking through the doors of his suite. "Noble, old friend, it is time to rise. We have much to do."

In an instant, Noble was at the doorway to his bedchamber, wearing only his sleeping gown.

"Why are you here, Dmitri?"

"Didn't you hear? My fiancée is back, and I am to be married tomorrow evening. This is my very last night as a lonely man. Rosemary..."

Noble was alarmed, hearing his wife's name. "What about Rosemary?"

"She has told me that she is willing to be without you tonight so that we may go into the city. So please, put something on that has not been slept in."

Charles entered the room and looked at his master. "Lady Rosemary asks permission to come into your rooms, milord."

"Of course, she need not ask."

Miss Stone led Rosemary into the room.

"Noble?"

Taking her hand as she reached out to him, he smiled. "I am here."

"I hope that your travels into the city are pleasurable this evening," she said with her own smile.

"Oh, they will be, dear lady," said Dmitri, taking her other hand and laying a kiss upon it. "I thank you for the release of your husband for the night."

"I hope you enjoy your last night as an unmarried man, Lord Addleton," she said with a curtsy.

Noble walked next to his old friend as they headed to a pub on the high street. "Why are you dragging me away from my wife's bed when I know your intended is most likely buried in the English countryside in an unmarked grave?"

Dmitri scoffed. "You have little faith in my ability to live as a man."

"I do ... but I know you."

Dmitri laughed. "You do. But maybe, like you, I wish to be a man."

"Hardly. At times, I question if you ever were one. You play with your meals and always dispatch them when you get bored with them. Little holds your interest, save the Luveatu ladies, but alas, they, too, are dead."

"They were fun, were they not?"

"No, they were monsters. Monsters you created but never completed."

"But they certainly made me miss the golden age of English living. You should have been here then. There were more beautiful women than you could count, and all of them happy to please. Their husbands were caught up in wars, leaving many a lonely wretch ready to pleasure you better than any wife. Heartache does that, you know?"

"I would rather not spend the night rehashing your long-dead conquests. I would surely age several hundred more years waiting for you to finish with your stories, and I do wish to see my wife tonight."

"So, you still haven't told her you're a monster?"

Noble stopped short of the public house door. "I do not want to talk about my marriage either."

Dmitri opened the door and walked into an old haunt.

"Let us drink and gorge ourselves on the blood of ready women," he said with a sly grin.

"You can have my share of whores, as I wish not for the touch of a woman who is ready to clear out my pockets, but of the one that awaits my return home."

"Dear Noble, trust me, come tomorrow, you will wish you had accepted my offer."

"I wish it not, nor will I ever again."

Dmitri turned to him. "You are not taking of human blood?"

Shaking his head, Noble pushed through the door of the Sly Dog Inn.

Within minutes of sitting down, Dmitri had two whores, one on each knee, his tongue invading their mouths while his fingers shoved coins down the fronts of their corsets and other places.

"Noble, I beg of you, drink something... human or not."

"I'll take of wine, but nothing more."

Dmitri smacked the hind end of one of the girls. "You, get my friend some wine. It may be the only way you see yourself lying with a lord of his stature."

The woman patted Noble's hand as he glowered at Dmitri across the table.

"Don't go nowhere, lord. I'll be back quite quickly." The girl laughed as she fought her way through the filled tables of the sparsely lit public house.

"All the more for me, isn't that right, Maggie?" Dmitri asked a jiggly-breasted woman, who filled her mouth with mead and snuck her hands into his shirt.

"You're right, milord. I am so much more for you."

His gold eyes gleamed over dark spectacles as they captured her attention. "May I have a nip of you, dear woman?"

"Of course, milord."

A sly smile played on his lips as he waved her closer with his fingers. "Closer still, milady."

She leaned in until Noble could no longer see his friend's face.

Dmitri ran his lips over hers and then pushed his tongue into her mouth. She did not fight him as he broke from her mouth and started running his tongue down her throat.

Noble heard his fangs pierce the skin of her neck. The woman moaned quietly as he fed.

"What are you doing?" Noble demanded in a whisper as the whore's heart slowed to a stop.

"What you should be, as a fellow monster." Wiping his mouth on a kerchief from his pocket, Dmitri settled the woman in the chair next to his. She fell forward on the table.

Shaking his head, Noble leaned toward his friend. "You endanger us?"

"I am trying to eat enough for the both of us."

"But here? Have you lost your senses?"

"No, but you have. Your pallor is terrible, your lips cracked, your eyes bloodshot and clouded. Being married to this woman is killing you."

"No, it's making me happy."

"Why are you not happy here with me, with these women who are begging to feed us? You once enjoyed drinking from them. Sharing them with me because you could not finish them yourself."

"I never fed in the middle of a room filled with men. You are playing a dangerous game, killing in public," Noble whispered across the table.

"Then join me in an upstairs room and let us feast. I promise I will take no more at this table."

"You know I cannot do that."

"I know that, at this moment, the pulses of every man, woman, and child are pounding in your head like a blacksmith's hammer striking an anvil."

"That worry is not yours, dear Dmitri."

"Fine, try to stifle your true hunger with wine. Pray you do not kill your wife. Prayer might be the only thing that saves her from the black-winged beast, but then again, history has a habit of repeating itself. For no matter how much you see yourself a man, that beast's eyes are staring out at me, and it is ravenous. You are foolhardy enough to starve it."

"I won't kill her."

"Quite foolish indeed," said Dmitri, leaning back in his chair, resting his arm on the back of the dead whore as the other returned, carrying three large bottles.

The table quickly filled with empty bottles. Dmitri made several trips upstairs with one or another whore, while Noble waited at the table, trying to avoid the prostitutes. Different girls, reeking of their trade mixed with cheap perfumes, shoved against him as they moved between tables.

Finally, sick of waiting and feeling the wine overtake his head, Noble stood up and listened intently for his companion. He heard moaning women and the prick of fangs as Dmitri drank the wine he preferred most; that is, something less than twenty-five years old, already opened and slightly staled by others.

Placing his mug on the table, Noble walked out of the pub and climbed into the carriage.

"Home, Thomas," he called out to the carriage boy.

"Yes, Milord Cross."

Noble's eyes fell upon the beauty lying in her bed. He watched the rise and fall of her breasts beneath her nightgown as she lay in slumber. He ignored the sharp pains of hunger in his midsection. What had it been, three or four weeks since he drank from a deer in the forest?

Noble then stumbled to his rooms and fell into his chair before the dying fire.

THE PATH
OF RUIN

Noble woke as the sun had started descending below the horizon. A knock sounded at the door. "Lord Cross?"

"Come in, Charles," said Noble, getting to his feet.

"Am I to help you dress for the wedding?"

"Wedding?"

"Yes, milord, Lord Addleton's wedding. Lady Rosemary has already gone to help her aunt prepare."

"Rosemary has gone?"

"Yes, milord, several hours ago."

"Why did no one tell me of this?"

"Lord Addleton sent a carriage and a messenger from Lady Ursula requesting her presence at Lord Addleton's manor. She asked that we not wake you since you were so late coming in last evening."

Alarmed, Noble picked up the coat he had dropped to the floor the night before. "I must take my leave now," said Noble, rushing into the hall.

Bursting through the front doors, he was met by the setting sun. His skin burned, and he recoiled, falling against the wall behind him. Charles slammed the doors closed and kneeled to tend to his master.

Noble pushed the man's hands away. "No, please, I'm fine, Charles, just please go and ready my carriage immediately!"

The old man looked confused, but nodded. "Yes, milord."

Thomas drove quickly through the city's streets, headed north to the manor Dmitri had laid claim to some years earlier. The sun was almost gone from the sky when the carriage pulled into the gates.

At six stories, it was more a castle than a house. Its foreboding stone walls and high windows, with statuary at the eaves, gave it a medieval feel. However, its gardens lay in waste, for the master of the house preferred to feast upon his servants.

Noble jumped from the carriage before it stopped. "Stay here, Thomas. But if I do not return in the next hour, or you feel danger closing in upon you, return home quickly."

Thomas looked confused, but nodded. "Yes, milord."

Noble burst through the front doors, and darkness surrounded him.

"Rosemary!" he shouted as he ran through the halls.

When no reply came from her, he called out, "Dmitri!" Reaching the rooms his friend slept in, he found clothes strewn about on the floor, some covering rotting corpses, along with toppled wine glasses and bottles that lay broken everywhere. The bed stood solid and empty, but the mattress was soaked through with blood.

The smell of putrid death turned Noble's alarm into distress as he moved through the house, his voice echoing in empty halls and rooms. "Rosemary, please call out to me! Tell me where you are!"

The house was as dead as the occupants Noble came across.

Breaking glass and screams sounded, but not inside the large home. Running, Noble went through the rear parlor doors until he stood outside behind the house. Nothing but dead plants and grasses stood behind the home, save a sizeable round greenhouse made of iron and glass.

"Rosemary!"

Another scream sent Noble across the yard in a flash.

Looking through the windows, Noble did not find relief. On one side of the greenhouse, Ursula was pulling at the chains and manacles binding her wrists and ankles, but she was no longer human. Her eyes were gold and bloodshot, her body gaunt from starvation. Her bloodied wedding gown hung from her shoulders. Fangs were prominent as she dug into her wrists with a shard of glass, causing blood to erupt. Crying out, she quickly fed on it. Her gold eyes gleamed as she met Noble's when he entered. She screamed, dropping the glass, her clawed hands reaching out to him. "Your bitch is taking my husband!"

Noble turned to see Dmitri, who glowered in the darkness. He held tight to something draped in a dark cloak.

"You've come, dear friend."

"Where is Rosemary?"

"Not even a congratulatory salutation? I am now married, and as you can see, I have not killed her yet."

"She would be better off in the ground than being that wretched creature. Where is my wife?"

Dmitri laughed. "Rosemary came of her own free will, though she was confused as to why her aunt would bite her. All because you never told her what you are, what we are. Playing the fool, you made one of her. You played upon her weakness, but you claim you are a kind and honest man. And she, so trusting, so loving, but nonetheless a fool."

Noble stepped toward Dmitri carefully. "You know I need you to let her go, Dmitri."

Shaking his head, Dmitri held up his hand, signaling Noble to stop. "Do I?"

Trying to hold back the panic he felt, Noble said, "Yes, please, let her go. I beg you," as calmly as possible.

Dmitri shook his head and pulled the cloak from the trembling woman who stood before him. She faced her captor, but she was gagged and her hands bound behind her back, her arms covered in small holes, staining her skirts in blood.

Noble could hear her heart beating faster than he had ever heard it. He sighed in relief. "Oh, thank God, Rosemary."

"Do not think to free her. I have been ravenously feeding while you have been pretending to eat roasted quail. If you want her, you will have to fight me for her. Is that not what noblemen do, Father Lincoln?"

"I'll not fight you, Dmitri."

Dmitri patted Rosemary's blonde hair gently. "I'm afraid your husband does not truly love you, Rosie."

"You know that is not so!" Noble shouted at Dmitri.

"Alright then, shall we come to a different accord," asked Dmitri with a taunting smile.

Noble's eyes narrowed. "What kind of accord?"

Dmitri stood as if in deep thought for a moment, and then a sly smile played upon his lips. "You cease this foolishness. You feed like the beast you are, and you join me once again as my companion. Forget this woman. Forget breaking your silly curse. Why would you ever want to be this weak? I could pull her pretty, fair-haired head right off her pretty little neck instantly, with the flick of my thumbs."

Rosemary struggled against Dmitri for a moment and cried out in fear around the gag.

"Shh, dear Rosie," Dmitri said, looking into her face.

Rosemary fell silent.

"Please, Dmitri, stop this. I know you do not want to hurt her. She has been so kind to you, and she is no threat."

"This idle chitchat is boring, and you cannot dissuade me of anything. I know what I want, and I know you won't give it to me."

Dmitri's claws grew, and his fangs descended. Rosemary screamed through the gag in her mouth as he ran a long nail down the side of her face.

Noble's anger was building. "Let her go!"

"No. Come and take Rosemary from me if you want her so badly." The golden-eyed monster's sly smile widened into a grin.

Within a moment, Noble's skin turned black. His ears extended up the side of his head. His shirt burst open in the back as his large black wings spread, his jaws jutted outward and moved upward, and his long, sharp, pointed teeth descended. Hooked claws stretched as he prepared to pounce.

"This is the moment I've waited for, dear Noble. I wanted to give you your wedding gift," he said, turning the girl from him while simultaneously yanking the gag from her mouth and snapping the ties from her wrists.

Clear, bright-blue eyes looked at Noble through the darkness. She screamed, recoiling from the monster before her.

Dmitri pulled her close and patted her hair awkwardly. "There, there, sweet girl. Do not worry, dear Rosemary, for that is your husband, come to save you from a monster."

Rosemary struggled against Dmitri. "You are a demon! How have I wronged God that he would have me marry a demon?" she sobbed. "I have lain with Satan. I am surely damned!"

"No, Rosemary, no," said Noble as he once again became a man. He sank to his knees, his eyes welling over with crimson tears.

"That is no demon, Rosemary. That is a wonder of God's earth. My only sadness is that he wanted you to take all of that away from him. He wanted to become weak, short-lived, and inane, like you."

Rosemary stopped fighting, collapsing in his arms. Dmitri released her, and she fell farther still to her knees. Her long hair fell over her face, and she cried.

The vampire waved her off. "Take your mortal girl and be gone."

Noble reached out his hand to her. "I'm so sorry, Rosemary." Watching Dmitri closely, Noble stood and moved toward his wife.

Frightened eyes looked up at him as he stepped closer to her. "No! Stay away from me," she screamed.

She struggled to her feet and fell over her skirts.

Ursula growled savagely at them from across the room. She looked longingly at her niece. "Oh, Rosemary, come to your Aunt Ursula. I will protect you," she said sweetly as she broke loose the chains bolted to the floor, taking slow steps toward her niece. "I'm sorry I bit you. I was just so hungry. Dmitri's left me here a month without so much as a nip of food," Ursula said as she shot across the room toward Rosemary.

Dmitri was behind Ursula in a second, and in that same movement, he pulled her head from her shoulders. The body of the newly born monster went up in flames, followed by her head, which Dmitri released as it disappeared into ash before it could hit the ground.

Rosemary screamed, closed her eyes, and sobbed into her hands.

Noble stood, watching her, his heart aching to reach out to her.

Rosemary stopped crying into her hands for a moment and looked up at Dmitri through a fall of blood-stained golden curls. "Please, monster, kill me now!"

Dmitri was startled by her request and furrowed his brow.

Resting her hand on her stomach for a moment, she met Dmitri's gaze. "Please, kill me, for I fear I am carrying the child of Satan in my belly. And I would rather die..."

A look of utter shock came over Noble's face, and his eyes met Dmitri's when the realization of a sound that had gone unnoticed by both monsters struck them. Neither could ignore the flutter of life that had yet to be born coming from Rosemary's womb as Noble moved toward his wife. "No, Dmitri!"

Dmitri moved faster still, grabbing Rosemary's head and twisting her neck.

To Noble, time slowed as he heard the snapping of bone and then the fall of her body on the greenhouse stone. Rosemary's bright blue eyes met his, and a single tear slid down her cheek. She seemed to smile as she dropped to the ground.

Noble felt himself cry out, "No!" but he could not hear it as he scrambled to his bride, lying on the floor in a broken pile.

Blood tears ran down Noble's face, and everything around him seemed to stop and fall silent. He pulled Rosemary into his arms, rocking on his knees, burying his face in her hair.

A MILLENNIA TOO LONG

December 15th 1799

    In my dreams, I, again and again, watch the fall of an angel. Pale her golden hair, ever beautiful her face, steady her grace. Love now lost in the shimmer of fading light that was my joy.

    Several months have passed in a blur. Sometimes, I do not believe those few months of bliss with Rosemary indeed occurred.

    Was Rosemary real, or was she a wondrous dream within a nightmare, a light meant to be followed out of this terrible darkness?

    Dmitri tells me I held her throughout the night until he ran out to the greenhouse as the sun rose and dragged me away from her corpse. He said I fought him until he broke my neck and left me lying in the darkness of his bedchamber amongst the bodies of his wedding guests.

    When I awoke, I felt a vast nothingness and just lay there in the putrid, rotting mess for days. I did not speak. I did not feel. I just lay there, waiting for the end, ready to accept the hell I so deserved.

    After he burned her body, Dmitri left me to mourn for the greater part of four months before he dragged me out fighting, which again concluded with him breaking my neck. This time, however, Dmitri threw me into a carriage and took me out of the city and into the countryside.

He ran off through the forest. When he finally appeared, he was carrying a deer, which he dropped at my feet as I sat leaning against an old oak. I watched as the doe breathed slowly, still alive but frozen by Dmitri's charm.

"You must feed, but I know of no whore who would allow herself to get close enough to your rot-smelling carcass to even give you a chance at her throat. So, I brought you this lovely creature."

I met his gaze. "You have ravaged every bit of my soul and destroyed my very will to live, yet demand that I feed and prolong this hell you find so splendid?"

"Noble, you can hate me for all eternity. You know, just as I do that we are not men, and we may not love like men. We may not be loved like men, not by them, not by humans. It is like telling a starving lion he can only befriend the antelope."

"Lions were never men."

Dmitri sat in the grass before me, patting the doe as she lay at his feet. "No, they were not, but we are all animals. The only difference is that you and I can talk about it, reason with it, and truly understand it."

We said nothing more, the both of us sitting there, patting the deer.

My profound sadness changes him. He is so desperate for my forgiveness and companionship but, at the same time, cares not what I think. In a single moment, he can change from the demon I greatly fear and then into the persecuted man filled with empathy and love that he once was.

Is this the madness that comes with a thousand years on Earth?

Is this what my future holds with him at my side?

Dmitri walked into Noble's bedchamber, smiling. "It is a night of celebration. It is certainly time for you to get up and act lively for once. It is New Year's Eve, and I want to enjoy the end of the century and the one-thousandth year since my rebirth. I have made plans for us. We are going to the theater. I've gotten us a lovely box we'll share with two couples with better-than-average bloodlines. Then there is a party."

Noble sat up in his bed. "I'll not be going."

"Noble, we have much to celebrate: the birth of a new era and you. Yesterday, you fed for the first time in months, though you still look a bit worse for wear. I can see you are coming around again, and I know you are still hungry. So, let us go and commemorate these little milestones in our lives and feast and make merry."

Dmitri started pulling clothing from the wardrobe for his friend. "Charles, come and help your master dress."

The older gentleman entered the room, a bandage around his neck.

"Dmitri, I ask that you stop feeding upon my servants," said Noble, very much annoyed.

Furrowing his brow, Dmitri grinned. "If you come out with me this night, I will never lay another finger on your help."

Fuming, Noble met the eyes of his companion. "Fine."

The golden-eyed monster smiled and walked out, leaving Noble with his servant.

Charles looked at his master and smiled for a moment. "Are you feeling better, milord?"

"I think I am starting to feel a bit better, yes, Charles."

"Yes, milord." The old man paused and finally met his master's eyes. "I just wanted to say that the rest of us miss her, too. There wasn't a nicer lady I ever met."

Noble nodded. "Thank you, Charles, for always reminding me of her affection. I'm so afraid I'll forget her. Swift are the hours of our lives, but we cannot lose what makes those hours worth living."

Charles nodded and helped his master dress.

Noble and Dmitri sat in the theater box, each drinking their share of champagne and *Hamlet*. The two couples shared the opera box in silence, as Dmitri had promised. Less blood flowed through their veins, but they were alive and would never remember the two gentlemen who had sat with them. This was Dmitri's gift to Noble.

After the final curtain, Noble and Dmitri's entrance was announced across the city at the Queen's Ball that Dmitri had charmed his way into.

Dmitri was pleased that Noble's face no longer looked as gaunt and gray as it had been at the beginning of the evening. He had even smiled a little.

Leaning against the railing two floors above the crowd, Dmitri poured wine into a glass for Noble and then one for himself. "I told you an evening out would make you feel better. You look much healthier with a little nobility flowing through your veins. And because it's a new era, I would like to toast you, dear Noble."

"Why?" asked Noble, furrowing his brow.

The thousand-year-old vampire smiled. "I want to salute you for finally embracing what you are and sharing my life with me, though you rarely agree with how I live it."

The longcase clock's chimes in the ballroom below began blaring its warning of the incoming century. The banging chimes caused a cheer from the crowd two floors down.

Dmitri clinked his glass into Noble's. "Cheers to almost a century for you and a thousand years for me."

Noble looked into his eyes. The clock chimes hammered his senses. The hand tucked behind his back started to turn black, and his claws grew longer. He set his glass down and smiled. "A thousand years is far too long for some."

Before Dmitri could react, Noble's claws ripped through the old vampire's waistcoat and into his chest. Feeling the slow beating of the heart in his palm, Noble ripped it out, blood spilling down his sleeve as he held it up.

In a flash, flames consumed it, turning it to ash.

"Noble?" the name whispered from Dmitri's lips, his eyes wide and his mouth hanging open as he fell to the floor.

Dmitri's body burst into flames, leaving swirling cinders floating around his murderer until finally settling on the aged oak.

Noble stood, waiting to die, as the ash on the floor scattered and dissipated as if it and Dmitri had never been there.

Noble wiped away the fading ashen blood on his hands and tucked the handkerchief into his sleeve.

Feeling nothing out of sorts as the final chime sounded, Noble downed Dmitri's drink, then poured more wine and gulped it down.

Nalini was right, he thought with a thin smile. Filling the glass again, he looked at the cheering crowd below, hugging and giving well-wishes to friends.

Noble held up his glass, looking upward to the ceiling. "I toast you, my beautiful wife, who was so kind as to return to me. May your soul be at peace," he whispered.

"I could not put it any better, Lord Lincoln," said a man's voice behind him.

Startled by a name he had not heard in years, Noble turned to see a famil-iar-looking face framed with golden hair.

The young man, maybe twenty, held out his hand. "Finally, we meet. I'm Silas Lincoln. This has been a very long time coming, Father."

To be continued...

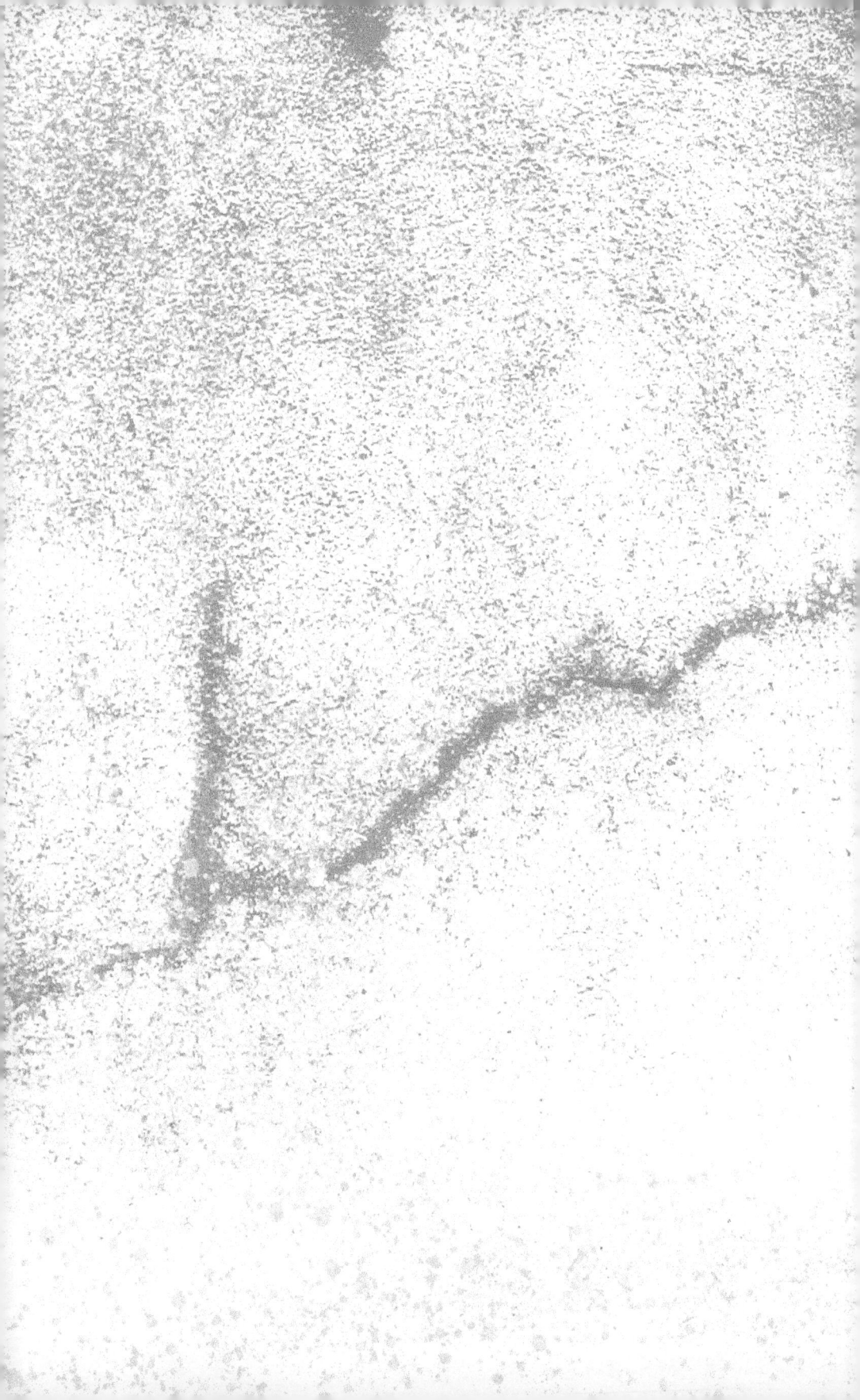

ABOUT THE AUTHOR

Sinara Ellis (Sinnie to her closest friends) lives and writes in New York City. When she is not writing novels, she spends time with her husband selling books in his bookshop, Not Just Another Story, in Greenwich Village. She is also known for telling her son stories about Larry the Dwarf, who is still unemployed.

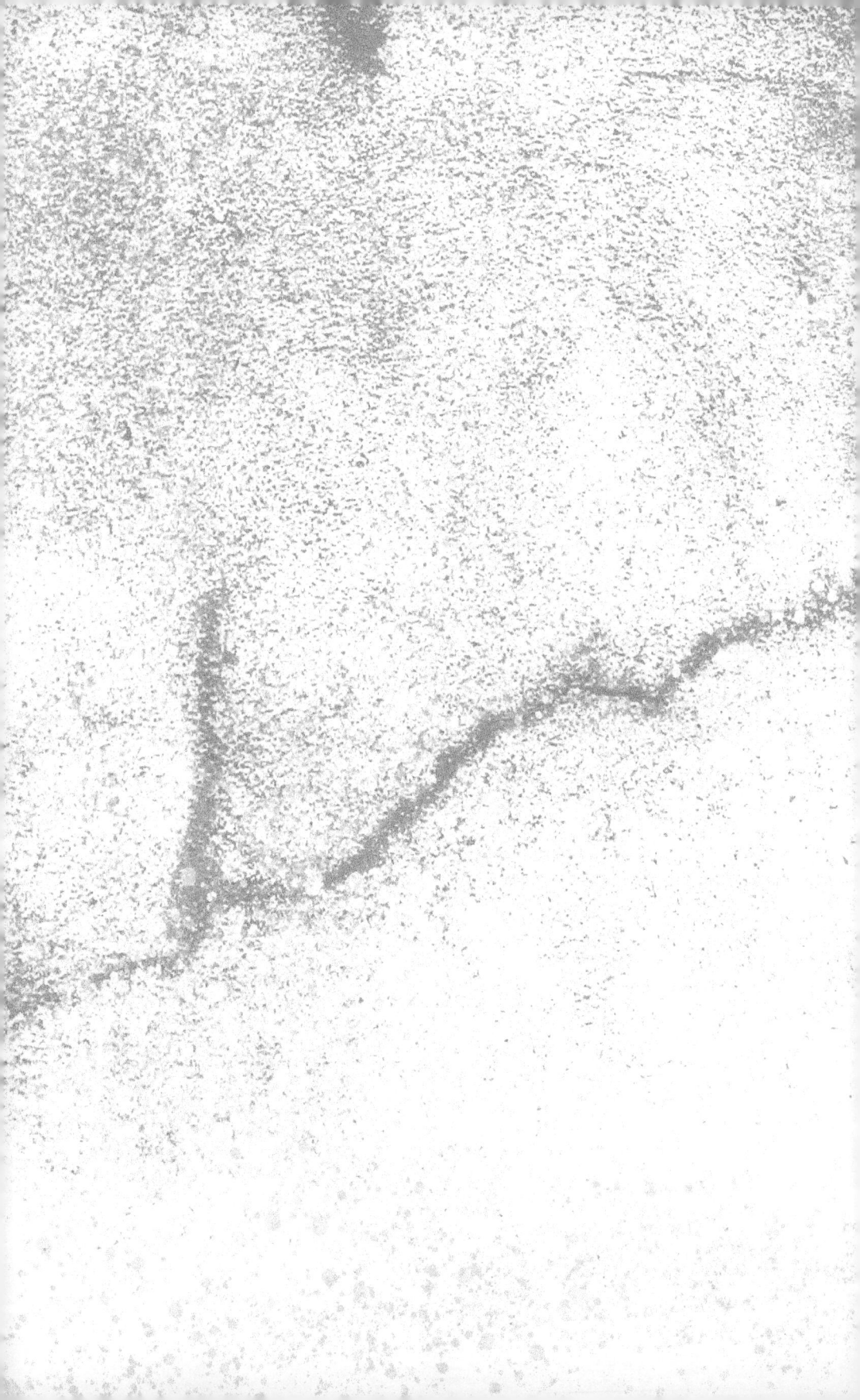

QUERIES FOR YOUR BOOK CLUB

1. What is the significance of the title? Did you find it meaningful? Why or why not?

2. What scene would you point out as the pivotal moment in the narrative? How did it make you feel?

3. Would you have given the book a different title? If yes, what would your title be?

4. What were the main themes of *God's Monsters*? How were those themes brought to life?

5. What did you think of the writing style and content structure of *God's Monsters*?

6. How important was the time period or the setting to the story? Did you think it was accurately portrayed?

7. How would the book have played out differently in a different time period or setting?

8. Which location in the book would you most like to visit and why?

9. Were there any quotes or passages that stood out to you? Why?

10. What did you like most about the book? What did you like the least?

11. What were the power dynamics between Noble, his family, his church, and Dmitri, and how did that affect their interactions?

12. How did the book make you feel? What emotions did it evoke?

13. What do you think will happen to the main characters next?

14. Did the ending leave you ready for the next book in the series?

**Discover more at
4HorsemenPublications.com**

10% off using HORSEMEN10

Milton Keynes UK
Ingram Content Group UK Ltd.
UKHW040815021124
450515UK00012B/63/J

9 798823 204361